Imitation in Death

Imitation in Death

Nora Roberts
writing as
J. D. Robb

First published in Great Britain 2004
by
Piatkus Books Ltd.

Published in Large Print 2009 by ISIS Publishing Ltd.,
7 Centremead, Osney Mead, Oxford OX2 0ES
by arrangement with
Little, Brown Book Group
An Hachette UK Company

British Library Cataloguing in Publication Data
Robb, J. D., 1950–
Imitation in death
1. Dallas, Eve (Fictitious character) - - Fiction.
2. Policewomen - - New York (State) - -
New York - - Fiction.
3. Detective and mystery stories.
4. Large type books.
I. Title
813.5'4–dc22

ISBN 978–0–7531–8302–1 (hb)
ISBN 978–0–7531–8303–8 (pb)

Printed and bound in Great Britain by
T. J. International Ltd., Padstow, Cornwall

No man ever became great by imitation.
SAMUEL JOHNSON

And the Devil said to Simon Legree,
'I like your style, so wicked and free.'
VACHEL LINDSAY

Prologue

Summer of 2059 was a mean and murderous bitch who showed no sign of lightening her mood. September dragged in on the sweaty heels of August and smothered New York in a wet blanket of heat, humidity, and foul air.

Summer, Jacie Wooton thought, was killing business.

It was barely 2a.m., prime time with the bars spitting out customers, and those customers looking for a little extra action before heading home. The heart of the night, as she liked to think of it, when those with a yen and the price to satisfy it came trolling for a companion.

She was licensed for street work, since she'd screwed herself up with a little illegals addiction and a couple of busts. But she was clean now, and intended to work her way back up the prostitution ladder until she was back on the arm of the rich and lonely.

But for now, she had to earn a goddamn living, and nobody wanted to have sex, and pay for it, in all this heat.

The fact that she'd seen only a couple of associates on the stroll in the last two hours told her there weren't many willing to have sex and be paid for it in the current climate either.

But Jacie was a pro, had considered herself a complete professional since the night, more than twenty years ago, she'd put her first license to use.

She might sweat in the heat, but she didn't wilt. Just as she'd cracked a bit under the probationary street license, but it didn't break her.

She'd stay on her feet — or her knees or her back, depending on the client's preference — and do the job.

Do the job, she told herself. Bank the pay, mark the time. And in a few months, she'd be back in a penthouse on Park where she belonged.

If the thought passed through her mind that she'd gotten a bit old and soft for street work, she blocked it out and focused on making one more score. Just one more score.

Besides, if she didn't make that one more score tonight, she wasn't going to have anything left over for body treatments after the rent. And she needed a tune-up.

Not that she wasn't still choice, she told herself as she strolled by a lamppost in the three-block area she'd staked as her own in the bowels of the city. She kept in shape. Maybe she'd traded the Push for a bottle of vodka — and she could sure as hell use a drink right now — but she still looked good. Damn good.

And she was showing off the merchandise in a go-glo halter and crotch skirt, both pulsing red. Until she hit the body sculptor, she needed the halter to boost up her boobs. But her legs were still her best feature. Long and shapely, and given an erotic touch with the silver spike sandals with lattice straps that crossed to her knees.

They were fucking killing her as she walked the streets looking for one more job.

To give her feet a break, she leaned on the next lamppost, cocked out a hip, and scanned the all-but-deserted street out of tired brown eyes. She should've gone for the long silver wig, she told herself. Johns always went for hair. But she hadn't been able to face the weight of a wig tonight, and had simply spiked up her own ink black, and given it a careless spray of silver netting.

A cab streamed by, and a couple of cars passed. Though she leaned over, gave them each the standard come-on, nobody so much as paused.

Ten more minutes and she'd call it a night. And she'd give the landlord a free blowjob if she was short on the rent.

She pushed off the post and began to walk, slowly on aching feet, in the direction of the one room she'd been reduced to. She remembered she'd once had a high-toned apartment on the Upper West Side, a closet full of beautiful clothes, and a full appointment book.

Illegals, as her counselor had told her, sent you into a downward spiral that often ended in miserable death.

She'd lived through it, Jacie thought, but she was right dead center of misery.

Six more months, she promised herself. And she'd be back on top again.

She saw him walking toward her. Rich, eccentric, and out of place — you didn't see many guys wandering around this area done up in evening clothes. With a cape and top hat, no less. He carried a black satchel.

Jacie put on her game face, and slicked a hand down her hip. "Hey, baby. Since you're all dressed up, why don't we have a party?"

He smiled at her, a quick, appreciative smile that showed her a flash of white, even teeth. "What did you have in mind?"

His voice suited his dress. Upper-class, she thought, with both pleasure and nostalgia. Style, culture. "Whatever you want. You're the boss."

"A private party then, somewhere . . . close." He glanced around, then gestured toward a narrow alley. "I'm afraid I'm a bit pressed for time right now."

The alley meant a quick bang, which was fine with her. They could get the business done, and if she played it right, she'd get herself the fee and a nice tip. More than enough for the rent and the boob job, she planned as she led the way.

"You're not from around here, right?"

"Why do you say that?"

"Don't sound like it, don't look like it." She shrugged, none of her business. "Tell me what you want, baby, and we'll get the financials out of the way."

"Oh, I want it all."

She laughed, then reached out to run a hand over his crotch. "Mmm. You sure do. You can have it all." *Then I can get out of these shoes and into a nice, cold drink.* She named a fee, elevating it as much as she thought possible. When he nodded, didn't blink at the inflated price, she cursed herself for not adding more.

"I need to have it up front," she told him. "Once you pay, we start having fun."

"Right. Payment first."

Still smiling, he spun her around to face the wall, jerked her head back by the hair. He slit her throat so she couldn't scream, sliced it with one stroke with the knife he'd held under his cloak. Her mouth opened as she gaped at him, and she made a gurgling sound as she slid down the dirty wall.

"And now the fun," he said, and went to work on her.

CHAPTER ONE

You never saw it all. No matter how many times you walked through the blood and the gore, no matter how often you looked at the horror man inflicted on man, you never saw it all.

There was always something worse, something meaner, or crazier, more vicious, more cruel.

As Lieutenant Eve Dallas stood over what had once been a woman, she wondered when she would see worse than this.

Two of the uniform cops on scene were still retching at the mouth of the alley. The sound of their sickness echoed back to her. She stood where she was, hands and boots already sealed, and waited for her own shuddering stomach to settle.

Had she seen this much blood before? It was hard to remember. It was best not to.

She crouched, opened her field kit, and took out her ID pad to run the victim's fingerprints. She couldn't avoid the blood, so she stopped thinking about it. Lifting the limp hand, she pressed the thumb to her pad.

"Victim is female, Caucasian. The body was discovered at approximately oh three-thirty by officers responding to anonymous nine-one-one, and is herewith identified through fingerprint check as Wooton, Jacie, age forty-one, licensed companion, residing 375 Doyers."

She took a shallow breath, then another. "Victim's throat has been cut. Spatter pattern indicates wound was inflicted while victim stood against the north-facing wall of the alley. Blood pattern and trail would indicate victim fell or was laid across alley floor by assailant or assailants who then . . ."

Jesus. Oh Jesus.

"Who then mutilated the victim by removing the pelvic area. Both the throat and pelvic wounds indicate the use of a sharp implement and some precision."

Despite the heat her skin prickled, cold and clammy as she took out gauges, recorded data.

"I'm sorry." Peabody, her aide, spoke from behind her. Eve didn't have to look around to know Peabody's face would still be pale and glossy from shock and nausea. "I'm sorry, Lieutenant; I couldn't maintain."

"Don't worry about it. You okay now?"

"I . . . Yes, sir."

Eve nodded and continued to work. Stalwart, steady, and as dependable as the tide, Peabody had taken one look at what lay in the alley, turned sheet-white, and stumbled back toward the street at Eve's sharp order to puke elsewhere.

"I've got an ID on her. Jacie Wooton, Doyers. An LC. Do a run for me."

"I've never seen anything like this. Just never seen . . ."

"Get the data. Do it down there. You're in my light here."

She wasn't, Peabody knew. Her lieutenant was cutting her a break, and because her head wanted to spin again, she took it, moving toward the mouth of the alley.

She'd sweated through her uniform shirt, and her dark bowl of hair was damp at the temples under her cap. Her throat was raw, her voice weak, but she initiated the run. And watched Eve work.

Efficient, thorough, and some would say cold. But Peabody had seen the leap of shock and horror, and of pity on Eve's face before her own vision had blurred. *Cold* wasn't the word, but *driven* was.

She was pale now, Peabody noted, and it wasn't just the work lights that bleached the color from her narrow face. Her brown eyes were focused and flat, and unwavering as they examined the atrocity. Her hands were steady, and her boots smeared with blood.

There was a line of sweat down the middle of the back of her shirt, but she wouldn't stumble away. She would stay until it was done.

When Eve straightened, Peabody saw a tall, lean woman in stained boots, worn jeans, and a gorgeous linen jacket, a fine-boned face with a wide mouth, wide eyes of gilded brown, and a short and disordered cap of hair nearly the same color.

More: She saw a cop who never turned away from death.

"Dallas —"

"Peabody, I don't care if you puke as long as you don't contaminate the scene. Give me the data."

"Victim's lived in New York for twenty-two years. Previous residence on Central Park West. She's resided down here for eighteen months."

"That's quite a change of venue. What she get popped for?"

"Illegals. Three strikes. Lost her top-drawer license, did six months in, rehab, counseling, and was given a probationary street license about a year ago."

"She roll on her dealer?"

"No, sir."

"We'll see what the tox screen tells us once she's in the morgue, but I don't think Jack here is her dealer." Eve lifted the envelope that had been left — sealed to prevent bloodstains — on the body.

LIEUTENANT EVE DALLAS, NYPSD

Computer-generated, she guessed, in a fancy font on elegant cream-colored paper. Thick, weighty, and expensive. The sort of thing used for high-class invites. She should know, she mused, as her husband was big on sending and receiving high-class invites.

She took out the second evidence bag and read the note again.

Hello, Lieutenant Dallas:

Hot enough for ya? I know you've had a busy summer, and I've been admiring your work. I can think of no one on the police force of our fair city I'd rather have join me on what I hope will be a very intimate level.

Here is a sample of my work. What do you think?

Looking forward to our continued association.

— Jack

"I'll tell you what I think, Jack. I think you're a very sick fuck. Tag and bag," she ordered with a last glance down the alley. "Homicide."

Wooton's apartment was on the fourth floor of one of the housing structures thrown up as a temporary shelter for refugees and victims of the Urban Wars. A number of them stood in the poorer sections of the city, and were always slated for replacement.

The city dickered back and forth between tossing out the low-rent LC's, chemi-heads, and dealers along with the working poor and mowing down the shaky structures or revitalizing.

While they dickered, the buildings decayed and nothing was done.

Eve expected nothing would be done until the dumps collapsed inward on their residents and the city fathers found themselves in the throes of a class-action suit.

But until that time, it was the sort of place you expected to find a down-on-her-luck whore.

Her room was a hot little box with a stingy bump-out for a kitchen and a thin sliver for a bathroom. Her view was the wall of the identical building to the west.

Through the thin walls Eve could clearly hear the heroic snoring from the apartment next door.

Despite the circumstance, Jacie had kept her place clean, and had made some attempt at style. The furniture was cheap, but it was colorful. She hadn't been able to afford privacy screens, but there were frilly curtains at the windows. She'd left the bed pulled out of the convertible sofa, but it was made, and the sheets were good cotton. Possibly salvaged from better times, Eve thought.

She had a low-end desk 'link on a table, and a prefab dresser covered with the various tools of her trade: enhancements, scents, wigs, tawdry jewelry, temporary tattoos. The drawer and closet held work clothes primarily, but mixed in with the whore-wear were a couple of more conservative outfits Eve imagined she'd used for off-hours.

She found a supply of over-the-counter meds, including half bottle of Sober-Up and a full, unopened bottle as backup. Which made sense with the two bottles of vodka and the bottle of home-brew in the kitchen.

She turned up no illegals, which caused her to assume Jacie had switched from chemicals to alcohol.

She opened the desk 'link and replayed the transmissions received and sent over the last three days. One to her counselor to request an upgrade in her license, one received and not answered or yet returned from the landlord regarding overdue rent, another made to an uptown body sculptor requesting rates.

No chats with pals, Eve mused.

She scrolled through, located the financials, and found Jacie's bookkeeping spare and efficient. Paid attention to her money, Eve mused, did the job, banked the pay, and pumped most of it back into the business. Expenses were high for wardrobe, body treatments, hair and face work.

Used to looking good, Eve decided. Wanted to keep looking good. Self-esteem wrapped around appearance, which was wrapped around sexual appeal, which was wrapped around selling yourself for enough money to maintain appearance.

A strange and sad cycle, in her opinion.

"She made a nice nest for herself in a very ugly tree," Eve commented. "I've got no transmissions or any correspondence from anyone named Jack, or any one guy in particular for that matter. No marriage or cohabitation on record?"

"No, sir."

"We'll talk to her counselor, see if there's anybody she was close to, or had been close to. But I don't think we'll find him there."

"Dallas, it seems to me, what he did to her . . . it seems to me that it was personal."

"Does, doesn't it?" She turned around, looked at the room again. Neat, girlie, with a desperate attempt at style. "I think it was very personal, but not specific to the victim. He killed a woman, and a woman who made her living from selling her body. That's the personal part. You not only kill her, but you hack out the part of her that made that living. It's not hard to find a street LC in this area any time of the night. You just have to choose your time and place. A sample of his work," she murmured. "That's all she was."

She walked to the window and, narrowing her eyes, visualized the street, the alley, the building just out of view. "He might have known her, or have seen her. Just as possible it was chance. But he was ready if chance presented itself. He had the weapon, he had the note written and sealed, and something — a case, a bag, a satchel, something to carry fresh clothes, or to store whatever he was wearing. He'd've been covered with her blood."

"She goes in the alley with him," Eve continued. "It's hot, it's late, business can't be very good. But here's a job, maybe one last job before she heads home. She's experienced, been in the life for two decades, but she doesn't make him as trouble. Maybe she's been drinking, or maybe he looked okay. And there's the fact that she's not used to street work, wouldn't have the instincts for it."

Too accustomed to the high life, Eve thought, to the sexual kinks of the wealthy and discreet. Coming down to Chinatown must've been like landing on Venus for her.

"She's up against the wall." Eve could see it, see it perfectly. The dark, spiked hair shimmering with silver, the come-on-big-boy red of the halter. "And she's thinking she needs the fee to make the rent, or she hopes he hurries because her feet hurt — Jesus, they had to be killing her in those shoes. She's tired, but she'll take one more mark before she calls it a night."

"When he slashes her throat, she's surprised more than anything. It had to be quick and clean. One quick slice, left to right, straight across the jugular. Sprayed blood like a son of a bitch. Her body's dead before her brain computes it. But that's only the beginning for him."

She turned back, scanned the dresser. Cheap jewelry, expensive lip dye. Perfumes, designer knockoffs, to remind you that you'd been able to bathe in the real thing once, and damn well would again.

"He arranges her, lays her out, then cuts the woman out of her. Had to have a bag somewhere to put what he's taken from her. He cleans his hands."

She could see him, too, the shadow of him crouched in the filthy alley, hands slick with blood as he tidied up.

"I bet he cleaned his tools, too, but he certainly cleans his hands. Takes the note he's written, sets it neatly on her breasts. He had to change his shirt, or put a jacket on. Something, because of the blood. What then?"

Peabody blinked. "Ah, walks away, figuring job well done. He goes home."

"How?"

"Um, walks if he lives close enough." She took a breath, pushing herself out of the alley and into her lieutenant's mind. Into the killer's mind. "He's on top of the world, so he's not worried about being hassled by a mugger. If he doesn't live close by, he's probably got his own ride because, even changing, or covering up, there's too much blood on him, and there'd be a smell. It'd be a stupid risk to take a cab or the subway."

"Good. We'll check the cab companies for pickups around the crime scene during our time frame, but I don't think we'll find anything. Let's seal this place up, canvass the building."

Neighbors, as was expected from neighbors in such places, knew nothing, heard nothing, saw nothing. The landlord operated out of a storefront in Chinatown, between a market that was running a special on ducks' feet and an alternative medicine joint that promised health, well-being, and spiritual balance or your money back.

Eve recognized Piers Chan's type, the beefy arms in shirtsleeves, the pencil mustache over thin lips. The humble surroundings and diamond pinky ring.

He was mixed-race, with enough Asian to have him set up in the business bustle of Chinatown, though she imagined his last ancestor to see Peking might have been at his prime during the Boxer Rebellion.

Just as she imagined Chan kept his home and family in some upscale suburb in New Jersey while he played slumlord of the Lower East Side.

"Wooton, Wooton." While two silent clerks busied themselves in the back, Chan flipped through his tenant book. "Yes, she's got a deluxe single on Doyers."

"Deluxe?" Eve repeated. "And what makes it deluxe?"

"Got a kitchen area with built-in friggie and AutoChef. Comes with the package. She's behind. Rent was due a week ago. She got the standard reminder call a couple days ago. She'll get another today, then an automatic evict notice next week."

"That won't be necessary as she's changed her address to the city morgue. She was murdered early this morning."

"Murdered." His eyebrows lowered into an expression Eve interpreted as irritation rather than sympathy or shock. "Goddamn it. You seal the place?"

Eve cocked her head. "And you ask because?"

"Look, I own six buildings, got seventy-two units. You got that many tenants, some of them are going to croak one way or another. You get your unattended death, your suspicious death, your misadventure, and your self-termination." He ticked them off on his fat fingers. "And your homicide." For that he used his thumb. "Then you guys come along, seal the place up, notify next of kin. Before I can blink some uncle or other is clearing the place out before I can put in a claim and get my back rent."

He spread his hands now, and sent Eve an aggrieved look. "I'm just trying to make a living here."

"So was she, when somebody decided to carve her up."

He puffed out his cheeks. "Person's in that kind of work, they're going to take some lumps."

"You know, this outpouring of humanitarianism is choking me up, so let's stick to the point. Did you know Jacie Wooton?"

"I knew her application, her references, and her rent payment. Never set eyes on her myself. I don't have time to make friends with the tenants. I've got too many."

"Uh-huh. And if somebody falls behind on the rent, wiggles around the evict, do you pay them a little visit, try to appeal to their sense of fair play?"

He rubbed a fingertip over his mustache. "I run by the book here. Costs me plenty in court fees annually to move the deadbeats out, but that's part of the operating expenses. That's part of the business. I wouldn't know this Wooton woman if she stopped in to give me a handjob. And I was home, in Bloomfield, last night with my wife and kids. I was there for breakfast this morning, and came into the city on the seven-fifteen, just like I do every day. You need more than that, you talk to my lawyers."

"Creep," Peabody stated out on the sidewalk.

"Oh yeah, and I'd make book he takes some of his rent in trade. Sexual favors, little party bags of illegals, stolen goods. We could squeeze him if we had nothing but time and righteousness." She angled her head as she studied the display of naked hanging fowls so skinny death must have been a relief, and the odd groupings of webbed feet for sale. "How do you eat feet?" Eve wondered. "Do you start at the toes and work up, or at the ankle and work down? Do ducks have ankles?"

"I've spent many sleepless nights pondering just that."

Though Eve slanted over a bland stare, she was glad to see her aide back in tune. "They do some of the butchering right here, don't they? Slice and dice the merchandise in the kitchens. Sharp knives, lots of blood, a certain working knowledge of anatomy."

"Cutting up a chicken's got to be a lot simpler than a human."

"I don't know." Considering, Eve rested her hands on her hips. "Technically, okay. There's more mass, and it's going to take more time, and maybe more skill than your average fowl plucker. But if you don't see that mass as human, it wouldn't be so different. Maybe you practice on animals, get the feel for it. Then again, maybe you're a doctor, or a vet, who's gone around the bend. But he had to know what he was doing. A butcher, a doctor, a talented amateur, but somebody who's been perfecting his technique so he could pay homage to his hero."

"His hero?"

"Jack," Eve said as she turned away to walk back to her vehicle. "Jack the Ripper."

"Jack the Ripper?" With her mouth dropping open, Peabody trotted to catch up. "You mean like over in London, back in . . . whenever?"

"Late 1800s. Whitechapel. Poor section of the city during the Victorian era, frequented by prostitutes. He killed between five and eight women, maybe more, all within about a one-mile radius over a period of a year."

She got behind the wheel, flicked a glance over to find Peabody gaping at her. "What?" Eve demanded. "I can't know stuff?"

"Yes, sir. You know great bundles of stuff, but history isn't generally your long suit."

Murder was, Eve thought as she pulled away from the curb. And always had been. "While other little girls were reading about fluffy as yet ungutted duckies, I was reading about Jack, and other assorted serial killers."

"You read about . . . that sort of thing when you were a kid?"

"Yeah. So?"

"Well . . ." She didn't quite know how to put it. She was aware that Eve had been raised in the system, in foster homes and state homes. "Didn't any of the adults in charge monitor your interests? What I mean is my parents — and they were big on not restricting our choices — would've brought the hammer down in that sort of area when we were kids. You know, formative years and all, nightmares, emotional scarring."

She'd been scarred, in every possible way, long before she could read more than a few basic words. As for nightmares, Eve didn't remember a time she hadn't had them.

"If I was scrolling the Internet for data on the Ripper or John Wayne Gacy, I was occupied and out of trouble. Those were the essential criteria."

"I guess. So, you always knew you wanted to be a cop."

She'd known she wanted to be something other than a victim. Then she'd known she'd wanted to stand for the victim. That meant cop to her. "More or less. The Ripper sent notes to the police, but only after a while. He didn't start off, like our guy. But this one wants us to know what he's about straight off. He wants the play."

"He wants you," Peabody said and got a nod of acknowledgment.

"I've just come off a highly publicized case. Lots of screen time. Lots of buzz. And the Purity case, earlier this summer. Another hot one. He's been watching. Now he wants some buzz of his own. Jack got plenty of it back in the day."

"He wants you involved, and the media focused on him. The city fascinated by him."

"That's my take."

"So he'll hunt other LCs, in that same area."

"That would be the pattern." Eve paused. "And what he wants us to think."

Her next stop was Jacie's counselor, who worked out of a three-office suite on the lower fringes of the East Village. On her large, overburdened desk was a bowl of colorful hard candies. She sat behind them in a gray suit that gave her a matronly air.

Eve judged her to be on the shadowy side of fifty, with a kind face and, by contrast, a pair of shrewd hazel eyes.

"Tressa Palank." She rose to offer Eve a firm handshake before gesturing to a chair. "I assume this concerns one of my clients. I've got ten minutes before my next session. What can I do for you?"

"Tell me about Jacie Wooton."

"Jacie?" Tressa's eyebrows lifted, a slight smile touched her lips, but there was a look in her eyes, a steady look of dread. "I can't believe she'd give you any trouble. She's on a straight path, determined to earn back her A-Grade license."

"Jacie Wooton was murdered early this morning."

Tressa closed her eyes, did nothing but breathe in and out for several seconds. "I knew it had to be one of mine." She opened her eyes again, and they remained direct. "As soon as I heard the bulletin about the murder in Chinatown, I knew. Just a feeling in the gut, if you understand me. Jacie." She folded her hands on the desk, stared down at them. "What happened?"

"I'm not free to give you the details as yet. I can only tell you she was stabbed."

"Mutilated. The bulletin said a female licensed companion had been mutilated in a Chinatown alley early this morning."

One of the uniforms, Eve thought, and there would be hell to pay for the leak when she found the source. "I can't tell you any more at this time. My investigation is in its earliest stages."

"I know the routine. I was on the job for five years."

"You were a cop?"

"Five years, sex crimes primarily. I switched to counseling. I didn't like the streets, or what I saw on them. Here, I can do something to help without facing that day after day. This isn't a picnic, by any means, but it's what I do best. I'll tell you what I can; I hope it helps."

"She spoke to you recently, about her upgrade."

"Denied. She has — had — another year's probation. It's mandatory after her arrests and addiction. Her rehab went well, though I suspect she'd found a substitute for the Push she was hooked on."

"Vodka. Two bottles in her flop."

"Well. It's legal, but it violates her parole requirements for upgrade. Not that it matters now."

Tressa rubbed her hands over her eyes and simply sighed. "Not that it matters," she repeated. "She couldn't think of anything but getting back uptown. Hated working the streets, but at the same time never considered, not seriously, any alternative profession."

"Did she have any regulars you know of?"

"No. She once had quite an extensive client list, exclusive men and women. She was licensed for both. But, to my knowledge, no one followed her downtown. I believe she would've told me, as it would've boosted her ego."

"Her supplier?"

"She wouldn't give a name, not even to me. But she swore there had been no contact since her release. I believed her."

"In your opinion, did she hold back the name because she was afraid?"

"In mine, she considered it a matter of ethics. She'd been an LC nearly half her life. A good LC is discreet and considers her clients' privacy sacred, much as a doctor or a priest. She considered this along the same lines. I suspect her supplier was also a client, but that's just a hunch."

"She gave no indication to you during your last sessions that she was concerned, worried, afraid of anything or anyone?"

"No. Just impatient to get her old life back."

"How often did she come in?"

"Every two weeks, per her parole requirements. She never missed. She had her regular medicals, was always available for random testing. She was cooperative in every way. Lieutenant, she was an average woman, a little lost and out of her element. She was not street savvy as she'd been accustomed to a more select clientele and routine. She enjoyed nice things, worried about her appearance, complained about the rate restrictions at her license level. She didn't socialize any longer because she was embarrassed by her circumstances, and because she felt those in her current economic circle were beneath her."

Tressa pressed her fingers to her lips a moment. "I'm sorry. I'm trying not to be upset, not to personalize it, but I can't help it. One of the reasons I was no good out there. I liked her, and wanted to help her. I don't know who could've done this to her. Just another random act, on one of the weaker. Just a whore, after all."

Her voice threatened to break, so she cleared her throat, drew air through her nose. "A lot of people still think that way, you and I both know it. They come to me beaten and misused, humiliated and battered. Some give it up, some handle themselves, some rise to a different level and live almost like royalty. And some are tossed into the gutter. It's a dangerous profession. Cops, emergency and health workers, prostitutes. Dangerous professions with a high mortality rate.

"She wanted her old life back," Tressa said. "And it killed her."

CHAPTER TWO

She stopped by the morgue. It was another chance, Eve thought, for the victim to tell her something. Without any real friends, known enemies, associates, family, Jacie Wooton was presenting a picture of a solitary woman in a physical contact occupation. One who considered her body her greatest asset and had chosen to use it to attain the good life.

Eve needed to find out what that body would tell her about the killer.

Halfway down the corridor of the dead house, Eve paused. "Find a seat," she told Peabody. "I want you to contact and harass the lab guys. Plead, whine, threaten, whatever works, but push them on tracking the stationery."

"I can handle it. Going in. I'm not going to lose it again."

She was already pale, Eve noted. Already seeing it once more — the alley, the blood, the gore. She'd stand up, Eve was sure of it, but at a price. The price didn't have to be paid, not here and now.

"I'm not saying you can't handle it; I'm saying I need the source of the stationery. The killer leaves something behind, we follow up on it. Find a seat, do the job."

Without giving Peabody a chance to debate, Eve strode down the hall and through the double doors where the body was waiting.

She'd expected Morris, the chief medical examiner, to take this one, and wasn't disappointed. He worked alone, as he often did, suited up in clear protective gear over a blue tunic and skin-pants.

His long hair was corded back in a shiny ponytail and covered with a cap to prevent contamination of the body. There was a medallion, something in silver with a deep red stone around his neck. His hands were bloody, and his handsome, somewhat exotic face set in stone.

He often played music while he worked, but today the room was silent but for the quiet hum of machines and the spooky whirl of his laser scalpel.

"Every now and then," he said without looking up, "I see something in here that goes beyond. Beyond the human. And we know, don't we, Dallas, that the human has an amazing capacity for cruelty to its own species? But every once in a while, I see something that takes even that one hideous step beyond. The throat wound killed her."

"Small mercy." Understanding, he lifted his head. His eyes behind his goggles didn't smile, as they usually did, nor did they show any spark of fascination with his work.

"She wouldn't have felt the rest that was done to her, wouldn't have known. She was comfortably dead before he butchered her."

"Was it butchery?"

"How would you define it?" He tossed the scalpel in a tray, gestured with one bloody hand over the mutilated body. "How the hell would you define this?"

"I don't have the words. I don't think there are any. Vicious isn't enough. Evil doesn't cover it, not really. I can't get philosophical now, Morris. That won't help her. I need to know, did he know what he was doing, or was it a hack job?"

He was breathing too fast. To steady himself, Morris yanked off his goggles, his cap, then strode over to wash the sealant and blood from his hands.

"He knew. The cuts were precise. No hesitation, no wasted motions." He stepped to a friggie, took out two bottles of water. After tossing one to Eve, he drank deeply. "Our killer knows how to color inside the lines."

"Sorry?"

"Your deprived childhood continues to fascinate me. I need to sit a minute." He did so, scrubbed the heel of one hand between his eyebrows, up to his hairline. "This one got to me. You can't predict when or how it might happen. With all that comes through here, day after day, this forty-one-year-old woman with her home-job pedicure and the bunion on her left foot got to me."

She wasn't sure how to handle him in this mood. Going with instinct, Eve dragged over a chair, sat beside him, sipped water. He hadn't turned the recorder off, she thought. It would be up to him whether he edited it or not.

"You need a vacation, Morris."

"I hear that." He laughed a little. "I was due to leave tomorrow. Two weeks in Aruba. Sun, sea, naked women — the sort who're still breathing — and a great deal of alcohol consumed out of coconut shells."

"Go."

He shook his head. "I've postponed. I want to see this one through." He looked over at her now. "There are some you have to see through. I knew as soon as I saw her, what had been done to her, I wouldn't be sitting on a beach tomorrow."

"I could tell you you've got good people working for you here. People who'd take good care of her, and whoever else comes in over the next couple of weeks."

She sipped the water as she studied the husk of Jacie Wooton, laid bare on a slab in a cold room. "I could tell you that I'm going to find the son of a bitch who did this to her, and build a case that ensures he'll pay for it. I could tell you all that, and all of it would be true. But I wouldn't go either." She rested her head back against the wall. "I wouldn't go."

He mirrored her position, head resting on the wall, legs kicked out. With Jacie Wooton's butchered body on the table a few feet in front of them.

And their silence, after a moment, became companionable.

"What the hell's wrong with us, Dallas?"

"Beats me."

He closed his eyes for a moment, knowing he was settling down again. "We love the dead." When she snorted, he grinned, eyes still closed. "And not in a sick, boink the corpse sort of way, gutterbrain. Despite whoever they were when they were alive, we love them because they were cheated and misused. The ultimate underdogs."

"I guess we're getting philosophical anyway."

"Guess we are." He did something he rarely did. He touched her. Just a pat of his hand over the back of hers. But it was, Eve realized, a kind of intimacy. An affectionate contact between comrades, and more personal than any act the victim had ever exchanged with a client.

"They come to us," Morris continued, "from babies to the doddering old, and everything between. No matter who loved them in life, we're their most intimate companions in death. And sometimes, that intimacy reaches down inside us and braids our guts like cornrows. Ah, well."

"She didn't seem to have anybody, not really, in life. From the look I got at her place, the lack of — I guess you could say sentiment — she didn't want anybody in life. So . . . it's you and me now."

"Okay." He took another drink, rose. "Okay." Setting the bottle aside, he sealed his hands again, replaced his goggles. "I put a rush on the tox, for what it's worth. Liver shows some wear, alcohol abuse. But even with that, I've found no major damage or disease. Last meal of pasta about six hours premortem. She's had breast augmentation and an eye tuck, butt lift and some jaw sculpting. All good work."

"Recent?"

"No. Couple of years, at least on the ass job, and I'd judge that as the last maintenance."

"Fits. Her luck took a turn, and she wouldn't've had the price of good body work in the last little while."

"Moving to the job most recently done on her: The killer used a thin, smooth-bladed knife, probably a scalpel for the throat cut, going left to right, downward stroke. From the angle, her chin was up, head back. He came in from behind, likely pulled her head back by her hair with his left hand, sliced with his right." Morris demonstrated, using both hands on an invisible form. "One stroke, severing the jugular."

"A lot of blood." Eve continued to study the body, but imagined Jacie Wooton alive and on her feet, face against the dingy wall of the alley. Then the jerk of the head, the quick shock of the pull, the bright pain and confusion. "Lots of gush and splash."

"A great deal. He got messy, even coming from behind. For the rest, it's one long incision." This Morris drew with a finger in the air. "Quickly, even economically done, I'd say. You can't call it neat, or surgical, but this wasn't his first time. He's cut into flesh before. More than sims, in my opinion. He had to have dealt with flesh and blood before this poor woman."

"Not surgical. Not a doctor then?"

"I wouldn't rule it out. He'd have been in a hurry, the light was poor, his own excitement, fear, arousal." Morris's exotic face mirrored his inner disgust. "Whatever drives this sort of . . . well, words fail me for once. Whatever drove him might very well have hampered his skill. He removed the female organs with, we'll say, dispatch. It's not possible to say if there was sexual contact before the removal. But from the time of death, the mutilation, there wouldn't have been time for games as they were done minutes apart."

"Would you peg him as a medical? MT, vet, nurse?" She paused, deliberately, cocked her head. "Pathologist?"

He gave Eve a small grin. "Possible, certainly. It took some considerable skill given the circumstances. But then again, he didn't have to concern himself about the patient's chances of survival. He needed some knowledge of anatomy, some knowledge of the tools he used on her. I would say he certainly studied, certainly practiced, but it may not have been with a medical license, and again may not have been with the goal of keeping the patient alive. I hear there was a note."

"Yeah. Addressed to me, which ensured I'd come on as primary."

"So he's made it personal."

"You could even say intimate."

"I'll have the test results and report to you as soon as I can. I want to run a few more, see if I can get a closer handle on the knives."

"Good. Take it easy, Morris."

"Oh, I just take it," he said as she started for the door. "Dallas? Thank you."

She glanced back. "Sure."

She gestured to Peabody as she headed down the corridor. "Tell me what I want to know."

"The lab, after considerable brown-nosing by yours truly, was able to discern that the material used in the note and envelope is of a particular grade of bond. It's not even recycled, which not only shocks my Free-Ager heart, but means it had to be sold and manufactured outside of the United States and its territories. We have laws here."

Eve lifted her eyebrows as she walked back out into the heat. "I thought Free-Agers didn't believe in man-made laws of government interference in society."

"We do when it suits our purposes." Peabody slid into the car. "It's English. The paper was manufactured in Britain, and is available in only a handful of outlets around Europe."

"Not available in New York."

"No, sir. In fact, it's difficult to buy it through the Internet or mail order as we have unrecycled paper products on our banned list in this country."

"Mmm-hmm." Eve's brain clicked several steps ahead, but as Peabody was studying for her detective's exam, she thought it was a good pop-quiz question. "So how did it get from Europe to an alley in Chinatown?"

"Well, people smuggle all sorts of banned products into the States. Or use the black market. Or if you're traveling on another passport, touring or visiting the U.S., you're allowed a certain number of personal possessions that aren't strictly kosher. You could even be a diplomat or something. But whatever, you'd have to pay the price, and it's high. That particular paper goes for twenty Euro dollars a pop. One sheet. The envelope's twelve."

"Lab boys tell you that?"

"No, sir. Since I was sitting out there, I checked it out myself."

"Good work. You got the outlets?"

"All the knowns. Though the paper's manufactured exclusively in Britain, there are sixteen known retailers and two known wholesalers who carry this particular style and weight. Two are in London."

"Is that so?"

"I thought, since he's copying Jack the Ripper, the London angle was the best."

"Start there. We'll pursue all the outlets, but London will be priority. See if you can get a list for purchases of that paper."

"Yes, sir. Lieutenant, about this morning. I know I didn't do the job —"

"Peabody," Eve interrupted. "Did I say you didn't do the job?"

"No, but —"

"Has there been any time since you came under my command that I've hesitated to tell you when I felt you didn't do the job to my requirements, or that I was dissatisfied with your performance, or that you'd screwed up in any way, shape, or form?"

"Ah, well, no, sir." Peabody puffed out her cheeks, expelled air audibly. "Now that you mention it."

"Then put it away, and get me those client lists."

At Central, she was waylaid in the detectives' bull pen with questions, rumors, speculation about the Wooton homicide. If cops were buzzing about a case, she knew the public would be screaming.

She escaped to her office, hit the AutoChef for coffee first, then called for her messages and missed transmissions.

She stopped counting the hits from reporters when she reached twenty. But six of those were from Nadine Furst at Channel 75.

With coffee in hand, Eve sat at her desk. Drummed her fingers on it. She'd have to deal with the media sooner or later.

Later would be better. In fact, sometime in the next millennium would suit her just fine. But she'd have to make a statement. Keep it short and official, she decided. Refuse and avoid any sound bytes and one-on-ones.

That's what he wanted. He wanted her going out, talking about him, getting airtime and print, giving him some glory.

Many of them did, she reflected. Most of them did. But this one wanted to be sensational. He wanted the media shouting:

MODERN DAY RIPPER
SLASHES THROUGH NEW YORK

Yeah, that was his style. Big, bold, splashy.

Jack the Ripper, she thought, and turned to her computer to make notes.

Grandfather of the modern serial killer.

Never caught, never positively identified.

Central figure in multiple studies, stories, speculations for nearly two centuries.

Subject of fascination and revulsion. And fear.

Media hype fueled panic and interest during his spree.

Copycat expects to escape detection. Wishes to instill fear and fascination, and pit himself against police. Would have studied the prototype. Would have studied medicine, formally or informally in order to commit initial crime. Classy stationery, possible symbol of wealth or taste.

Some of the main suspects in the Ripper case had been upper-class, Eve mused. Even royalty. Above the law. Considering themselves above the law.

Other speculation had run to the Ripper being an American in London. She'd always thought that bogus, but . . . was it possible her killer was a Brit in America?

Or maybe a — what did you call it — an Anglophile? Somebody who admired things British. Had he traveled there, walked the streets of Whitechapel? Relived it? Imagined himself as the Ripper?

She started to type up a report, stopped, then put in a call to Dr. Mira's office and wrangled an appointment.

Dr. Charlotte Mira wore one of her elegant suits, an icy blue she'd matched with a trio of long, thin gold chains. Her soft brown hair had a few sunny highlights around her pretty face. They were new, Eve noted, and wondered if that was the sort of thing she was supposed to comment on or pretend she didn't notice.

She was never fully at ease in girl territory.

"I appreciate you making time," Eve began.

"I wondered if you'd contact me today." Mira gestured to one of her scoop chairs. "Everyone's talking about your case, your particularly gruesome case."

"The more gruesome, the more talk."

"Yes, you're right." Because she imagined Eve had subsisted on coffee all day, Mira programmed her AutoChef for tea. "I don't know how much of what I've heard is accurate."

"I'm in the middle of writing my report. I know it's early to ask you for a profile, but I don't want to wait on this one. If I'm right, he's just getting started. Jacie Wooton wasn't his target, not specifically. I don't think he knew her, or she him."

"You believe it was random."

"Not exactly. He wanted a particular type of woman, an LC. A whore. A street prostitute in a poor area of the city. He had very specific requirements; Wooton's dead because she met them. Nothing more or less than that. I'll give you everything I've got orally, then once I've worked it up, I'll send you everything in a file. But I want, I need," she corrected, "some sense that I'm going down the right road."

"Tell me what you know." Mira handed her a delicate china cup, then sat and balanced her own on her knee.

She began with the victim, giving Mira a sketch of Jacie Wooton, as she had been, as she'd been found. She described the note, her fieldwork thus far, and Morris's preliminary findings.

"Jack," Mira murmured. "Jack the Ripper."

Eve leaned forward. "You know about him?"

"Any criminal profiler worth her salt has studied Saucy Jack. You think we're dealing with a copycat?"

"Do you?"

Settling back, Mira sipped her tea. "He's certainly laid the groundwork for that conclusion. He'd be educated, egocentric. He abhors women. The fact that he chose that particular style of killing is telling. His prototype for this crime assaulted and mutilated women in different ways. He's elected to mimic the one that attacks and removes that which makes the victim female."

She saw by Eve's slow nod that the lieutenant had already reached that same conclusion.

"He has, essentially, desexed her. Sex is equated for him with lust, violence, control, humiliation. His relationships with women are neither healthy nor traditional. He sees himself as elite, canny, even brilliant. So only you would do, Eve."

"Do for what?"

"For his adversary. The greatest and most elusive killer of modern time couldn't settle for just any cop to pursue him. He didn't know Jacie Wooton, I agree. Or if he did, his knowing of her was only to select the right victim. But he knows you. You're as much a target as she. More. She was a pawn, a momentary thrill. You're the game."

She'd thought of that, too, and was still circling around how to make it useful. "He doesn't want me dead."

"No, at least not yet." A faint crease of concern marred Mira's brow. "He wants you alive so that he can watch you chase him. Watch the media report his deeds and your pursuit. The style of note was taunting, and he'd want to continue to taunt you. You, not just a cop, but a high-profile cop, and a *female*. He'll never lose to a woman, and his certainty that he'll crush you, serve you your biggest defeat, is a large part of the excitement for him."

"Then he's going to be seriously bummed when I take him down."

"He could turn on you if he feels you're getting too close, ruining his fantasy. At first it's a challenge, but I don't believe he'll tolerate the humiliation of being stopped by a woman." She shook her head. "Much of this depends on how much of the Ripper personality he's taken on, and which persona ascribed by the various theories to the Ripper he, himself, believes. It's problematic, Eve. When he said, 'sample of my work,' did that mean his first, or has he killed before and gone undetected?"

"It's his first here, in New York, but I'm going to do a check through IRCCA. Some psycho tries to emulate Jack the Ripper every now and then, but I don't know of anywhere he wasn't caught."

"Keep me updated, and I'll work up a more substantial profile."

"I appreciate it." She rose, hesitated. "Listen, Peabody had a little trouble this morning. The vic was in pretty bad shape, and . . . well, she got sick. She's brooding about it. Like she's the first cop to puke on her shoes," Eve muttered. "Anyway, she's under some stress prepping for the detective's exam, and then she's hunting for a place to cohab with McNab — which I don't really want to think about, but she does. So, maybe you could find a minute to pat her on the head about it or something. Whatever. Shit."

Mira let out a quick, bubbling laugh. "It's very sweet for you to be worried about her."

"I don't want to be very sweet," Eve said with some passion. "Or to worry about her. This isn't the time for her head to be up her ass."

"I'll talk to her." Mira cocked her head. "And how are you?"

"Me? Fine. Good. No complaints. Um . . . things good with you?"

"Yes, they are. My daughter and her family are visiting for a few days. It's always nice for me to have them, and the chance to play Grandma."

"Uh-huh." Mira with her icy suit and pretty legs wasn't Eve's picture of anybody's grandma.

"I'd love for you to meet them."

"Oh, well —"

"We're having an informal cookout on Sunday. I'd very much enjoy it if you and Roarke could come. About two," she said before Eve could think of a response.

"Sunday." A little bubble of panic lodged in her throat. "I don't know if he's got anything going or not. I —"

"I'll check with him." There was a laugh in Mira's eyes as she set her cup aside. "It's just family. Nothing fancy. Now, I'd better let you get back to work."

She walked to the door, opened it, and all but scooted Eve out. Then she leaned back on the door and laughed. It delighted her, absolutely, to see that slightly horrified and completely baffled expression on Eve's face when confronted with the idea of a family cookout.

She checked the time, then hurried to her desk 'link. She'd just contact Roarke immediately and box Eve in before she could find an escape hatch.

Eve was still horrified, still baffled when she reached the Homicide Division again. Peabody leaped out of her cube and hot-footed after her. "Sir. Lieutenant. Dallas."

"What do you do at a cookout?" Eve muttered. "Why are you cooking at all, much less out? It's hot out. There are bugs. I don't get it."

"Dallas!"

"What?" Brows lowered, Eve spun around. "What is it?"

"I've got the customer lists. It took some fast talking, but I convinced the two outlets to give me the names of purchases, those on record, for the stationery found with Jacie Wooton."

"Did you run the names?"

"Not yet. I just got them."

"Let me have them. I've got to do something to get my brain back in gear."

She snatched the disc out of Peabody's hand and plugged it into her desk unit. "I don't have a cup of coffee in my hand," Eve commented as the names began to scroll. "And I'm sure I need it, immediately."

"Yes, sir, you certainly do. Did you see? There's a duchess and an earl, and Liva Holdreak, the actress, and —"

"The coffee isn't in my hand. How can this be?"

"*And* Carmichael Smith, the international recording star, has a standing order for a box of a hundred sheets and envelopes, every six months." As she spoke, Peabody put the mug into Eve's outstretched hand. "His music's too wanky for me, but he, himself? Totally iced."

"I'm glad to know that, Peabody. It's important for me to know he's both wanky and iced should I arrest him for the murder of this very unfortunate LC. We need to keep these things in the forefront."

"Just saying," Peabody grumbled.

She scanned the names, shuffling those with only European residences on record to the bottom. She'd hit the ones with secondary residences in the States first.

"Carmichael Smith keeps an apartment on the Upper West Side. Holdreak has a U.S. residence, but it's in New L.A. We'll just drop her down a notch or two."

She started a standard run, studying the names. "Mr. and Mrs. Elliot P. Hawthorne, Esquire. Ages seventy-eight and thirty-one, respectively. You wouldn't think Elliot would be out cutting up LCs at his age. Married two years, third time around. Elliot likes them young, and I just bet he likes them stupid, too."

"Doesn't seem stupid to marry a rich old guy," Peabody replied. "Calculating."

"You can be stupid and calculating at the same time. Keeps houses in London, Cannes, New York, and Bimini. Made his money the old-fashioned way. Inherited it from his father. No criminal record, no nothing much. Still, we'll see if he's in New York at the moment. Could have servants, staff, assistants, crazy relatives hanging around him with access to his fancy paper."

She continued on down. "Take the names, Peabody. See if you can find out if any of them are in New York."

Would it be that easy? she wondered. Would he be that arrogant to leave something so easily traced back to him? Maybe, maybe. She'd still have to prove it, even if she targeted him through his fancy writing paper.

"Niles Renquist," she stated. "Thirty-eight. Married, one child. Brit citizen with residences in London and New York. Currently chief of staff for the U.N. delegate from Britain, Marshall Evans. Got yourself digs on Sutton Place, don't you, Niles. Fancy stuff. No criminal on you either, but you're worth a look-see."

She sipped coffee, thought vaguely about food.

"Pepper Franklin. What the hell kind of name is Pepper? Actress? Of course you are. Brit actress currently starring in Broadway revival of *Uptown Lady*. No criminal. Nothing but squeaky-clean on this list."

It was a little depressing.

But she hit with Pepper Franklin's cohabitation partner, Leo Fortney.

Sexual assault, indecent exposure, sexual battery.

"Bad boy," Eve reprimanded. "Bad and busy boy."

When Peabody came back, Eve already had her list in order of priority and was shrugging back into her jacket.

"Carmichael Smith, Elliot Hawthorne, Niles Renquist, and Pepper Franklin are all in New York, or reputed to be in New York at this time. Suit up. We're going to go pay some of our English friends a visit." She started out. "Is the U.N. in session?"

"U.N.? As in United Nations?"

"No, U.N. as in Unidentified Numbskulls."

"I recognize sarcasm when I hear it," Peabody said with some dignity. "I'll check on it."

CHAPTER THREE

It irritated her to jump through hoops. Every time she cleared one, there was another stack to hurdle. No amount of reason, demand, or threat got her through the maze of assistants, staffers, coordinators, and personal attendants to Carmichael Smith or Niles Renquist.

She was forced to settle for appointments the following day.

Which might have made her slightly less than diplomatic with the blonde touting herself as Mr. Fortney's social secretary.

"This isn't a social call. See this?" Eve all but pressed her badge to the woman's nose. "This means I'm probably not feeling particularly sociable. This is what we NYPSD people like to call an official inquiry."

The blonde set her face into stern lines and succeeded in looking like a cranky baby doll. "Mr. Fortney is very busy," she said in an indignant lisp Eve just bet some brainless guy found sexy. "He can't be disturbed."

"If you don't tell your boss that Lieutenant Dallas of the NYPSD is out here waiting to speak to him, everyone in this building's going to be disturbed."

"He's unavailable."

Eve had taken that line on Smith, who might very well have been at his health center having a complete physical workup. And she'd taken it on Renquist, who quite possibly had been in back-to-back meetings with various heads of state.

But she wasn't taking it from some actress's bimbo companion.

"Peabody," she said without taking her eyes off the blonde, "call for an Illegals sweep. I believe I smell Zoner."

"What are you talking about? That's just silly." Obviously incensed, the blonde danced on her four-inch platforms that had her impressive breasts bobbing like soccer balls. "You can't do something like that."

"Oh, I bet I can. And you know what happens sometimes, on an Illegals sweep? It leaks to the media. Especially when there's a celebrity type involved. I bet Ms. Franklin's going to be a little annoyed about that."

"If you think you can intimidate me into —"

"Illegals team will be here within thirty, Lieutenant." Peabody tried her cold cop voice. She'd been practicing. "You're authorized to lock down the building."

"Thank you, Officer. That was quick work. With me."

"What?" The blonde clattered after her as Eve strode out of the office. "Where are you going? What are you doing?"

"I'm going to lock down. Once a sweep's been authorized, no one is allowed to enter or leave the premises."

"You can't — Don't." She grabbed Eve's arm.

"Oh-oh?" Eve paused enough to look at the lily-white hand with its baby pink nails that clutched her sleeve. "That might be construed as assaulting an officer, and an attempt to obstruct a police investigation. Since you seem a little dim to me, I'll just cuff you instead of knocking you on your ass, then cuffing you."

"I wasn't!" The blonde dropped Eve's arm as if it had burst into flame, and scrambled back. "I didn't! Oh, damn it, okay, okay, o-*kay*! I'll tell Leo."

"Hmm. You know, Peabody." Eve took another testing sniff of air. "I don't think that's Zoner after all."

"I think you're right, Lieutenant. I think it's gardenia." Peabody let the grin spread as the blonde rushed back into the office. "She must be dim if she thinks you can call for a sweep that way."

"Dim or guilty. Bet she's got a little goodie stash in here. Who did you call?" Eve asked.

"Weather. It's hot, and it's going to stay hot. In case you wondered."

Chin up, the blonde stepped out again, and announced in her best lisp, "Mr. Fortney will see you now."

Eve followed in the wake of the woman's intense dislike.

Fortney was set up in one of the five office suites. The area appeared to have been decorated by the color-blind or the insane — possibly both — as even Eve's casual sense of style was bombarded with the clashing colors and patterns that dominated walls, floors, ceiling.

Fortney's space had taken it one step further by adding animal prints that ran rampant over the walls in a jungle madness of leopard spots, tiger stripes, and splotches of unknown wildlife. Clear tables fashioned of glossy plates atop oddly phallic columns were used as accents.

His desk was a larger version of the tables, with the penis-like columns painted a virulent red. He was pacing behind it as they entered, talking rapidly into a headset.

"We need to move on this within twenty-four. Up or down, no in between. I've got the outline, the projections, and the Q-factor. Let's wrap it up."

He gave a come-ahead gesture with a hand glittering with gold and silver bands.

While he continued to talk and pace, Eve sat in one of the tiger-striped chairs and studied him. He was posing for her, she had no doubt of it. So, she'd accommodate him.

He was artfully dressed in a tunic-jacket and pants, both the color of green grapes. His hair was a dark magenta, worn long and sleek around a narrow, deeply carved face. His eyes too closely matched the shade of his suit to be natural.

Like his fingers, his ears glittered with gold and silver bands.

About six two, Eve judged — with the heeled sandals — and well turned out for his type. Took his body seriously, she imagined, and enjoyed showing it off in fancy duds.

Since he was working hard to show her what a busy and important man he was, she assumed he was neither.

He removed the headset, smiled at her. "I'm so sorry, Lieutenant Dennis. I'm just swamped today."

"Dallas."

"Dallas, of course, Dallas." He made a little ha-ha sound and walked to a long counter, bent down to the minifriggie beneath. He continued to speak in his rapid-fire style, in a accentless tone that said West Coast to Eve. "It's just madness around here, my mind's going a thousand directions at once. Parched. Just parched. Drink?"

"No, thank you."

He took out a bottle of something orange and frothy and poured it into a glass. "Suelee tells me you were very insistent about seeing me."

"Suelee was very insistent I wouldn't see you."

"Well, ha-ha, just doing her job. Don't know what I'd do without my Suelee guarding the gates."

He beamed, sat in an I'm-a-busy-but-personable-son-of-a-bitch style on the edge of his horrible red desk. "You'd be amazed how many people try to get in to see me on any given day. Comes with the territory, of course. Actors, writers, directors." He threw up a hand, waved it dramatically. "But I don't often have an attractive policewoman looking for a meeting."

His smile glittered, white and perfectly even. "So, tell me, what've you got? Play, vid, disc book? Cop drama's cooled off recently, but there's always room for a good story. The girl cop angle's good. What's your pitch?"

"Your whereabouts between midnight and 3a.m. this morning."

"I don't understand."

"I'm primary on a homicide investigation. Your name's come up. I'd like to know your whereabouts during the time frame I just gave you."

"Murder? I don't — *Oooh!*" With another laugh, he shook his head so his hair shook fashionably. "Interesting pitch. Let's see, my first reaction would be what? Shock, insult, fear?"

"A licensed companion was brutally murdered early this morning in Chinatown. You can speed up this process, Mr. Fortney, by telling me where you were between midnight and three."

He lowered his glass. "You're serious?"

"Midnight and three, Mr. Fortney."

"Well, my God. My God." He laid his free hand on his heart, patted it there. "I was home, of course. Pepper comes straight home after the show. We tend to go to bed early during a run. It's both physically and emotionally exhausting for her. People don't understand the strain of performing, night after night, and how few reserves one has left after —"

"I'm not interested in where Ms. Franklin was," Eve interrupted. *Or in your stalling tactics*, she thought. "Where were you?"

"Well, home, as I said." His tone was a little testy now. "Pepper would have arrived by midnight, and she needs a bit of company and care after a show, so I always wait up to be there for her. We had a nightcap while she ran down, then we were tucked in before one, so she could get her beauty sleep. I can't understand why you'd possibly question me. An LC, in Chinatown? What could that have to do with me?"

"Can anyone verify that you were home during the time frame?"

"Pepper, of course. Pepper. I was right there to greet her when she arrived home, just before midnight. And we were in bed, as I said, by one. She's a very light sleeper. It comes from being so creative and sensitive. She'll tell you she'd have known if I so much as stirred from the bed in the night."

He took another drink, a longer one. "Who was this woman who was killed? Do I know her? I don't use the services of companions. I do, naturally, know many people, from various walks. Certainly some actors and hopefuls might moonlight as LCs."

"Jacie Wooton."

"It means nothing to me. Nothing." The color that had come into his face during his rambling alibi began to diminish. He shrugged, carelessly now. "I don't believe I've ever been to Chinatown."

"You bought stationery in London several months ago. Fifty sheets and envelopes, plain, cream-colored, unrecycled stock."

"Did I? It's certainly possible. I buy quite a lot of things. For myself, for Pepper, as gifts. What in the world does stationery have to do with anything?"

"It's very expensive, very distinctive stock. It would be helpful if you could produce it."

"Paper, bought months ago, in London?" He made his ha-ha sound again, but this time it carried annoyance. "For all I know it's still in London. I think I should call my lawyer."

"That's your choice. You can ask your representative to meet us downtown, at Central, to discuss your priors. Assaults and sex crimes."

His face turned nearly the same shade as his hair. "Those incidents are in my past. If you must know the sexual assault charge was completely unwarranted. An argument with a woman I'd been dating that escalated, and her revenge when I broke things off with her. I didn't fight the charge as I felt it would only generate more ugly publicity and drag things out."

"Indecent exposure."

"A misunderstanding. I'd had a bit too much to drink after a party and, impaired, was relieving my bladder when a group of young women happened to pass. It was foolish and ill-advised, but hardly criminal."

"And the battery?"

"A shoving match with my ex-wife. Who started the incident, by the way. Just an unfortunate display of temper, which she used to skin me in the divorce. I don't appreciate having all this thrown in my face, or being accused of murder. I was at home and in bed last night. All night. And that's all I have to say without my lawyer."

"Funny," Eve commented as she headed uptown. "A guy can be arrested and charged three times, but none of it was his fault. All misunderstandings."

"Yeah, the law's a bitch."

"What we've got here, Peabody, is a weasely little man who likes to put on a big show. Look at me. I'm important, I'm powerful. I'm somebody. And he has a history of knocking women around, showing off his dick and losing his temper. Surrounds himself with phallic symbols and has a big-breasted blonde playing guardian of the gates."

"I didn't like him. But it's a pretty big leap from shaking his wang to slicing up an LC."

"Steps and stages," Eve declared. "Let's see if Pepper's home, and how she slept last night."

The brownstone was lovely, old and elegant. And meant, Eve calculated as she walked toward the door, private security. The sort the owner could turn on and off at whim.

She rang the bell, considered the entrance, the flow of flowers in pots running up the short set of steps, the proximity of neighboring houses.

When the door opened, she had an immediate flash, and not very pleasant, of Roarke's majordomo, and the bane of her existence, Summerset.

The butler was dressed in stark black, as was Summerset's habit. He was long and thin with pewter hair atop a narrow face.

She actually felt her gorge rise.

"May I help you?"

"Lieutenant Dallas, Officer Peabody." Prepared to plow through him if necessary, she flipped out her badge. "I need to speak with Ms. Franklin."

"Ms. Franklin is engaged in her yoga/meditation hour. May I be of some assistance?"

"You can assist me by getting out of the way, telling Ms. Franklin she's got a cop at the door who wants to question her regarding an official investigation."

"Of course," he said so genially, she actually blinked. "Please come in. If you'd make yourself comfortable in the living area, I'll inform Ms. Franklin. Would you care for any refreshment while you wait?"

"No." She eyed him suspiciously. "Thanks."

"I'll just be a moment." After gesturing them into a large, sunny room with long white sofas, he turned toward a staircase.

"Maybe we can trade Summerset for him."

"Hey, Dallas, check it out."

Eve turned and studied what Peabody was currently gaping at. The life-sized portrait of Pepper Franklin rose above the sea green mantel of a white hearth. In it, she appeared to be dressed in nothing but mists. They curled and draped around her, shimmering and thin so that her impressive body was displayed. Her arms were stretched out as if welcoming an embrace.

She was smiling, dreamily, her lips painted deep rose. Her hair was a tumble of gold around a heart-shaped face set off by wide, deep blue eyes.

Striking, Eve mused. Sensual. Powerful.

Just what, she wondered, was a woman with that much style and strength doing with a loser like Fortney?

"I've seen her on-screen and in mags and stuff, but this is — you know — wow. She looks like, I don't know, a fairy queen."

"Thank you." The voice was silver wrapped in fog. "That was the goal," Pepper said as she walked into the room. "It's taken, more or less, from my role of Titania."

She wore a skin-suit now, in dark purple, and had a short towel hooked around her neck. Her face, still striking, was sheened with perspiration, and her hair was bundled up carelessly.

"Lieutenant Dallas?" She offered a hand. "Excuse my appearance. I'm in the middle of yoga. It helps keep me in shape — body, mind, spirit. It also makes me sweat like a pig."

"I'm sorry to interrupt."

"I assume it's important." She sat, dropping down on the white sofa, letting out a long sigh. "Please, have a seat. Oh God, Turney, thanks." She took the large bottle of water the butler brought her on a silver tray.

"Mr. Fortney is on the 'link. He's called three times in the last thirty minutes."

"He should know better than to call during yoga hour. Tell him I'll get back to him."

She took a long drink, angled her head. "Well, what's this about?"

"I'd like you to verify Mr. Fortney's whereabouts this morning between midnight and three."

The easy smile vanished. "Leo? Why?"

"His name has come up in the course of an investigation. If I can verify his whereabouts during that period, we can eliminate it and move on."

"He was here, with me. I got home about eleven forty-five. Maybe a few minutes later. We had a drink. I allow myself one glass of wine before bed after a performance. We talked about various things, then I went upstairs. I suppose I was in bed and asleep by twelve-thirty."

"Alone?"

"Initially. I'm always beat after a show, and Leo's a night owl. He was going to watch some screen, make some calls. Something." She lifted one elegant shoulder.

"You a light sleeper, Ms. Franklin?"

"Hell, I sleep like the dead." She started to laugh, then caught the implication. "Lieutenant, Leo was here. Honestly, I can't imagine what sort of investigation you might be pursuing where Leo's name came up in any way."

"You're aware it's not the first time his name's come up in a police investigation."

"Those incidents are in the past. He had some bad luck with women, until me. He was here when I got home, and we had coffee together this morning at about eight. What's this about?"

"Last fall Mr. Fortney purchased, in London, some stationery."

"Oh for God's sake." Pepper tipped the bottle back for another drink. "I'm still angry with him about that. Ridiculous, and careless. Unrecycled. I don't know what he was thinking. Don't tell me he brought it with him into the U.S.?" She rolled her eyes, then stared at the ceiling. "Really, I know it's against the law, technically. I'm very active in environmental groups, which is why I could have skinned him for buying that stationery. In fact, we had a row about it, and I made him promise to get rid of it. I'm sure there's a fine, and I'll see he pays it."

"I'm not a Green Cop. I'm Homicide."

Those brilliant blue eyes went blank. "Homicide?"

"Early this morning, a licensed companion identified as Jacie Wooton was murdered in Chinatown."

"I know." Pepper's hand crawled up to her throat. "I heard the report this morning. You can't possibly believe . . . Leo? He'd never do such a thing."

"Stationery, of the type Mr. Fortney purchased in London, was used for a note left with the body."

"He . . . he's certainly not the only idiot who bought that stationery. Leo was home last night." She bit off the words so that each one was highlighted. "Lieutenant, he's occasionally foolish, tends to be a bit of a show-off, but he's not vicious or violent. And he was home."

She was going home herself, dissatisfied. She'd done all she could for Jacie Wooton in one day, but it wasn't enough.

She needed to clear her mind. Take a couple hours' downtime, then go back, read over the reports, the notes, juggle it around in her home office.

Fortney and Franklin just didn't match for her. The guy was a putz, a braggart, a fake with a handsome face. Her impression of Franklin was that the woman was the real deal. Smart, strong, stable.

Then again, you never could tell why people ended up together.

She'd given up trying to figure out how she and Roarke had become a unit.

He was rich, gorgeous, sneaky, just a little dangerous. He'd been everywhere and had bought most of it. He'd done everything, and a great deal of what he'd done didn't fall on her side of the law.

And she was a cop. Solitary, short-tempered, and unsociable.

He loved her anyway, she mused, as she drove through the iron gates of home.

Because he did, she'd ended up here, living in the huge stone palace draped in trees and flowers, surrounded by the stuff of fantasy. It was ridiculous, really, she thought, that someone who'd lived in reality, often the harshest wells of it, should end up in some sort of dreamscape.

She parked in front of the house. She'd leave her pea green cop issue there, as sort of an homage to Summerset, the gnome in her personal dreamscape.

He might've still been on holiday — sing hallelujah — but since he despised her habit of parking out front of the spectacular entrance, she saw no reason to stop.

She stepped inside, into the cool and rarified air of the house that Roarke built, and was immediately greeted by the cat. The pudgy and obviously irritated Galahad pranced up, batted his head against her ankle, and mewed shrilly.

"Hey, I've got to work for a living. I can't help it if you're alone all day with He Who Shall Not Be Named out of the country." But she bent down, scooped the cat up. “You need a hobby. Or hey, maybe they make VR for pets. If not, Roarke will jump right on that.”

She scratched the cat as she headed out of the foyer and downstairs to the gym. “Little VR goggles for cats, with programs about war on mice, kicking a Doberman’s ass, that sort of thing.”

She dumped him on the floor of the gym, and knowing the true path to his heart, got a bowl of tuna from the AutoChef.

With the cat occupied, she stripped down, changed into workout gear, and set herself a twenty-minute run on the video track. She opted for a beach run, and set out at a light jog, feeling her feet slap sand.

By the time she was at full pace, she’d worked up a nice sweat and was enjoying the salty breeze of the sea, the sound of the surf.

You could keep your yoga, Eve thought. Give her a good, full-out run, then maybe a couple rounds with a workout droid, follow it with a good strong swim, and you’d have your mind, body, and spirit tuned right up.

When the machine blinked end of program, she grabbed a towel, scrubbed it over her sweaty face. With the intention of challenging the droid to a little hand-to-hand, she turned.

And there was Roarke, sitting on a weight bench with a cat in his lap, and his eyes on his wife.

Spectacular eyes, she thought. Violently blue in a face carved by clever angels. The dangerous poet, the poetic danger, whichever way you looked at it — at him — he was amazing.

"Hey." She tunneled her fingers through her damp hair. "How long have you been here?"

"Long enough to see you wanted a hard run. You've had a long day, Lieutenant."

There was Ireland in his voice, dreamy wisps of it that could, unexpectedly, wind around her heart. He set the cat aside, and walked over to tip up her chin. Rubbed his thumb in the shallow dent in its center.

"I heard about what happened in Chinatown. That's what pulled you out of bed so early this morning."

"Yeah. She's mine. Just clearing my head before I get back to it again."

"All right." He touched his lips to hers. "You want a swim, then?"

"Eventually." She rolled her shoulders to loosen them up. "Hand-to-hand's next up. I was going to use the droid, but since you're here . . ."

"Want to fight with me, do you?"

"You're better than the droid." She stepped back, began to circle him. "Marginally."

"And to think some men come home after a day of work and are greeted by their woman." He rolled up to his toes, and back, glad he'd changed with the idea of a workout. "A smile, a kiss, perhaps a cold drink." His grin flashed. "How tedious for them."

She lunged, he countered.

She kicked out, her foot coming within a half-inch of his face. He slapped it away, then swept her standing leg out from under her. She went down, rolled, and was up again in seconds.

"Not bad," she acknowledged, and scored a hit mid-body before their forearms slapped together in a block. "But I was holding back."

"Can't have that."

She came in on a spin — left hook, right cross — that would have knocked his head back if she'd connected. His backhand stopped a hairbreadth from her nose.

With the droid, she'd have pounded and gotten pounded in return. But this — the demand for control — was more challenging. And a hell of a lot more fun.

She got under his guard, flipped him, but when she leaped on the mat to pin him, he was already up again. She had to somersault aside, and came up just enough off balance to give him the opening.

Her breath whooshed out as she hit the mat, flat on her back, with his weight pinning her.

She stared up into his eyes as she got her wind back, lifting a hand so she could trail her fingers through the wonderful mane of black hair that nearly hit his shoulders.

"Roarke," she murmured, and with a little sigh, tugged his hair to bring his lips to hers.

And when he relaxed, started to sink into her, she scissored her legs, arched, and flipped him over.

She was looking in his eyes again, and grinning as she pressed the point of her elbow lightly to his throat. "Sucker."

"I do tend to fall for that one, don't I? Well then, it appears you've taken this —" He broke off, winced.

"What? You hurt?"

"No. Just must've jammed my shoulder a bit." He rotated it, winced again.

"Let me take a look." She eased back, shifting her weight.

And found herself flat on her back under him again.

"Sucker," he said and laughed when her eyes went to slits.

"Foul."

"No more foul than the seductive murmur of my name. You're down, darling." He touched his lips to the tip of her nose. "Well pinned." His fingers linked with hers as he held her hands down. "Now I'm going to have you."

"You think?"

"I do. Victor, spoils, all that. Not going to be a sore loser, are you?" he asked with his mouth rubbing hers.

"Who says I lost?" She arched her hips. "Like I said, you're better than the droid." She arched again. "Touch me."

"I will. Let's start with this."

His mouth came down on hers, warm and soft, sliding her into the kiss, deepening it until, once again, she lost her breath.

"It's never quite enough," he whispered, trailing his lips over her face, down her throat. "Never will be."

"There's always more."

So he took more, skimming those lips, scraping his teeth over the swell of her breasts beneath the loose cotton T-shirt.

Her heart began to thud, anticipation. Her fingers curled tighter against the ones that held her hands prisoner. She didn't try to free herself, not yet. Here, too, was control. His and hers. And trust. Absolute.

When he drew her hands down to her waist, roamed with that busy mouth over her torso, she braced herself for the onslaught of pleasure.

Her skin was already damp, her muscles taut. He loved the feel of them, hard and strong, under all that smooth skin. He loved the lines of her, and the subtle, almost delicate curves.

He released her hands, then drew the shorts down. With a slight frown, he traced a fingertip over her thigh. "You've a bruise here. You're always coming up with bruises."

"Hazard of the job."

She faced worse hazards, they both knew. He lowered his head, touched his lips lightly to the faint discoloration.

Amused, she stroked his hair. "Don't worry, Mom. It doesn't hurt."

The laugh caught in her throat as his mouth got to work.

Her hand fisted in his hair now, and her other hand dug into the mat as her system shot from rest to revved. A shockwave of heat, a stunning ache that gathered in a fist of pressure, then imploded inside her.

"Teach you to call me mum," he said, and nipped lightly at her thigh while she shuddered.

She got her breath back, whistled it out again. "Mom," she repeated, and made him laugh.

He wrapped his arms around her so they rolled, playfully now. Hands sliding over flesh, tugging off clothes, lips meeting for nibbles or longer tastes.

She felt free and careless, and foolishly in love as she held him against her. Easy enough to laugh even as her body quaked, to rub her cheek against his in innocent affection even as he slid into her.

"Looks like I've pinned you again."

"How long do you think you can keep me down?"

"Another challenge, is it?" His breath was backed up in his lungs, but he moved slowly, watching her watch him.

With long, smooth, almost lazy strokes he urged her up again until he saw her eyes begin to blur, and the flush deepen in her cheeks. And then heard her low sound, that helpless sound, of pleasure.

"There's always more," he said and captured her lips with his again and let himself fly with her.

CHAPTER FOUR

They ate in the dining room at Roarke's suggestion that they have a meal like people who have lives outside their professions. The remark was pointed enough to have Eve checking her intention of grabbing a burger at her desk in her home office. But her initial enjoyment of the crab salad was spoiled by his reminder that they had plans the following evening.

"Charity dinner dance," he prompted when she stared blankly. "Philadelphia. We need to make an appearance." He sipped his wine and smiled at her. "Not to worry, darling. It won't hurt very much, and we won't have to leave until after seven. If you're running late, you can change on the shuttle."

She poked sulkily at chilled crab. "Did I know about this?"

"You did. And if you ever glanced at your personal calendar, you wouldn't so often be surprised and appalled by these little obligations."

"I'm not appalled." Dinner, dancing. Fancy outfit, fancy people. God. "It's just that if something breaks at work —"

"Understood."

She bit back a sigh because it was true. He understood. She heard enough comments from other cops about spouses or lovers who didn't, or couldn't, or wouldn't, to appreciate it.

And she knew she wasn't nearly as flexible and understanding about the role she had to play as the wife of one of the richest and most influential men on or off planet.

She stabbed more crab and made an effort to pull her marital weight. "It shouldn't be a problem."

"It might actually be fun. Sunday promises to be."

"Sunday?"

"Mmm." He topped off her wine, figuring she'd need it. "The cookout at Dr. Mira's. It's been a very long time since I attended something I suppose would be termed a kind of family picnic. I hope there's potato salad."

She picked up her wine, drank deep. "She talked to you. You said yes."

"Of course. We should take a bottle of wine or I wonder if beer's more appropriate." Enjoying himself, he lifted an eyebrow. "What do you think?"

"I can't think. I don't know about this stuff. I've never been to a cookout. I don't understand the ritual. If we're both off on Sunday, we could just stay home, in bed. Have sweaty sex all day."

"Hmm. Sex or potato salad. You've hit me at two basic levels." Then he laughed at her, and passed her half a roll he'd already buttered. "Eve, it's a simple family gathering. She wants you there because you're important to her. We'll sit around and talk about, I don't know, baseball or some such thing. We'll eat too much and enjoy ourselves. And you'll have the chance to meet her family. Then we'll come home and have sweaty sex."

She scowled at the roll. "It just makes me nervous, that's all. You like having conversations with strangers. I don't get that about you."

"You have conversations with strangers all the time," he pointed out. "You just call them suspects."

Defeated, she filled her mouth with bread.

"Now, why don't we talk about something that won't make you nervous? Tell me about the case."

There was a lovely twilight outside the windows, and candles flickering prettily on the table. Wine sparkled in crystal and silver gleamed. And her mind, she realized, kept slipping back to a hacked body in a cold drawer at the morgue. "It's not exactly dinner conversation."

"Not for normal people. But it works for us. The media reports were sketchy."

"I'm not going to be able to keep them that way if and when he hits again. I ducked reporters all day, but I'm going to have to give them something tomorrow to stem the appetite. She was an LC, bumped down to street level because of some illegals busts. She seemed to be clean now, though I'd still like to find her supplier just to knot that thread."

"A down-on-her-luck LC shouldn't have the media slathering very long."

"No, it won't be who, it'll be how that gets them drooling. He took her in an alley. The way it looked, she went in to do the job. He faced her to the wall, slit her throat. Even from behind, he couldn't have avoided all the blood spatter."

She picked up her wine again, staring into it rather than drinking. "Then he laid her out, across the alley floor. Morris thinks a laser scalpel. He cut her pelvis out, took the whole works. You could all but swim in the blood."

She drank now, let out a breath. There was something about blood, she thought, the scent of death blood. Once you smelled it, you never completely got it out of your system.

"Clean job, though, almost surgical. Had to have a bag to take it away in, had to work fairly quickly, had to clean himself up before he walked back out again. Even down there, that time of night, somebody's going to notice a guy covered in blood."

"And no one did."

"No." They'd check again, she thought. And again. But odds were they'd come up zero. "See no evil, hear no evil, speak all you want as long as it doesn't put you in the mix. He didn't know her, I'm almost sure. Otherwise, he'd have gone for the face some. That's what they do. Thrill crime, lust driven. Woman hater. Peabody got dog sick, and spent a good part of the day kicking herself about it."

He thought of what the victim, what the alley must have looked like and rubbed a hand over Eve's. "Have you ever? Gotten sick?"

"Not on scene. It's like saying you did more than I can take, more than I can handle, and I can't stand over this body and look at what you did. But sometimes, later, it comes back on you. Middle of the night mostly. Then you get sick."

She drank now. "Anyway . . . he left a note, addressed to me. Don't freak," she said when she felt his fingers tighten over her hand. "It's professional rather than personal. He's admired my work, wanted to give me a chance to see his. He wanted me on this one, an ego thing. I've had two very hot cases this summer, with wall-to-wall media attention. He wants that sort of buzz."

His fingers stayed over hers. "What did it say?"

"Just that — cocky. He signed it Jack."

"Emulating the Ripper then."

"You save me a lot of steps when you get it. Yeah, the choice of victim, the location, the method, even the note to a cop. Too much of it's already leaked to the media, and if they get their teeth in it, it's going to be a frenzy. I want to shut him down fast, before the panic. Been working with the note — the paper."

"What's unique about it?"

"Unrecycled, very pricey, manufactured in England, sold exclusively in Europe. Do you manufacture unrecycled paper products?"

"Roarke Industries is green. Just our little contribution to environmental responsibility, which also earns a healthy tax break in most markets." He ignored the server droid who came to clear the plates and bring out small dessert parfaits and coffee.

"Where's the paper taking you?"

"I'm focusing on London outlets first, playing the Ripper angle. I've got a couple of celebs, a politician type, a retired financier, and the asshole lover of some actress named Pepper."

"Pepper Franklin?"

"Yeah, she strikes me as straight up, but the guy . . ." She trailed off, narrowing her eyes as Roarke scooped up a spoonful of parfait. "You know her."

"Mmm. This is very nice, refreshing."

"You banged her."

Though his lips twitched he managed to maintain a sober expression as he sampled more parfait. "That's a very unattractive term. I prefer saying we had a brief and mature relationship, which included the occasional banging."

"I should've known. She's just your type."

"Is she?" he queried.

"Gorgeous, elegant, sophisticated sex."

"Darling." He sat back to sip his coffee. "How conceited of you. Not that you aren't all those things, and more."

"I'm not talking about me." She scowled at him a moment, then went to work on the parfait. "I should have figured her for one of your formers the minute I saw the portrait."

"Ah, she still has that, does she? The Titania portrait?"

She shoveled parfait in her mouth. "You're going to tell me you gave it to her."

"As what you might call a parting gift."

"What, like on a game show?"

His laughter was rich and full of fun. "If you like. How is she? I haven't seen her in, Christ, seven or eight years, I suppose."

“She’s dandy.” Watching him, she licked her spoon. “But her taste in men has seriously declined.”

“Why, thank you.” He grabbed her hand, kissed it. “While mine, in women, has seriously improved.”

She wouldn’t have minded working up a good head of jealousy steam, to see what it felt like. But it just didn’t work for her. “Yeah, yeah, yeah. She’s hooked up with a guy named Leo Fortney. Operator. He’s got operator all over him, and a couple of pops, including sexual assault.”

“Doesn’t sound like Pepper’s usual fare. Is he your prime suspect?”

“He’s number one right now, though he was home in bed during the time involved. She’s corroborating, but since she was sleeping, I’m not putting much weight there. Plus, he lied, said they went nighty-night together, and she said different before she realized she’d be blowing it for him. Still, she struck me as a straight shooter.” She paused, waited.

“She is, yes.”

“So whether or not he was there, she thinks he was. We’ll see where it goes. Meanwhile, I’ve got informals set up tomorrow with Carmichael Smith to start.”

“Pop music king. Irritatingly saccharin lyrics, over-orchestrated melodies.”

“So I’m told.”

“You may not have been told, as I’ve been, that Smith enjoys young women, preferably more than one at a time. And makes considerable use of groupies, as well as professionals, to help him . . . relax between recording sessions and gigs.”

"Minors?"

"There've been rumblings that there might have been an underage fan now and again, though he's usually more careful. No violence that I've heard of. Though he likes bondage games, he prefers being the one bound."

"He one of yours?"

"No, he's still with his original label. I could probably poach him, but his music just annoys me."

"Okay, moving on. There Niles Renquist, works for U.N. Delegate Marshall Evans."

"I know Renquist, slightly. So do you."

"I do?"

"You met him, I think it was last spring, at another appalling obligation." He watched her eyebrows draw together as she tried to place it — the place, the meet, the man. "More a quick introduction than a meet, actually. A silent auction benefiting, well, there you have me," he murmured. "I'd need my book for that. But it was a few months ago, here in New York. You'd have been introduced to him and his wife at some point."

Because she couldn't bring it in, she let it go. "Did I have an impression?"

"Apparently not. He's, let's see . . . conservative, leaning toward stuffy. Late thirties, I'd say, well-spoken, well-educated. What you might call a bit prissy. His wife's quite pretty in the British tea party style. They have homes here and in England, I know, as I recall his wife telling me she enjoyed New York, but much preferred their home outside London where she could garden properly."

"Did *you* have an impression?"

"Can't say I liked either of them overmuch." He lifted a shoulder in a vague shrug. "A bit on the pompous side, and very aware of class distinctions and levels of society. The sort I'd find tedious if not downright annoying with regular exposure."

"You know a lot of people who fit that box."

His lip twitched. "I do. Yes, I do."

"Elliot P. Hawthorne?"

"Yes, I've had dealings with him. Seventies, sharp, lives for golf. Apparently dotes on his third, considerably younger wife, and travels quite a lot now that he's retired. I like him quite a bit. Is that helpful at all?"

"Anybody you don't know?"

"Not worth mentioning."

The evening at home with Roarke had helped clear her mind, Eve decided as she rode up in the jammed elevator to the Homicide Division. Not only did she feel rested, well-fed, and tuned up, but his informal rundown of some of the names on her list gave her a different insight. It was more personal and certainly more informative than the dry facts from a standard ID run.

She could shuffle his data around in her head as she questioned each party, and angle those questions around the more personal information. But first, she needed to check for any updates on lab and ME reports, round up Peabody, and face the media music.

She elbowed her way out of the elevator and turned toward her sector.

And all but ran into Nadine Furst.

The on-air reporter had a new short and sleek hairdo. What was it, Eve thought, with new hair on everybody? It was blonder, swingier, and swept back from Nadine's perfect, angular face.

She was wearing a short, fitted jacket over slim, fitted pants, both in power red, which told Eve she was camera-ready.

And she carried a huge white bakery box that smelled gloriously of fat and sugar.

"Doughnuts." There was no mistaking that scent, and Eve homed in on it like a hound on a fox. "You've got doughnuts in there." She tapped a finger to the box. "That's how you get through the bull pen, avoid the civilian and media lounges, and end up in my office. You bribe my men."

Nadine fluttered her lashes. "And your point is?"

"My point is, how come I never get a damn doughnut?"

"Because generally I time it better, dump my offering in the bull pen, sometimes it's brownies, and while every cop in Homicide descends like a pack of coyotes, I settle down in your office and wait for your arrival."

Eve waited a beat. "Bring the doughnuts, leave the camera."

"I need my camera," Nadine said, gesturing to the woman beside her.

"I need a sunny Sunday at the beach where I can romp naked as a puppy in the surf, but I'm not going to get it anytime soon either. Doughnuts in, camera out."

To ensure obedience, and to prevent her men from rioting, she snatched the bakery box herself before striding into the bull pen.

Several heads lifted, noses sniffed the air. "Don't even think about it," Eve ordered and kept right on walking through choruses of protests and complaints.

"There are three dozen in there," Nadine told her as she followed Eve into her office. "You can't possibly eat them all."

"I could, just to teach those greedy hogs a lesson. However, this is a lesson in discipline and authority." She opened the box, sighed deep as she perused her choices, all glossy, all hers. "I'll let them think I'm keeping them all, and have my fill, then have them weeping with gratitude when I take out the leftovers to share."

She plucked one out, brought up coffee on the AutoChef, then bit in. "Cream filled. Yum." Chewing, she checked her wrist unit, then counted back from ten as she crossed to the door. Peabody rushed to the doorway as Eve hit one.

"Dallas! Hey! I was just —"

Taking another enormous bite, Eve closed the door in her aide's sorrowful face.

"That was really cold," Nadine commented and did what she could to swallow the laugh.

"Yeah, but fun."

"Now that we've had our fun, I need an update on the Wooton murder, and a one-on-one. It would've been easier to set this up if you'd bothered to return any of my calls."

Eve sat on the corner of the desk. "Can't do it, Nadine."

"I need to verify if there was, as rumored, some sort of communication left at the crime scene, and the contents therein. Also what progress has or has not been made since —"

"Nadine, I can't."

Undaunted, Nadine helped herself to coffee, sat in Eve's battered visitor's chair, crossed her legs. "The public has a right to know, and I, as media representative, have a responsibility to —"

"Save it. We can go through the dance, but you've brought me these nice doughnuts and I don't want to waste your time." Giving Nadine a moment to stew, Eve licked sugar off her thumb. "I'm going to issue a press release, give a statement, and you'll have it along with the other media reps within the hour. But I can't give you a head start, or agree to a one-on-one. I need to pull back a little —"

Nadine was finished stewing and ready to cut to the core. "What makes this case different? If there's to be some sort of media shutdown —"

"Stop. Shift out of reporter mode for one goddamn minute. You're a friend of mine. I like you, and beyond that I think you do a good job, a responsible one."

"Great, fine, and right back at you, but —"

"I'm not shutting you out. The fact is, I'm treating you as I would any other media rep."

Except, Eve thought, for the doughnut gorging and private chat. "My tendency to show favoritism toward you is one of the reasons you were pulled into the Stevenson case last month."

"That was —"

"Nadine." It was the quiet patience in Eve's tone — something rarely heard — that had Nadine subsiding again. "There were complaints. And there's speculation of the sort that could bring us both grief if I don't throttle back on the cop/reporter relationship a bit. So I can't feed you this time. I need the rumbles to quiet down before I start to be known as Furst's pet, or you as mine. Enough reporters get together and start crying foul and favoritism, it's not going to be good for either of us."

Nadine hissed through her teeth. She'd heard the complaints, and the speculation, and had already weathered some resentment among her own rank and file. "You're right, and that's a pisser. Doesn't mean I won't hound you, Dallas."

"Goes without saying."

The battle light shone in her eyes again, and matched the sharp little smile. "Or bribe your men."

"I like brownies, especially the ones with those chunks of chocolate in them."

Nadine set the coffee down, got up. "Listen, if you need to leak something, give Quinton Post a try. He's young yet, but he's good, and the work matters to him as much, maybe even a little more, than the ratings.

That won't last," she added cheerfully. "But you might as well get him while he's fresh."

"I'll keep it in mind."

Alone, Eve refined her official statement, then ran it through channels. Carting the bakery box back into the bull pen, she dropped it on the communal AutoChef.

All movement stopped. Silence fell.

"Peabody," she said into the breathless hush, "with me."

She'd barely hit the doorway when the riot of rushing feet and clamor of voices erupted behind her.

Cops and doughnuts, she thought. A well-honored tradition that almost brought a sentimental tear to the eye.

"I bet there were jelly-filled. I bet there were," Peabody muttered as they muscled onto an elevator.

"Some of them had those little colored sprinkle things on top. Like edible confetti."

Peabody's square and sturdy jaw wobbled with emotion. "All I had time for this morning was reconstituted banana slices on a stale bagel."

"You're breaking my heart." At garage level, Eve strolled off the elevator. "Carmichael's first stop. We're catching him between his morning aqua therapy and daily skin treatment."

"You could've saved me one. One little doughnut."

"I could have," Eve agreed as they climbed in her vehicle. "I could have done that. In fact . . ." She rummaged around in her pocket, pulled out an evidence bag. Inside was a jelly doughnut. "I believe I did."

"For me?" Overjoyed, Peabody snatched it, sniffed through the bag. "You saved me a doughnut. You're so good to me. I take back everything I was thinking — you know, how you're a cold, selfish, doughnut-hogging bitch and all that. Thanks, Dallas."

"Don't mention it."

"I really shouldn't eat it though." Peabody caught her bottom lip between her teeth, stroking the bag as Eve backed out of the slot. "I really shouldn't. I'm on a diet. I've just got to lose some of the square footage of my ass, so I —"

"Oh, for Christ's sake. Give it back then."

But when Eve reached out, Peabody cringed back, doughnut bag clutched at her breasts, face screwed into dangerous lines. "Mine."

"Peabody, you continue to be a fascination to me."

"Thanks." Slowly, savoring the moment, Peabody unsealed the bag. "Anyway, I deserve it. I'm using up lots of calories studying for the detective's exam, and stressing about it. Stress sucks up calories like a vacuum. That's why you're so thin."

"I'm not thin, I'm not stressed."

"If you've got an excess ounce of body fat, I'll eat it. Respectfully, sir," Peabody added with a mouthful of jelly doughnut. "But I've really been hitting the discs and the simulators. McNab's helping me out. He's hardly even being an asshole right now."

"Wonder of wonders."

"It's coming up really soon. I was wondering if you could tell me where you think my weak areas are so I could work on them."

"You question yourself. Even when your gut tells you you're right, you don't trust it enough. You've got good instincts, but you tend to be afraid to go with them without confirmation from a superior. You often question your own competence, and when you question yours, you're questioning mine."

She glanced over, unsurprised to see Peabody keying her comments into her notebook between bites of doughnut. "You're writing this down."

"It helps to see it, you know. Then to do these affirmations in the mirror. I'm a confident, competent officer of the law, and like that." She flushed a little. "It's just a method."

"Whatever."

Eve nosed into a narrow space at the curb. "Let's confidently and competently see where Carmichael Smith was night before last."

"Yes, sir, but I also have to stress and obsess about having eaten that jelly doughnut. That'll work off the calories and even it out. It'll be like I never ate it at all."

"Then you might want to wipe the jelly off your lip."

Eve stepped out of the car, studied the building. It had been, she supposed, a small three-level apartment building at one time. Now it was a single residence on a tony street. Private security again, two entrances in the front. At least one in the back, she assumed.

Not so far from an alley in Chinatown geographically, but worlds away in every other form. No LCs on the stroll here, no glide-carts on the corners. High maintenance and low crime.

She circled around the walk and up to the main entrance on the second level.

Security panel, palm plate, and a retinal scan. A very careful man. She engaged the panel and frowned at the music that soared out. A lot of strings and keyboard around a creamy male voice.

" 'Love Lights the World,' " Peabody identified. "It's sort of his signature song."

"It's got more calories than your doughnut."

WELCOME, the computer said in polite, female tones. WE HOPE YOU'RE HAVING A WONDERFUL DAY. PLEASE STATE YOUR NAME AND YOUR BUSINESS.

"Dallas, Lieutenant Eve." She lifted her badge for a scan. "Police business. I've got an appointment with Mr. Smith this morning."

ONE MOMENT, PLEASE . . . THANK YOU, LIEUTENANT. MR. SMITH IS EXPECTING YOU. YOU'RE CLEARED.

Almost immediately the door was opened by a dark-skinned woman in snowy white. There was more music here, quietly dripping its sweetness in the air.

"Good morning. Thank you for being prompt. Please come in, make yourself at home in the living area. Carmichael will be right with you."

She glided, Eve thought, like a woman on rollers instead of feet, as she ushered them into a large room with blond walls. There was a mood screen taking up one of those walls, with an image of a white boat drifting on a blue sea as calm as a plate of glass. Thick gel cushions were spread over the floor in lieu of actual furniture, and all were in pastels. Tables were long and low, in that same blond tone.

A fuzzy white kitten curled on one of the tables, and blinked emerald eyes at Eve.

"Please relax. I'll let Carmichael know you're here."

Peabody walked over and poked at one of the floor cushions. "I guess you sink right in and it molds to your butt." Experimentally, she reached back and patted a hand over her ass. "That could be embarrassing."

"That music is making my teeth ache." Eve ran her tongue around them, then turned as Carmichael Smith made his entrance.

He was tall, about six three with a well-toned body he was currently showing off in a fluid white vest that left his pecs and abs on display. His pants were black and snug, so he could display his other attributes. His hair was dramatically streaked black and white, and worn back in a queue to leave his face — wide, high-boned, and narrowed to a sharp, pointed chin — unframed.

His eyes were deep, melted chocolate brown, his skin the color of coffee light.

"Ah, Lieutenant Dallas. Or do I call you Mrs. Roarke?"

Eve heard Peabody's smothered snort, ignored it. "You call me Lieutenant Dallas."

"Of course, of course." He strode in, vest streaming, and took the hand she'd yet to offer in both of his. "It's just that I only made the connection this morning." He gave her hand an intimate squeeze, then turned his charm on Peabody. "And who might you be?"

"My aide, Officer Peabody. I have some questions, Mr. Smith."

"More than happy to answer them." He took Peabody's hand as he had Eve's. "Please, please, sit. Li's bringing us some tea. I have a special morning blend for energy. It's simply fantastic. Call me Carmichael."

He lowered smoothly to a peach-colored cushion and took the little cat into his lap. "There now, Snowdrop, did you think Daddy had forgotten you?"

She didn't want to sit on one of the cushions, nor did she want to remain standing and towering over him. So she sat on the table.

"Can you tell me where you were, early yesterday morning, between midnight and 3a.m.?"

Like the cat, he blinked. "Well, that sounds very official. Is there some problem?"

"Yes, the murder of a woman in Chinatown."

"I don't understand. Such negative energy." He breathed deep. "We try to keep a positive flow in this house."

"Yeah, I'm sure Jacie Wooton found being sliced up a pretty negative experience. Can you verify your whereabouts, Mr. Smith?"

"Li," he said as the black woman in flowing white streamed in. "Do I know anyone named Jacie Wooton?"

"No."

"Do we know where I was night before last, between midnight and three?"

"Yes, of course." She poured pale gold tea from a pale blue pot into pale blue cups. "You were attending the dinner party hosted by the Rislings until ten. You escorted Ms. Hubble home, had a nightcap with her in her apartment, and returned here about midnight. You spent twenty minutes in your isolation tank to eliminate any negativity before retiring. You were in bed by one-thirty, and had your usual wake-up call at eight the following morning."

"Thank you." He picked up the teacup she'd set on the table. "It's difficult for me to keep all those details in my head. I'd be lost without Li."

"I'd like the names and addresses of the people you were with, to verify this information."

"I'm feeling very unsettled about this."

"It's routine, Mr. Smith. When I confirm your alibi, I can move on."

"Li will provide you with anything you need." He made a gesture with his hand. "It's important to my well-being, to my work, to keep my senses stimulated by the positive, by love and by beauty."

"Right. You have a standing order from Whittier's in London for a certain type of stationery. Your last purchase of it was four months ago."

"No. I never purchase anything. I can't go into shops, you see. My fans are so enthusiastic. I have things brought in to me, or Li, or one of my staff goes into the shops. I do enjoy good stationery. I feel it's important to send personal notes, on good paper, to friends or those who've made some contribution."

"Cream-colored, heavy-eight bond. Unrecycled."

"Unrecycled?" He ducked his head, smiling into his cup like a small boy caught with his hand in the cookie jar. "I'm ashamed to say I have been using something like that. Not very green of me, but it's gorgeous paper. Li, does my writing paper come from London?"

"I can check."

"She'll check."

"Fine. I'd like a sample of it, too, if you don't mind, and the names of any staff members who were authorized to make purchases for you in London."

"I'll take care of that." Li glided out again.

"I don't quite understand how my writing paper could interest you."

"There was a note, written on that style of paper, left with the body."

"Please." He lifted both hands, drawing them up his own body as he breathed in, pushing them outward as he exhaled. "I don't want that sort of image corrupting my senses. That's why I listen only to my own music. I never watch the media reports, except for specially selected features on entertainment or society. There's too much darkness in the world. Too much despair."

"Tell me about it."

When Eve left, she had a sample of his writing paper, and the names of his staffers in London.

"He's weird," Peabody commented. "But he's built. And he just doesn't seem like the type who'd go hunting LCs."

"He likes to have multi-partner sex, occasionally with minors."

"Oh." Peabody wrinkled her nose as she glanced back toward the house. "So much for my instincts on this one."

"Maybe he figures underage groupies have less negativity, sexually speaking, than any grown woman who could listen to that crap he plays and not run screaming after five minutes."

She got into the car, slammed the door. "If that stinking 'Love Lights the World' sticks in my head, I'm coming back here and beating him with a club."

"Now that's positive," Peabody decided.

CHAPTER FIVE

Knowing the security at the U.N. was tight, Eve decided to avoid a possible pissing match with guards and parked in a second-level street ramp on First Avenue.

The little cross-block hike would help work off the doughnuts.

They still allowed tours — she'd checked — but they were stringently regulated with the threat of terrorism always a thunderhead ready to storm. But nations throughout the world, and the recognized off-planet factions, had their meetings and assemblies, their votes and their agendas, inside the huge white building that dominated its six-block stretch.

The flags still waved, a colorful symbol, Eve supposed, of man's willingness to get together and talk about the problems of humanity. And occasionally do something about them.

Even with their names on the visitors' list, she and Peabody went through a series of checkpoints. At the first, they surrendered their weapons, a requirement that always made Eve twitchy.

Their badges were scanned, their fingerprints verified. Peabody's bag was scanned, then hand-searched. All electronics, including 'links, PPCs, and communicators, were taken through analysis.

They passed through a metal detector, an incendiary device detector, a weapon identifier, and a body scanner, all before being cleared through entry level.

"Okay," Eve declared. "Maybe they've got to be careful, but I'm drawing the line at a cavity search."

"Some of these security levels were added after the Cassandra incident." Peabody stepped with Eve and a uniformed guard into a bomb-proof elevator.

"Next time we need to talk to Renquist, he comes to us."

They were escorted off the elevator and directly to another checkpoint where they were scanned, analyzed, and verified again.

They were passed from the guard to a female aide who was equally military in bearing. The aide's retina scan and voice command unlocked a bomb door. Through it, they moved from paranoid security to daily business.

It was a hive of offices, but a very big hive with very efficient chambers. Here, the high-level drones wore conservative suits and headsets, with heels that clicked briskly on tiled floors. The windows were triple-sealed and equipped with air-traffic detectors that would slam down impact shields at any threat. But they let in the light and a decent view of the river.

A tall, thin man in unrelieved gray nodded at the aide, smiled at Eve.

"Lieutenant Dallas, I'm Thomas Newkirk, personal assistant to Mr. Renquist. I'll escort you from here."

"Some security you've got here, Mr. Newkirk." She spotted cameras and motion sensors along the corridor. Eyes and ears everywhere, she thought. Who could work that way?

He followed the track of her gaze. "You stop noticing. Just a price to be paid for safety and freedom."

"Uh-huh." He had a square face, a jaw so sharp and straight it might have been sliced off with a sword. Very pale, very cool blue eyes and a ruddy complexion under short, bristly sandy hair.

He walked very erect, with a purposeful stride, his arms straight at his sides.

"You former military?"

"Captain, RAF. Mr. Renquist has a number of former military on staff." He used a key card to access another door, and Renquist's suite of offices.

"Just one moment, please."

While she waited, Eve studied the area. Another warren of rooms, most separated by glass panels so that the staffers were exposed to each other, and the cameras. It didn't seem to bother them as they worked away at keyboards or headsets.

She glanced in the direction Newkirk had taken and saw that it ended in a closed door with Renquist's name on it.

It opened, and Newkirk stepped out again. "Mr. Renquist will see you now, Lieutenant."

It was a lot of buildup for an ordinary man, which was her first impression of Renquist. He stood behind a long, dark desk that might have been wood, might have been old, with an East River view at his back.

He was tall, with the kind of build that told her he used a health center regularly or paid good money to a body sculptor. She also figured his build was wasted in the dull gray suit, though the suit had probably cost him a great deal.

He was attractive enough, if you went for the polished and distinguished type. He was fair-skinned, fair-haired with a prominent nose and a wide forehead.

His eyes, a kind of sooty gray, were his best feature, and met hers directly.

His voice was clipped, and oh-so-British she expected crumpets — whatever the hell they were — to come popping out of his mouth along with the words.

"Lieutenant Dallas, I'm very pleased to meet you. I've read and heard quite a bit about you already." He held out a hand, and she was treated to a firm, dry, politician's shake. "I believe we met once, some time back, at a charity function."

"So I'm told."

"Please have a seat." He gestured, and sat behind his desk. "Tell me what I can do for you."

She sat in a sturdy cloth chair. Not a comfortable one, she noted. Busy man, can't have people sitting around in his office taking up too much of his time.

His desk was another hive of industry. The data and communication system with the screen blinking on hold, a short stack of discs, another stack of paper, the second 'link. Among the work was a duet of framed photographs. She could see a slice of a young girl's face and curly hair — both fair like her father's — and assumed the other shot would be of his wife.

She knew enough about politics and protocol to at least start out playing the game. "I'd like to thank you, for myself and on behalf of the NYPSD for your cooperation. I know you're extremely busy and appreciate you taking the time to speak with me."

"I believe strongly in assisting the local authorities, wherever I am. The U.N. is, on an elemental level, the world's police force. In a way, we're in the same profession, you and I. How can I help you?"

"A woman named Jacie Wooton was murdered the night before last. I'm the primary investigator."

"Yes, I heard of the killing." He leaned back, but his eyebrows lowered. "A licensed companion, in the Chinatown district."

"Yes, sir. In the course of my investigation, I've had reason to research and trace a certain brand of stationery. You purchased this brand of writing paper six weeks ago in London."

"I was in London this summer for a few days, and did, indeed, buy stationery. Several different types, as I recall. Some for personal use, some for gifts. Am I to understand that this purchase makes me a suspect in this woman's death?"

He was cool, she thought. More intrigued than worried or annoyed. And, if she wasn't mistaking that faint curve of mouth, he was a little amused. "In order to expedite my investigation, I need to check all the names of purchasers, and verify their whereabouts on the night in question."

"I see. Lieutenant, can I assume this line of investigation is secure and discreet? Having my name linked, however loosely, with a licensed companion and a murder would generate considerable unwanted media attention on myself, on Delegate Evans."

"The name won't be made public."

"All right. Night before last?"

"Between midnight and three."

He didn't reach for his book, but instead steepled his fingers, watched Eve over the tips. "My wife and I attended the theater. A production of *Six Weeks* by William Gantry, a British playwright. At Lincoln Center. We were in the company of two other couples, left the theater at about eleven, then had a post-theater drink at Renoir's. I believe we left there, my wife and I, around midnight. We'd have been home by twelve-thirty. My wife went to bed, and I worked in my home office for perhaps an hour. It might've been a little longer. Following habit, I would have watched about thirty minutes of news, then retired for the night."

"Did you see or speak with anyone after your wife went to bed?"

"I'm afraid I didn't. I can only tell you that I was home, tending to my work when this murder took place. I'm confused how buying this paper connects me to this woman, or her death."

"Her killer wrote a note on that stationery."

"A note." Now Renquist's eyebrows lifted. "Well. That was rather arrogant of him, wasn't it?"

* * *

"He's not really covered for the time of the murder either," Peabody pointed out as they walked back to the car.

"That's the problem when somebody buys it at two in the morning. Most of the suspects are going to claim they were home, innocently tucked into their own beds. They got their own security, or a way around hotel or apartment security, it's tough to call them a stinking liar."

"Do you think he is a stinking liar?"

"It's early yet."

She tracked Elliot Hawthorne down on the eleventh hole of a private club on Long Island. He was a sturdy, tough man, with a shock of white hair fluttering around under a tan cap, matched by the luxurious white mustache that set off his tanned face. There were lines scored around his mouth, fanned out from his eyes, but the eyes themselves were sharp and clear as he drove the ball off the tee.

He passed the driver back to his caddy, hopped in a small white cart, then signaled for Eve to join him. "Talk fast" was all he said as he sent the cart zipping forward.

She did, giving him the details as Peabody and the caddy followed on foot.

"Dead whore, fancy writing paper." He gave a little grunt as he stopped the cart. "Used whores from time to time, never kept track of their names." He jumped out, circled his ball, studied the lay. "Got a young wife, don't need whores now. Don't remember the paper. You got a young wife, you buy all sorts of useless shit. London?"

"Yes."

"August. London, Paris, Milan. I still got my fingers in some business, and she likes to shop. If you say I bought the paper, I bought the paper. So what?"

"It's tied to the murder. If you could tell me where you were between midnight and three, night before last —"

He let out a bark of laughter, stood from where he'd crouched by the ball and gave her his full attention. "Young lady, I'm more than seventy. I'm fit, but I need my sleep. I play eighteen holes every morning, and before I do, I have a good breakfast, read the paper, and check the stock reports. I'm up every morning at seven. I'm in bed every night by eleven unless my wife drags me out to some shindig. Night before last I was in bed by eleven, and after making love to my wife — a process that doesn't take as long as it once did — I was asleep. Can't prove it, of course."

He brushed her back, turned to the caddy. "Gimme the seven iron, Tony."

She watched him set, sight, then smack the ball into a pretty arch. It bounced on the green and rolled to within about five feet of the cup.

From Hawthorne's wide grin, she assumed it was a good shot.

"I'd like to speak with your wife."

He shrugged, handed the club back to the caddy. “Go ahead. She’s over at the courts. Got a tennis lesson today.”

Darla Hawthorne was dancing around on a shaded court in a candy pink romper with a flippy skirt. She was doing more dancing than actual connecting with the ball, but she looked damn good doing so. She was built like a teenager’s wet dream, lots of soft, jiggling breast barely contained, and long, long legs shown off by the little skirt and matching pink shoes.

She was so evenly tanned, she might have been painted.

Her hair, which must have hit her waist when unrestrained, was tied back in a ribbon — pink, natch — and scooped through the hole in her little pink visor. It swung happily back and forth as she pranced over the court and missed the bright yellow ball.

When she bent over to retrieve it, Eve was treated to the sight of her heart-shaped butt in tight, high-cut panties under the skirt.

Her instructor, a hunky guy with lots of streaky hair and white teeth, called out direction and encouragement.

At one point, he came over to stand behind her, nuzzling her back against him as he adjusted her swing. She sent him a big, lash-fluttering smile over her shoulder.

“Mrs. Hawthorne?” Before the balls could start flying again, Eve stepped onto the court.

Tennis guy immediately rushed forward. “Boots! You can’t walk on this surface without the proper foot attire.”

“I’m not here to whack balls.” She held up her badge. “I need a moment with Mrs. Hawthorne.”

“Well, you have to take those off, or stand on the sidelines. We have rules.”

“What’s the problem, Hank?”

“There’s a policewoman here, Mrs. H.”

“Oh.” Darla bit her lip, and patting her heart walked over to the end of the net. “If this is about that speeding ticket, I’m going to pay it. I just —”

“I’m not Traffic. Can I have a minute?”

“Oh, sure. Hank, I could use a break anyway. Getting all sweaty.” She walked, with a lot of swinging hip, to a bench, opened a pink bag and took out a bottle of designer water.

“Could you tell me where you were night before last? Between midnight and three.”

“What?” Beneath the glow on her perfect oval face, Darla paled. “Why?”

“It’s just a routine stop in a matter I’m investigating.”

“Sweetie knows I was home.” Her eyes, mermaid green, began to swim. “I don’t know why he’d have you investigating me.”

“I’m not investigating you, Mrs. Hawthorne.”

Hank walked over, handed her a small towel. “Any problem, Mrs. H?”

“No problem here, go flex your muscles someplace else.” Dismissing him, Eve sat beside Darla. “Midnight and three, night before last.”

"I was home in bed." She shot Eve a defiant look now. "With Sweetie. Where else would I be?"

Good question, Eve thought.

She asked about the writing paper, but Darla shrugged it off. Yes, they'd been in Europe in August, and she bought a lot of things. Why shouldn't she? How was she supposed to remember everything she'd bought or that Sweetie bought for her?

Dallas circled around for another few minutes, then stood so Darla could walk back, and be comforted by Hank. He shot Eve a nasty look before leading his student toward what Eve assumed was the clubhouse.

"Interesting," Eve stated aloud. "Looks like our Darla was out, practicing on Hank's balls during at least part of the time in question."

"Definitely getting more than instruction on her back-swing," Peabody agreed. "Poor Sweetie."

"If Sweetie knows his wife's playing singles with her tennis pro, he could've used the time she was out pulling his racket to get downtown, do Wooton. You got a wife's running cross-court on you, it pisses you off. So you not only kill a whore — and what's your young, unfaithful wife but a whore — but you use the cheating bitch as your alibi. Game, set, match. Very neat."

"Yeah, and I liked your tennis metaphors, too."

"We do what we can. Anyway, it's a theory. Let's go see what else we can dig up on Hawthorne."

He'd been married three times, as Roarke had stated, with each successive spouse younger than the preceding one. He'd divorced both former Mrs. Hawthornes, and had nipped them off with the lowest possible financial package, as arranged through a premarital agreement. An iron-clad one from the results, Eve mused.

The man was no fool.

Would such a careful and canny man be oblivious to his current wife's activities?

He had no criminal record, though he'd been sued a number of times in civil court for various financial deals. A quick scan told her most of them were nuisance suits, brought by unhappy and unlucky investors.

He owned four homes, and six vehicles, including a yacht, and was associated with numerous charities. His reported worth was just under a billion.

Golf, according to the various media articles and features' she scanned through, appeared to be his god.

Every name on her list had an alibi corroborated by a spouse or partner or employee. Which meant none of them held much weight.

Sitting back, Eve propped her feet on her desk, closed her eyes, and took herself back into the Chinatown alley.

She walks in ahead of him. She leads the john. Her feet hurt. She's got a bunion. Shoes are killing her. Two in the morning. Hot, airless. Not much business tonight. Only two hundred in her cash bag.

Gives her four, maybe five johns on this circuit, depending what they wanted.

Been in the game a long time, knows to get payment upfront. Did he take it back, or didn't he give her a chance to take it? No chance, she decided. He'd want to move fast. Spins her around. Wants her facing the wall.

Does he touch her? Run his hand over her breast, her ass, slide it over her crotch?

No, no time for that. Not interested in that. Especially after the blood gushes out on his hands.

Warm blood. That's what got him off.

Against the wall. Tug her head back by the hair. Left hand. Slice the scalpel over her throat with the right. Left to right, slight downward path.

Blood gushes, splashes on the wall, splashes back at her face, her body, his hands.

She's alive for a few seconds, just a few, shocked seconds when she can't scream, and her body jerks a little as it dies.

Lay her down, head toward the opposite wall. Get out your tools.

A light, some sort of light. Can't do that sort of precision work in the dark. Laser scalpel, use the light from the laser scalpel to guide the way.

Put what you came for in a leakproof bag, clean off your hands. Change your shirt or take off what you were wearing over it. Everything in a bag or case now. Check yourself, make sure you'll pass on the street.

Take out the note. Smile at it, amuse yourself. Place it carefully on the body.

Walk out of the alley. Fifteen minutes, maybe. No more than fifteen, and you're walking away. Carrying your prize back to your car. Excited, but controlled. Need to drive carefully. Can't risk a routine stop when you smell of death and have that part of her with you.

Back home. Reset security. Shower. Dispose of your clothes.

You did it. You've imitated one of the great killers of the modern age, and no one's the wiser.

She opened her eyes, stared up at the ceiling. If it was one of her five current candidates, he'd have to dispose of the body part as well, or have a very secure place to keep it as a souvenir.

Would a regular household recycler handle that sort of thing, or would you need something that handled medical waste? She'd need to check on that.

Bringing up a map on-screen, she calculated time and distance from the murder site to each of the suspect's residences. Giving fifteen minutes in the alley, the time to hunt the victim — likely scoped out at some point earlier — clean up, drive home. Any of them could have done the job in under two hours.

Straightening up, she began to type up a report, hoping inspiration would strike. When it didn't, she read over the facts, finished it off, and filed it.

She spent another hour learning about recyclers and the availability of laser scalpels. And decided to go back to the scene.

The street did a decent business during the day. A couple of bars, a storefront eatery, a market, and a money exchange were the closest businesses to the alley.

Only the bars had been open after midnight, and both of them were at the far ends of the block. Though the neighborhood had already been canvassed, she swung through each place again, running the routine, asking the questions, coming away empty.

She ended up standing at the mouth of the alley again with the beat cop, the neighborhood security droid, and Peabody.

"Like I said," the cop named Henley told her, "I knew her, the way you know the locals LCs. She never caused any trouble. Technically, they're not supposed to use the alley or any public access for work, but most of them do. We roust them now and again for it."

"She ever complain about any john getting rough or hassling her?"

"Wouldn't have." Henley shook his head. "She steered clear of me, and the droid. Give me a little nod if we passed each other on patrol, but she wasn't the friendly sort. We get some rough stuff in this sector — johns and janes slapping an LC around. You got some mopes coming through mugging them, and sometimes they wave a sticker around. Had some use 'em, but not like this. Never had anything like this."

"I want a copy of any reports where they used a sticker, any kind of blade."

"I can get that for you, Lieutenant," the droid told her. "How far back do you want to go?"

"Give me a full year. Keep it to attacks on women, with LCs the priority. Maybe he practiced first."

"Yes, sir. Where should I transmit?"

"Send it to me at Central. Henley, where's the safest place to park in this area? Street or underground, not a surface lot or port."

"Well, you want quiet, lower crime, probably you'd go west, maybe Lafayette. You want busy, so there's too much going on for anybody to mess with your ride, you could hike it up the other side of Canal, into Little Italy. Restaurants stay open late."

"Okay, we're going to try this. One of you take from here to Lafayette, the other head north. Ask residents, merchants who might have been around at that time of night, if they noticed a guy alone carrying a bag. Some kind of bag, good-sized one. He'd've been moving along pretty quick, no meandering, and going for a car. Talk to the LCs," she added. "One of them may have tried to hustle him and got brushed off."

"Long shot, sir," Peabody said when they'd split off again.

"Somebody saw him. They don't know it, but they saw him. We get lucky, jog a few memories." She stood on the sidewalk, baking in the heat as she scanned the street.

"We're going to have to see how much we can stretch the budget for added security and surveillance for a square mile around this scene. He'll stick to the mile, stick to the script. And it played too well for him the first time — he's not going to want to wait too long before act two."

CHAPTER SIX

It was a difficult meeting for him to take. It had to be done, and Roarke could only hope that some of the weight he was carrying at the base of his skull would lift once it was over.

He'd put it off too long already, and that wasn't like him. Then again, he hadn't felt completely like himself since he'd met Moira O'Bannion, and she'd told him her tale.

His mother's story.

Life, he thought, as he stared out the wide window wall of his midtown office, could take a big chunk out of your ass when you were least prepared for it.

It was after five already, and his timing had been deliberate. He'd wanted to meet with Moira at the end of the day, so that there was no business to be done afterward. So that he could go home and try to shift it all aside with an evening out with his wife.

His interoffice 'link beeped, and damn him, he nearly jolted.

"Yes, Caro."

"Ms. O'Bannion's here."

"Thanks. Bring her back."

He watched the traffic, air and sky, and thought idly that the trip home would be a bit of a bitch just now. The commuter trams were already loaded, and from his lofty perch he could see dozens of tired, irritable faces packed together like rowers on a slave ship for the hot journey home.

On the street below, buses were chugging, cabs standing like a clogged river, and the walks and people glides were mobbed.

Eve was down there somewhere, he expected. No doubt having an annoyed thought at the prospect of having to dress up and socialize after a day of chasing a killer.

More than likely, she'd rush in, flustered, with minutes to spare and struggling to make that odd transition from cop to wife. He doubted she had any idea how it thrilled and delighted him to see her make that slippery change.

At the knock on his door, he turned. "Yes."

His admin brought her in, so that he found himself amused, for a moment, at the sight of two neat, trim, well-dressed women of a certain age stepping into his office.

"Thank you, Caro. Ms. O'Bannion, thank you for coming. Won't you have a seat? Would you like anything? Coffee? Tea?"

"No. Thank you."

He took her hand, felt hers tremble lightly as he shook it. He gestured to a chair, knowing his manner was smooth, practiced, cool. He couldn't quite help it.

"I appreciate you making the time for me," he began, "especially so late in the day."

"It's not a problem."

He could see her taking in his office — the space of it, the style. The art, the furniture, the equipment, the *things* he was able to surround himself with.

Needed to surround himself with.

"I thought to come to Dochas, but it occurred to me that having a man around the shelter too often may make some of the women, the children, nervous."

"It's good for them to be around men. Men who treat them as people and wish them no harm." She folded her hands in her lap, and though she met his eyes levelly, he could almost hear the quick beat of her heart. "Part of breaking the cycle of abuse is overcoming fear, and reestablishing self-esteem and normal relationships."

"I wouldn't argue that, but I wonder — if Siobahn Brody had had more fear, would she have survived? I don't know precisely what to say to you," he continued before she could speak. "Or precisely how to say it. I thought I did. First, I want to apologize for taking so long to meet with you again."

"I've been waiting to be fired." Like his, her voice carried Ireland in it, in wisps and whispers. "Is that why you brought me here today?"

"It's not, no. I'm sorry, I should've realized you'd be concerned after the way I left things. I was angry and . . . distracted." He gave a short laugh and had to stop himself from raking a hand through his hair. *Nerves*, he thought. Well, she wasn't the only one dealing with them. "That's one way to put it."

"You were furious, and ready to boot me out on my ass."

"I was. I told myself you were lying." His eyes stayed on hers, level and serious. "Had to be. Had to be some angle in there for you telling me this girl you knew back in Dublin was my mother. It was counter to everything I'd known, believed, my whole life, you see."

"Yes. I do see it."

"There have been others, from time to time, who've wormed their way to me with some story of a relation. Uncle, brother, sister, what have you. Easily refuted, ignored, dealt with."

"What I told you wasn't a story, Roarke, but God's truth."

"Aye, well." He looked down at his hands and knew in their shape — the width of palm, the length of fingers — they were his father's hands. "I knew that, somewhere in the belly, I knew it. It made it worse. Almost unbearable really."

He looked up again, met her eyes again. "You've a right to know I checked on you, deeply."

"I expected you would."

"And I checked on her. On myself. I'd never done so before, not carefully."

"I don't understand that. I wouldn't have told you the way I did if I hadn't thought you'd know some of it. A man like you would know whatever he needed to know."

"It was a point of pride to me that it didn't matter. Wouldn't matter, particularly when I believed my mother was Meg Roarke and I was as glad to see the back of her as she was of me."

Moira let out a long breath. "I said no to coffee before because my hands were shaking. I wonder if I might trouble you for some after all."

"Of course." He rose and walked over to open a panel in the wall. Inside was a fully equipped minikitchen. When she laughed, he turned in the act of programming coffee.

"I've never seen the like of this office. So posh. My feet nearly sank to the ankles in the carpet. You're young to have so much."

The smile he sent her was more grim than amused. "I started early."

"So you did. My stomach's still jumping." She pressed a hand to it. "I was certain you were bringing me in to fire me, maybe to threaten legal action of some sort. I didn't know how I was going to tell my family, or the guests at Dochas. I hated thinking I'd have to leave. I've gotten attached."

"As I said, I checked on you. They're lucky to have you at the shelter. How would you like your coffee?"

"Plenty of cream, if you don't mind. Is this whole building yours, then?"

"It is."

"It's like a great black spear, powerful and elegant. Thanks." She accepted the coffee and took the first sip. Her eyes widened, then narrowed as she sniffed the contents of the cup. "Is this *real* coffee?"

And that weight at the base of his skull vanished with a quick, appreciative laugh. Gone, at last. "It is, yes. I'll send you some. The first time I met my wife, I gave her coffee and she had a similar reaction. I sent her some as well. Might be why she married me."

"I doubt that very much." She kept her gaze steady on his now. "Your mother is dead, and he killed her, didn't he? Patrick Roarke murdered her, as I always believed."

"Yes. I went to Dublin and verified it."

"Will you tell me how?"

Beat her to death, he thought. *Beat her bloody and dead, with hands so much like my own. Then threw her away in the river. Threw away the poor dead girl who'd loved him enough to give him a son.*

"No, I won't. Only that I tracked down a man who'd been with him in those days, and who knew of it. Knew her and what happened."

"If only I'd had more experience and less arrogance . . ." Moira began.

"It wouldn't have mattered. If she'd stayed in the shelter in Dublin, or gone back to her family in Clare, or run. As long as she'd taken me, it wouldn't have mattered. For whatever reason, pride, meanness, bloody-mindedness, he wanted me."

The knowledge of that would haunt him for all of his days. Maybe it was meant to. "And he'd have found her."

"That's the kindest thing you could say to me," she murmured.

"It's just truth." And he needed to get past it as best he could. "I went to Clare. I saw her family. My family."

"Did you?" She reached out, laid a hand on his arm. "Oh, I'm so glad. I'm so glad for that."

"They were . . . extraordinary. My mother's twin, Sinead, she opened her home to me. Just like that."

"Well, West County folks, they're known for their hospitality, aren't they?"

"I'm still baffled, and grateful. I'm grateful to you, Ms. O'Bannion, for telling me. I wanted you to know that."

"She'd have been pleased, don't you think? Not only that you know, but that you've taken these steps. I think she'd be very pleased." She set her coffee aside, opened her purse. "You didn't take this when you were in my office before. Will you have it now?"

He took the photograph of a young woman with red hair and pretty green eyes holding the dark-haired little boy. "Thank you. I'd very much like to have it."

A guy in a white suit sang about love being quiet and tricky. Eve sipped champagne and had to agree. At least about the tricky part. Why else was she struggling to take her mind off murder and pretending to do something more than taking up space in a Philadelphia ballroom?

God knew love — and she would kick Roarke's ass later for deserting her — was the only reason she was standing here while some woman in lavender silk rambled on and on and *on* about fashion designers.

Yes, yes, yes, she knew Leonardo personally. Jesus, he was married to her oldest friend. And she could've used a good dose of Mavis at the moment. Yes, for God's sake, he'd designed the dress she was wearing.

So the fuck *what?* It was clothes. You put them on and you weren't naked or cold.

Love obliged her to edit her thoughts so her part of the conversation — when she could shove a word through the wall of noise the woman built around her — went something like: *Yes*.

"Ah, there's the most striking woman in the room. Excuse us, won't you?" Charles Monroe, smooth and handsome, beamed a smile at Eve's tormentor. "I simply have to steal her."

"Kill me," Eve muttered as Charles drew her clear. "Take my weapon out of my bag, press it to the pulse in my throat, and fire. End my torment."

He only laughed and swung her to the dance floor. "When I spotted you I thought you might be on the point of drawing that weapon and blasting the woman between the eyes."

"I imagined ramming it into her mouth. It was never shut anyway." She gave a quick shudder. "Anyway, thanks for the rescue. I didn't know you were here."

"Running a bit late, only just arrived."

"Working?" Charles was a top-level LC.

"I'm with Louise."

"Oh." And because he was a man who made his living selling himself, Eve couldn't quite figure how he and the dedicated Dr. Louise Dimatto developed, and maintained, a relationship.

Took all kinds, she reminded herself.

"I was going to get in touch with you," he continued. "About Jacie Wooton."

The cop shifted back to the forefront. "You knew her?"

"I used to. Not well, really. I don't think anyone knew Jacie well. But we ran in similar circles, so we'd bump into each other now and then. Or did, before she got busted."

"Let's find a corner somewhere."

"I don't know that this is the time —"

"Works for me." Taking charge, she pulled him from the dance floor, scanning the little packs of people, the tables, and decided to take it outside.

There was a terrace festooned with flowers, scattered with more tables, more people. But it was quieter.

"Tell me what you know."

"Next to nothing." He wandered to the edge of the terrace, looked out over the lights of the city. "She was well-established before I got into the life. She liked everything top drawer. The best clothes, the best venues, the best clients."

"The best dealer, then?"

"I don't know about her dealer. I don't," he insisted. "I'm not going to claim I don't know anything about that end of the business, but I stay clean. Spotless now that I'm dating a doctor," he added with a smile. "Jacie's busts took everybody by surprise. If she was an addict, she hid it well. If I knew anything, Dallas, I'd tell you. No hesitation, no bullshit. As far as I know she didn't have friends. Not real friends. Or enemies. She *was* the job."

"Okay." She started to slip her hands into her pockets, remembered the little copper-colored number didn't have any. "If something occurs to you, however small or remote, I want to hear about it."

"That's a promise. It's shaken me, the way it happened, the rumors I'm hearing. Louise is worried." He glanced back toward the terrace doors. "She hasn't said anything, specifically, but she's worried. When you love someone you can tell when they're carrying stress."

"Yeah, I guess so. You're going to want to be careful, Charles. You don't fit the vic profile on this, but you're going to want to be careful."

"Always," he replied.

She didn't say anything to Roarke about the conversation on the shuttle ride home. But she turned it over in her mind, replayed it, considered it.

When they were back in their bedroom and she was shimmying out of the tiny dress, she ran it by him.

"Doesn't sound like he'll be much of a source on this," Roarke commented.

"No, but that's not what I'm thinking about. After we went back in, I watched him and Louise together. They're practically like turtledoves or something. You know they're going to roll around naked tonight."

"Naked turtledoves. No, not an attractive visual. Let me think of another."

"Ha-ha. What I'm saying is how can she roll naked with him tonight knowing he's going to be doing the same deal with however many clients are on his book tomorrow?"

"Because it's not the same." He flipped down the bedspread. "One's personal, one's professional. It's his job."

"Oh, that's just bullshit. That's just a bullshit rationalization. And if it's not, can you stand there and tell me if I was a sex pro, you'd be perfectly fine, just iced with me riding some other guy's stick?"

"You have such a way with words." He looked at her, standing with the glittery dress in one hand. She wore nothing but a matching triangle over her crotch, too small to be called panties, a triple chain of multicolored stones she'd yet to remove, and high, backless heels.

And an annoyed scowl.

"No, I wouldn't be fine with it, or iced, or anything remotely like it. But then I don't share. Christ, you look sexy. Why don't you come over here and we'll roll around, naked as turtledoves?"

"We're having a conversation."

"You are," he corrected, as he stepped off the bed platform and toward her.

"And speaking of conversations . . ." She evaded, nipping neatly behind the sofa. "I still have to beat you brainless for leaving me with that woman, the one who looked like a skinny purple tree."

"I was unavoidably detained."

"My ass."

"Oh, darling Eve, I'm thinking very fondly of your ass." He feinted, she countered. And they circled the sofa. "Better run," he said softly.

And with a quick whoop, she did. When they were both breathless, she let him catch her.

She had nothing. No breaks, no fresh leads, no old ones that looked promising. She juggled her list of suspects and possibles, looked for openings. She recanvassed the area around the crime scene, studied lab reports.

She ran the elements through IRCCA, searching for similar crimes, and found one in London more than a year before that could fit. Still open. It wasn't exact, she mused. Messier, sloppier.

Practice session?

There was no note on elegant stationery, just the mutilated body of a young LC. Not the same type as Wooton, Eve acknowledged, and wondered if she was grasping at straws.

There were plenty of slice-and-dice, a number of LCs, especially on street level, who'd been assaulted, even killed, by clients or would-be clients. But nothing that matched the barbaric elegance of Jack.

She spoke with neighbors, coworkers, associates of those on her possible list, keeping the interviews informal and discreet. Pushing, poking for that crack. But nothing broke.

She faced her Sunday off with annoyance and irritability. Hardly a picnic of a mood. Her only hope of getting through it, Eve decided, was to get Mira in some quiet spot and pick her brain.

"Maybe you should give her brain, and your own, a day off."

She frowned over at Roarke as they crossed the sidewalk to Mira's pretty house, set in her pretty neighborhood. "What?"

"You're muttering out loud." He patted her shoulder supportively. "I don't know if talking to yourself when knocking on the door of a shrink is the best of behaviors."

"We're only staying a couple of hours. Remember? We agreed on that."

"Mmm." With this noncommittal sound, he pressed his lips to her forehead. And the door opened.

"Hello. You must be Eve and Roarke. I'm Gillian, Charlotte and Dennis's daughter."

It took her a beat as she rarely thought of Mira by her given name. But Mira was stamped, clearly, on her daughter's face.

Though her hair was longer, well past her shoulders and curling, it was the same rich sable. Her eyes were the same mild and patient blue, but they were homed in on Eve's, looking deep. Her frame was longer, lankier like her father's, and she'd draped it in some loose, airy top and pants that stopped inches short of her ankles.

One of those ankles carried a tattoo, a trio of connecting chevrons. Bracelets jangled on her wrists, rings jingled on her fingers. Her feet were bare with the toes painted a pale pink.

She was Wiccan, Eve recalled, and responsible for a couple of Mira's grandchildren.

"It's lovely to meet you." Roarke was already taking Gillian's hand, and smoothly stepping between two women who were obviously taking each other's measure. "You favor your mother, who I've always considered one of the world's loveliest of women."

"Thanks. Mom said you were very charming. Please come in. We're spread out" — she glanced back to where a baby's strong wails poured down the stairs — "as you can hear, but most of us are in the back. We'll fix you a drink, so you'll be braced for the onslaught of a day at the Miras."

There were a considerable number of them there already, gathered in the kitchen/activity room that was as big as a barn, and nearly as noisy. Through the two-story glass wall of the back, others could be seen on a wide patio decked with chairs and tables and some sort of large, outdoor cooking device that was already smoking.

She could see Dennis, Mira's delightful and absent-minded husband, manning it with a long fork of some kind. He had a Mets cap over his explosion of gray hair, and baggy shorts nearly down to a pair of knobby knees Eve found secretly adorable.

Another man was with him, his son maybe, and they seemed to be holding an intense and spirited debate with a lot of laughter and beer-swilling from bottles.

There were kids of various ages milling or running around. And a girl of about ten who sat on a stool at the big work counter, sulking.

Food was spread out all over, and urged on them while introductions were made. Someone pushed a margarita in her hand.

When he opted for beer, Roarke was told he'd find them outside in a cooler. A young boy — Eve was already losing the names as they came at her like grapeshot — was given the task of escorting Roarke out and introducing him to the rest.

With the boy's hand clasped in his, Roarke looked over his shoulder, shot a wicked grin at Eve, and strolled outside.

"It looks chaotic now, but . . . it'll get worse." With a laugh, Mira took a bowl of yet more food out of an enormous refrigerator. "I'm so glad you came. Lana, stop pouting and run upstairs. See if your aunt Callie needs any help with the baby."

"I don't see why I have to do *everything*." But the kid scooted down and away.

"She's irritable because she broke the rules and can't have screen or comp privileges for a week," Gillian commented.

"Oh."

"Her life, as she knows it," Gillian said as she bent to pick up a toddler — sex undetermined for Eve — from the floor, "is over."

"A week's an endless stretch of time when you're nine. Gilly, taste this coleslaw. I think it could use a bit of dill."

Obediently, Gillian opened her mouth, accepted the bite her mother held out on a fork. "Bit more pepper, too."

"So, um . . ." Eve already felt as if she'd entered a parallel universe. "You're expecting a lot of people."

"We are a lot of people," Mira said, chuckling.

"Mom still thinks we all have the appetites of teenagers." Gillian rubbed a hand absently over Mira's back. "She always makes too much food."

"Makes it? You *made* all this?"

"Hmm. I like to cook, when I can. Especially when it's for family." Her cheeks were pink with pleasure, her eyes laughing as she winked at her daughter. "And I drag the girls into helping out. It's shamefully sexist, of course, but none of my men are worth two damns in the kitchen." She glanced out the window wall. "Give them a big, complicated smoking grill, however, and they're right at home."

"All our men grill." Gillian gave the toddler a little bounce on her hip. "Does Roarke?"

"You mean, like, food?" Eve looked out to where he stood, apparently enjoying himself, picnic casual in jeans and a faded blue T-shirt. "No. I don't think he has one of those."

There were soy dogs and burgers, the potato salad of Roarke's fantasy, cold pasta, big chunks of fruit swimming in some sweetened juice, fat slices of tomatoes, the slaw, and deviled eggs. Bowls, platters, trays of those and more were shuffled around. The beer was cold and the margaritas kept coming.

She found herself in a conversation with one of Mira's sons about baseball, and to her frozen shock had a small, blond child climb up her leg and into her lap.

"Want some," he burbled at her and grinned with his ketchup-smeared mouth.

"What?" She looked around in mild panic. "What does he want some of?"

"Whatever you've got." Mira patted the boy's head as she passed by to take the baby from her daughter-in-law and cuddle it.

"Okay, here." Eve offered her plate with the hope the boy would take it and go back about his business. But he just dipped his fat little fingers into her fruit salad and came out with a slice of peach.

"Like it." He took a bite, then generously offered her the rest.

"No, you go ahead."

"Off you go, Bryce." Gillian hefted him off Eve's lap and instantly became her new best friend. "See what Granddad's got for you."

Then she plopped down beside Eve, arched her eyebrows at her brother. "Go away," she told him. "Girl talk."

He ambled away, good-naturedly. Amiability, Eve thought, appeared to be a common trait for the men in this family. "You're feeling overwhelmed and just a little out of place," Gillian began.

Eve picked up what was left of her burger, bit in. "Is that an observation or the result of a psychic scan?"

"A little of both. And a little of being the daughter of two observant and sensitive people. Large family gatherings can be odd for those who don't have one of their own. Your Roarke adjusts more seamlessly." She glanced around to where he sat with Dennis and Bryce. "He's more a social animal than you, and part of it's from the work he does, part's just his nature."

Gillian took a forkful of pasta salad. "There are a couple of things I feel compelled to say to you. I hope you won't be offended. I don't mind offending people, but I prefer to do it deliberately, and this wouldn't be deliberate."

"I don't bruise easy."

"No, I don't suppose you do." She switched her food for her margarita. "Well, first, I have to say that your husband is, without question, the most magnificent piece of work I've ever seen in real life."

"I'm not offended by that, as long as you remember the *mine* part."

"I don't poach, and if I did — and there was anything left of me after you'd got done, he wouldn't even notice. Added to that, I'm very much in love with my husband. We've been together a decade now. We were young, and it concerned my parents. But it was right for us." She nibbled on a slice of carrot. "We have a good and satisfying life, three beautiful children. I'd like to have another."

"Another what?"

Gillian laughed, turned back. "Another child. I'm hoping to be blessed with one more. But I've wandered from my purpose, and I doubt this group will give me much more time alone with you. I've been jealous of you."

Eve's eyes narrowed, flicked back in the direction where Roarke sat, then back when Gillian let out a low, almost purring laugh. "No, not because of him, though one could hardly be blamed there. Jealous of you and my mother."

"You lost me."

"She loves you," Gillian said, and watched something like embarrassment pass over Eve's face. "She respects you, worries about you, admires you, thinks of you. All the things she does for and about me. And this relationship, well, annoyed me on some primal level."

"It's not at all the same," Eve started to say, and Gillian shook her head.

"It's very much the same. I'm the daughter of her body, her heart and spirit. You're not of her body, but you are, without question, of her heart and her spirit. I was of two minds when she told me you were invited today."

She licked salt from the rim of her glass as she studied Eve. "The first was purely selfish — why is she coming? You're my mother. The other was rampant curiosity. At last, I'll get a good look at her."

"I'm not in competition with you for Mira's . . ."

"Affections?" Gillian finished with a little smile. "No, you're not. And it was my flaw, my self-absorption that caused those unattractive and destructive feelings in me. She's the most extraordinary woman I've ever known. Wise, compassionate, strong, smart, giving. I didn't always appreciate it, you don't when it's yours. But as I've gotten older, had children of my own, I've come to treasure everything about her."

Her gaze swept the patio, then stopped, held on her own daughter. "I hope, one day, Lana will feel that way about me. In any case, I felt you were stealing little bits of my mother from me. I was prepared to dislike you on sight — an attitude that is in direct opposition to what

I believe, to what I am, but there you are." She lifted her glass in a little toast, sipped. "I just couldn't pull it off."

Gillian picked up the pitcher of margaritas, poured more in each of their glasses. "You came here today for her. Probably with a little persuasion from your gorgeous husband, but primarily you're here for her. She matters to you, on a personal level. And I noticed the way you look at my father, with a kind of charmed affection. It tells me you're a good judge of character, and I know from my mother — who's one as well — that you're a good cop, a good woman. It makes it easier for me to share her with you."

Before Eve could think of a response, Mira walked over, carrying the now sleeping baby on her shoulder. "Did everyone get enough?"

"More than," Gillian assured her. "Why don't you give him to me? I'll take him upstairs."

"No, he's fine. I don't get to hold him nearly often enough." Agilely, she sat, lightly patting the baby's back. "Eve, I should warn you, Dennis has convinced Roarke he can't live without a grill."

"Well, he has everything else." She polished off her burger. "And it works great."

"Dennis would tell you it's all in the cook, not the cooker. Which I'll claim when you've tasted my strawberry shortcake and peach pie."

"Pie? You made pie?" Obviously, Eve realized, there was a great deal to be said for family cookouts after all. "I could probably —"

Eve's communicator beeped. Her face closed down; Mira's cheerful smile vanished.

"I'm sorry. Excuse me a minute."

She rose, pulling it out of her pocket as she walked back inside the kitchen, back into the quiet.

"What is it?" Gillian demanded. "What's the matter?"

"Her work," Mira murmured, thinking of how Eve's eyes went cool and flat. "Death. Take the baby, Gilly."

She was rising when Eve stepped back out. "I have to go," Eve began, then lowered her voice as Mira walked over, took her arm. "I'm sorry. I have to go."

"Is it the same?"

"No. It's him, but it's not the same. I'll get you the details as soon as I can. Damn, brain's a little sloshy. Too many margaritas."

"I'll get you some Sober-Up."

"Appreciate it." She nodded to Roarke when he joined her. "You can stay. This is going to take awhile."

"I'll take you, and if need be I'll get myself home and leave you the car. Another LC?"

She shook her head. "Later." She took a breath, studying the patio, with its family sprawl, its flowers and food. "Life's not always a goddamn picnic, is it?"

CHAPTER SEVEN

"Drop me off on the corner. You don't have to go down the block."

Roarke ignored her and breezed through the light. "But your associates would miss the opportunity to witness your arrival in this particular vehicle."

The vehicle was a shiny silver jewel with a smoked glass retractable top and a snarling panther of an engine. It mortified her, they both knew, for other cops to whistle and hoot about her connection with Roarke's fancy toys.

She sucked it up, yanked off her sunshades. They were new, one of the items that habitually, and mysteriously, appeared among her things. She suspected they were stylish, knew they were ridiculously expensive. To save herself a little grief, she stuck them in her pocket.

"There's no reason for you to hang. I don't know how long I'll be."

"I'll stick around awhile and stay out of your way." He eased in behind a black-and-white and an emergency services vehicle.

"That is *some* ride, Lieutenant," one of the uniforms said even as she climbed out. "Bet it burns on a straightaway."

"Button it, Frohickie. What've we got here?"

"Sweet," he murmured, sliding a hand over the gleaming hood. "Female vic, strangled in her apartment. Lived alone. No sign of forced entry. Name's Lois Gregg, age sixty-one. Son became concerned when she didn't show up at a family event or answer her 'links. Came over, let himself in, found her."

He spoke briskly, though he did shoot one more look over his shoulder at the car as they trooped into an apartment building.

"Strangled?"

"Yes, sir. Definite signs of sexual assault with object. Fourth floor," he said when they were in the elevator. "Looks like he used a broomstick on her. It's pretty bad."

She said nothing, letting the new data filter through.

"He left a note," Frohickie said. "Addressed to you. Bastard stuck the envelope between her toes."

"DeSalvo," she muttered. "Good Christ."

Then she blanked it out, blanked it all out so she would walk into the scene with no set images or preconceptions in her head.

"I need a field kit and a recorder."

"Brought them up when we got word you were tagged away from home."

She forgave him for his comments about the car. "Scene's secured?" she questioned.

"Yes, sir. We've got the son in the kitchen, with a uniform and an MT. He's in bad shape. He says he didn't touch her."

"My aide's on her way. Send her in when she gets here. You have to stay out," she said to Roarke.

"Understood." But he felt a quick wrench that he would remain closed out while she walked into what was going to be another nightmare.

She marched in the open door, noted there were no signs of forced entry nor of struggle in the neat, simple living area. There were plain blue curtains at the window, sheer enough to let in the light. No privacy screens were engaged.

She squatted down to examine a few drops of blood on the edge of an area rug.

She could hear weeping from another room. The son in the kitchen, she thought, then blocked it out. Rising, she gestured the other cops back, sealed up, fixed on her recorder, then went into the bedroom.

Lois Gregg lay on the bed, nude, still bound, with the sash that had strangled her around her neck tied just under her chin in a festive bow.

The creamy envelope with Eve's name printed on the front was stuck between the toes of her left foot.

There was more blood — not as much as Wooton — on the plain white sheets, on her thighs, on the broomstick he'd left on the floor.

She was a small woman, probably no more than a hundred and ten pounds, with the caramel complexion that indicated mixed-race heritage.

Broken capillaries in her face, in her eyes, the distended and swollen tongue, were signs of the strangulation. The body fought back, Eve thought. Even after the mind went dark, the body fought for air. For life.

Eve spotted the long green robe beside the bed. He'd used the robe sash to strangle her.

He'd have wanted you conscious when he hurt you. He'd want to see your face, the pain, the horror, the terror. Yes, he'd want that this time. He'd want to hear you scream. Nice building like this ought to have decent soundproofing. He'd checked it out, checked you out before today.

Did he tell you what he was going to do to you? Or did he work in silence while you begged?

She recorded the scene, documenting the position of the body, the placement of the robe, the broomstick, the carefully drawn curtains.

Then she took the envelope, opened it, and read.

Hello again, Lieutenant Dallas. Isn't it a gorgeous day? A day that just begs for heading down to the shore or strolling through the park. I hate to interrupt your Sunday, but you seem to enjoy your work so much — as I do mine — that I didn't think you'd mind.

I'm a little disappointed in you, however, for a couple of reasons. First, tsk, tsk, on stonewalling the media reports on me. I was really looking forward to the buzz. Then again, you're not going to be able to keep a lid on the barrel too much longer. Second, I thought you'd be giving me just a bit more of a challenge by this point. Hopefully, my latest offer will inspire you.

Best of luck!

— Al

"Self-important bastard, aren't you?" she stated aloud, then sealed the note and envelope before opening the field kit.

She'd completed the preliminary exam when Peabody came in. "Lieutenant, I'm sorry. We were in the Bronx."

"What the hell were you . . ." She broke off. "What is that? What are you wearing?"

"It's a, um, ah, it's a sundress." Flushing a little, Peabody brushed a hand over the poppy pink skirt. "It took us so long to get back, I thought I should come straight here instead of heading home to change into uniform."

"Huh." The dress also had skinny little shoulder straps and a very low bodice. It demonstrated what McNab was fond of saying: Peabody sure was built.

Peabody's ruler-straight hair was covered by a wide-brimmed straw hat, and she was wearing lip dye that matched the sundress. "How are you supposed to work in that getup?"

"Well, I —"

"You said we? You brought McNab?"

"Yeah. Yes, sir. We were at the zoo. In the Bronx."

"That's something anyway. Tell him to go check the outside security, and the discs for the lobby level and elevators. This building should have them."

"Yes, sir."

She went out to relay the order as Eve walked into the adjoining bath.

He could've washed up after, she figured, but there was no sign of it. The bath was tidy, the towels looked fresh. Lois hadn't liked fuss, Eve mused, or clutter.

Must have brought his own soap and towel, too, or took some away with him.

"We'll want the sweepers to check the drains. Might get lucky," she said as Peabody came back in.

"I don't get it. This isn't like Wooton. Nothing like Wooton. Different type of victim, different method. There was another note?"

"Yeah. It's sealed."

Peabody studied the scene, tried to commit it to memory as the recorder did. She noticed, as Eve had, the little vase of flowers on the nightstand, the square catchall box on the dresser that said I LOVE GRANDMA in pink swirly letters on the top, and the framed photos and holos that stood on the dresser, the nightstand, the small desk by the window.

It was sad, she thought. It was always sad to see those bits and pieces of a life when the life was over.

But she tried to shake it off. Dallas would shake it off, she knew. Or bury it, or use it. But she wouldn't let herself be distracted by the pity.

Peabody looked again, making the deliberate shift from woman to cop. "Do you think there's more than one killer? A team?"

"No, there's only one." Eve lifted one of the victim's hands. No polish, she noted. Short nails. No rings, but a faint pale circle where one had been, and habitually. Third finger, left hand. "He's just showing us how versatile he is."

"I don't understand."

"I do. See if you can find where she kept her jewelry. I'm looking for a ring, band style."

Peabody started on the dresser drawers. “Maybe you could explain what you understand, so I can.”

“Victim is an older woman. No sign of forced entry or struggle. She let him in because she thought he was okay. He was probably suited up as maintenance or repair. She turns her back, and he hits her over the head. She’s got a laceration on the back of the skull, and there’s some blood on the living room rug.”

“Was she an LC?”

“Doubtful.”

“Got her jewelry.” Peabody lifted out a clear-sided box with insets of varying sizes. “She liked earrings. Got a few rings, too.”

She brought the case over, holding it while Eve poked through. Exposure to Roarke, and his propensity for dumping glitters on her had taught her to spot the real stuff from the costume. Lois’s body adornments were mostly costume, but there were a few good pieces as well.

He hadn’t bothered with those. Unlikely he’d even looked. “No, I don’t think so. I think she was wearing a ring, a kind of wedding ring, and he took it off her finger. A symbol, a souvenir.”

“I thought she lived alone.”

“She did. Another reason he picked her.” She turned away from the box of pretty stones and metal, looked back at Lois Gregg. “He carries her in here. He’s got his equipment again, likely in a toolbox this time. Restraints for her hands and feet. Strips off her robe, ties her up. Finds what he wants to use to rape her.

He's going to wake her up then. He didn't get to play with the other, but this one's different."

"Why?" Peabody set the jewelry box back on the dresser. "Why is she different?"

"Because that's what he's looking for. Variety. She screams when she comes around and realizes — when it comes into her like a flood what's happened, and what will happen. Even though part of her rejects it, refuses to believe, she screams and struggles, and begs. They like it when you beg. When he starts on her, when the pain spurts into her, hot, cold, impossible, she screams more. He'd get off on that."

Eve lifted one of Lois's hands again, then moved down to her feet. "She bloodied her wrists and ankles trying to get free, straining and twisting against the restraints. She didn't give up. He'd have enjoyed that, too. It's exciting for them when you fight, makes their breath come fast in your face, makes them hard. It gives them power when you fight and can't win."

"Dallas." Peabody kept her voice low, laid a hand on Eve's shoulder as her lieutenant had gone pale and clammy.

Eve shrugged, carefully took a step back. She knew everything Lois Gregg had felt. But it wouldn't take her down, not now, into the memory, into the nightmare. The blood and the cold and the pain.

Her voice was level and cool when she continued. "When he's done raping her, he takes the sash from her robe. She's incoherent now, from the pain and the shock. He gets on the bed, straddles her, looks into her eyes when he strangles her, listens to her fight to breathe, feels her body convulsing under his in that sick parody of sex. That's when he comes, when her body bucks under his and her eyes bulge. That's when he gets his release.

"When he comes back to himself, he ties the sash into a bow, wedges the note between her toes. He takes the ring off her finger, amused by it. Such a female thing, to wear the symbol when there's no man to go with it. He slips the ring in his pocket, or puts it in his toolbox, then checks how it all looks, and he's pleased. Just as it's supposed to. An excellent imitation."

"Of what?"

"Of who," Eve corrected. "Albert DeSalvo. The Boston Strangler."

She stepped out into the hallway, where cops were milling around, doing what they could to keep people from the neighboring apartments inside.

And there was Roarke, she thought. There was a man with more money than God sitting cross-legged on the hallway floor, his back supported by the wall as he worked with his PPC.

And would probably be content to do so, for reasons she could never understand, for hours.

She moved to him, squatted down so their eyes were level. "I'm going to be here awhile. You ought to go on home. I can catch a ride into Central."

"Bad, is it?"

"Very. I've got to talk to the son, and he's . . ." She let out a long breath. "They tell me the MT gave him something, but he's still pretty messed up."

"One is, when their mother's murdered."

Despite the presence of other cops, she laid a hand over his. "Roarke —"

"Demons don't die, Eve, we just learn to live with them. We've both known that all along. I'll deal with mine, in my way."

She started to speak again, then looked up when McNab came off the elevator.

"Lieutenant, no disc run since eight this morning. Nothing from the outside unit, elevator, or the hall on this floor. Best I can tell, he jammed it by remote from outside before entering the building. I could verify, but I don't have any tools on me."

He held out his hands, a half-ass smile on his face, to indicate his baggy red shorts, blue cinch vest, and toeless airsneaks.

"Then go get some," she began.

"I happen to have a few things in the car that might help with that," Roarke interrupted. "Why don't I give you a hand, Ian?"

"That would be mag. It's pretty decent security, so I figure if he went remote, it had to be police-issue level or above. Can't tell unless I can get into the panel and check the board."

Eve straightened, then held out a hand. Roarke grasped her forearm, and she his, to help him to his feet. "Go ahead. Get me best guess on what he used."

Oh eight hundred for entry, she thought. With the time of death she'd established, he'd spent no more than an hour on Lois Gregg. More time than Wooton, more time to play, but still fast.

She went back in, walked to the kitchen.

Jeffrey Gregg wasn't weeping now, but the tears already shed had wrecked his face. It was red and swollen, much like his mother's.

He sat at a small laminated table, his hands cupped around a glass of water. His brown hair stood up in tufts from where she imagined he'd pulled at it, raked his fingers through it, in his grief.

She judged him to be somewhere in his early thirties, and dressed in brown shorts and a white T-shirt for a casual summer Sunday.

She sat across from him, waited until those damaged eyes lifted to hers.

"Mr. Gregg, I'm Lieutenant Dallas. I need to talk to you."

"They said I couldn't go in and see her. I should go in. When I — when I found her, I didn't go in. I just ran out again, and called the police. I should've gone in — something. Covered her up?"

"No. You did exactly the right thing. You helped her more by doing just exactly what you did. I'm sorry, Mr. Gregg. I'm very sorry for your loss."

Useless words, she knew. Goddamn useless words. She hated saying them. Hated not being able to count the number of times they'd forced themselves out of her mouth.

"She never hurt anybody." He managed to lift the glass to his lips. "I think you should know that. She never hurt anybody in her life. I don't understand how somebody could do this to her."

“What time did you come here today?” She knew already, but would take him through the details, the repetition.

“I, ah, came over about three, I think. Maybe closer to four. No, nearer to three. I’m so mixed up. We were supposed to have this afternoon cookout at my sister’s in Ridgewood. My mother was supposed to come by our place. We’re over on 39th. We were all going to take the train over to New Jersey. She was supposed to be at our place by one.”

He gulped some water. “She runs late a lot. We tease her about it, but when it got to be like two, I started calling to move her along. She didn’t answer, so I figured she was on her way. But she didn’t show. I called her pocket number, but that didn’t answer either. My wife and kid were getting restless and annoyed. Me, too. I was getting pissed off.”

Remembering that, he began to cry again. “I was really steamed that I had to come over here and get her. I wasn’t worried so much, not really. I never thought anything had happened to her, and all the time she was . . .”

“When you got here,” Eve prompted, “you let yourself in. You have a key?”

“Yeah, I got access to the outside door and her apartment. I was thinking, something wrong with her ’links, that’s all. She forgets to bump them sometimes and they go out. Something’s wrong with her ’links and she’s lost track of time. That’s what I was thinking when I let myself in. I called out to her, like: ‘Mom! Damn it, Mom, we were supposed to leave for Mizzy’s two hours ago.' And when she didn't answer, I thought, Oh crap, she's on her way to my place and I'm over here, and this is so irritating. But I walked to the bedroom door anyway. I don't even know why. And she was . . . God. God. Mom."

He broke down again, and Eve shook her head at the MT before he could move in with a tranq. "Mr. Gregg. Jeff, you have to hold it together. You have to help me. Did you see anyone near the apartment, anyone outside?"

"I don't know." He mopped at his streaming face. "I was irritated and in a hurry. I didn't see anything special."

"Did your mother mention being uneasy about anything, noticing something, someone who worried her?"

"No. She's lived here for a dozen years. It's a nice building. Secure." He took deep breaths to steady his voice. "She knows her neighbors. Leah and me, we're only ten blocks away. We see each other every week. She'd've told me if something was wrong."

"How about your father?"

"They split, God, twenty-five years ago. He lives out in Boulder. They don't see each other much, but they get along okay. Jesus, Jesus, my father wouldn't have done this." The hitch came back in his voice, and he began to rock himself. "You'd have to be crazy to do this to somebody."

"It's just routine. Was she involved with anyone?"

"Nobody special now. She had Sam. They were together for about ten years. He was killed in a tram wreck about six years ago. He was the one for her, I guess. There hasn't been anybody else special since."

"Did she wear a ring?"

"A ring?" He looked at Eve blankly, as if the question had been posed in some strange foreign language. "Yeah. Sam gave her a ring when they moved in together. She always wore it."

"Can you describe it for me?"

"Um . . . it was gold, I think. Maybe with stones on it? God. I can't remember."

"It's okay." He'd had enough, she judged. And this line was a dead end. "One of the officers is going to take you home now."

"But . . . isn't there something? Shouldn't I do something?" He stared beseechingly at Eve. "Can you tell me what I'm supposed to do?"

"Just go home to your family, Jeff. That's the best thing you can do for now. I'm going to take care of your mother."

She walked out with him, turning him over to a uniform for escort home.

"Tell me something," she demanded of McNab.

"Definitely a remote zap. He has to have a superior skill with electronics and security, or enough money to buy a jammer, and we're talking mucho black-market buckaroos for a unit like this."

"Why?" she wanted to know. "A building like this, security's good, but it's not top level."

"Okay, it's not that it jammed security, it's *how* it jammed." He pulled a pack of gum from one of his many pockets, offered Eve some, then folded a cube into his mouth when she shook her head.

"It shut everything down — security-wise — without messing with other ops. Lights, climate control, home and personal electronics weren't touched. Except —" Busily chewing, he pointed to the living room lamps. "In here. This apartment unit, and this specific room. Lights on," he ordered, and Eve nodded when the lamps stayed dark.

"Yeah, that fits. 'Sorry to bother you, ma'am, but we've had reports of electronic malfunction in the building.' He's dressed like a workman. I'd make book he's got a toolbox. A big helpful smile. Maybe he even tells her to try the lights, and when they don't work, she opens the door."

McNab blew an impressive purple bubble, snapped it. "Plays for me."

"Check out the 'links, let's be thorough. You find anything, I'm at Central. Peabody!"

"With you, sir."

"Not while you're wearing that stupid hat. Lose it," Eve ordered and strode out.

"I like the hat." McNab kept his voice low. "Sexy."

"McNab, you think brick's sexy," Peabody replied. But with a quick check to see if the coast was clear, she gave his ass a fast squeeze. "Maybe I'll wear it later. You know, *just* the hat."

"She-Body, you're killing me."

He took a quick peek, saw Eve was gone, then dragged Peabody close for a sloppy kiss.

"Blueberry." Amused, she blew a purple bubble with the gum he'd passed to her. Then hurrying after Eve, she pulled the hat off her head.

She found Eve outside standing beside the totally iced vehicle with the totally iced Roarke.

"No point in it," Eve was saying. "We'll hitch in a black-and-white. If I'm going to be really late, I'll let you know."

"Let me know regardless, and I'll have transpo arranged to bring you home."

"I can arrange my own transpo."

"This isn't transpo." Peabody gave a feline purr as she stroked the car. "This is a total *ride*."

"We could easily squeeze in."

"No." Eve cut Roarke off. "We're not squeezing anywhere."

"Suit yourself. Peabody, you look delicious." He took the hat from her hand, arranged it back on her head. "Absolutely edible."

"Oh. Well. Golly." Under the hat, her head went wonderfully light.

"Wipe that ridiculous look off your face, lose the hat, and get us a ride to Central," Eve snapped.

"Huh?" She let out a long sigh. "Oh, yes, sir. Doing all that."

"Do you *have* to do that?" Eve demanded of Roarke when Peabody walked dreamily away.

"Yes. When she makes detective, I'm going to miss seeing our girl in uniform, but it should be interesting to see how she suits up otherwise. I'll see you at home, Lieutenant." And not caring if it annoyed her, he caught her chin in his hand, pressed his lips firmly to hers. "You are, as always, delicious."

"Yeah, yeah, yeah." Jamming her hands in her pockets, she stalked away.

It was dark when she got home. Whether it was bullheadedness or not, she hadn't tagged Roarke for transpo even after realizing she didn't have cab fare on her. But she had dug up subway tokens, and found the underground ride jammed with people going home after a Sunday out on the town.

She opted to stand, swaying with the rhythm of the train as it headed uptown.

She didn't ride the subway enough anymore, Eve thought. Not that she missed it. Half the ads were in languages not her own, half the passengers were zoned or irritated. And there would always be one or two who smelled as if they had a religious objection to soap and water.

Such as the wizened, toothless beggar with his license around his grubby neck who gave her a gummy grin. Still, it only took one steely stare to have him looking elsewhere.

She supposed she'd missed that, just a little.

She shifted, whiling away the trip by studying the other passengers. Students, buried in their disc books. Kids heading out to the vids. An old man snoring loud enough to make her wonder if he'd slept through his stop already. Some tired-looking women with children, a couple of tough guys looking bored.

And the skinny, geeky guy in the unseasonable trench coat currently masturbating at the far end of the car.

"Oh, for Christ's sake." She started over, but one of the tough guys spotted the geek, and obviously taking exception to the activity smashed a fist into the whacker's face.

Blood spurted. Several people screamed. Though his nose was now a fountain, the geek kept himself in hand.

"Break it up." Eve surged, reached down to grab tough guy number one when a fellow passenger panicked, sprang to his feet, and knocked Eve into the fist of tough guy number two.

"Goddamn it to hell!" She saw a couple of shooting stars, shook her head clear. "I'm the frigging police." With her cheek throbbing, she smashed her elbow into tough guy number one to stop him from pounding on the giggling pervert still whacking off on the floor of the car, then stomped her foot on the instep of tough guy two.

When she hauled up the geek, snarled, everyone else stepped back. Something about the glint in her eye did what the tough guy's fist hadn't. The geek went limp.

She glanced down as he deflated, and let out a sigh. "Put that thing away," she ordered.

Screw the subway, she grumbled as she strode up the long drive toward home. The ride had given her a sore jaw and a headache, and cost her the time it had taken to get off the damn car and turn the idiot over to the transit authority.

She didn't much care that there was a nice breeze stirring up, an almost balmy one. Or that it carried hints of something sweet and floral into the air. She didn't care that the sky was so clear she could see a three-quarter moon hanging in it like a lamp.

Okay, it looked nice, but *hell*.

She stomped inside, and after a terse inquiry, was told by the house system that Roarke was in the family media room.

Which was opposed to the main media room, she thought. Where the hell was it again? Because she wasn't entirely sure and the hike from the subway stop to the front door had been considerable, she went into the elevator.

"Family media room," she ordered, and was whisked up, and east.

The main media room was for parties and events, she remembered. It could fit more than a hundred people in plush chairs, and offered a wall screen as wide as a theater's.

But the family media room was — she supposed he'd say — more intimate. Deep colors, she recalled, cushy seats. Two screens — one for vids, one for games. And the complex and complicated sound system that could play anything from the old-fashioned clunky vinyl records Roarke liked to fiddle with on occasion to the minute sound sticks.

She stepped into the room to a blast of sound that seemed to come from everywhere. Her eyes widened in reaction to the fast-moving space battle being waged over the wall screen.

Roarke was kicked back in a lounge chair, the cat in his lap, a glass of wine in his hand.

She should go to work, she told herself. Do more research on the Boston Strangler, keep digging for a connection between Wooton and Gregg. Though she was dead sure there would be no connection.

She should hound the sweepers, the ME, the lab. None of whom, she knew, would pay much attention to her at nearly ten on a Sunday night. But she could harass them anyway.

She could run probabilities, go over her notes, her suspect lists, stare at her murder board.

Instead, she walked over, plucked the cat off Roarke's lap. "You're in my seat," she told him, and set him on another chair.

She slid into Roarke's lap, took his wine. "What's this one about?"

"It seems water is the commodity in fashion. This particular planet in the Zero quadrant —"

"There isn't any Zero quadrant."

"It's fictional, my darling, literal-minded Eve." He snuggled her in, pressing an absent kiss to her head as he watched the action. "Anyway, this planet's all but out of water. Potable water. And there's a rescue attempt being made to get the colony there a supply, and the means to clean up what they have. But there's this other faction who wants the water for themselves. There've been a couple of bloody battles over it already."

Something exploded on screen, a shower of color, an ear-splinting boom of sound.

“Nicely done,” Roarke commented. “And there’s a woman, head of the environmental police — the good guys — who’s reluctantly in love with the rogue cargo captain who’s helping deliver the goods — for a price. It’s about thirty minutes in. I can start it over.”

“No, I’ll catch up.”

She intended to sit with him for a few minutes only, let her mind rest. But she got caught up in the story, and it was so nice, so simple to stay, stretched out in the chair with him while fictional battles raged.

And good overcame evil.

“Not bad,” she said when the credits began to roll. “I’m going to get another hour or two of work in.”

“Are you going to tell me about it?”

“Probably.” She climbed out of the chair, stretched, then blinked like an owl when he turned on the light.

“Well, damn it, Eve, what have you done to your face now?”

“It wasn’t my fault.” Sulking a little, she touched fingers gingerly to her jaw. “Somebody knocked me into this guy’s fist when I was trying to stop him from beating this other guy who was whacking off in the subway to a bloody pulp. I couldn’t blame the guy, the guy with the fist, because he wasn’t aiming it at me. But still.”

“My life,” Roarke said after a moment, “was gray before you walked into it.”

“Yeah, I’m a rainbow.” She wiggled her jaw. “My face anyway. You up for some drone work?”

“I might be persuaded. After we put something on that bruise.”

"It's not so bad. You know, the transit cop told me that guy's a regular on that line. They call him Willy the Wanker."

"That's a fascinating bit of New York trivia." He pulled her toward the elevator. "It makes me yearn to ride the subway."

CHAPTER EIGHT

In Peabody's cramped apartment, McNab ran her through a series of intense computer simulations. He'd proven himself, Peabody had discovered in the last few weeks, a strict and fairly irritating instructor.

With her shoulders hunched, she carefully picked her way through a murder scene, selecting her choices and options in a field investigation of a double homicide.

And cursed when her selection resulted in a blasting buzz — McNab's personal addition to the sim — and a stern-faced figure of a robed judge shaking his finger at her.

Ah-ah-ah — improper procedure, scene contamination. Evidence suppressed. Suspect gets a free walk due to detective investigator's screwup.

"Does he *have* to say that?"

"Cuts through the legal mumbo," McNab pointed out, and stuffed potato chips in his face. "Digs down to the point."

"I don't want to do any more sims." Her face fell into a pout that had McNab's libido jiggling. "My brain's going to leak out of my ears in a minute."

He loved her, enough to mostly ignore the image of peeling her out of her clothes and doing her on the rug.

"Look, you're aces on the written. You've got a memory for details and points of law, blah blah. You get thumbs-up on the oral, once your voice settles down from a squeak."

"It does not squeak."

"Sort of like how it does when I bite your toes." He grinned toothily when she scowled at him. "And while I like how it sounds myself, the test team's going to be less romantically inclined. So you're going to want to oil the squeaks."

She continued to pout, then her mouth dropped open in shock when he slapped her hand away from the bag of chips. "None for you until you get through a sim."

"Jesus, McNab, I'm not a puppy performing for a biscuit."

"No, you're a cop who wants to make detective." He moved the bag out of her reach. "And you're scared."

"I'm not scared; I'm understandably anxious about the testing process and proving myself ready to . . ." She hissed out a breath as he merely studied her with patient green eyes. "I'm terrified." Because his arm came around her, she snuggled into his bony shoulder. "I'm terrified I'll blow it, and I'll let Dallas down. And you, and Feeney, the commander, my family. Jesus."

"You're not going to blow it, and you won't let anyone down. This isn't about Dallas, or anybody else. It's all about you."

"She trained me, she put me up for it."

"So she must figure you're ready. It ain't no snap, She-Body." He gave her cheek a quick nuzzle. "It's not supposed to be. But you've got the training, you've got the field time, the instincts, the brains. And, honey, you've got the guts and heart, too."

She turned her head to look up at him. "That's so damn sweet."

"It's a fact, and here's another one, here's what you don't have right now. You don't have the balls."

Her gooey affection toward him transformed into brittle insult. "Hey."

"And because you don't have the balls," he continued calmly, "you're not trusting your gut, or your training. You're second-guessing yourself. Instead of going with what you know, you keep wondering what you don't know, and that's why you keep missing up on the sims."

She'd pulled away from him. Her breath hissed out. "I hate you for being right."

"Nah. You love me because I'm so damn good looking."

"Asshole."

" 'Fraidy cat."

" 'Fraidy cat." Her lips twitched into a reluctant smile. "Jeez. Okay, set up another one. Make it tough. And when I nail it, I not only get the chips, but . . ." Her smile widened. "You wear the hat."

"You're on."

She rose to pace and clear out her head while he programmed the sim. She'd been afraid, she admitted. Afraid she wanted it too much. So she hadn't used the hunger, but had let it eat away at her confidence. That had to stop. Even if her palms were damp and her stomach in knots it had to stop.

Dallas never let nerves get in the way, she thought. And she had them, nerves and something deeper, darker. It had peeked through on the Gregg scene, for just a moment that afternoon. Now and again on a sexual homicide, it peeked through. It turned her lieutenant's cheeks pale. Took her back, Peabody was sure, to something horrible. Something personal.

Rape, Peabody was sure, just as she was sure it had to have been brutal. And she'd have been young. Before the job. Peabody had studied Eve's career with the NYPSD like a template, but there'd been no report of a sexual assault on Dallas.

So it had been before, before the Academy. When she was a teenager, or possibly younger. In automatic sympathy, Peabody's stomach roiled. It would take guts, and balls, to face that, to revisit whatever had happened every time you walked into a scene that reverberated with sexual violence.

But to use it, instead of being used by it, that took more, Peabody determined. It took what she could only define as valor.

"Ready here," McNab told her. "And it's a doozy."

She sucked in a breath, squared her shoulders. "I'm ready, too. Go in the bedroom or something, okay? I want to do it on my own."

He looked at her face, saw what he'd hoped to see, and nodded. "Sure. Nail the bad guy, She-Body."

"Damn right."

She sweated through it, but stayed focused. She stopped asking herself what Dallas would want her to do, even after a point what Dallas would do, and just concentrated on what needed to be done. Preserve and observe, collect and identify. Question, report, investigate. It began to click for her, the pattern emerging. She waded her way through conflicting witness statements, shaky memories, facts and lies, forensics and procedure.

She built, she realized with rising excitement, a case.

Though she wanted to hesitate on the final stage, the arrest, she bore down and selected. And was rewarded with the graphic of a prosecuting attorney.

Pick him up. Murder One.

"Yes!" She popped up from the chair, did her little victory dance. "I got an arrest. Nailed the murdering bastard. Hey, McNab, bring me those damn potato chips."

"Sure." He stepped out, grinning. He carried the bag in one hand, and was naked but for her summer straw hat. Since it was perched jauntily at his crotch, she assumed her success made him as happy as it made her.

She laughed until she thought her ribs would crack. "You're such a moron," she managed, and jumped him.

For Eve it was a matter of merging bare facts with educated speculation. "He had to know their routines, which means he knew them. Doesn't mean they knew him, doesn't connect them, but *he* knew. He's too cocky for them to have been random. He trolled first."

"That's the usual pattern, isn't it?" Roarke cocked his head at her look. "If my one true love was a dentist, I'd study up a bit on the latest thoughts on dental hygiene and treatments."

"Don't say dentist," Eve warned, automatically running her tongue warily over her teeth.

"By all means let's stick with bloody murder." And knowing there was no talking her out of another cup of coffee at midnight, had another himself. "The trolling, the selecting, the stalking, the planning. They are all essential parts of the whole for the typical, if the word can be used, serial killer."

"There's a rush in it, the control, the power, the details. She's alive now because I allow it, she'll be dead because I want it. It's clear he admires the serial killers who made names for themselves. Jack the Ripper, the Boston Strangler, so he emulates them. But he's very much his own man. Better than they were, because he's versatile."

"And he wants you pursuing him because he admires you."

"In his own sick way. He wants the buzz. It isn't enough to kill. That doesn't heat the blood enough. The hunt, being both hunter and prey, that does it for him. He hunted these women."

She turned to the board she'd set up in her home office, with pictures of Jacie Wooton and Lois Gregg, alive and dead. "He watched them, learned their routines and patterns. He needed a prostitute for the Ripper imitation, and a certain type of LC. She fit the mold. He *expected* her to walk along that street at that time. It wasn't chance. Just as Lois Gregg fit his need for a Strangler vic, just as he knew she'd be home alone on a Sunday morning."

"And knew someone would find her before the end of the day?"

"Yeah." Sipping coffee, she nodded. "Quicker gratification that way. More and more likely he called in the anonymous nine-one-one. Wanted Wooton found as soon as possible so the adulation and horror could begin."

"Which tells me he feels very safe."

"Very safe," Eve agreed. "Very superior. If Gregg hadn't had family or friends who were bound to check on her in a few hours, he'd have to wait to get the next kick, or risk another nine-one-one. So he targeted these women specifically, just as he's targeted the next."

She sat, rubbed her eyes. "He'll imitate someone else. But it'll be someone who created a stir, and who left bodies where they could and would be found. We eliminate historic serial killers who buried, destroyed, or consumed their victims."

"Such a fun group, too."

"Oh yeah. He's not going to copy someone like Chef Jourard, that French guy in the twenties, this century."

"Kept his victims in a large freezer, didn't he?"

"Where he carved them up, cooked them up, and served them to unsuspecting patrons of his fancy bistro in Paris. Took them nearly two years to catch him."

"And he was famed for his sweetbreads."

She gave a quick shudder. "Anybody who eats internal organs of any species baffles me. And I'm off the track."

He trailed a hand down her arm. "Because you're tired."

"Maybe. He'll stay more straightforward, won't go for a play on someone like Jourard, or Dahmer, or that Russian maniac Ivan the Butcher. But people being what they are, he's got plenty of others to work with. He'll stick with women."

She walked back to the board. "When you kill women the way he did these two, you've got a problem with them. But he's not connected to the actual victims. I'll go back and push the paper — the note. See if anyone on the list has a particular interest in celebrity killers."

"There's another you might want to speak with," Roarke suggested. "Thomas A. Breen. He's written what some consider the definitive book on twentieth-century serial killers, another on mass murderers throughout history. I've actually read some of his work, as the subject matter is of some interest to my wife."

"Breen, Thomas A. I might've read some of his stuff. Sounds vaguely familiar."

"He lives here in the city. I looked up the particulars when you were at Central, as I thought you might want a word with him."

"Smart guy."

This time when she reached for the coffeepot, he laid a hand over hers to stop her. "Smart enough to know you've had over your quota of coffee for the day, and despite it you're starting to droop."

"I just want to run a couple of probabilities."

"Set them up then, and they can run while you're sleeping. You'll have the results in the morning."

She'd have argued, but she was too damn tired. Instead, she did as he suggested, and still her gaze was drawn back to the board. Back to Lois Gregg.

She could hear the way the woman's son, a grown man, had sobbed. She could see the utter devastation on his face when he'd pleaded with her to tell him what he should do.

"Mom," he'd said, the way she imagined a child would. Though over thirty he'd said "Mom" with a little boy's helpless loss.

She knew Roarke had felt some of that same helplessness, that young boy's lost grief, when he'd learned the mother he'd never known had been murdered. Dead for three decades. Still he grieved.

And just that afternoon, a grown woman had studied her with suspicion and resentment over a relationship with her mother.

What was it that bound the child, so inexorably, with the mother? Was it blood, she wondered, as she stripped down for bed? Was it imprinted in the womb or something learned and developed after birth?

Killers of women, lust killers, were often bred due to their unhealthy feelings or relationships with a mother figure. Just as she supposed saints were bred from healthy ones. Or all the normality of the human race between the extremes.

Had this killer hated his mother? Abused or been abused by her? Was he killing her now?

And thinking of mothers, she slipped into sleep to dream of her own.

It was the hair, golden hair, so shiny and pretty, so long and curly. She liked to touch it, though she knew she wasn't supposed to. She liked to pet it, as she'd seen a boy pet a puppy dog once.

Nobody was home, and it was all quiet, the way she liked it best. When they were gone, the mommy and the daddy, nobody yelled or made scary noises or told her not to do everything she wanted to do.

Nobody slapped or hit.

She wasn't supposed to go into the room where the mommy and daddy slept, or where the mommy sometimes brought other daddies to play on the bed without their clothes.

But there were so many *things* in there. Like the long golden hair, or the bright red hair, and the bottles that smelled like flowers.

She tiptoed toward the dresser, a thin girl in jeans that bagged and a yellow T-shirt that was stained with grape juice. Her ears were keen, as the ears of prey often were, and she listened carefully, prepared to dart out of the room at any moment.

Her fingers reached out and stroked the yellow curls of the wig. The pressure syringe tossed carelessly beside it didn't interest her. She knew the mommy took medicine every day, sometimes more than once a day. Sometimes the medicine made her sleepy, sometimes it made her want to dance and dance. She was nicer when she wanted to dance; even though her laughing was scary, it was better than the yelling or the slapping.

There was a mirror over the dresser and she could just see the top half of her own face if she strained up high on her toes. Her hair was ugly brown and straight and short. It wasn't pretty like the mommy's play hair.

Unable to resist, she put the wig over her own hair. It fell all the way to her waist and made her feel pretty, made her feel happy.

There were all sorts of toys on the dresser, for painting faces with color. Once when the mommy had been in a good mood, she'd painted her lips and cheeks and said she'd looked like a little doll.

If she looked like a doll, maybe the mommy and daddy would like her better. They wouldn't yell and hit, and she could go outside and play.

Humming to herself, she painted on lip dye, rubbing her lips together as she'd seen the mommy do. She brushed on cheek color and clumsily fit her feet inside the high-heeled shoes that were in front of the dresser. She teetered on them, but was able to see even more of her face.

"Like a little doll," she said, pleased with the golden curls and the smears of color.

She began to use more, with enthusiasm, and was so intent on the game, on the fun, she failed to listen.

"You stupid little *bitch!*"

The scream had her stumbling back, tripping out of the shoes. She was already falling when the hand slapped across her face. It hurt where she banged her elbow, but even as the tears spurted out in response, the mommy was grabbing her by her sore arm and yanking her to her feet.

"I told you never to come in here. I told you never to touch my things."

The mommy's hands were white, so white, and painted red on the nails like they were bleeding. She used one to slap, and it stung the little painted cheek.

The girl opened her mouth to wail as the hand raised up to strike again.

"Goddamn it, Stel." The daddy burst in, grabbing the mommy, shoving her away and onto the bed. "The soundproofing in here's next to nothing. You want to bring the fucking social workers down on us again?"

"The little shit's been into my things." The mommy jumped off the bed, curling those bloody fingertips into claws. "Look at the mess she made! I'm sick and tired of having to clean up after her and listening to her whine."

On the floor, curled up tight with her arms over her head, the child struggled not to make a sound. Not any sound at all so they'd forget she was there, so she'd be invisible.

"I never wanted the brat in the first place." There was a bite in the mommy's voice, like sharp teeth snapping. The child imagined them snapping down on her fingers, her toes. Terror made her mewl like a cornered kitten and press her hands to her ears to block the sound.

"Having her was your idea. You deal with her."

"I'll deal with her." He scooped the child up, and though she feared him, feared him on a deep and instinctual level, at the moment she feared the mommy more with her words that bit and her white hands that slapped.

So she curled herself into him, and shuddered when he stroked a hand over the wig that had fallen over her eyes, and down her back, over her rump.

"Have a hit, Stella," he said. "You'll feel better. I get this deal through, we'll buy a droid to look after the kid."

"Yeah, right. About the same time we'll have that big house and the fleet of fancy cars and all the other shit you promised me. The only thing I got out of you so far, Rich, is that whiny brat."

"An investment in the future. She's going to pay off for us one day. Aren't you, little girl? Have a hit, Stella," he said again as he started out of the room with the child on his hip. "I'll clean the kid up."

The last thing the child saw as he left the room with her was the mommy's face. And the eyes, brown eyes painted gold on the lids that were, like the words, full of teeth and hate.

Eve woke, not with the strangled panic of the nightmares that plagued her, but with a kind of cold, dull shock. The room was dark, and she realized she'd rolled herself to the far edge of the bed, as if she'd needed privacy for the dream.

Shaken, vaguely ill, she rolled back, curled herself against Roarke. His arm came around her, drawing her in. Circled in his warmth, she pretended to sleep again.

* * *

She said nothing to Roarke of the dream the next morning. Didn't know if she should, or could. She wanted to lock it away, but she felt it pushing at her as she went through her morning routine.

It was a relief that Roarke had a morning full of meetings and she could slip around him and out of the house with little conversation.

He read her too well and too easily — a talent that was both a wonder and an irritation to her — and she wasn't ready to explore what she'd remembered.

Her mother was a whore and a junkie, and had never wanted the child she'd made. More than not wanted. Had despised and abhorred.

What difference did it make? Eve asked herself as she drove downtown. Her father had been a monster. Was it any worse to know her mother had been the same? It changed nothing.

She parked at Central, made her way up to her office. With every step inside the busy hive of Central, she felt more herself. The weight of her weapon comforted her, as did the knowledge that her badge was in her pocket.

Roarke had called them her symbols once, and so they were. Symbols of who and what she was.

She walked through the bull pen where the morning shift was settling in. She detoured by Peabody's cube just as her aide was knocking back the last of a glide-cart coffee.

"Thomas A. Breen," Eve began, and rattled off an East Village address. "Contact him, set up a meeting ASAP. We'll go to him."

"Yes, sir. Rough night?" At Eve's silent stare Peabody shrugged. "Don't look like you got much sleep, that's all. Neither did I. Cramming for the exam. It's coming up soon."

"You want regular eight straights, you don't pick up the badge. Set up the interview. Then we're doing follow-ups on the list, starting with Fortney." She started to walk away, then turned back. "You can overstudy, you know."

"I know, but I was really blowing the sims. I nailed two last night. That's the first time I felt like I had a handle."

"Good." Eve stuck her thumbs in her pockets, drummed her fingers. "Good," she repeated and headed to her office to nag the lab for updates on Gregg.

The bickering with Dickhead put her in a cheerier mood as she read over the ME's reports. Morris was going with surgical grade on the weapons used on Wooton. Her tox screen confirmed that her system was clear of chemicals.

Since she wasn't using, spending time trying to find her former dealer wasn't priority.

The canvasses of Chinatown and the surrounding areas had come up zero, one more time.

"No trace of semen with Gregg," Eve told Peabody as they headed to the Village. "ME findings indicate she was raped and sodomized, with the broomstick only. No prints on-scene other than hers, family members, and two neighbors who're clear. Hair fibers, man-made. Dickhead thinks wig and mustache, but isn't ready to commit."

"So we think he wore a disguise."

"In case he was seen around the neighborhood. He had to keep tabs on her, a few weeks, I'd say. Solidify her Sunday routine. How'd he pick her, though? Out of a fucking hat? How does he target this particular LC, this particular woman?"

"Maybe there's some connection. A place they shopped, ate, did business. A doctor, a bank."

"Possible, and it's a good line for you to tug. I'm more inclined to think it was the area first. Neighborhood. Select the setting, then the character, then put on your play."

"Speaking of neighborhoods, this is really nice." Peabody gazed out at shady sidewalks, large old houses, pretty urban gardens planted in window boxes or pots. "I could go for this one day. You know, when I settle down, start thinking family and stuff. You ever think about that? Kids and all."

Eve thought of the hate-filled eyes, staring at her out of a dream. "No."

"Tons of time and all. I figure maybe to think about it in six, eight years anyway. Definitely going to be taking McNab on a long test drive before I commit to more than cohabbing. Hey, your eye didn't twitch."

"Because I'm not listening to you."

"Are, too," Peabody muttered when Eve pulled to the curb. "He's been really great working with me for the exam. It makes a difference having somebody rooting for me. He really wants it for me because I want it. That's . . . well, that's just solid."

"McNab's a moron the majority of the time, but he's in love with you."

"Dallas!" Peabody shifted in her seat so sharply her cap tipped over one eye. "You said the 'L' word and 'McNab' in the same sentence. Voluntarily."

"Just shut up."

"Happy to." With a happy smile, she squared her cap. "I'm just going to savor in silence."

They walked three houses down to a three-story home that Eve imagined had once been a multifamily dwelling. Writing about killers was obviously profitable if Breen could afford something this up-market.

She went up a short flight of flagstoned steps to the main entrance, noted the full security system that must have made the man confident enough to keep the etched glass panes on either side of the front door.

There was a wife as well, she knew from her quick background check, and a two-year-old boy. Breen collected partial professional father pay from the government as primary at-home parent while his wife earned a substantial salary as a VP and managing editor of a fashion rag called *Outre*.

A nice, tidy setup, Eve mused, as she rang the bell and held up her badge for scan.

Breen answered the door himself with his son sitting astride his shoulders. The boy was holding on to Breen's blond hair like the reins on a horse.

"Go, ride!" the boy shouted and kicked his feet.

"Only this far, partner." Breen hooked his hands around the boy's ankles, either to anchor him, Eve thought, or to stop the busy little heels from digging holes in his armpits. "Lieutenant Dallas?"

"That's right. I appreciate you taking the time to talk to me, Mr. Breen."

"No problem. Always happy to talk to the cops, and I've followed your work. I'm hoping to do a book on New York murders eventually, and figure you'll be one of my prime sources."

"You'll have to talk to public relations at Central about that. Can we come in?"

"Oh yeah, sure. Sorry."

He stepped back. He was in his thirties, of strong, medium build. From the definition in his arms, Eve doubted he sat at a computer all day. He had a good face, handsome without being soft.

"Blaster!" the boy called out as he spotted Eve's weapon under her jacket. "Zappit!"

Breen laughed, flipped the child off his shoulders in a rapid and smooth move that had the kid squealing in delight. "Jed here's a little bloodthirsty. Runs in the family. I'm just going to set him up with the droid, then we can talk."

"No droid!" The kid's face went from angelic to mutinous in a heartbeat. "Stay with Daddy!"

"Just for a little while, champ; then we'll go out to the park." He tickled the boy into giggles as he charged up the steps with him.

"Nice to see a guy handle a kid that way, and enjoy it," Peabody commented.

"Yeah. Wonder what a guy, a successful guy, thinks about pulling in a professional father stipend, dealing with an offspring, while the mother's being a busy exec at a major firm every day. Some guys would resent that. Some might think the little lady's pushy, domineering. Maybe his mother was the same — Breen's mother is a neurologist and his father went the professional parent route. You know," Eve added, looking up the stairs, "some guys would build up a nasty little resentment of women over that kind of setup."

"That's really sexist."

"Yeah, it is. Some people are."

Peabody frowned up the steps. "It's some brain that could take a nice, homey scene like we just witnessed and turn it on its head into a motive for murder."

"Just one of my natural-born talents, Peabody."

CHAPTER NINE

Breen set them up in a roomy office just off the kitchen. Two large windows faced the rear, where they could see a kind of tidy patio skirted by a low wall. Behind the wall were leafy trees. With the view, they might have been in some quiet suburb rather than the city.

Someone had put pots of flowers on the patio, along with a couple of loungers. There was a small table shaded by a jaunty blue-and-white striped umbrella.

A couple of big plastic trucks lay on their sides, along with their colorful plastic occupants, as if there had been a terrible vehicular accident.

Why, Eve wondered, were kids always bashing toys together? Maybe it was some sort of primitive cave-dweller instinct that, if things went well, the kid outgrew or at least restrained into adulthood.

Jed's father looked civilized enough, sitting in his rolly chair that he'd scooted around from his workstation. Then again, he made the bulk of his living writing about people who restrained nothing, and rather than outgrowing any destructive instincts, had bumped it up from plastic toys to flesh and blood.

It took, Eve was very aware, all kinds.

"So, how can I help?"

"You've done considerable research into serial killers," Eve began.

"Historical figures, primarily. Though I have interviewed a few contemporary subjects."

"Why is that, Mr. Breen?"

"Tom. Why?" He looked surprised for a moment. "It's fascinating. You've been up close and personal with the breed. Don't you find them fascinating?"

"I don't know if that's the word I'd use."

He leaned forward. "But you have to wonder what makes them who they are, don't you? What separates them from the rest of us? Is it something more or something less? Are they born to kill, or does that need evolve in them? Is it a single instance that turns them, or a series of events? And really, the answer isn't always the same, and *that's* fascinating. One guy spends his childhood in poverty and abuse" — he tapped his index fingers together — "and becomes a productive member of society. A bank president, faithful husband, good father, loyal friend. Plays golf on the weekend and walks his pet schnauzer every night. He uses his background to springboard himself into something better, higher, right?"

"And another uses it as an excuse to dive into the muck. Yeah, I get it. Why do you write about the muck?"

He sat back again. "Well, I could give you a lot of jive about how studying the killer and the muck he wades in gives society insight into how and why. And understanding, *information*, is power against fear. It would be true," he added with his quick and boyish smile. "But on another level entirely, it's just fun. I've been into it since I was a kid. Jack the Ripper was the big one for me. I read everything about him, watched every vid ever produced, surfed the Web sites, made up stories where I was a cop back then and tracked him down. Along the way I expanded, studied up on profiling and types, the steps and the stages — you know, trolling, hunting, the rush and the lull."

He shrugged now. "I went through a phase where I thought I'd be a cop, chase the bad guys. But I got over that one. Considered going into psychology, but it just didn't suit me. What I really wanted to do was write, and that's what I was good at. So I write about my lifelong interest."

"I hear some writers need to experience the subject they're writing about. Need that hands-on approach before they can put it down in words."

Amusement bloomed on his face. "So, you're asking if I've gone out and carved up a couple of street LCs in the name of research?" His laughter rolled out, then stopped, like a wave hitting a wall as Eve only continued to watch him.

He blinked, several times, then swallowed audibly. "Holy shit, you really are. I'm a suspect?" The healthy color in his face had drained away to leave it pale and shiny. "For real?"

"I'd like to know where you were on September second, between midnight and 3a.m."

"I was home, probably. I don't . . ." He lifted both hands, rubbed the sides of his head. "Man, my brain's gone fuzzy. I figured you wanted me to consult. Was pretty juiced about it. Ah . . . I was here. Jule —

Julietta, my wife — had a late meeting, and didn't get home until about ten. She was whipped and went straight up to bed. I put in some writing time. With Jed, the only time the house is really quiet is the middle of the night. I worked until one, maybe a little after. I can check my disc log."

He opened drawers in his workstation, began to root around. "I, ah, Jesus, did the man of the house routine. I go through it every night before I turn in. Check the security, make sure everything's locked up. Look in on Jed. That's it."

"How about Sunday morning?"

"This Sunday?" He glanced up, over. "My wife got up with Jed."

He paused, and Eve could see the change taking place. The shock was ebbing and the interest, the enjoyment, even the pride in being considered a murder subject was rolling in.

"Most Sundays I sleep in and she takes over. She doesn't get as much one-on-one time with him as I do. She took him to the park. They go out early and have a picnic breakfast if the weather's good. Jed loves that. I didn't surface till close to noon. What's Sunday? I'm not following . . ."

Then he did. She could see it click. "The woman who was found strangled in her apartment on Sunday. Middle-aged woman, living alone. Sexual assault and strangulation."

His eyes were narrowed now, his color back. "The media reports were sketchy, but strangulation and sexual assault, that's not Ripper style. An older woman, at home in her apartment, that's not Ripper style either. What's the connection?"

At Eve's steady stare, he scooted forward in the chair. "Listen, if I'm moonlighting as a killer, I already know so you won't be telling me anything. If I'm just an expert on serial killers, giving me some details might let me help. Either way, how can you lose?"

She'd already decided what she would and wouldn't tell him, but held his gaze another moment. "The sash of the victim's lounge robe was used as the murder weapon, and tied in a bow under the chin."

"Boston Strangler. That was his signature." He snapped his fingers, and began to push through the piles of discs and files on his desk. "I've got considerable notes on him. Wow. You've got two killers imitating the famous? Teamwork, like Leopold and Loeb? Or . . ." He paused, took a long breath. "Not two, just one. One killer working his way down a list of his heroes. That's why you're looking at me. You're wondering if the people I write about are heroes to me, and if I'm mixing up my work and my life. If I want to be one of them."

He pushed to his feet, pacing with what looked to Eve to be energy rather than nerves. "This is fucking *amazing*. He's probably read my books. That's sort of creepy, but icy in a strange way, too. DeSalvo, DeSalvo. Different type from Jack," Breen mumbled. "Blue collar, family man, a sad sap. Jack was probably educated, likely a member of the upper class."

"If the information I just gave you finds its way to the media, I'll know where it came from." Eve paused until Breen stopped pacing and looked at her. "I'll make your life hell."

"Why would I give it to the media, and let somebody write about it first?" He sat again. "This has bestseller written all over it. I know that sounds cold, but in my line of work I have to be as detached as you do in yours. I'll help however I can. I've got mountains of research and data accumulated on every major serial killer since the Ripper started it all, and a few interesting minor ones. I'll make it all available to you, pitch in as a civilian consultant, and waive the fee. And when it's over, I'll write it."

"I'll think about it." Eve got to her feet. And saw, under the mess he'd made of his desk, a box of cream-colored stationery.

"Fancy writing paper," she commented, stepping over to pick up the box.

"Hmm? Oh yeah. I use it when I want to impress somebody."

"Is that so?" Her eyes flashed to his like lasers. "Who did you want to impress lately?"

"Hell, I don't know. I think I used it a couple weeks ago when I sent what my dad always called a bread-and-butter note to my publisher. A thanks for a dinner party thing. Why?"

"Where'd you get it? The paper?"

"Jule must've bought it. No, wait." He rose himself, looking baffled as he took the box from Eve. "That's not right. It was a gift. Sure, I remember now. Came through my publisher with a fan letter. Readers send stuff all the time."

"A token from a reader, to the tune of about five hundred dollars?"

"You're kidding! Five hundred. Wow." He was watching Eve more carefully now as he set the box back on his desk. "I should be more careful with it."

"I'll want a sample of that paper, Mr. Breen. It matches the type left at both homicides I'm investigating."

"This is just too fucking weird." He sat, heavily. "Take it." Several emotions seemed to run across his face as he scooped a hand through his luxurious hair. "He knows about me. He's read my stuff. What the hell did the note say? I can't remember, just something about how he appreciated my work, my attention to detail or something like that, and my — what — enthusiasm for the subject."

"Do you have the note?"

"No, I wouldn't keep it. I answer some of the mail personally, have a droid do the bulk. If it's snail mail, we recycle the paper after it's answered. He's using my work as research, don't you think? That's horrible, and really flattering at the same time."

Eve passed one of the sheets and envelopes to Peabody to seal into evidence. "Give him a receipt for it," she ordered. "I wouldn't be flattered if I were you, Mr. Breen. This isn't research, or words in a discbook."

"I'm part of it now. Not just an observer this time, but part of something I'll write about."

She could see he was more pleased than appalled.

"I plan to stop him, and soon, Mr. Breen. Things go my way, you're not going to have much of a book."

* * *

"I don't know what to think about him," Peabody said when they were outside. She turned back, studied the house and imagined the good-looking Breen swinging his handsome son onto his shoulders and taking him to the park to play. And dreaming of fame and fortune written in blood. "The stationery was right out of the blue. He didn't try to hide it."

"Where's the excitement if we don't find it?"

"I get that — and he likes the rush, no question. But his story sounds solid, especially if the killer has read his stuff."

"He can't prove where it came from, and we have to waste time trying to trace it. And Breen's juiced by it."

"I guess it's the sort of thing that'd juice him. His job's on the sick side."

"So's ours."

Surprised, Peabody hiked with Eve to the car. "You liked him?"

"I haven't made up my mind. If he's no more than he claims to be, I've got no problem with him. People like murder, Peabody. They jive on it when it's got at least one of those degrees of separation. Reading about it, watching vids about it, turning on the evening news to hear about it. As long as it isn't too close. We don't pay to watch a couple of guys hack each other to death in an arena anymore, but we've still got the blood lust. We still get off on it. In the abstract. Because it's reassuring. Somebody's dead, but we're not."

She remembered, as she climbed into the car out of the vicious heat, how that thought raced through her head, again and again, when she'd huddled in the corner of that frigid room in Dallas and looked at the bloody waste of the thing that had been her father.

"You can't feel that way when you see it all the time. When you do what we do."

"You can't," Eve said as she started the car. "Some can. Not all cops are heroes just because they're supposed to be. And not all fathers are good guys just because they give their little boys a ride on their shoulders. Whether I like him or not, his lack of alibi, his line of work, and his possession of the notepaper put him on the list. We're going to do a very careful check on Thomas A. Breen. Let's run the wife, too. What didn't we hear from him in today's conversation, Peabody?"

"I'm not following you."

"He told us she came home from a late meeting. She went to bed. He worked. He slept in. She took the kid to the park. But I never heard anything about *we*. My wife and I, Jule and I. Me and my wife and Jed. That's what I didn't hear. And what impression do you suppose I get from that?"

"You're thinking the marriage isn't good, that there's friction or disinterest between Breen and his wife. Yeah, I can see that, but I can see how with two careers and a kid a couple could get into a routine that revolves around work and pass the toddler."

"Maybe. Doesn't seem much point in being together if you never are though, does there? Good-looking guy like that might start getting resentful and frustrated with that sort of routine. Especially if he sees it as a repeat of his own childhood. A guy doesn't want to look in the mirror at thirty-something and see his father looking back at him. We'll take a good close look at Thomas A. Breen," she repeated. "And see what we see."

Eve decided her next stop would be Fortney. But it was time to play it, and him, a different way. "I want to nudge Fortney on the second murder, revisit the first. His alibi's bullshit. And since I tend to get cranky when people lie to me, I'm not going to be particularly friendly."

"As you are the epitome of cheer and goodwill by nature, sir, this will be somewhat of a stretch."

"I smell the distinct aroma of lame-ass sarcasm in this vehicle."

"We'll have it fumigated."

"But fortunately I'm the epitome of cheer and goodwill and will not rub your nose in it at this time. A few minutes into my unfriendly conversation with Fortney, I'm going to get a tag on my pocket 'link."

"As I'm in awe of you in all ways, I'm unsurprised by this sudden psychic ability."

"I'll be annoyed, but will have to take the communication, thereby passing the interview to you."

"Do you also know who'll be tagging . . . What? To me?"

That, Eve thought, had wiped the sassy little smirk off her aide's face. "You'll pick it up as good cop. The long-suffering, somewhat inexperienced, and apologetic underling. Play that up, fumble around."

"Sir. Dallas. I *am* the long-suffering, somewhat inexperienced, and apologetic underling. I don't have to play it up or pretend to fumble around."

"Use it," Eve said simply. "Make it work for you. Let him think he's leading you. He'll see a girl cop in uniform, who takes orders from me. Second-string. He won't see past that to what you're made of."

I don't know what I'm made of, Peabody thought, but drew a deep breath. "I can see how it could work."

"Make it work," Eve said again, and parked outside the office building to set the timer on her 'link.

Eve bullied her way into Leo Fortney's office and set the mood. Enjoyed setting it, she admitted. She put a little swagger in her step as she broke in on his holo-conference with a video producer.

"You're going to want to reschedule your little confab, Leo," she told him. "Or let Hollywood here in on our conversation."

"You have no right pushing your way in here, throwing your weight around."

She flipped out her badge so the images in the room had a clear view. "Bet?"

Fortney's color was edging toward magenta. "I'm sorry, Thad. I need to take care of this . . . disturbance. I'll have my assistant reschedule, at your convenience."

He shut the hologram down before Thad could do more than raise two thin eyebrows into sharp, questioning points.

"I don't have to tolerate this kind of ambush!" His magenta hair was pulled severely back from his face today, and the sleek tail of it whipped wildly as he flung out his arms. "I'm calling my lawyer, and I'll see you're reprimanded by your superior."

"You do that. And we'll take this to Central where you can explain to me, your lawyer, and my superior why you handed me a pile of bullshit as an alibi."

Eve toed in, and punched a finger toward his chest. "Lying to a primary during a homicide investigation doesn't earn you any points, Leo."

"If you think you can insinuate that I'm covering up some crime —"

"I'm not insinuating anything." She got right up in his face as she spoke, and enjoyed that as well. "I'm saying it. Flat out. Your meal ticket didn't back you up, pal. You did not, as you claimed, retire with her on the night in question. She went to bed alone, and *assumes* you joined her at some point. Assume ain't dick. So let's start this over. Your place or mine, it doesn't mean a damn to me."

"How *dare* you!" He lost all color now, insult and temper robbing his cheeks. "If you think I'm going to stand here and be insulted, have the woman I love insulted by some two-bit dyke bitch cop —"

"What're you going to do about it? Take me out, like you took out Jacie Wooton and Lois Gregg? You're going to find it tougher. I'm not a used up LC or a sixty-year-old woman."

His voice piped out now, like an adolescent boy's threatening to crack. "I don't know what the hell you're talking about."

"Couldn't get it up, could you, Leo?" She was careful to keep her hands off him, though she'd have liked to have given him a couple of mild shots. "Even when you had her tied up, and helpless, you couldn't get the wood on."

"Get away from me. You're crazy." Little darts of fear shone in his eyes now as he danced behind his desk. "You're out of your mind."

"You're going to see just how crazy if you don't tell me where you were on the night of September second, and the morning of September fifth. Shuffle me again, Leo," she said and slapped her hands on the desk. "And you'll see how crazy."

On cue, her 'link beeped. With a snarl, she ripped it out of her pocket. "Text only," she snapped. Waited a few beats as if reading. "Goddamn it." She muttered it, then rounded on Peabody. "Get the goddamn information from this asshole. I've got to take this, and I don't have time to waste. Five minutes, Leo," she said over her shoulder as she marched to the door. "Then I'm coming back for the next round."

He sat heavily when the door slammed behind Eve. "That woman is a menace. She was going to strike me."

"Sir. I'm sure you're mistaken." But Peabody cast an uncertain eye toward the door still shuddering on its hinges. "My lieutenant is . . . it's been a difficult few days, Mr. Fortney, and Lieutenant Dallas is under a great deal of stress. I'm sorry she lost her temper. Can I get you some water?"

"No. No, thank you." He pressed a hand to his brow. "I just need to settle down. I'm not used to being treated that way."

"She's very colorful." Peabody tried a half smile when he looked up. "I'm sure we can straighten this all out before she gets back. There were some discrepancies in your earlier statement, sir. It's easy to get confused or mix up times and dates when you're not expecting to have to remember your movements."

"Well, of *course* it is," he said with obvious relief. "I certainly wasn't expecting to be questioned about a murder. For God's sake."

"I understand that. And it seems to me if you'd killed Ms. Wooton or Ms. Gregg, you'd have arranged a solid alibi. You're obviously an intelligent man."

"Thank you, Officer . . ."

"It's Peabody, sir. If I could take out my notebook, we could try to put things together for the times in question." She smiled at him with whiffs of sympathy and nerves. "May I sit down?"

"Yes, yes. That woman's shaken my manners loose. I don't see how you stand to work with her."

"It's really for her, sir. I'm in training."

"I see." He was relaxing, Peabody could see. Just as she could see his amusement at thinking he'd escaped the lion and gotten himself a pussycat. "Have you been with the police long?"

"Not very. I do mostly administrative work. The lieutenant hates paperwork." She started to roll her eyes, seemed to catch herself and worked up a blush.

Fortney laughed. "Your secret's safe with me. Still, I wonder what an attractive woman like you is doing in such a difficult field?"

"Men still outnumber women on the job," she heard herself saying, and felt the quick, flirtatious smile curve her lips. "That can be a pretty strong incentive. I'd just like to say how much I admire your work. I'm such a fan of musical theater, and you've been involved in wonderful projects. It seems so glamorous and exciting to someone like me."

"It has its moments. Maybe you'd like me to give you a tour of the theater, backstage, where the action really is."

"That would be . . ." She trailed off breathlessly. "I'd just love it." She glanced back at the door again. "I'm not supposed to do something like that. You won't say anything?"

He mimed zipping his lip and made her giggle.

"If I can just clear up some of these discrepancies before she gets back. Otherwise, she'll skin me."

"Sweetheart, you can't really believe I'd kill anyone."

"Oh no, Mr. Fortney, but the lieutenant . . ."

He got up from the desk, came around, and sat on the corner of it. "I'm not interested in the lieutenant. The fact is, Pepper and I . . . well, our relationship has devolved, you could say. We're really just business partners at this point, keeping up appearances for the public. I don't want anything to damage her while she's working so hard in this play. I have a great deal of affection and respect for her even though . . . even though things aren't what they were between us."

He gave Peabody a puppy dog look, and she did her best to respond with one of sympathy. Even as she thought: Putz. *Do I look that green?* "It must be awfully hard for you."

"Show business is a demanding mistress, on both sides of the curtain. I did tell nearly the truth about that night. I didn't mention that Pepper and I didn't really speak or have contact with each other when she came back from the theater. I spent that night as I've spent far too many of them. Alone."

"So you have no one to corroborate your whereabouts?"

"I'm afraid I don't, not directly, though Pepper and I were in the same house together all night. It was just another lonely night, and to be frank, they blur together now. I wonder, maybe you and I could have dinner?"

"Ummm . . ."

"Privately," he added. "I can't be seen having dinner with a beautiful woman while Pepper and I still have to keep up this pretense. Gossip would hurt her, and she's so temperamental. She needs to focus on the play. I have to honor that."

"That's so . . ." The words that ran through her head were anything but flattering, but she choked out an alternative. ". . . so brave. I'd love to, if I can get the time off. These murders have the lieutenant working practically 24/7. And when she works, I work."

"Murders." For a moment he looked genuinely puzzled. "Is that what all this business about this Gregg person is? Another prostitute's been killed?"

"There was another attack," Peabody evaded. "It would help me out a lot if you could tell me where you were Sunday morning, between eight and noon. That would cover you, and I could probably smooth things out with Lieutenant Dallas so she won't bother you again."

She tried a simper, but didn't think it was her best look.

"Sunday morning? Sleeping the sleep of the just until tenish. I indulge myself on Sundays. Pepper would have been up and out early. Dance class, she never misses. I would have had a light brunch, lingered over the Sunday paper. I doubt I was even dressed until noon."

"And alone again?"

He gave a sad, crooked smile. "Afraid so. Pepper would have gone directly to the theater after class. Sunday matinee. I did go to the club, but not until at least one. For a swim, a steam, a massage." He lifted his hands, let them fall. "I'm afraid I did nothing of any interest all day. Now, if I'd had a companion. Someone . . . simpatico . . . we'd have taken a leisurely drive in the country, stopped at some charming little inn for a champagne lunch, and whiled away our Sunday in a much more entertaining fashion. As it is, I have nothing but work, illusion, and solitude."

"Could you tell me the name of your club? Then I can give Lieutenant Dallas something solid."

"I use the Gold Key, on Madison."

"Thanks." She rose. "I'll see if I can head her off."

He took Peabody's hand, looking into her eyes as he brought it to his lips. "Dinner?"

"It sounds mag. I'll contact you as soon as I know when I'm clear." She hoped she had one more blush in her. "Leo," she said shyly.

She hurried out and straight to where Eve stood with her 'link. "I can't break character yet," Peabody reported. "He might ask one of his bimbos what went on out here, so you should look annoyed and doubtful, and like you could ream my ass at any moment."

"Fine. Then I don't have to break character either as that's the one I walk around in on a daily basis."

"He's a total sleaze, and he doesn't have a solid for either murder. Hard for me to see somebody that slimy being our guy, but he's not covered."

She looked down at her shoes, studying the shine, and hoping the body language looked subservient. "He also cheats on Pepper, regularly by my take. He hit on me, and it seemed like a natural rhythm. Guy's got more tired lines than an afternoon soap and less talent at selling them."

"You hit back?"

"Enough to keep the rhythm up, not enough to get me a reprimand should there be an official inquiry. Maybe you could stomp off to the elevator now. It's getting hard to keep looking naive and subservient."

Eve obliged and timed it so Peabody barely had time to nip in with her before the doors shut. "I thought that was a good touch."

"Good thing my butt isn't any bigger than it already is. He's shifting his story for the night of the Wooton murder. Says he and Pepper are just business partners now, and keeping up the pretext of otherwise so there isn't any negative publicity through the run of the play. Still says he was at home all night, though, and home all Sunday morning. Alone. The original Lonely Guy."

"What kind of moronic female falls for that crap?" Eve wondered.

"Lots, I guess, depending on the delivery." She moved her shoulders. "His wasn't bad, actually. But it was too quick, and too obvious. Anyhow, he claims he went to the Gold Key on Madison about one on Sunday. I say he's twinking at least one of those bimbos on the side. He's not the type for an LC. Isn't going to pay for it when he can bullshit and brag his way into it. And I'd say it'd be news to Pepper that they're just business partners now. I'd also say he doesn't think much of women as a species."

Go, Peabody, Eve thought, and leaned back against the elevator wall as her aide ran it through. "Thinks about them, because he probably imagines fucking any woman who's remotely attractive. But he doesn't like them. He kept calling you *that woman*. Never referred to you by name or rank. And there was a lot of passion in the way he said it."

"Good job."

"I don't know that I found out anything really useful. Except now that I think about it, I *can* see him doing the murders."

"You found out he's lying to his lover, and if he isn't actively cheating — which he likely is — he's open to cheating. You found out that he had the opportunity to commit both murders. So he's a liar and a cheat. Doesn't make him a murderer, but he's a liar and a cheat with opportunity, with access to the stationery found at both crime scenes, and that he has an attitude toward women. That's not bad for the day."

Carmichael Smith was in the studio — in New L.A. — so she gave him a pass for the day. She found Niles Renquist so heavily wrapped in red tape that she decided to do an end run around him and aim for his wife.

The Renquists' New York home wasn't Breen's upwardly mobile family neighborhood, or Carmichael's trendy loft. It was all dignity and restrained grace in faded brick and tall windows.

The entrance hall, where they were admitted with considerable reluctance and disapproval by a uniformed housekeeper who could have given Summerset a run for his money, was done in creams and burgundies and the subtle sheen of religiously polished antiques.

Lilies, white and burgundy in a crystal vase, sat on a long narrow table along the staircase and scented the air. Along with it was an echoing hush she associated with empty houses or churches.

"It's like a museum," Peabody said out of the corner of her mouth. "You and Roarke have all this cool, rich people stuff, but it's different. People live there."

Before Eve could respond there was the female sound of heels on wood. People lived here, too, Eve thought, but she had a feeling they were a different type altogether.

The woman who walked toward them was as beautiful, as dignified, and as quietly elegant as the home she'd made. Her hair was a soft blonde, carefully coiffed into a short bob that caught the light. Her face was pale and creamy, with a hint of rose on cheeks and lips. This one, Eve thought, never left the house without sunscreen, top to toe. She wore wide-legged pants, killer heels, and a blousy shirt with a faint sheen, all in cream.

"Lieutenant Dallas." There was a high-toned drift of England in her voice, and the hand she offered was cool. "Pamela Renquist. I'm sorry, but I'm expecting company shortly. If you'd contacted my secretary, I'm sure we could have arranged an appointment at a more convenient time."

"Then I'll try to keep the inconvenience short."

"If this is about the stationery, your time would be of more use speaking with my secretary. She handles the bulk of my correspondence."

"Did you buy the stationery, Mrs. Renquist?"

"Quite possibly." Her face never changed, held its mildly pleasant expression as she spoke with the kind of undiluted politeness Eve always found insulting. "I enjoy shopping when in London, but I rarely keep track of every little purchase. We certainly have the paper, so it hardly matters if I bought it myself, or Niles, or one of our assistants made the purchase for us. I was under the impression my husband had discussed this with you."

"He did. There is considerable repetition and overlap in a homicide investigation. Could you tell me where you and your husband were on the night —"

"We were precisely where Niles has already told you we were on the night of that unfortunate person's murder." Her tone became frigid and dismissive. "My husband is a very busy man, Lieutenant, and I know he's already taken the time to speak with you regarding this matter. I have nothing to add to what he's already told you, and I'm expecting guests."

Not so fast, sweetheart. "I haven't yet spoken to your husband regarding a second murder. I'd like you to tell me where you both were on Sunday, between eight and noon."

For the first time since the woman had walked down the hall, she looked flustered. It was momentary, just a slight heightening of color on that creamy skin, a slight frown around the rosy mouth. Then it was smooth and pale again.

"I find this very tedious, Lieutenant."

"Yeah, me, too. But there you go. Sunday, Mrs. Renquist."

Pamela drew air sharply through her chiseled nostrils. "We have brunch on Sundays at ten-thirty. Prior to that, my husband would have enjoyed a well-deserved hour in our relaxation tank, as he does every Sunday, when schedule permits, between nine and ten. While he was doing so, I would have joined him in our home health center for my own Sunday morning hour of exercise. At eleven-thirty, after brunch, my daughter would have gone with her au pair to a museum, while my husband and I prepared to go to the club for a doubles match with friends. Is that detailed enough, Lieutenant?"

She said *lieutenant* as another woman might have said *nosy, insolent bitch*. Eve had to give her credit for it. "You and your husband were home on Sunday from eight until noon."

"As I've just said."

"Mummy."

They both turned and looked at the young girl — gold and pink and white, as pretty as a frosted cake — on the stairs. A woman of about twenty-five, with a spill of black hair clipped back neatly at her nape, held the girl's hand.

"Not now, Rose. It's impolite to interrupt. Sophia, take Rose back upstairs. I'll let you know when the guests have arrived." She spoke to her daughter and the woman in the same polite and distant tones.

"Yes, ma'am."

She gave the girl's hand a little tug — Eve saw it, and the slight resistance of the child before the girl went obediently back up the stairs.

"If there's nothing more, Lieutenant, you'll have to make an appointment with either myself or my husband through our offices." She walked to the door, opened it. "I hope you find who you're looking for soon, so this can be put to rest."

"I'm sure Jacie Wooton and Lois Gregg feel exactly the same way. Thanks for your time."

CHAPTER TEN

With the help of Lois Gregg's daughter-in-law, Eve mapped out the daily routine of the victim's life.

Leah Gregg served iced tea in the compact nook off her compact kitchen. She wanted to keep her hands busy, Eve could see. And her mind occupied. More, Eve saw a woman who wanted to take some active part in standing for her husband's mother.

"We were close. Actually, Lois was closer to me than my own mother. Mine lives in Denver with my stepfather. We have issues." She smiled when she said it, a tight-lipped grimace that indicated they were big issues. "But Lois was the best. Some of my friends have trouble with their in-laws. Unwanted advice, little digs, interference."

She shrugged, and sat across from Eve at the narrow service bar. Then she nodded at the ring on Eve's left hand. "You're married, so you know how it can be — especially with mothers of sons, who don't want to let go of their baby boy."

Eve made a noncommittal sound. There was no point in saying no, she didn't know how it could be. Her husband's mother had been forced to let go of her baby boy a long, long time ago.

"But I didn't get any of that from Lois. Not that she didn't love her kids. She just knew how to keep it all balanced. She was fun, and smart, and had a life of her own. She loved her kids, she loved the grands, she loved me." Leah had to take a long, calming breath. "Jeff and his sister, all of us really, are just flattened by this. She was young and healthy, vital and active. The sort of woman you expect to live forever, I guess. To lose her this way, it's just cruel. But well . . ." She took another breath. "I guess you know that, in your line of work. And it's not why you're here."

"I know this is hard, Mrs. Gregg, and I appreciate you taking the time to talk to me."

"I'll do anything, absolutely anything, to help you find the bastard who did this to Lois. I mean that."

Eve saw that she did. "I take it you talked to her often."

"Two, three times a week. We got together very often: Sunday dinners, shopping sprees, girl days. We were friends, Lieutenant. Lois and I . . . she was, I guess I've just realized, she was my best friend. Oh, *shit*."

She broke off, pushing off to grab some tissue. "I'm not going to lose it, it won't help her or Jeff or the kids for me to lose it. Just give me a second."

"Take your time."

"We're having a memorial tomorrow. She didn't want anything formal or depressing. She used to joke about it. 'When my time comes,' she'd say, 'I want you to have a nice, tasteful memorial service and make it short. Then, break out the champagne and have a party. Celebrate my life.' That's what we want to do, we will do because she wanted it. But it wasn't supposed to be *now*. It wasn't supposed to be like this. I don't know how we'll get through it. One minute at a time, I guess."

She sat again, breathed again. "Okay. I know what was done to her. Jeff told me. He tried not to, but he fell apart and it all came pouring out, so I know what was done to her. You don't have to be delicate with me."

"She must've liked you a lot." It was the first time Peabody had spoken, and the comment had Leah's eyes tearing again.

"Thanks. Now what can I do?"

"She wore a ring, third finger, left hand."

"Yes, she considered it her wedding ring though she and Sam never made it formal. Sam was the love of her life. He died a few years ago in an accident, and she continued to wear his ring."

"Can you describe it?"

"Sure. Gold band, channel set with little sapphires. Five little sapphires because he gave it to her on their fifth anniversary. Very classic, very simple. Lois didn't like flashy jewelry."

She paused a moment, and Eve could see it sink in. "He took it? He took her ring? The bastard, the filthy son of a bitch. That ring *mattered* to her."

"The fact that her killer took the ring may help us find and identify him. When we find it, and him, you'll be able to positively identify it. That will help us build our case."

"All right, all right. Thanks. I can think of it that way now, think of it as a way to lock him up. That helps."

"Did she mention anything, however casually," Eve began, "about meeting someone, seeing someone hanging around the neighborhood?"

"No." Her kitchen 'link beeped, and she ignored it.

"You can get that," Eve told her. "We can wait."

"No, it's someone calling with condolences. Everyone who knew her is calling. This is more important now."

Eve angled her head. "Officer Peabody's right. She must've liked you very much."

"She'd have expected me to handle this, the way she would've handled it. So I will."

"Think carefully then. Any mention of anyone she might've met or seen in the last few weeks."

"She was friendly, the sort who talks to strangers in line at the market or strikes up conversations in the subway. So she wouldn't have mentioned anything like that unless it was out of the ordinary for her."

"Take me through the places she'd go, the routes she'd take. Daily business sort of thing. I'm looking for repetition and habit, the kind of thing someone who was tracking her could use to determine she'd have been alone in the apartment Sunday morning."

"Okay." Leah began to outline Lois's basic routines as Eve took notes.

It was a simple life, if an active one. Fitness classes three times a week, bi-weekly sessions at a salon, market on Fridays, Thursday evenings out with friends for a meal and a vid or play, volunteer work Monday afternoons at a local day-care center, her part-time job at a lady's boutique on Tuesdays, Wednesdays, and Saturdays.

"She dated once in a while," Leah added. "But not so much recently, and nothing serious. As I said, Sam was it for her. If she'd been seeing anyone, even very casually, I'd have known about it."

"Customers in the shop? Men?"

"Sure, she'd tell us about some of the guys who'd come in and throw themselves on her mercy, looking for something for a spouse or girlfriend. Nothing lately, not that she mentioned. Wait."

Her back went steel straight. "Wait. I remember her saying something about a man she ran into when she was shopping for produce. A couple of weeks ago. Said he looked sort of lost over the tomatoes or something."

As if to nudge the memory clear, Leah rubbed her temples. "She helped him pick out some vegetables and fruit, that was just like her. She said he was a single father, just moved to New York with his little boy. He was worried about finding good day care, so she told him about Kid Time, that's the place she volunteers, gave him all the information. Being Lois, she pumped him for personal information. She said he was a good-looking guy, concerned father, looked lonely, and she was hoping he checked out Kid Time so she could maybe fix him up with a woman she knew who worked there. God, what did she say his name was? Ed, Earl, no, no, Al. That's it."

"Al," Eve repeated and felt it hit her gut.

"She said he walked her part of the way home, carried her bags. Said they talked kids for a few blocks. I didn't pay much attention, it was the kind of thing she did all the time. And knowing Lois, if they talked kids, she talked about hers, about us. She probably said how we got together Sunday afternoons, and how she looked forward to it. About how she knew what it was like to raise kids alone."

"Did she tell you what he looked like?"

"She just said he was a good-looking boy. That doesn't mean anything. Damn it! She'd call any guy under forty a boy, so that's no help."

Yes, it was, Eve thought. It eliminated Elliot Hawthorne, as her own instincts already had.

"She was a born mother, so if she saw this guy puzzling over tomatoes, she'd have automatically stepped up to give him a hand and talk to him, try to help him out with his problems. Southern," Leah said on a rise of excitement. "That's what she said. A good-looking Southern boy."

"She was a jewel. You know what I'm saying?"

Rico Vincenti, proprietor of the family-run market where Lois Gregg did her weekly shopping, unashamedly wiped his tears with a red bandanna, then stuffed it away in the back pocket of khakis that bagged over his skinny butt. He went back to stacking a fresh supply of peaches in his sidewalk bin.

"That's what I'm hearing," Eve said. "She came in here regularly."

"Every Friday. Sometimes she'd come by other times, pick up a couple things, but she was in every Friday morning. Ask me about my family, give me grief about prices — not bitchy," he said quickly. "Friendly like. Some people they come in here, never say a word to you, but not Mrs. Gregg. I find the bastard . . ." He made an obscene gesture. "*Finito*."

"You can leave that part to me. You ever notice anybody hanging around, look like he was watching her?"

"I see somebody bothering one of my customers, even if it ain't a regular, I move 'em along." He jerked his thumb over his shoulder like an umpire calling out a base runner. "I been here fifteen years. This is my place."

"There was a man, a couple of weeks ago. She helped him pick out some produce, struck up a conversation."

"Just like her." He pulled out the bandanna once more.

"He went out with her, carried her bags. Nice-looking guy, probably under forty."

"Mrs. Gregg, she was always talking to somebody in here. Let me think." He raked his hands through his thatch of salt-and-pepper hair, screwed up his narrow face. "Yeah, couple Fridays back, she took this guy under her wing, picked out some nice grapes for him, some tomatoes, head of romaine, radishes, carrots, got a pound of peaches."

"Can you tell me as much about him as what he bought?"

Vincenti cracked his first smile. "Not so much. She brought him up with her — I always checked Mrs. Gregg out — and she says: 'Now, Mr. Vincenti, I want you to take good care of my new friend, Al, when he comes in here by himself. He's got a little boy who needs your best produce.' I say something like, 'I got nothing but the best.' "

"What did he say?"

"Don't recall that he did. Smiled a lot. Had on a ball cap, now that I think. And sunshades. This heat, most everybody's got on a cap and shades."

"Tall, short?"

"Ah, damn me." He mopped at his sweaty face with the bandanna now. "Taller than me, but who the hell isn't? I top out at five six. We were busy, and I wasn't paying much attention. She was doing all the talking, like always. She asked me to put some peaches aside for her the next week. She was going to her daughter's in Jersey Sunday next, whole family deal, and she wanted to take her some peaches 'cause her girl had a fondness for them."

"She come in for them?"

"Sure, this past Friday. Five pounds. I put them in a little basket for her, let her take them home in it 'cause she's a good customer."

"The guy who went out with her, has he come back?"

"I haven't seen him again. I don't come in on Wednesdays, like to golf on Wednesdays, so he coulda come in and I wouldn't know. But if he'd come back any other day, I'm here. You think that's the guy? You think that's the sick prick who killed Mrs. Gregg?"

"Just covering the ground, Mr. Vincenti. I appreciate the help."

"You need any more, you need anything, you come see me. She was a jewel."

"You think he might be the killer," Peabody said as they walked the neighborhood, following the route Leah had outlined for them.

"I think he was being a smart-ass, introducing himself with the name Al — Albert DeSalvo, the method he planned to use for her murder. I think it would have been a very smart way to feel her out, coming to the market, putting on the baffled single-daddy routine. If he'd scoped out the area, looking for a woman, a single woman of her age group, spotted her, considered her while he was trolling, he'd have watched her routine, gotten her name, looked up her data, so he'd know she volunteered at a kid care place."

He knew how to research, Eve thought. Knew how to take his time, get the data, digest it before he made a move.

"A woman does time in day care, voluntarily, she's into kids, so he tells her he's got a kid when he makes his first contact."

She nodded as she spoke, as she studied the neighborhood. It was smart. It was simple. "Good place to make that contact is the market. Ask her for advice, give her a story about having a kid needing day care.

Walk her part of the way home. Not all the way. He doesn't have to, he knows where she lives. Just like he knows her plans for Sunday. Not the next Sunday, the following, so he can have plenty of time to watch her, get it all down, plan it out, enjoy the anticipation."

She stopped on the corner, watched people walk by, most with the native New York stare that stopped well short of eye contact. Not a tourist sector, she acknowledged. People lived and worked here, went about their business.

"She'd have strolled, though," Eve said aloud. "Strolled along with him, chatting, giving him what seemed like harmless little details of her life. Peaches for her daughter, but there wasn't a basket of peaches in the apartment on Sunday. He took them. A nice edible souvenir to go with the ring. Walked out of her place after he did what he did, carrying a little basket of fruit. I bet he got a real kick out of that, really enjoyed taking a big juicy bite."

Feet planted, she hooked her thumbs in her pockets, too intent on what she was seeing in her head to notice the quick and wary glances tossed her way when her stance revealed her weapon. "But that's a mistake, a stupid, cocky mistake. People might not notice some guy walking out of an apartment building with a toolbox, but they might, just might, notice one walking out with a basket of peaches and a toolbox."

She crossed the street, stood on the next corner, and judged the ground. "Glide-carts aren't going to be up and running that early on a Sunday, not around here. But the newstands, the coffee shops, the delis, they would be. I want them canvassed. I want to know if anyone noticed a man in maintenance wear, carrying a toolbox and a friggin' basket of peaches."

"Yes, sir. Lieutenant, I just want to say it's a real pleasure to watch you work."

"What're you angling for, Peabody?"

"No, seriously, it's an education to watch you, see what you see, and how you see it. But now that you mention it, it's pretty hot. Maybe we could, since they are up and running this time of day, get a drink from the glide-cart there. I'm doing a Wicked Witch of the West here."

"A what?"

"You know . . . I'm *melting*."

With a half-snort, Eve dug credits out of her pocket. "Get me a tube of Pepsi, and tell him if it's not cold I'm going to come over there and hurt him."

While Peabody clomped off, Eve stood on the corner, her imagination running. He'd have left her here, she decided. Most likely here, a couple blocks short of the apartment. Had to part ways on a corner, makes the most sense. Probably told her he lived nearby, what he did for a living, little stories about his kid. Lies, all of them, if this was their man.

And every cell of the cop told her it was.

Southern, she thought. Had he told her he was from the South? Most likely. Used an accent, or had one. Used, she decided. Just another little flourish.

Peabody came back with the drinks, a scoop of fries, and a veggie kabob. "Got you the scoop, heavy on the salt, so you wouldn't sneer at my kabob."

"I can still sneer at a kabob. I'll always sneer at veggies on a stick." But she dug into the scoop. "We'll head down this way, swing into the dress shop. Maybe he paid a visit there, too."

There were two clerks on duty at the boutique and both began to weep openly the minute Eve mentioned Lois's name. One of them went to the door, put up the Closed sign.

"I just can't take it in. I keep expecting her to walk in and tell us it was some sort of horrible joke." The tall clerk, with her greyhound's lithe body, patted her companion's back as the younger woman sobbed into her hands. "I was going to close the shop for the day, but I don't know what we'd do with ourselves."

"This your place?" Eve asked.

"Yes. Lois worked for me for ten years. She was great, with the staff, with the customers, with the stock. She could've run the place single-handedly if she'd wanted. I'm going to miss her so much."

"She was like a mother to me." The sobbing woman lifted her head. "I'm getting married in October, and she was helping me with so much of it. We were having the best time with all the plans, and now, now she won't be there."

"I know this is hard, but I need to ask you some questions."

"We want to help. Don't we, Addy?"

"Anything." The woman got her sobbing under control. "Absolutely anything."

Eve took them through the usual questions, wound her way around to the man Vincenti had described.

"I don't remember anyone like that coming in recently. Addy?"

"No, at least not by himself. We get men who come in with their wives or girlfriends, and the occasional solo. But nobody like that in the past few weeks. No one Lois helped or talked to while I was working."

"How about someone who came in, asked about her?"

"There was that man last week, no, the week before. Remember, Myra? He had on a totally mag suit, carried a Mark Cross briefcase."

"Yes, I remember. He said Lois had helped him the month before on some gifts for his wife, and they were such a big hit he'd stopped by to thank her."

"What did he look like?"

"Mmm. Late thirties, tall, nicely built, neat little goatee and wavy brown hair on the long side. He wore it tied back. He never took off his sunshades."

"Pradas, Continental style." Addy added. "I bought my fiancé a pair for his birthday. They cost a mint. He smelled like money, and had a clipped Yankee accent. Ivy League type, I thought. I tried to steer him to accessories because he looked like he could afford to drop a bundle, and we've got some terrific new handbags, but he wasn't biting. Just said he'd hoped to give his thanks and regards to Mrs. Gregg. I said I was sorry she wasn't working today, because she'd have appreciated that. If he wanted to stop by again, he should shoot for Tuesday, Wednesday, or Saturday, and gave him her hours. Oh God."

Her face went sheet-white. "Was that wrong?"

"No. This is just routine. Do you remember anything else?"

"No, he just said he'd try to come by again if he was in the area, and left. I just thought how nice that was, because customers don't usually bother, and the men sure don't."

They followed Leah's list and found that at every point there was someone who remembered a man, of subtly varied descriptions, who'd made some casual inquiry about Lois Gregg.

"He stalked her," Eve said. "Gathering data, taking his time. Had a couple of weeks for it anyway. He was going to do Wooton first, and she was easy. All you have to do to pick an LC at her level is wander around and watch the stroll, zero in on one who fits your requirements. You don't have to worry about getting her alone because that's her job, but with Lois, it had to be in her place to fit the imitation. She had to be home, she had to be alone, and not expecting anyone."

"He had to have plenty of time," Peabody pointed out. "Had to be able to hit the market on Friday, the boutique, the day care, the fitness center — all on weekdays, all during regular work hours. Doesn't sound like he's a nine-to-fiver."

"No, and if we go back to our own list, anyone on it so far has the flexibility."

She'd tugged Baxter and Trueheart out to do the neighborhood canvass, and was hoping to get a call any minute telling her they'd found someone who'd seen the killer with his souvenir basket of peaches.

Meanwhile, she had to keep it moving. He'd killed twice, and she was certain he'd already selected his next victim.

She left Peabody to do the deeper runs on Breen and his wife, and headed out to beg or bribe a short consult with Mira.

She had to wait, and pace the outer office, and ask herself, yet again, who their deadly mimic might imitate next.

So far he'd picked two notorious and deceased killers, and she was willing to bet he'd stick to pattern. No one, she thought, who was still among the living. The Ripper had never been caught, DeSalvo had died in prison. So capture and incarceration were okay. That left the field pretty wide, even excluding anyone who'd destroyed or hidden or consumed their victims.

Her communicator beeped as she was staring holes through Mira's door and willing it to open.

"Dallas."

"Baxter. I think we've got one for you, Dallas. A witness from the neighboring building who was heading out to church and saw a guy in a city maintenance uniform — or so she believes — walking out of the vic's building carrying a toolbox and a plastic fruit basket."

"Time right?"

"It's dead on. Our witness knew Gregg. She insists on coming downtown and talking to the primary personally."

"Bring her on."

"We're heading back. I'll meet you in the break room."

"My office —"

"Break room," he insisted. "Some of us haven't eaten our lunch as yet."

She opened her mouth to protest, and heard the click of Mira's door. "Fine. I'm in a meeting. I'll be there as soon as I'm clear."

Before Mira's assistant could repeat the fact that the doctor had only a scant ten minutes free, Mira was stepping out, gesturing Eve inside.

"I'm glad you found the time to come in. I've read all the available data."

"I have more," Eve told her.

"I need something cold. Cool enough in here," Mira said as she went to the minifridge. "But just knowing what it's like outside makes me *feel* hot. Mind over matter."

She took out a container of juice, poured two glasses. "I know you live on caffeine, in one form or another, but this is better for you."

"Thanks. The two vics are distinct types. Very distinct."

"Yes." Mira sat.

"The first, a recovering junkie LC, busted down to street level. A lifer, with no friends, family, or support group, though it appears her own choice. He wasn't concerned about who she was, but what she was. A street whore, working the dingier section of Chinatown. But the second was a who and what."

"Tell me about the second."

"A single woman, living alone in a nice neighborhood. A woman who'd raised her family and kept close ties with them. Active in her community, friendly, well-liked by everyone. More well-liked than I think he understood, because he doesn't get that."

"He has no strong feelings for anyone, but himself, so he doesn't relate to those who do. Doesn't understand the circle." Mira nodded. "It was her situation — living alone, age, neighborhood, and the fact that she would be found quickly. That's what drew him to her."

"But it was a mistake, because she had impact on everyone she was associated with. People liked her, loved her, and they're not just willing to cooperate with the police, they're eager to. She isn't going to be forgotten like Wooton, not ever. Everyone I've spoken to had something specific to say about her, something personal and positive. It's like what I imagine people would say about you when you . . ." She caught herself, coughed, but it was too late. "Jesus, that sounded creepy. I meant —"

"It didn't." Mira cocked her head and quite simply beamed. "What a nice thing to hear. Why do you say it?"

She wished to hell and back she hadn't, but she was stuck now. "It's just" — she downed the juice like medicine, in one huge gulp — "I — ah — interviewed

Gregg's daughter-in-law earlier, and it reminded me, that's all, of the way your daughter talked about you. There was this real bright . . . connection. A total bond. And I got that same sort of thing from the guy at her market, the people she worked with, everybody. She left her mark. So do you. It's that he wasn't considering, the way people would rally for her. Stand for her."

"You're right. He'd have expected the event itself to be the big story. Meaning *he'd* be the story. She, beyond her convenience for him, was incidental. Though the first victim made her living through sex, and the second was sexually brutalized, the killings aren't a sexual act but a rage against sex. Against women. And this act makes him powerful, and makes them nothing."

"He stalked Gregg," Eve said and led Mira through it.

"He's very careful. Meticulous in his way despite the fact that both killings were messy. His preparation is precise, as his imitations are. Each time he succeeds, he proves not only that he's more powerful, more important than the women he kills, but more than the men he emulates. He doesn't have to stick with a pattern — or so he tells himself because, of course, there is a pattern. He believes himself capable of any sort of murder, and the getting away with it. The outwitting you — the female he's chosen, deliberately chosen, to play against. He beats you, a woman, and proves you're less than him every time he leaves you a note."

"The notes, they're not his voice. It doesn't fit with everything else you're saying. They're broad and jokey. He's not."

"Another disguise," Mira agreed. "Another persona."

"He's making himself sound different in them, the way he made himself sound different to the people he spoke with when stalking Gregg. Mr. Versatility again."

"It's important to him that he not be pegged, labeled, pigeonholed. It's very likely that he was, just that, during his upbringing, and by the female authority figure. He may maintain the illusion of the image she forced on him, but it's not how he sees himself. It is the mother he kills, Eve. The mother as whore with Wooton, and now the mother as nurturer with Lois Gregg. Whoever he mimics next, the victim will be, in his mind, another form of mother."

"I've run probabilities, but even if I narrow down who he'll copy, I don't know how that leads me to the next victim before he gets to her."

"He'll need some time to prepare, to assume the new face, the new method."

"Not much," Eve replied. "He won't need much, because he's already worked it all out. He didn't start this last week."

"Quite true. It began years ago. Some of his need would have manifested in childhood. The typical route of tormenting or killing small animals, secret bullying, sexual dysfunction. If his family or caregivers knew and were concerned, there may have been some therapy or counseling."

"And if they didn't?"

"If they did, or didn't, we know his needs and his acts escalated. From the profile and your witness statements this man is in his mid to late thirties. He didn't begin to kill at this age, didn't begin with Jacie Wooton. There'll be others. You'll find them," Mira said, "and they'll create a path to him."

"Yes, I'll find them. Thanks." Eve rose. "I know you were squeezed, and I've got a witness heading in." She started to speak again, then changed gears. "And thanks for the invitation for Sunday. Sorry I had to duck out the way I did."

"It was lovely to have you both there while you were." Mira got to her feet as well. "I hope you'll tell me what's on your mind. There was a time you wouldn't have — or wouldn't have let me see there was something troubling you. I thought we were past that now."

"My ten minutes are up."

"Eve." With that quiet word, Mira laid a hand on hers.

"I had a dream." The words came out fast, as if they'd been waiting to be disgorged. "Sort of a dream. About my mother."

"Sit." Mira stepped to her desk, buzzed her assistant. "I'll need another few minutes here," she said and clicked off before her assistant could respond.

"I don't want to hold you up. It wasn't a big deal. It wasn't a nightmare. Exactly."

"You've had no real memory of your mother up until this."

"No. You know. Just one time before, I remembered hearing her voice, yelling at him, bitching about me. But I saw her this time. I saw her face. I have her eyes. Fuck it."

She sat now, just dropping down and pressing the heels of her hands against those eyes. "Why is that? Goddamn it."

"The luck of the gene pool, Eve. You're too smart to think the color of your eyes means anything."

"Screw the science, I hate it. That's all. I saw the way she looked at me with them. She hated me, gut-deep hate. I don't get it, I just don't get it. I was . . . I'm not good at judging ages of little kids. Three, four maybe. But she hated me the way you hate a lifelong enemy."

Mira wanted to go over, to enfold. To *mother*. But knew it wasn't the way. "And that hurt you."

"I wondered, I guess." She drew in air, let it out explosively. "I guess I wondered if — even though I knew from what I remembered — I wondered if maybe, somehow, he snatched me from her at some point. Beat the crap out of her maybe, and took off with me. I wondered if, even though she was on the junk, she had some feeling for me. I mean, you cart somebody around inside you for nine months, you ought to feel *something*."

"Yes, you ought." Mira spoke gently. "Some people aren't capable of love. You know that, too."

"Better than most. I had this fantasy. Didn't even know I had it until it shattered on me. That she was looking for me, worried about me. Trying to find me all this time because . . . under everything she loved me.

But she didn't. There wasn't anything but hate in her eyes when she looked at me. Looked at the child."

"You know it wasn't you she hated because she never knew you. Not really. And her lack of feeling wasn't — isn't — your fault. It was — and is — her lack. You're a difficult woman, Eve."

She laughed a little, jerked a shoulder. "Yeah. So?"

"A difficult woman, often abrasive, moody and demanding, and impatient."

"Are you going to get to my good parts anytime soon?"

"I don't have that much time." But Mira smiled, pleased to hear the habitual sarcasm. "But your flaws, as some might see them, don't prevent those who know you from loving you, respecting you, admiring you. Tell me what you remembered."

Eve blew out a breath, and ran through it with the cool dispassion and attention to detail she'd use in a police report.

"I don't know where we were. I mean what city. But I know she whored for money and drugs, and that was okay with him. I know she wanted to ditch me, and that wasn't okay with him because he had other plans for me. For his investment."

"They weren't your parents."

"I'm sorry?"

"They conceived you — egg and sperm. She incubated you, and expelled you from her body when it was time. But they weren't your parents. There's a difference. You know there is."

"I guess I do."

"You didn't come from them. You overcame them. There's another difference. Let me say one more thing before my assistant chews through my door and punishes me for ruining her schedule. You've also left your mark, and had an impact on more lives than either of us can count. Remember that when you look in the mirror, and into your own eyes."

CHAPTER ELEVEN

When Eve walked into the break room, Baxter was chowing down on an enormous sandwich that smelled too good and looked too fresh to have come out of the facility's AutoChef, any of the vending machines, or the take-out counter at the Eatery.

It looked civilian and delicious.

Beside him at the square table, the sweet-faced Trueheart was making neat work of a leafy salad topped with chunks of chicken. Across from them, a woman who looked to have seen the dawn and dusk of a couple of centuries beamed goodwill over them.

"There now," she said in a reedy voice, "isn't that better than anything you can get out of a machine?"

"Glump," Baxter responded over bread and meat in what was obviously delirious agreement.

Trueheart, who was younger, nearly as green as his salad, and whose mouth wasn't quite as full at the time, scraped back his chair when he spotted Eve. "Lieutenant." He shot to attention as Baxter rolled his eyes in amusement over the rookie, and adoration over his sandwich.

He swallowed. "Jeez, Trueheart, save the brown-nosing until after I digest. Dallas, this is the amazing and wonderful Mrs. Elsa Parksy. Mrs. Parksy, ma'am, this is Lieutenant Dallas, the primary investigator you wanted to see."

"Thanks for coming in, Mrs. Parksy."

"My duty, isn't it? As a citizen, not to mention as a friend and neighbor. Lois looked after me when I needed it, now I'll look after her, best I can. Sit down, dearie. Have you had your lunch?"

Eve eyed the sandwich, the salad, and ignored the envy that swirled in her mostly empty stomach. "Yes, ma'am."

"I told these boys I'd fix extra. Can't abide food out of a machine. It's not natural. Detective Baxter, you offer some of that sandwich to this girl. She's too skinny."

"I'm fine, really. Detective Baxter told me you saw a man leaving Mrs. Gregg's apartment building on Sunday morning."

"Did. I didn't talk to the police before as I went straight on to my grandson's after church and stayed overnight. Didn't get back home until this morning. Heard about Lois on the news yesterday, of course."

The countless wrinkles in her withered raisin of a face shifted in what Eve took for sorrow.

"I've never been so shocked and sad, even when my Fred, God rest him, fell under the Number Three train back in 2035. She was a good woman, and a good neighbor."

"Yes, I know she was. What can you tell us about the man you saw?"

"Hardly paid him any attention. My eyes are pretty good yet. Got them fixed up again last March, but I wasn't paying him much mind."

Absently, she pulled a pack of nap-wipes out of a cavernous handbag, and passed them to Baxter.

"Thank you, Mrs. Parksy," he said in a humbled, respectful voice.

"You're a good boy." She patted his hand, then turned her attention back to Eve. "Where was I? Oh yes. I was just coming out to wait for my grandson. He comes by every Sunday at nine-fifteen, to take me to church. You go to church?"

There was a quick and beady gleam in Mrs. Parksy's eyes, causing Eve to hesitate between the truth and a convenient lie.

"Yes, ma'am," Trueheart spoke up, his face solemn. "I like to go to Mass at St. Pat's when I can get into Midtown on Sunday. Otherwise, I go to Our Lady of the Sorrows, downtown."

"Catholic, are you?"

"Yes, ma'am."

"Well, that's all right." She patted his hand in turn, as if it wasn't his fault.

"You saw the man come out from Mrs. Gregg's building," Eve prompted.

"Said I did, didn't I? He came out just a minute after I stepped out my own front door across the street. Had on a gray uniform and carried a black toolbox. Had a blue plastic basket in his other hand, like the kind they have down at the market. Couldn't see what was in it, 'cause it was a ways, and I wasn't staring at the man."

"What can you tell me about how he looked?"

"Looked like a repairman, is all. White man, or maybe mixed. Hard to tell as the sun was blasting. Don't know how old. Not as old as me. Thirty, forty, fifty, sixty, that's all the same when you hit your century mark, and I hit mine seventeen years ago last March. But I'd say thirty or forty as a best guess."

"Congratulations, Mrs. Parksy," Trueheart said and she smiled at him.

"You're a very nice young man. This other, he had a cap on, uniform cap, and sunglasses. Dark ones. Had mine on, myself. Sun was blazing even though it was early. He saw me. Couldn't see his eyes, of course, but he saw me, as he sent me a big as life grin and gave me this little bow. Sassy's what I call it, and I just sniffed and looked the other way, as I don't hold with sass. Sorry about that now. Wish I'd watched after him more."

"Which direction did he go?"

"Oh, he headed east. Spring in his step, like a man pleased with his morning's work. Bad business, bad business when a man can all but skip out the door and onto the sidewalk when he's killed a woman. Lois went to the market for me more than once when I was feeling poorly, and she brought me flowers to cheer me up. Always had a minute to chat. I wish I'd known what he'd done when I saw him. My grandson drove up just a minute or two later. He's always prompt. I'd've told him to run that murdering bastard down on the street. As God is my witness, I would've."

She worked Mrs. Parksy until she was sure she had everything the woman could give her, then passed her to Trueheart, asking him to escort her to a uniform for transport home.

"Baxter, another minute here." She dug in her pocket and discovered she'd given Peabody all her credits earlier. "Got enough on you for a Pepsi?"

"What's wrong with using your badge number? You over your limit?"

She gave him a disgusted look, with a sulk right on the edges. "I plug in my badge number, the machine will give me grief. The one up by our squad hates me, has a personal vendetta. And they talk to each other, Baxter. Don't think they don't communicate."

He studied her for one long minute. "You need a vacation."

"I need a friggin' Pepsi. You want an IOU?"

He walked to the machine, keyed in his badge number, ordered the tube.

GOOD AFTERNOON. YOU HAVE ORDERED ONE EIGHT-OUNCE TUBE OF PEPSI. IT'S ICED! HAVE A SAFE AND PRODUCTIVE DAY, AND DON'T FORGET TO RECYCLE.

He tugged it out of the slot, walked back, and handed it to her. "My treat."

"Thanks. Listen I know you've got backlog. I appreciate you taking the time for the canvass."

"Just put it in your report. I could use the shine."

She gave a head nod toward the door, so they'd walk and talk. "Trueheart looks good. He steady enough?"

"Doc cleared him physically. Kid's healthy as a horse. Shrink gave him thumbs-up, too."

"I read the evals, Baxter. I'm asking you."

"Truth is, I think what happened to him — nearly happened — a couple weeks ago shook me more than him. He's solid, Dallas. He's gold. Gotta tell you, I never figured on taking on a rookie, or putting on a trainer's hat, but he's a gift."

Baxter shook his head as they caught a glide. "Kid loves the job. Hell, he *is* the job, like nobody I know except you. He bounces in each shift, raring. I tell you, he makes my fucking day."

Satisfied, Eve headed down the hall with him.

"Speaking of trainees," Baxter continued, "I hear Peabody's going to take the detective's exam in a few days."

"Nothing wrong with your hearing."

"Nervous, Mom?"

She shot him a narrow look. "Funny. Why should I be nervous?"

He started to grin, then they both turned at the high-pitched howl. A skinny guy in restraints broke away from the uniform escorting him, sent another to his knees with a well-placed groin kick, then came flying toward the glide, eyes wild, spittle flying.

Since her Pepsi was in her weapon hand, Eve winged it. It caught him between the eyes with an audible thud. It surprised more than hurt him, so that he stumbled, righted himself, then lowered his head and charged her like a battering ram.

She had just enough time to pivot. She brought her knee up sharply, connecting with his chin. There was a nasty crunching sound that she figured was either his jaw snapping or the cartilage in her knee shifting.

In either case, he went down hard on his ass, and was immediately tackled by two uniforms and one passing plainclothes cop.

Baxter reholstered his weapon, scratched his head at the melee on the floor. "Want another Pepsi, Dallas?" What was left of hers was making a brown puddle on the floor.

"Goddamn it. Who's in charge of this asshole?"

"Me, sir." One of the uniforms staggered up. He was winded, and bleeding from the bottom lip. "I was taking him to holding for —"

"Officer, why didn't you have control of your prisoner?"

"I thought he was controlled, Lieutenant. He —"

"Obviously, you thought incorrectly. It appears you need to refresh yourself on proper procedure."

The prisoner bucked and kicked, and began to scream like a woman. To demonstrate proper procedure for controlling prisoners, Eve crouched, ignoring the twinge in her knee. She grabbed the screamer by a hank of his long, dark hair, jerked his head until his crazed eyes met hers.

"Shut up. If you don't shut up, if you don't cease resisting immediately, I will pull your tongue out of your mouth, drag it around your neck, and strangle you with it."

She saw from his eyes that he'd been enjoying some chemicals, but the threat got through, or maybe it was the tone that warned him she meant it, literally.

When he sagged, Eve rose and gave the uniform the same cold glare. "Add resisting and assaulting an officer to our guest's prize package today. I want to see a copy of your report before you file it, Officer . . ." She deliberately scraped her gaze down and scanned his name tag. "Cullin."

"Yes, sir."

"Lose him again, and I'll use his tongue to strangle you. Move."

There was a scramble as a couple of uniforms moved in, a show of solidarity, to drag the prisoner up and haul him away.

Baxter handed Eve a fresh tube of Pepsi. "Figured you'd earned this."

"Goddamn right," she shot back, and limped into Homicide.

She wrote her own report, and hand-carried it to Commander Whitney. He gestured her to a chair, which she took, grateful to get off her aching knee.

When she'd finished her oral briefing, he nodded. "Is your block on the media going to fuel him or frustrate him?"

"With or without the media, he's hunting again. While his victims are random, they are deliberate, and the deliberation takes time. As for the media, I've fed a few statements through the department liaison. They're concentrating on the first murder. It's flashier than the rape and murder of a sixty-one-year-old woman in her apartment. We're not going to be pressed too hard on that end until one of them gets the connection. They will eventually, especially if he hits again, but we've got some room."

"You're misleading the media?"

"No, sir. I'm just not leading them. I've given my statement to Quinton Post at 75, rather than Nadine Furst, as I felt that would cool any mumbling about favoritism. He's sharp, but still a bit green. Once Nadine gets her teeth into this, she'll make the connection. Until then, I don't have to answer what isn't asked."

"Good enough."

"On another front, sir, I don't think, despite his claims, he cares overmuch about the media attention. Not at this time. He wants my attention, and he has it. Dr. Mira's profile confirms his need to dominate and destroy women. The female authority figure is his nemesis. That's me, that's why he picked me."

"Are you a target?"

"I don't believe so, not as long as he sticks to pattern."

Whitney grunted, then steepled his fingers. "You should be aware that I've had complaints."

"Sir?"

"One from Leo Fortney, who's crying harassment, and threatening a suit against you and the department. A second from the offices of Niles Renquist, intimating

. . . displeasure at having the wife of a diplomatic figure interrogated by a member of the New York Police and Security Department. And a third from the representative of Carmichael Smith, who ranted vigorously about the possibility of damaging publicity due to the hounding of his client by a . . . what was it? An insensitive, abrasive hotshot with a badge."

"That would be me. Leo Fortney gave false information during initial questioning. He's changed his story, somewhat, during subsequent questioning by my aide, but it still reeks. Both Niles Renquist and his wife have been questioned, not interrogated. And while both were cooperative, neither was forthcoming. As for Carmichael, if anyone leaks his involvement in my investigation to the media, it would be him."

"You intend to pursue each of these individuals as suspects in this investigation."

"Yes, sir, I do."

"All right." Satisfied, he nodded. "I have no problem fielding the complaints, but walk softly here, Dallas. Each of these people has considerable power in his own way, and all of them know how to spin the media."

"If one of them is a murderer, I'll make the case. They can spin until they revolve to Saturn and back, but they'll do it from a cage."

"Wrap them up then, carefully."

Dismissed, she got to her feet. Whitney lifted an eyebrow as she started out. "What's wrong with the leg?"

"It's just the knee," she said, annoyed she hadn't remembered to control the limp on the way out. So she smiled, a little. "I ran into something stupid," she said, and closed the door behind her.

She left later than she'd intended, and got stuck in some bad traffic. Instead of fighting it, Eve waited it out, using the time to think, to review her notes, to think some more.

She had suspects, though she was thin on evidence. She had threads that wove through both murders. The notes, the tone of them, the imitation.

She had no DNA, no trace evidence, and no evidence that led her to believe the killer had known his victims. Witness reports described a white or possibly mixed-race male, of indeterminate age and coloring. He used accents, she thought. Because his voice was distinctive?

Renquist, with his British tones. Carmichael, with his famous ones.

Possible.

Then again, Fortney ran his mouth to the media and the public often enough. He might assume someone would recognize his voice.

Or it could just be ego again, and any one of them. I'm so important, everyone will recognize me if I don't disguise myself.

Look for the female authority figure, she told herself. That's the core and that's the key. What was the phrase? *Cherchez la femme*. She thought that was right.

She stripped off her jacket on the way from the car to the house. The air felt close, heavy, and just a bit electric. Maybe a storm coming. Rain couldn't hurt, she thought, and tossed the jacket over the newel. A good bitch of a storm might keep her man inside, and off the hunt.

Before she went back to work, back to her own hunt, she'd track down another man.

The home locator told her Roarke was on the rear patio, off the kitchen. She couldn't figure out why he'd be out in the nasty air when the house was blissfully fresh and cool, and provided a room for any possible activity.

But she walked the long stretch of it, and out the kitchen to find him. Then simply stood, struck speechless.

"Ah, good, you're here. We can get started."

He was wearing jeans — not his usual around-the-house attire — and a white T-shirt. He was barefoot, and a little sweaty, which appealed to her. The fact was, he would have appealed to her, or any woman, regardless of his attire, or the fact that he was standing on a sun-baked patio on a September evening where the air quality index had simply waved the white flag and surrendered the field.

But at the moment, she was more interested in the enormous, shiny silver contraption beside him.

"What is that thing?"

"It's an outdoor cooking system."

Warily, relieved she was still wearing her weapon just in case, she approached. "Like a barbecue deal?"

"That, and more." He stroked one of his beautiful hands over the lid, as a man might stroke a woman who bewitched him. "Gorgeous, isn't she? Just arrived an hour ago."

It was massive, and the glare of the sun off its surface nearly blinding. There was, she noted, more than one lid as it had extensions on either side, and some doored compartment beneath the main unit.

There were countless buttons, controls, dials. She wet her lips. "Um. It doesn't look exactly like the one the Miras used."

"Newer model." He opened the main lid and revealed another gleaming surface, this one full of shiny bars, with a bunch of silver cubes beneath, and a side surface of solid metal. "No reason not to have the latest."

"It's really big. You could almost live in it."

"After a couple of practice runs, I thought we might have a barbecue of our own. In a few weekends perhaps."

"By practice run, I don't guess you mean you're going to drive it somewhere." She gave one of its big, sturdy wheels a quick, testing kick.

"Totally under control." He crouched, opened one of the doors. "Refrigerator unit. We've got steaks, potatoes, some vegetables we'll put on these skewers."

"We will?"

"It's just a matter of shoving them on." He assumed. "And a bottle of champagne, to christen it. Though I thought we'd drink it rather than whack the unit with the bottle."

"I can get behind that part. Have you ever cooked a steak?"

He sent her a mild look as he opened the champagne. “I read the tutorial and I watched how it was done at the Miras. It’s hardly rocket science, Eve. Meat, heat.”

“Okay.” She took the glass he’d poured for her. “What happens first?”

“I turn it on, then according to the timetable in the tutorial, the potatoes would go first. They take the longest. While they’re cooking, we’ll sit in the shade.”

The idea of him turning on the monster unit had her taking a cautious step back. “Yeah, well, I’ll just get started on the sitting in the shade part.” Several buffering feet away.

Still, she loved him, so she prepared to leap to his defense if the machine got testy. She watched Roarke arrange two potatoes on some of the smaller sections of grill, fiddle with controls.

Whatever he did had a red light, like a single, unfriendly eye, beam on. Apparently this pleased him, as he closed the lid, patted it, then pulled a little tray of crackers and cheese out of the lower compartment.

He looked pretty cute, she had to admit, carrying the tray, crossing the sunny patio in his bare feet, with his hair tied back as he often did for serious work.

She grinned at him, popped a cube of cheese in her mouth. “You put all this together.”

“I did. Very gratifying, too.” He stretched out his legs, sipped champagne. “I don’t know why I haven’t fiddled about in the kitchen before this.”

The umbrella over the table broke the blast of the sun, and the champagne was ice cold. Not, she decided, such a bad deal after a long day. "So, how do you know when the potatoes are done?"

"There's a timer. It also suggested we might want to jab them with a fork."

"Why?"

"Something to do with doneness. I assume it'll be self-evident. What did you do to your knee?"

Never missed a trick, she thought. "Some jerk in uniform let an asshole get away from him. I used my knee to discourage said asshole from ramming me down the glide. Now he's crying because his jaw was dislocated, and he has a mild concussion."

"Knee to jaw. Sensible. How'd he get the concussion?"

"He says it was from the tube of Pepsi I pitched at him, but that's bogus. I figure he got it when a bunch of cops landed on him."

"You threw your Pepsi at him."

"It was handy."

"Darling Eve." He picked up her free hand, kissed it. "Ever resourceful."

"That may be, but I had to waste time on more paperwork. Officer Cullin is going to rue this day."

"No doubt."

He poured more champagne, and they drank it in the shade. When she heard the distant rumble of thunder, she lifted her eyebrows, glanced toward the grill. "You may be rained out."

"There's time yet. I'll just turn it up a bit, and put on the steaks."

Fifteen minutes later, Eve sipped champagne and watched a little burst of flame erupt from one end of the grill. Since it wasn't the first, she was no longer alarmed by it.

Instead, she watched Roarke fight his new toy, curse it in two languages, and eye it with frustration.

When jabbed, the potatoes proved to be hard as stone inside their blackened skin. The skewered vegetables were burned to a crisp, and had been on fire twice.

The steaks were a sickly gray on one side, and black on the other.

"This isn't right," he muttered. "It must be defective."

He stabbed one of the steaks, lifting it off the grill to scowl at it. "This doesn't appear to be medium rare."

When the juice dripping from it sparked another pocket of flame, he tossed it back on the bars.

More fire spurted, and the machine, as it had a number of times before, issued a dour warning:

ACTIVE FIRE IS NEITHER ADVISABLE NOR RECOMMENDED. PLEASE REPROGRAM WITHIN THIRTY SECONDS, OR THIS UNIT WILL GO INTO SAFETY MODE AS EXPLAINED IN THE TUTORIAL, AND SHUT DOWN.

"Bugger it, you bloody bitch, how many times do you need to be reprogrammed?"

Eve took another hit of champagne, and decided not to point out that *bitch* was inappropriate as the unit's voice mode was distinctly male.

Men, she'd observed, habitually termed the inanimate objects they cursed by uncomplimentary female names. Hell, she did the same herself.

A couple of lightning bolts popped in the sky, and the thunder rolled closer in one long, menacing growl. Eve felt the first splat of rain in the rising wind.

She walked over to rescue the bottle of champagne while Roarke stared at the grill.

"I'm thinking pizza," she said and started into the house.

"It's just a glitch." Roarke scraped what was left of the food into the unit's garbage disposal feature. "This isn't finished," he grumbled to it, and followed Eve into the house. "I'll have another look at it tomorrow," he told her.

"You know . . ." She crossed to the AutoChef, which was, in her opinion, the sensible way to cook. ". . . it's sort of nice to see that you can screw up like the rest of us mortals. Get all sweaty and frustrated and curse out inanimate objects. Though I'm not convinced that thing outside is inanimate."

"A factory defect, no doubt." But he was grinning now. "I'll see to it tomorrow."

"Bet you will. You want to eat in here?"

"That's fine. We won't likely eat in the kitchen much after tonight, with Summerset due home tomorrow."

She stopped dead, the glass halfway to her lips. “Tomorrow? That can’t be right. He just left five minutes ago.”

“Tomorrow, noon.” He walked over to flick a finger over the dent in her chin. “It’s been considerably longer than five minutes.”

“Make him extend it. Tell him to . . . he should take a trip around the world. In a boat. One of those boats you row by hand. It’ll be good for him.”

“I offered him more time. He’s ready to come home.”

“Well, *I’m* not ready.” She threw up her hands.

He only smiled, leaned in, and kissed her forehead as he might a child’s.

She huffed out a breath. “Okay then. Okay. But now we have to have sex on the kitchen floor.”

“I beg your pardon?”

“It’s on my to-do list, and we didn’t get to it yet, so we’ll have to go for it now. Pizza can wait.”

“You have a to-do list?”

“It was supposed to be spontaneous, and uncontrolled, but we’ll have to go with what we’ve got.”

She drained the glass of champagne, set it down, then released her weapon harness. “Go on, strip it off, pal.”

“A sexual to-do list?” Amused, fascinated, he watched her dump her harness on the counter, then start on her boots. “Was that bout we had last week on the dining room table, and the floor, on your list?”

“That’s right.” She pried off a boot, kicked it aside.

"Let me see the list." He held out a hand, wiggled his fingers.

Bent over for the second boot, she lifted her head. "It's what you'd call a mental list." She tapped her head. "All up here. You're not stripping."

"I love your mind."

"Yeah, well, let's just get this little chore ticked off, then we can —"

She broke off when he swooped her up, then dumped her butt first on the kitchen counter. Taking her hair in two fists, he yanked her mouth to his, and ravished.

"Spontaneous enough for you?" he asked when she sucked in a breath.

"It might be —" The words tumbled back down her throat when he ripped her shirt open.

"How's that for uncontrolled?"

It was a little hard to comment when her mouth was being assaulted again. He yanked what was left of her shirt down to her wrists. Her hands were trapped, tripping an instinctive panic that tangled messily with a spurt of excitement as he tugged the tattered material like a rope.

Her hands were behind her back now, and the blood was buzzing in her ears. She couldn't seem to draw a full breath. The champagne she'd drank began to spin giddily in her head, and her thigh muscles quivered.

"My hands," she managed.

"Not yet." He was mad for her. It seemed he spent his life mad for her. The shape and the scent of her, the taste and the feel of her. And now the sound she made as his hand raced over her.

He feasted on her skin, the lovely rise of her breast with her heart raging under his mouth. She moaned again, trembled, losing herself, he knew, as he used his tongue, his teeth.

Let go. There was nothing more arousing to him than when she let go.

She still couldn't breathe, but no longer cared. Sensations were storming her, too brutal, too dark, to be called something as mild as pleasure.

She let him take, would have begged him to take more if she'd had the words. When he yanked her pants down her hips, she opened for him. And those hands, those wonderful hands, drove her over.

She cried out as she came, as the orgasm flashed through her with such intense heat.

Her head dropped weakly on his shoulder, and she managed one word. "More."

"Always." His lips were on her hair, her cheek, then on hers again. "Always."

His arms came around her, and once freed, hers around him. She locked her legs around his waist and struggled to speak as her breath came in short, strained pants. "We're not on the floor."

"We'll get there." He nipped at her shoulder, her throat, wondered how he could stop himself from simply eating her whole.

He hitched her off the counter, taking her weight as their mouths fused again, as heartbeat slammed against heartbeat. Her hands had worked their way under his shirt, her short nails scraping over his damp skin.

Then she tugged it up, tugged it off, and fixed her teeth on his shoulder. "God, your body. Mine, mine, mine."

They were on the floor, pulling at clothes, pulling in air as lungs threatened to burst. And this time when her legs locked around him, he buried himself inside her.

Hot, so viciously hot, she trapped him there, rising up to take more of him, dragging him down to follow her. His hands slid off her slick skin, then found purchase on her hips. They dug in while he plunged.

CHAPTER TWELVE

They were lying on their backs on the floor in a sweaty heap. Her throat was wild with thirst, but she wasn't entirely sure she could swallow. Just breathing took all the energy she had left.

As far as spontaneous, uncontrolled sex went, she thought they had a winner. She felt his fingers brush hers, and gave him top marks for recovery.

"Is there anything left on your to-do list?" he asked softly.

"No." Her breath whistled in, whistled out. "That cleans it up."

"Thank God."

"We have to get up from here, before noon tomorrow," Eve warned.

"I think it has to be sooner. I'm starving."

She thought it over. "So am I. I don't suppose you could pull one of your macho routines and carry me."

"I don't suppose. I was hoping you'd carry me."

"Well." They lay where they were another full minute. "Maybe we can try this together."

"On three then." He counted it off. On three, they managed to pull each other to sitting positions, then just sat there, grinning.

"That was really good. My idea," she reminded him.

"And one for the record books. We'd better try to stand up."

"Okay, but let's not rush it."

They staggered to their feet, swayed, then held each other up like a pair of drunks.

"Wow. I'd say I got a little trashed watching you lose a round to that grill, but that's not it. You trashed me. Appreciate it."

"My pleasure." He rested his head on hers. "Just hold a minute, until the blood starts circulating again."

"Your blood has a tendency to circulate straight to your dick, and I need pizza. And a shower," she realized. "A shower, then pizza, because, pal of mine, we are a mess."

"All right. Let's get what's left of these clothes."

She found the rag of her shirt, what used to be her underwear, and other assorted apparel. Together, they carried the evidence out of the kitchen.

"And don't think you're going to nail me again in the shower. We're done."

He nailed her again in the shower, but only because she'd brought it up in the first place.

They ate pizza in the sitting area of the bedroom. By the time she was working on the third piece, she felt the hollow in her belly might just fill again.

"What did you do today?" she asked him.

"About what?"

She cocked her head. "Every now and again, I like to touch base with what it is you do. It reminds me you're not just a pretty sex object."

"Ah, I see. I had meetings." He lifted his shoulders as she continued to stare at him. "Most often, when I explain what it is I do, you get this glassy look in your eye, or fall into unconsciousness."

"I do not. Well, okay, the glassy look maybe, but I've never lost consciousness."

"I had a meeting with my broker. We discussed current market trends and —"

"I don't need every minute detail. Broker meeting — stocks and bonds and blah blah. Check. What else?"

His lips twitched. "A conference regarding the Olympus Resort. Two new areas are ready to open. I'm expanding the police and security force. Chief Angelo sends her regards."

"Right back at her. Any trouble up there?"

"Nothing major." He washed down pepperoni pizza with champagne. "Darcia wondered when we might be coming back for a visit."

"The next time I pass out and can be dragged into a space shuttle." She licked pizza sauce off her finger. "What else?"

"Internal staff meeting, a number of security checks. Routine. Discussion of preliminary reports on a sheep farm in New Zealand I'm considering buying."

"Sheep? Baa-baa?"

"Sheep, wool, lamb cutlets, and other by-products." He passed her a napkin and that made her think of Mrs. Parksy. "I had an extended business lunch with a couple of developers and their rep, who'd like me to come aboard their project. A massive indoor recreation center in New Jersey."

"Will you?"

"Doubtful. But it was entertaining to hear them out, and eat on their expense account. Is that enough for you?"

"That was just through lunch?"

"That's right."

"You're a busy guy. Is it harder for you to handle all this stuff out of New York than it was when you traveled?"

"I still travel."

"Not like you used to."

"It used to hold more appeal for me. Before I had a wife who invited me to nail her on the kitchen floor."

She smiled, but he knew her too well. "What's troubling you, Eve?"

She nearly told him about her dream, her memory, but pulled back from it. The subject of mothers had to be sensitive for him yet. Instead she used work. It wasn't an evasion. Work did trouble her.

"My gut knows who he is already, has from the first time I saw him. But I can't see him, so I don't know for sure. Not in my head. He changes, and he'll change again, so I can't see him. Not his type, or even his mind. Because that changes, too. He's good at what he does because he changes. Because he assumes the personality of what he imitates. I don't know if I can stop him."

"Isn't that what he's hoping for? That he'll frustrate you by assuming a different personality, different method, different victim type, all of it?"

"So far, mission accomplished. I'm trying to separate him from, let's say, the cloak he wears. To see him as he is so I'll know if my gut's right. So I can move from instinct to evidence to arrest."

"And what do you see?"

"Arrogance, intelligence, rage. Focus. He has excellent focus. Fear, too, I think. I'm wondering if it's fear that makes him imitate others, instead of striking out in his own way. But what does he fear?"

"Capture?"

"Failure. I think it's failure. And maybe that fear of failure has its roots in the female authority figure."

"I think you see him more clearly than you give yourself credit for."

"I see the victims," she continued. "The two he's killed already, and the shadow of the one who'll be next. I don't know who she'll be, or where, or why he'll choose her. And if I don't figure it out, he'll get to her before I get to him."

Her appetite was gone, as was the euphoria of good sex. "You're a busy guy, Roarke," she said. "Got a lot on your plate."

"I prefer that to an empty one. So do you."

"Good thing for us. I need to look into my list of suspects. I need to find this female authority figure, because when I do, I find him. I could use a hand."

He took hers, squeezed it. "I happen to have one available."

* * *

The most practical way to begin, she thought, was alphabetically. And, though it still scraped the pride a bit, to let Roarke man the computer.

He may have gotten spanked by a barbecue grill, but on a desk unit, he was king.

"We'll start with Breen," she told him. "I want everything I can get on Thomas A. Breen and his wife, without trampling on privacy laws."

He sent her a pained look as he sat at her desk. "Now, what fun is that?"

"Keep it clean, ace."

"Well then, I want coffee. And a cookie."

"A cookie?"

"Yes." The cat leaped on the desk to bump his head against Roarke's hand. "You have a cookie cache in here. I want one."

She stuck her hands on her hips, tapped her fingers. "How do you know I have a cache?"

He stroked the cat and smiled at her. "Unsupervised, you forget to eat half the time, and when you remember, you go for the sugar."

She took some exception to the "unsupervised" remark, but had another priority. Eyes slit, she came closer, watched his face as keenly as she would a prime suspect. "You haven't been sneaking into my office at Central and riffling my candy stash?"

"Certainly not. I can get my own candy."

"You could be lying," she said after a moment. "You're pretty slippery."

"And so you said in the shower."

"Har-har. But I don't see you skulking around Central lifting my chocolate just to drive me buggy."

"Not when I can easily find more convenient ways to do so. Where's my coffee?"

"Okay, okay. Thomas A. Breen."

She went into the kitchen off her home office, felt the cat ribbon around her legs despite the fact he'd had a slice of pizza. She programmed a pot of coffee, got down mugs, then — sending a cautious glance toward the office — went to the small utility closet and dug into the space behind the cat food for the bag of triple chocolate chunk cookies.

She started to take one out for Roarke, decided she could go for one herself. Then thought, what the hell, he was helping her out. They'd blow what was left in the bag.

Sensing dessert, Galahad went into serious purr-and-rub mode. She poured a handful of cat treats into his bowl, watched him pounce on them like a lion on a gazelle as she loaded the coffee and cookies on a tray.

"Initial data's up, though I assume you already have the basics," Roarke said. "More's coming. Why are you looking at Breen?"

"First, it's standard to run anybody I interview during an investigation." She set down the tray. "I'm going deeper because he flicked my switch. Don't know why, exactly."

She walked toward the wall screen where Roarke had already brought up the standard data. "Thomas Aquinas Breen, age thirty-three, married, one child, male, age two. Writer and professional father. Decent reported income. He makes a solid living, and appears to be on the track to making more. One bust for illegals — Zoner — age twenty-one. College smoke, nothing surprising. Native New Yorker, NYU grad: fine arts with post-grad work in criminology — I like that one — and creative writing. Earns his living writing magazine articles, short stories, and the two published nonfiction books to date, both substantial bestsellers. Married five years, both parents living and in Florida. Sounds normal."

"Yeah." But it wasn't, Eve thought. It wasn't quite the pretty picture it presented. "Got a nice house in a nice neighborhood. Couldn't afford it on what he made prior to the second hit book, but the wife has a high-powered job, so you assume they combined incomes as they've lived there since their second year of marriage. He deals with the kid, she makes the more regular bucks."

He sampled a cookie. His wife, he thought as the chocolate exploded in his mouth, had an unerring sweet tooth. "I have any number of employees with a similar setup."

"There was just something off, that's all. Hard to pin. Then you add that this guy spends his day thinking about murder, reconstructing it with words, reading about it, imagining it."

"Really?" He poured coffee for both of them. "Who would devote so much time and energy to murder?"

"I heard the sarcasm. The difference is a murder cop's supposed to find murder abhorrent. This guy gets off on it. Not that big a leap between fascination and experimentation. He's got the education, the flexible schedule, the knowledge, and a motive if you figure over and above the thrill, these murders, once it hits the media big, will juice up sales of his books. His wife's a fashion exec, and I bet she knows the value of publicity, too."

Studying the screen, she rocked back and forth on her heels. "He's got the paper. Claims it was a gift from a fan, one he doesn't remember. No way to prove or disprove. Yet. Be interesting if I find out he or his wife bought it though. That would be interesting."

"I could smudge those privacy lines a bit, see what I can dig up on that."

It was tempting, but Eve shook her head. "It wasn't charged to his or his wife's account. Not that we've found. Pushing that angle would mean more than a little smudge. We'll stick to the bio for now."

"Spoilsport."

"He has the paper, and that's enough. He has it, and he let me see it. That's interesting enough for now."

"If he's your man, wouldn't the wife know?"

"Seems to me, unless she's an idiot. Her bio doesn't read idiot to me. Julietta Gates, same age, another NYU grad. Bet they met in college. Fashion and public relations, double major. She had her path mapped out, and she's moved right along it. Minimal break for birthing, then back to work. Made double what he did up until two years ago, and still pulls in about the same annually, and more regularly. Wonder how their financials are set up?"

"What are you looking for?"

"Who runs the show? Money's power, right? I bet she calls the shots in that household."

"If that's the criterion, I feel I'm not as fully in charge as I should be around here."

"Too bad for you. I don't give a damn about your money. I bet Tom cares about hers." She brought him, the house, the child, the *feeling* of the home back into her mind. "Needs her share to run that nice house, raise the kid the way he wants, until he rises up another level in his own line. Good clothes, good toys, good child-care droid as backup, while he works at his own pace, so he can take time off to play horsey with his son, take him to the park."

"And those marks of a good father make him a murder suspect. As I'm following you, I'm afraid that makes us a very cynical pair."

She glanced over her shoulder just to look at him. Cynical or not, she reflected, they *were* a pair. "He never talked about her as a partner, or as one of the points of the family triangle. You saw his stuff and the boy's lying around. Toys, shoes, and so on, but nothing of hers. Interesting, that's all. Interesting that they're not a unit. Bring up the parental data."

She scanned it, filling in the blanks from the bare essentials she'd studied earlier. "See, the mother's the alpha dog here, too. Important career, the main wage earner. Father retired from his job to take over as professional parent. And look here, Mom served as an officer, including president, of the International Women's Coalition, and is a contributing editor to *The*

Feminist Voice. An NYU alum, while Dad went to Kent State. Yeah, that's interesting."

"Scenario being, Breen grew up in a female-dominant household, controlled by a woman with strong ideas and a political bent while his father changed the nappies and so forth. The mother pushed him to study at her alma mater, or he did so to gain her approval. And when choosing a mate, he selected another strong personality who would control his world while he took the more historically typical female role of nurturer."

"Yeah, which doesn't make him a whacked-out psychopath, but it's something to consider. Copy and file the data here and to my unit at Central."

He smiled as he did so. "It appears I've selected a strong personality as well. What does that say about me, I wonder?"

"Please," she added, and remembering the cookies walked over to take one. "I'll have a face-to-face with Julietta Gates tomorrow. Meanwhile, let's move on to Fortney, Leo."

Fortney was thirty-eight, and had two marriages, two divorces, no offspring. With Roarke's quick work, and his understanding of what she wanted, she read that his first wife had been a minor vid star, in the porn category. The marriage had lasted just over a year. The second was a successful theatrical agent.

"There's some buzz here," Roarke added. "The juicy gossip sort from media reports. You want them up, or do you want the highlights?"

"Start with the highlights."

"It appears Leo was a very bad boy." Roarke sipped coffee as he read from his own screen. "Got caught with his pants down, literally, in a hotel suite in New L.A., entertaining a pair of well-endowed starlets. Besides the two naked nubile starlets — that's a quote, by the way — there were rumors that considerable chemical enhancements and appliances of a sexual nature were also involved. Obviously, suspecting something of the sort, his wife had a P.I. on him. He was skinned to the bone in the divorce, and endured considerable snickering publicity as several other women were happy to talk to the media about their experiences with the hapless Leo. One is quoted as saying: 'He's a walking hard-on, always coming on and usually petering out at the sticking point.' Ouch."

"Sexually promiscuous, unable to maintain, and embarrassed publicly by a woman. Got a sheet with a couple of sexual assaults and an indecent exposure. I like it. And look at his financials. No way he can maintain the lifestyle he wants on what he pulls in. He needs a woman — currently Pepper Franklin — to keep him."

"I don't like him," Roarke muttered, continuing to read. "She deserves better."

"He hit on Peabody."

He looked up now, a dark gleam in his eye. "I really don't like him. Did he move on you?"

"Nah. He's scared of me."

"At least he isn't completely brainless then."

"What he is, is an ego-soaked liar who likes to take bimbos to bed — Peabody played up the bimbo angle on him — and use stronger women to take care of him, then cheat on them. He's educated, knows how to put on a polished front. Likes the good life, including high-dollar writing paper, is theatrical enough to enjoy the imitation route, and has the necessary freedom to troll and hunt. What have we got on his parents, family background?"

"On screen. You can see his mother's an actress. Largely supporting roles, character parts. I actually know some of her work. She's good, stays busy."

"Had Leo with husband number two out of five. I'll say she stays busy. So he's got a number of step- and half-sibs. Father's a theatrical broker. Same as Leo. Somebody who puts projects together, right?"

"Mmm. There you go. There are snippets of gossip here, too." He was scanning quickly on this first pass, looking for buzz words. "Our man would've been six when his parents divorced, both having very public affairs during the marriage, and afterward. His mother also claimed the father was physically abusive. Then again, he claimed the same about her. Reading bits and pieces here, it sounds as if the household was a war zone."

"So add a violent childhood and potential parental neglect. Mom's a public figure, which makes her powerful. They probably had household staff, right? Maids, gardeners, full-time child care. You could see what you could dig up on who looked after little Leo while you display the Renquists for me."

"Then I'm having another cookie."

She glanced back as he spoke, ready to make some sarcastic comment. But the look of him, just the look of him sitting there at her desk, his hair shining from the shower, his eyes vivid and focused on the screen, had her heart tripping.

Ridiculous, it was ridiculous. She *knew* what he looked like, and he could still turn her inside out without even trying.

He must have sensed her stare as he shifted his eyes, met hers. An absurdly handsome man with a cookie in his hand. "I think I deserve it."

Her mind blanked. "What?"

"The cookie," he said and took a bite. Then he cocked his head. "What?"

"Nothing." Vaguely embarrassed, she turned around again and ordered her heart to settle back down. Time, she told herself, to move to the next.

Renquist, Niles, she thought. Self-important, snotty bastard. But that was just personal opinion. Time for facts.

He'd been born in London, to a society deb who was half Brit, half Yank. Fourth cousin to the king on her mother's side and tons of money on her father's. His father was Lord Renquist, a member of Parliament and a staunch conservative. One younger sister who'd settled in Australia with husband number two.

Renquist had the full British educational package. The Stonebridge School to Eton, Eton to Edinburgh University. Served two years in the RAF, as commissioned officer, rank of captain. Fluent in Italian and French and joined the diplomatic corps at age thirty, the same year as his marriage to Pamela Elizabeth Dysert.

She had a similar background and education. Well-placed parents, high-class education, which had included six years at a boarding school in Switzerland. She was an only child, and had considerable money of her own.

They were, Eve supposed, what people of that class would call a good match.

Eve remembered the little girl who'd come to the steps while she'd been questioning Pamela Renquist. The little pink-and-gold doll, Rose, who'd given the nanny's hand one impatient tug before falling in.

No, not nanny. She'd called her the "au pair." People of that ilk always had a fancy name for everything.

Wouldn't Renquist have had an au pair growing up?

His schedule, daytime, wasn't as flexible as the others. But would an assistant or admin question him if he told them to block out a couple of hours? She studied the ID image of Renquist on-screen, and doubted it.

No criminal on him or the wife. No little smudges as there had been with Breen and Fortney. Just a perfect picture, all polished and shiny.

She didn't buy it.

He hadn't married until thirty, she thought. A reasonable age, if you were going the "till death" route. Plus, a man with political ambitions did better in the field if he presented the package of wife and family. But unless he'd taken a vow of celibacy, there'd have been other relationships before the marriage.

And maybe after it.

It might be worth having a conversation with the current au pair. Who knew family dynamics better than live-in help?

She went back for more coffee. "You could shoot up the data on Carmichael Smith."

"Do you want that before the data on the Fortney nanny?"

"You've got that already?"

"What can I say? I earn my cookies."

"Fortney first, smart guy. Let's keep it ordered."

"Difficult, as it appears there were several child-care providers used. It appears his mother chewed through them like gumdrops. Baby nurses, au pairs, whatever. Seven total over a period of just under ten years. None stayed on the job longer than two years, with an average stay of six months."

"Doesn't seem long enough to have any serious impact. So my thought would be the mother remained the authority figure."

"And from this data, one assumes an incendiary one. Three of the former employees filed hardship suits against her. All were settled out of court."

"I'm going to have to take a closer look at the mother." She paced back and forth in front of the screen while she ran it through her head. "Leo has a mother who's an actress, and his current lover is in the same profession. He goes into a profession where he'll deal with actors, have some control over them — be controlled, I imagine, by them. That says something. The killer is acting. Assuming a role, and proving he can play the part better than the original, and with more finesse. When I run a probability with this data, it's going to come out high on Leo."

She considered. "Let's go down the list before we do another layer. Find me Renquist's nanny, or whatever they call them over in England."

"Roberta Janet Gable," Roarke announced, then smiled. "I'm multitasking."

"Usually do," she replied, then looked up at the image on-screen. "Man." Eve gave a mock shudder. "Scary."

"This is current. She'd have been considerably younger when working for Renquist's mother, but" — having anticipated her, Roarke called up the earlier photo — "still scary."

"I'll say." She studied the split-screen images of a thin face with dark, deep-set eyes and an unsmiling mouth. The hair was brown in the younger, gray in the current, and in both cases pulled severely back. The lines that bracketed the no-nonsense mouth on the earlier image had dug themselves into disapproving grooves on the older woman.

"I bet nobody called her Bobbie," Eve commented. She started to struggle with the math, and could only be grateful Roarke had gotten there before her.

"She took the job when Renquist was two, and held it until he was fourteen. He didn't board at Stonebridge, but was a day student. Headed off to Eton at fourteen, and no longer required the services of a nanny. Roberta, don't call me Bobbie, would have been twenty-eight when she took the position, and forty when she left it to take another position as private child-care provider. She's now sixty-four and has recently retired. Never married, nor had any offspring of her own."

"She looks like she pinches," Eve commented. "One of the providers at the state school was a pincher. She's got all the credentials, but so did that bitch who decorated my arms with bruises when I was ten. Born in Boston, and went back there when she retired. Yeah, that's a New England bedrock face, the kind that says shit like 'spare the rod, spoil the child.' "

"She could be an unfortunate-looking woman with a heart of gold who keeps sugarplums in her pocket to pass out to rosy-cheeked children."

"Looks like a pincher," Eve said again, and sat on the edge of the desk. "Financially solid. I bet she saved her pennies and didn't squander them on sugarplums. What is a sugarplum, anyway?"

He was thinking of Eve at ten, with bruises on her arms. "I'll buy you some. You'll like them."

"Odds are. I think we'll chat, and see what she has to say about Renquist's early childhood training. Let's see the annoying Mr. Smith."

"Come sit on my lap."

She tried a severe look, but couldn't come close to Roberta Gable's expression. "There'll be no hanky or panky during a work session."

"As there was hanky on the kitchen floor followed by panky in the shower, I think we can shelve that activity. Come sit on my lap." He sent her a persuasive smile. "I'm lonely."

She did it, and tried not to soften too much when his lips brushed her hair.

"Carmichael Smith," he said, but he was still thinking of the child she'd been, at the mercy of the system she now stood for. And wanted, more than anything, to lavish her with everything she'd done without. Especially love.

"Thirty-one, my ass. I bet he greased some palms to have that stat adjusted. Born in Savannah, but spent part of his childhood in England. No sibs, and his mother opted for professional parent status, right up until his eighteenth birthday. Sealed juvie record, here and abroad, which might be worth the hassle of breaking. Not rolling in as much dough as he should be, considering. Must have himself some high expenses or habits."

"Parents divorced, father remarried and moved permanently to Devon. England, right?"

"The last I checked, yes."

"No adult criminal, but I bet there's something. Something paid off or expunged. Looks like he's done some time in a couple of snazzy rehab facilities. Let's have a closer look at the mother."

"Suzanne Smith. Age fifty-two. Young when he was born," Roarke commented. "And the marriage took place nearly two years later. Attractive woman."

"Yeah, he looks like her some. Well, lookie here. Mommy had an LC license for a while. Street level. And she's got herself a sheet."

Intrigued, Eve started to rise, but Roarke clamped his arms around her waist. "If you can't see the screen from here, I can put the data on audio."

"Nothing wrong with my eyes. Looks like she did some grifting, and got caught with illegals, tried a little minor fraud. Pleaded them all down," she added. "Never served time. Rolled on somebody, I bet. Held on to the license after she applied for PP status, but claimed no income. Just kept it off the books, that's all. She was still turning. Why pay the fee if you're not going to turn tricks? So, little Carmichael's sex education was likely early and hands on."

She considered, put herself in the scenario. "Let me see his medicals," she asked. "As far back as you can find."

"Am I smudging now?"

She hesitated, but her instincts were humming. "Keep it to a minimum."

He gave her hip a little pat, signaling her up so he could work. While he did, she poured the last of the coffee.

"Standard exams and inoculations as an infant," Roarke said. "He appeared to become accident-prone at about two."

"Yeah, I see." She scanned the various reports, from various doctors, different health centers. Stitches, minor fractures, one fairly serious burn. Dislocated shoulder, a broken finger.

"She knocked him around," Eve noted. "The abuse continued after the divorce, and right up until he hit the teen years and probably got too big for her to risk it. So it was the mother, the female authority figure. She moved around enough to get away with it. Relocating here and there in the States, doing some time in England. And look at her earned income, Roarke, as opposed to her assets."

"The first is all but nil, while the second is very comfortable."

"Yeah. I'd say she's still sucking on her little boy. Guy's bound to resent that sort of thing. Maybe enough to kill."

CHAPTER THIRTEEN

Eve had very rational reasons for starting her shift in her home office. It was quiet. Of course anything compared to the division at Central — including an Arena Ball match — was quiet.

She needed more thinking time. She wanted to set up a murder board here as well, so she could stare at it and study it whenever she was in the room.

And, the number-one reason for loitering there rather than heading straight downtown was the expected arrival of Summerset. She intended to be well away before noon, but she wanted to brood, just awhile, over the fact that once she left the house today, he would have reclaimed the field upon her return.

So she set up her board, sat, put her feet up on her desk. And drinking coffee, studied it.

There were crime-scene photos — the Chinatown alley, the Gregg bedroom. There were maps, and the notes left on-scene. Victim photos, before and after. With them, she pinned copies of the original crime scenes these were based on. Whitechapel and Boston, and two of those victims that most closely matched hers.

He'd studied those, too, she thought. Stared at those old photographs, read those old reports.

He'd be studying others now. Refreshing himself, preparing for the next act.

She had the lab reports, the ME's, the sweepers'. She had statements from witnesses, next of kin, suspects, neighbors. She had the timelines. She had her own notes, her own reports, and now a mountain of background data on those who remained on her shortlist.

She would go over them all again, and she would do more leg work, more interviews. She'd dig deeper, wider. But he would beat her to the next. Her gut told her he'd beat her in the short run, and someone else would die before she caught up.

He'd made mistakes. She sipped coffee and stared at the board. The notes were a mistake. That was pride and a kind of glee. He had a need not only to toot his own horn, but to do it with a flourish. Notice me! See how smart I am, see what excellent taste I have.

But the paper could be traced, could give her a list of names to pursue.

The basket of peaches was another. That was arrogance. I can walk right out of here, leaving the brutalized dead behind, and eat a nice ripe peach.

There might be other mistakes. She would pick everything apart until she found them. He would make other mistakes, because however smart he was, he was cocky.

She looked toward the open door when she heard the sound of footfalls, and her forehead creased.

"Hey," she said, as Feeney walked in. The neatly pressed shirt told her his wife had handed it to him out of the closet. The broken-in shoes said he'd gotten away from her before Mrs. Feeney could nag him into putting on a less disreputable pair.

He'd probably combed his hair, but it was already frizzing out in its usual wiry thatch of ginger and silver. There was a little nick on his chin because he claimed a man couldn't shave proper unless he used an actual razor.

"Got your message," he said.

"It was late, that's why I dumped it to voice mail. I didn't mean for you to come around this morning, go out of your way."

"It's only out of my way if there aren't any danishes back there."

"Probably are. If not there, somewhere else."

Taking that as invitation, he walked back to the kitchen. She could hear him scanning the menu, giving a grunt of approval as he found something that pleased him, calling it up.

He came back in with a pastry and an enormous mug of coffee. "So," he said, and sat, studying the board as she had. "He's two for two."

"Yeah, and I'm batting zero. Clipped the ball a couple times, but it keeps curving foul. Once he hits again, the media's going to pick up the scent, and we'll have a holy mess on our hands: 'Deadly Mimic Stalking New York.' 'Chameleon Killer Baffles Police.' They love that shit."

Feeney scratched his cheek, ate more pastry. "Public does, too. Sick bastards."

"I've got a lot of data, a lot of angles. Thing is, I pull one line and six more drop down. I can push Whitney for more manpower, but you know how it goes. I keep it low profile, and the budget only stretches so far. Once it breaks and people start screaming, politics come into play and I can stretch it further."

"EDD's got more manpower, more funds," he finished.

"I've got no direct need for EDD on this. The research and runs are standard stuff, nothing fancy. I've got no 'links or security to probe. But . . ."

"My boys can always use the practice." Feeney called his detectives and drones 'boys,' no matter how their skin was shaped.

"I'd appreciate it. It would free me up for interviews and fieldwork. I started thinking last night: This guy, he's careful and he's precise. Look at the vic photos — the old ones, and his. Positioning, basic build and coloring of the vics, method of death. Everything. They're good copies, careful copies. So how do you get so good?"

Feeney polished off the danish, gulped coffee. "You practice. I'll run that myself, through IRCCA, see if we get a pop."

"It won't be exact," she said, grateful. "I've got a hit on the first, and it's not exact. But when I did the run I was only looking for the one style. Now we've got two styles, and the potential for others. He's too careful for an exact match — he might do it that way, but he'd change it after. Wouldn't leave the scene precisely as he intended to leave the ones he'd make public."

"Doesn't want to show off until he's got it down to a science," Feeney said with a nod.

"Yeah. Any that were exact, he'd get rid of the bodies. Bury them, dump them. But he's not a kid. Not twenty. He's mature, and he didn't start killing with Wooton. He's been at this awhile."

"I'll work both styles, and whatever else you think he might go for."

"Everybody on my shortlist, but one I haven't pinned yet," she said, thinking of Breen, "travels. The States, Europe especially. They get around, and they get around well. First-class. If he's on that shortlist, the world's been his fucking playground."

"Send me the files."

"Thanks. I should tell you, there are some sensitive names on my list. We've got a diplomat, a well-known entertainer, a writer making a name for himself, and an asshole entertainment broker who's hooked up with a top-name actress. There've already been complaints of police harassment and blah blah. There'll be more."

He grinned. "Now this sounds like fun." He pushed to his feet, set his empty cup aside, and rubbed his hands together. "Let's get started."

Once Feeney left, she organized the files, sent them to his unit in EDD, noted the action in a memo to the commander. She ran another spurt of probabilities, toyed with some simulations, but they were really no more than an exercise to let her mind work.

By the time she was done, the computer and she agreed on a list of prototypes her killer might emulate next.

She eliminated any who had worked with a partner or targeted males. Any who concealed or destroyed the bodies. And highlighted any whose notoriety had outlived them.

She was just beginning to wonder where Peabody was when one of the domestic droids came to her door.

The droids always spooked her. Roarke rarely used them, and she rarely saw them in the house. She would have withstood any manner of hideous torture before admitting she actually preferred the flesh-and-blood Summerset to the automated staff.

"Excuse me for interrupting, Lieutenant Dallas."

The droid was female, with a husky voice. The dignified black uniform did nothing to disguise the fact she'd been built to rival a porn star.

Eve figured she didn't have to be a trained investigator to deduce her amused husband had activated this one purposefully, just so she could compare the big-titted blonde to the bony-assed Summerset.

She'd have to pay him back for this one, eventually.

"What's the problem?"

"There is a visitor at the gate. A Ms. Pepper Franklin who wishes to speak with you. Are you available?"

"Sure. She's saving me a trip. Is she alone?"

"She has arrived in a private car, with driver. But she has no companion."

Left Fortney at home, Eve thought. "Let her in."

"Shall I bring her up?"

"No, show her into the — what is it — the front parlor."

"Would you care for refreshments?"

"I'll let you know."

"Thank you, Lieutenant."

When the droid backed out of the room. Eve drummed her fingers for a moment. She glanced at the door that adjoined her home office with Roarke's. Probably just as well he was off doing what he did all day. It would keep the social portion of this visit to a minimum.

Deliberately, she strapped on her weapon harness, left the jacket where she'd hung it over the back of her chair. A not-so-subtle way, Eve decided, to let Pepper know she was on the job.

Then she finished off her coffee, sat and hummed for another couple of minutes.

When she went down to the parlor, Pepper was waiting.

The actress was dressed in perfect summer style: a breezy white blouse over a thin blue tank that matched the cropped pants. She'd added heeled sandals that made Eve's arches ache and had bundled her masses of gilt hair in some complicated up-do.

Eve caught her scent, something cool and floral, as she crossed the room.

"I appreciate you seeing me." Pepper flashed her professional smile. "And so early in the day."

"I'm Homicide. My day starts when yours ends." At Pepper's blank look, Eve shrugged. "Sorry. Little cop joke. What can I do for you?"

"I take it Roarke's not home?"

"No. If you want to see him, you might be able to catch him in Midtown."

"No. No, actually, I'd hoped to catch you alone. Could we sit?"

"Sure." Eve gestured to a chair, took one of her own.

Pepper rested her hands on the arms of the deep chair, sighed as she scanned the room. "This remains the most incredible home I've ever seen. Such wonderful style, but then it would have to be, since it's Roarke's."

"Keeps the rain off."

Pepper laughed. "It's been some time since I've been here, but I recall a formidable manservant rather than the splashy domestic droid who let me in."

"Summerset. He's on vacation. He'll be back later today." *Unless he's captured by desperados and held for ransom. Or falls madly in love with a young nudist and moves to Borneo.*

"Summerset. Yes, of course."

"You're not here to see him either."

"No." Pepper nodded. "My motive for coming is a woman-to-woman thing. I know you saw Leo again yesterday. He was very upset by it, feels hounded, and that you have some sort of personal grudge against him."

"I don't have a personal grudge against him. Even if he's a killer, it wouldn't be personal. It's my job to hound people."

"Maybe it is. But the fact is there is a personal connection here. Through me. Through Roarke. I wanted to address that frankly with you."

"Go ahead," Eve invited.

Pepper sat a bit straighter in her chair, folded her hands neatly in her lap. "You're aware, I'm sure, that Roarke and I had a relationship at one time. I can certainly understand how you might feel uncomfortable or irritated by this. But it was several years ago, before he met you. I'd hate for any annoyance or resentment, however understandable it might be, to influence your attitude toward Leo."

Eve let the silence hang for a moment. "Let me see if I have this straight. You're wondering if because you and Roarke rolled around naked a few years ago, I'm personally pissed off, and because I'm pissed off about it, I'm giving the guy you're currently rolling around naked with a rough time."

Pepper opened her mouth, shut it again, then delicately cleared her throat before speaking. "In a nutshell."

"Let me ease your mind on this score, Ms. Franklin. If I were to get personally pissed off about every woman Roarke banged, I'd spend my life in a perpetual state of annoyance. You were one of many." Eve lifted her left hand, tapped her wedding ring with her thumbnail. "I'm the only. You don't worry me."

For a moment, Pepper did nothing but stare. Then she blinked, very slowly. And the corners of her mouth twitched. "That's very . . . sensible, Lieutenant. And a very clever way to slap me back at the same time."

"Yeah, I thought so."

"But, in any case —"

"There is no other case. Roarke and I were grown-ups when we met. What happened before doesn't mean dick to me. And if I let petty jealousies interfere with or influence my work, I wouldn't deserve my badge. I deserve my badge."

"I bet you do," Pepper replied. "Just as I bet you deserve Roarke, too. He's the most fascinating man I've ever known, just like his house, full of color and style and surprises. But he didn't love me, and never pretended he did."

"And Leo does. Love you?"

"Leo? Leo needs me. And that's enough."

"I have to say, it sounds to me like you're selling yourself short."

"That's nice of you. But I'm no prize, Lieutenant. I'm selfish and demanding." She gave a light, amused laugh. "And I like that about me. I expect to be given my own time and space when I require it, and any man in my life must understand that my work is the priority. If he does, and he's loyal, needing me is enough. Leo's weak, I know that," she continued with an elegant little shrug. "Maybe I need a weak man, maybe that's why I couldn't hang on to Roarke for more than a few weeks. Leo suits me. And being weak, Lieutenant, is just one more reason he can't be the man you're looking for."

"Then neither of you have anything to worry about. He lied during our initial interview. Someone lies to me, I'm going to wonder why."

Her face softened in a way that told Eve whatever she said about need being enough, she loved Leo Fortney. "You frightened him. That's natural, isn't it, for someone to be frightened when they're questioned by the police? Especially about a murder."

"You weren't."

Pepper blew out a breath. "All right. Leo has trouble with the truth occasionally, but he'd never hurt anyone. Not seriously."

"Can you tell me where he was on Sunday morning?"

Pepper's lips firmed, and her eyes stayed direct. "I can't. I can only tell you where he said he was, and he's already told you that. Lieutenant, don't you think I'd know if I was living with, sleeping with, if I were intimate with a murderer?"

"I can't say. You may want to tell him that if he wants to get clear of this, he can start being straight with me. As long as he . . . has trouble with the truth, I'm going to keep looking at him."

"I'll talk to him." She got to her feet. "Thanks for seeing me."

"No problem." Eve walked her to the door, and opening it saw the waiting car. And her aide huffing down the drive on foot.

"Officer . . . what was her name?" Pepper asked.

"Peabody."

"Oh yes. Officer Peabody looks to have had a difficult morning already. That storm last night cooled things off a bit, but not enough. Not nearly enough yet."

"Last gasp of summer in New York. What else can you expect?"

"Teach me to stay in London." She offered her hand. "I'd still love for you and Roarke to come to the play. Just contact me anytime and I'll arrange for seats."

"Soon as things cool off for me a bit, we'll take you up on it."

She watched the driver get out, open the rear door of the small town limo. And waited until a breathless and sweaty Peabody rushed up the steps.

"Sir. Sorry. Overslept, then the subway . . . breakdown. Should've contacted you, but didn't realize —"

"Inside, before you fall over with heatstroke."

"I think I'm a little dehydrated." Peabody's face was lobster red and starting to drip. "Can I have a minute? Splash some water on my face."

"Go. Christ, next time take a cab!" she called out as she jogged upstairs to get her jacket and what she needed for the day.

She grabbed two bottles of water from her kitchen, and met Peabody coming out of the powder room. Her aide's color had calmed down, her uniform was straightened, her hair neatly combed and dry again.

"Thanks." Peabody took the water, and glugged at the bottle to add to the water she'd slurped up in the powder room. "Hate to oversleep. I was up late studying."

"Didn't I tell you that you can overstudy? You won't do yourself any good going into the exam burned out."

"I just gave it a couple hours. Wanted to make up the time I took checking out apartments with McNab. I didn't realize we had a meet with Pepper Franklin."

"We didn't. She stopped by to defend Fortney." Eve headed out the door and around to the garage. She hadn't thought to tell one of the droids to have her car brought out in front. Summerset did it without her asking. The fact that it was the sort of detail that slipped her mind, and never slipped his, just annoyed her.

"Well, as least I know I'm not losing my mind," Peabody managed as she quickened her pace to match Eve's. "So much going on right now. Jesus, Dallas, we signed a lease. It's a good space. Got an extra bedroom we can set up as a shared office, and it's close to Central. It's in your old building, so Mavis and Leonardo will be neighbors, and that's mag, and it was really great of Roarke to put us on to it, but . . ."

"But what?"

"I signed a *lease*, with McNab. It's like, huge. We're going to be moving in together in thirty days."

Eve coded into the garage, waited for the doors to open. "I thought you were already cohabitating."

"Yeah, but informally. Real informally. He just hangs at my place most of the time. This is the real deal. I got the jitters." She pressed a hand to her stomach as she walked to Eve's police issue. "So I dove into studying as soon as we got back, then I got the jitters from that. Then I couldn't sleep because of the jitters, so I jumped McNab to sort of remind myself why I'm doing this, and that took awhile because, you know, I was pretty jittery —"

"I don't want to hear that part."

"Right. Well, I didn't settle down until pretty late, and was so conked I must've deactivated the alarm before I was fully awake. Next thing I knew it was an hour later."

"If you got up an hour late, why are you only . . ." She checked her wrist unit. "Fifteen minutes behind?"

"I skipped some of my usual morning stuff. Was okay until the subway breakdown. That threw me off, and now I've got the jitters again."

"You can just forget about jumping me to take your mind off them. Look, Peabody, if you're not prepped for the exam by now, you're not going to be."

"That doesn't do a lot to calm me down." She brooded out the window as Eve drove through the gates. "I don't want to tank. Embarrass myself, you."

"Shut up, you're giving me the damn jitters. You're not going to embarrass anybody. You're going to do your best, and it's going to be good enough. Now pull yourself together so I can brief you on Smith before we talk to him again."

Listening, making her own notes, Peabody shook her head. "None of this stuff is in his official biographical data, or on any of the unofficial fan sites. I don't get it. Guy's a total publicity hound, and he likes to go for the heartstrings. So why not play up how he came from an abusive home, overcame it, and believes in the power of love, cha-cha-cha."

"Cha-cha-cha?" Eve repeated. "I can think of a couple reasons. First, it doesn't fit his image. Strong, handsome, romantic male of the so-clean-I-squeak variety. Doesn't mesh with the poverty level, physically abused son of a part-time LC — who's still tapping him for money."

"I get that, but you could play that angle and sell discs out the yang."

"Yang. Does that go with cha-cha-cha?" Eve wondered. "Okay, yeah, it might make some women feel sorry for him, even respect him, and plunk down the price of a disc. But that's not what he wants."

"What does he want?" Peabody asked, though she thought she was beginning to connect the dots.

"It's not money. That's just a handy by-product. He wants adulation, hero worship, and fantasy. He boinks young groupies because they're less likely to be critical, and he plays to older women because they're more forgiving."

"And he surrounds himself with female staff because he needs to be taken care of by women, because he wasn't taken care of by the woman who should have done so when he was a kid."

"That's how it shakes for me." Eve turned a corner and swung around a maxibus that was lumbering its contingent of commuters to their hives and cubes. "The public image doesn't want to have to overcome anything, but just to be. The man of your dreams isn't some kid who got knocked around by his mother after she turned a trick. Or I should say, his view of the man of your dreams isn't. He's built himself into an image, and he has to stick with it."

"So, theoretically, the pressure of concealing all that, his resentment, and the cycle of violence could have caused him to snap. And snapping, he killed two parts of the person who abused him. The LC and the mother."

"Now you're thinking."

It was kind of like a sim, Peabody thought. She was a little slow, but she hoped she was picking her way through it. "You said a couple reasons. What's another?"

"Another is he just wants to bury it, put it away. This isn't relevant to his life now — that's what he tells himself. He's wrong, it's always part of the whole, but it's private. It's one thing he doesn't want chewed over by a lip-smacking public."

Peabody slid her gaze toward Eve, but there was nothing to read on her lieutenant's face. "So he could just be an abuse survivor who's made a successful life for himself despite all the trauma and the violence."

"You're feeling sorry for him."

"Yeah, maybe. Not enough to spring for a disc," she added with a chuckle. "But maybe some. He didn't ask to be hurt, and by the one person who should have been looking out for him most of all. I don't know what it's like to have a parent turn on you like that. Mine . . . well, you've met mine. My mom, she can pin your ears back with a look, but she'd never have hurt any of us. And my parents may be nonviolent New Agers, but you can believe they'd have ripped into anybody who tried to hurt us. That's what I know," Peabody added. "But it's not all I know, because I've seen the other side. Handling double Ds before I transferred to you. Just being on the streets in uniform. And what I've worked on since I've been in Homicide."

"Nothing wipes the all-American family image out of a cop's head faster than their first couple of domestic disturbances."

"One of the best reasons to be off patrol," Peabody agreed, with feeling. "What I'm saying is I've seen what it can be like, and it's toughest on the kids."

"Everything's always toughest on the kids. Some get over it, under it, through it. Others don't. And another theory on Smith is he feeds on the female adulation in one part of his life — and revels in it. Meanwhile he considers them whores and bitches — and he kills them in the most vicious and theatrical way he can devise."

"I guess that's a pretty decent theory."

"Either way, he's not going to like me throwing his background up in his face. So be ready."

Taking Eve at her word, Peabody rested a hand on her stunner as they walked from the vehicle to Smith's front door. "Not that ready, Peabody. Let's try to play nice first."

They were admitted by the same woman, and walked into the same music. At least Eve thought it was the same. How could you tell, she wondered, when everything the guy sang had the same sugar rush to it?

Before they could be led into the room with floor cushions and the fluffy white kitten, Eve laid a hand on the woman's arm. "Any place in here have actual chairs?"

Li's mouth turned down in disapproval, but she nodded. "Of course. Come this way, please."

She showed them into a room with wide, deep chairs done in pale gold, accented with tables of clear glass.

On one table was a small fountain where blue water burbled over smooth white rocks. Another held a white box filled with white sand where some linear patterns had been drawn with, Eve assumed, the little rake that lay beside it.

The curtains were closed, but when they entered the room the rim of the tables illuminated.

"Please be comfortable." Li gestured to the chairs. "Carmichael will be with you in just a moment."

Ignoring her, Eve studied a mood screen. Soft pastels dripped down in this one, melting from pinks into blues into golds into pinks again. Smith's voice crooned in the background.

"I already feel queasy," Eve muttered. "I should've pressed to have him come into Central, where things are normal."

"I heard you dislocated some mope's jaw yesterday." Peabody kept her face sober. "Some people don't consider that actually normal in the day to day."

"Some people don't know diddly." She turned back as Smith made his entrance.

"How nice to see you both again." He made a flowing movement with his arms to indicate chairs. It had the wide sleeves of his shirt fluttering. "We're having something cool and citrus. I hope you'll enjoy it."

He arranged himself in a chair as one of his staff placed a tray on a long glass table. "I'm told you've been trying to get in touch," he continued as he poured liquid from pitcher to glasses. "I can't imagine why, but must apologize for being unavailable."

"Your rep called my commander," Eve said. "So I imagine you have some idea."

"Another apology forthcoming." He picked up one of the glasses, held it in both of his handsome hands. "My agent is overprotective, which, naturally, is his job. Just the idea that the media could get wind that I'd spoken to you regarding such a terrible matter worries him. I told him I trusted you to be absolutely discreet, but . . ." He shrugged elegantly, sipped.

"I'm not looking for publicity, I'm looking for a murderer."

"You won't find one here. This is a place of peace and tranquillity."

"Peace and tranquillity." Eve nodded, watching his face. "I'd guess that sort of thing's important to you."

"Vital, as it should be to everyone. The world is a canvas, and on it is painted great beauty. All we have to do is look."

"Peace and tranquillity and beauty are more vital to someone who grew up without them. To a man who was systematically and regularly abused as a child. Battered and beaten. Do you pay your mother to keep quiet about it, or just to keep her away?"

The glass in Smith's hand shattered, and a thin line of blood dripped down his palm.

CHAPTER FOURTEEN

Shards of glass hitting the floor had, in Eve's opinion, a more interesting musical note than the continued coo of Smith's recorded voice.

She doubted any of his fans would recognize him now, with all the negative energy twisting his face. His bloody hand still clenched the shattered drinking glass.

She could hear his labored breaths before he sprang to his feet. She got to her own, slowly, and prepared to deflect any assault.

But he simply threw his head back, like a great dog about to bay, and howled out for Li.

She came on the run, bare feet slapping the floor and filmy robes flapping the air.

"Oh, *Carmichael!* Oh, you poor thing. You're *bleeding*. Should I call the doctor? Should I call an ambulance?" She patted her own cheeks in rapid tat-tats.

While tears welled in his eyes, he held out his bleeding hand. "Do something."

"Jesus." Eve stepped forward, grabbed his injured hand, twisted it over to take a look at the cut. "Get a towel, some water, antiseptic, bandages. It's not deep enough to worry the MTs."

"But his hands, his beautiful hands. Carmichael is an artist."

"Yeah, well, he's an artist with a cut across his palm. No puncture. Peabody? Got a handkerchief?"

"Right here, Lieutenant."

Taking it, Eve wrapped the cut while Li raced off, probably to call up a cosmetic surgeon.

"Sit down, Carmichael. You're barely scratched."

"You have no right, no right to come into my home and upset me this way. No right, no *decency*. You can't come here, upset the balance. Threaten me."

"I don't recall threatening you, and I've got a pretty good memory for that kind of thing. Officer Peabody, did I threaten Mr. Smith?"

"No, sir, you did not."

"You think because I live an ordered and privileged life I don't know the darker corners." His lips curled now, and he held his injured hand to his heart in a loose fist. "You want to extort money from me, payment to keep quiet about matters that are none of your business. Women like you always want to be paid."

"Women like me?"

"You think you're better than men. You use your wiles or your sex to control them, to suck them dry. You're nothing but animals. Bitches and cunts. You deserve to . . ."

"Deserve to what?" Eve prompted when he stopped himself, when she watched the war for composure rage over his face. "To suffer, to die, to pay?"

"You won't put words in my mouth." He collapsed in the chair again, holding his hand by the wrist and rocking as if for comfort.

Li rushed back in carrying a fluffy white towel, a bottle of water, and what looked to be enough bandage to wrap an entire squadron after a bloody battle.

"Let my aide take care of it," Eve told him. "She's just going to mess it up, and hurt you considerably while she's at it."

Smith nodded curtly, and turned his head away from Peabody and the blood.

"Li, please go out now. Close the door."

"But, Carmichael . . ."

"I want you to go."

She blinked at the slap in his voice and fled.

"How did you learn about . . . her?" he asked Eve.

"It's my job to learn about things."

"It could ruin me, you know. My audience doesn't want to know about that sort of . . . They don't want the unseemly, the unattractive. They come to me for beauty, for romantic fantasy, not for the ugliness of reality."

"I'm not interested in your audience or in making any information public, until and unless it applies to my case. I told you, I'm not interested in publicity."

"Everyone is," he retorted.

"Think what you like, it doesn't change why I'm here. Your mother was an LC. She was abusive to you."

"Yes."

"You support her, financially."

"As long as she's taken care of, she stays away, and out of my life. She's smart enough to know that coming forward, selling her story, might net her some quick money, but it would kill the golden goose. If my income suffers, so does hers. I explained this to her, very carefully, before the first payment was made."

"Your relationship with your mother is adversarial."

"We don't have a relationship. I prefer not to think of the connection. It unbalances my chi."

"Jacie Wooton was an LC."

"Who?"

"Wooton. The woman who was murdered in Chinatown."

"It has nothing to do with me." More composed now, he waved it all away with his uninjured hand. "I also choose not to dwell on the darker shades of the world."

"A second woman was murdered on Sunday. The mother of a grown son."

He flashed her a look now, and there was a hint of fear in it. "That doesn't have anything to do with me, either. I survived violence. I don't perpetuate it."

"Victims of abuse often become abusive. Children who were beaten often become violent adults. Sometimes a killer is born, sometimes he is made. A woman hurt you, a woman who had control over you, authority over you. She hurt you for years when you were helpless to stop her. How do you make her pay for that pain, for that humiliation, for all the years you lived in fear?"

"I don't! She'll never pay. Her type never pays. She wins, again and again. Every time I send her money, she wins again." Tears tracked down his cheeks now. "She wins because you're standing there pushing her into my head again. My life is not an illusion because I *made* it. I created it. I won't let you come into it and try to shatter it, to smear it."

Empathy rolled into her stomach. His words, the passion behind them, could have been her own. "You have a home here, and one in London."

"Yes, yes, yes! What of it?" He jerked his hand, and glanced down at the tug of Peabody's. When his gaze landed on the bloody cloth, his face went white as bone.

"Go away. Can't you go away?"

"Tell me where you were Sunday morning."

"I don't know. How can I remember everything? I have people to take care of me. I'm entitled to be taken care of. I give pleasure. I take pleasure. I deserve it."

"Sunday morning, Carmichael, between eight and noon."

"Here. Right here. Sleeping, meditating, detoxifying. I can't live with stress. I need my quiet times."

"Were you alone?"

"I'm never alone. She's in every closet, under every bed, waiting in the next room to strike out. I lock her away, but it doesn't mean she isn't waiting."

She hurt, looking at him. Understanding the words, she hurt. "Did you leave the house on Sunday morning?"

"I don't remember."

"Did you know Lois Gregg?"

"I know so many people. So many women. They love me. Women love me because I'm perfect. Because I don't threaten them. Because they don't know that I know what they are under it all."

"Did you kill Lois Gregg?"

"I have nothing more to say to you. I'm going to call my attorneys now. I want you to leave my home. Li!" He put his injured hand behind his back as he rose, swaying a little. He stepped carefully to the side, away from the blood-smeared towel.

"Li, make them go away," he ordered, as she hurried into the room again. "Make them leave. I have to lie down now. I don't feel well. I need my quiet room."

"There now, there." Cooing, she put an arm around his waist, took his weight. "I'll take care of everything, don't you worry. Poor baby. Don't you worry."

She shot a vicious look at Eve over her shoulder as she led Smith from the room. "I want you gone when I get back. If not, your superior will hear about this."

Eve pursed her lips, listening to Li's voice fade as she cooed Smith away.

"Guy's got some serious problems," Peabody commented.

"Yeah. Maybe he thinks he can cover it up with meditation, herb drinks, and mind-numbing music." Eve shrugged. "Maybe he can. He couldn't look at the blood," she added, studying the towel. "Made him sick to see blood. Hard to do what was done to those two women if blood makes you sick. Then again, maybe it's just the sight of his own blood that does it."

She checked the time as they left the house. "We're running a little early."

"Yeah?" Peabody perked right up. "Then maybe we could hit a cart, or a 24/7. I missed breakfast."

"Not that early." When Peabody's face fell, Eve sighed. "You know I hate that kicked puppy look. Whatever we pass first. And you have one minute to do the transaction, which will include getting me coffee."

"Deal."

They hit a cart, so Peabody settled for a scrambled egg wrap that Eve assumed tasted better than it smelled. The coffee didn't but that was par. "We're going to talk to Breen's wife. I got a hassle when I called her office for her schedule, so I pulled in the reserves."

Peabody's response was an egg-substitute-filled mumble. She swallowed. "I'm supposed to arrange the appointments."

"You're going to bitch because I cut you a break?"

"No." But she had to fight the pout. "I don't want you to think I can't fulfill my duties because I've got all this stuff going on."

"If I have a complaint about your work, Peabody, you'll be the first to know."

"That's a given," Peabody muttered and took a slug of her orange-flavored energy drink. "You said reserves?"

"Julietta does fashion. I happen to know somebody in the fashion forefront. Ms. Gates's schedule miraculously cleared when she got a call from Leonardo's main squeeze."

"You tagged Mavis. Mag."

"It's not a girl outing, Peabody, it's a murder investigation."

"Silver linings, sir. I like a nice silver lining." Peabody washed down egg substitute with reconstituted citrus product. "I can't wait to tell her we're going to be neighbors. At least until she has the baby. I guess they're going to want a bigger place."

"Why? How much room could a baby take up?"

"It's not the baby so much, it's all the stuff. You got your crib, your changing table, your activity center, your diaper unit, your —"

"Never mind. Jeez." It gave her the mild weirds just to think about it.

"It was really smart to horn in using Mavis."

"I have my moments."

"Of course, you could've just told them you were Mrs. Roarke, and they'd have bowed to you."

"I don't want them to bow to me, I just want a damn interview. And don't call me Mrs. Roarke."

"Just saying." Cheerful now, Peabody polished off the wrap. "Boy, nothing like a good breakfast to lift your mood. It's not such a big deal, getting a place with McNab. It's just another step in an evolving relationship. Right?"

"How the hell do I know?"

Fastidiously, Peabody dug out a wipe for her fingers, and made a mental note to replace the bloody handkerchief she'd left at Smith's. "Well, when you moved in with Roarke you didn't get all stupid and nervous and knotted up."

There was a long pause, a long silence.

"You did?" Peabody's head thunked back on the seat. "That's so great. It makes me feel so much better. If you can get all screwed up over moving in with the god of men, into that palace, it's okay for me to get wigged about moving to an apartment with McNab. It's okay."

"Now that we've solved that thorny dilemma, maybe we can concentrate on the case."

"I just have one more question. When did you get over it? I mean, how long did it take for you to feel normal about hooking up with Roarke — living in the same space and all that?"

"I'll let you know when it happens."

"Wow. That's . . ." She thought it over, and a dreamy smile bloomed on her face. "That's sweet."

"Please shut up before I have to hurt you."

"Dallas, you said *please*. You're mellowing."

"Insults," Eve grumbled. "All I get are insults. Mrs. Roarke, sweet, mellowing. We'll see how mellow I am when I stuff your head up your ass."

"And she's back," Peabody announced, and rode in contented silence.

You could always count on Mavis, Eve thought. For a favor, for a laugh, for a shoulder. And most of all for sheer surprise.

Being four months pregnant hadn't depleted her energy or affected her bent for fashion risks. At least Eve assumed they were risks as nobody, absolutely nobody, looked quite like Mavis Freestone.

She'd gone for summer pastels, for her hair in any case, and had swooped it up in some sort of snaky twists that twined gleaming hunks of blue and pink and greens together. They were anchored here and there with lavender pins in the shapes of what Eve took for tiny flowers, until she got a closer look and realized they were naked babies curled into the embryonic position.

Talk about the weirds.

A dozen thin chains of gold and silver dangled from each ear. On each chain, colorful balls hung that clanged together every time she moved. Which meant constantly.

Her tiny body was decked out in a skirt the size of a table napkin, matched with a swingy vest, both in white, and both covered with tiny question marks that echoed the hues of her hair. She wore shoes with one clear strap. The thick soles and clunky heels were filled with more little balls that jingled with each step. Her toenails were painted in every color of the rainbow.

For Mavis, it was business attire.

"This is absolutely magalicious," Mavis claimed. "*Outre* is like the cutting edge. It was my bible of style before I met my honeybear. I still go through it every month, but now I never have to think how I'm going to afford all the friggin' clothes. Leonardo is the ult."

"I need five minutes with her."

"It's a dunk, Dallas. If she could've kissed my ass over the 'link, I'd have lip dye smears on my butt. Just watch."

They crossed the wide lobby. It was done in sharp geometric patterns of white, red, and black. Fanning out from the central data desk were pathways that led to boutiques, a fancy café, and a home decor center.

Between them on the walls were screens on which elongated models walked runways in outfits that might have been designed by a mental patient on Pluto.

"Fall fashion shows," Mavis told her. "New York, Milan, Paris, and London." She let out a squeal and pointed. "See that? That's my babycakes's designs. Nobody comes close."

Eve studied the ensemble of skintight red stripes that boasted an explosion of gold tail feathers and a transparent skirt that glowed with little white lights at the hem.

How could she argue?

Mavis marched by the data center to the security station that guarded a bank of glossy red elevators. "Mavis Freestone to see Julietta Gates."

"Yes, Ms. Freestone, you're to go right up to thirty. Someone will meet you." The guard's hand came up to stop Eve and Peabody. "Only Ms. Freestone is cleared for thirty."

"You don't really think I travel alone, do you?" Mavis spoke in icy tones before Eve could work up a snarl. "If my entourage isn't welcome, neither am I."

"I beg your pardon, Ms. Freestone. I just need to check upstairs."

"Quickly." Mavis shot her little nose in the air. "I'm a very busy woman."

She made a show out of tapping her foot, examining her nails in the twenty seconds it took the guard to clear them.

"You and your entourage are cleared for thirty. Thank you for your patience."

Mavis maintained the diva mode until the elevator doors shut behind them. "Subzero! I could eat that with a spoon. 'You and your entourage are cleared for thirty.' Is that hot shit, or what?"

She did a quick butt-wiggling dance, then patted her belly. "I only said entourage because I thought you might punch him."

"I was thinking about it."

"I'm keeping the baby away from displays of violence. Not even watching much screen. I heard how serenity and positive energy's really good for brewing babies."

With some trepidation, Eve glanced down at Mavis's belly. Could the thing hear in there? "I'll try not to punch anybody when you're around."

"That'd be good." Mavis shut off her beaming smile as the doors opened. The diva was back. She lifted her eyebrows at the woman who waited for them.

"Ms. Freestone, such a pleasure to meet you. I'm an enormous fan of yours, and of Leonardo's, of course."

"Of course." Mavis extended a hand.

"If you'll just come with me, Ms. Gates is very anxious to see you."

"I dig this to China," Mavis said out of the corner of her mouth as they walked through another generous lobby.

In this one, clear cubes were set up for busy drones. Headsets and keyboards were fully manned by a troop that had obviously watched the fashion shows and tried to outdo them.

The space once again fanned out, and at the far curve were double doors in what Eve now assumed was *Outre*'s signature murder red.

Their escort hurried along in a skirt snug as a bandage, on heels sharp as scalpels. She pressed a button at the center of the left door. Seconds later, a brisk impatient voice snapped: "Yes."

"Ms. Freestone is here to see you, Ms. Gates."

Rather than a response, the doors slid back into the wall, revealing an enormous office, ribboned with privacy-screened windows.

The black-and-white theme continued here. Black carpet, white walls, a massive white workstation. Wide chairs were covered in thin black-and-white stripes.

The red came from the scarlet roses massed in a tall black vase, and from the sharp, powerful business suit that decked Julietta's impressive body.

She was tall, curvy with a simple sweep of honey blonde hair that swung around a diamond-shaped face. Keen cheekbones, keen chin, keen nose, with a mouth just a shade too thin for beauty. But the eyes, a deep, deep brown, pulled the attention away from the minor flaw.

She was crossing the room as the doors opened, her hand extended, a delighted expression on her face. "Mavis Freestone, what a pleasure. I'm so glad you got in touch. I've been wanting to meet you for the longest time! Of course, I've known Leonardo forever. He's such a sweetheart."

"He's certainly mine."

"Please, sit down. What can I offer you? Iced coffee perhaps?"

"I'm dodging caffeine these days." Mavis remained standing, patted her belly.

"Yes, of course. Congratulations. When are you due?"

"February."

"What a nice Valentine's present." Ignoring Eve and Peabody, she drew Mavis toward a chair. "Get off your feet, and we'll have a cold, sparkling juice."

"We'd love one. Got time for a drink, Dallas?"

"I can make time, since Ms. Gates found an opening in her busy calendar." Resting an arm on the back of Mavis's chair, Eve cocked her hip. "My questions shouldn't take long."

"I'm afraid I don't understand."

"Lieutenant Dallas, NYPSD." Eve took out her badge. "My aide, Officer Peabody. Now that we all know each other, and we're all cozy, maybe you could answer some questions."

"I repeat" — Julietta walked around her desk to assume a position of command — "I don't understand. I agreed to see Ms. Freestone. We'd very much like to do a major article on you, Mavis, with a photo layout."

"Sure, we can talk about that. After Dallas is done. Dallas and I go way back," she added with a wonderfully guileless smile. "When she mentioned she was having trouble getting an interview, I said I was sure it was just a communication glitz, and you'd make time. Supporting our local police is a really important issue with me and Leonardo."

"Cleverly done," Julietta replied.

"I thought so." Eve stayed on her feet as Julietta sat down. "If you're not comfortable, I'm sure Mavis wouldn't mind waiting outside the office until we're finished."

"No need for that." Julietta leaned back, swiveled in her chair. "You've already spoken to Tom. I don't know what I can possibly add. I don't get involved in his work, and he doesn't get involved in mine."

"How about each other's lives?"

Her tone remained perfectly pleasant. "Which area of our lives do you have in mind?"

"When was the last time you were in London?"

"London?" Her brow creased. "I don't see what that has to do with anything."

"Humor me."

"I was there a few weeks ago on business." With the annoyance still creased between her eyebrows, she picked up a small pocket calendar, keyed in for the date. "July eight and nine and ten."

"Alone?"

There was a quick flicker in her eyes before she set the calendar down. "Yes, why?"

"Your husband ever go over with you?"

"We went in April. Tom thought the experience would be fun for Jed. I had business, and he wanted to do some research. We took an extra two days for a family holiday."

"Buy any souvenirs?"

"What are you getting at?"

"I guess you travel to Europe pretty regularly," Eve said, changing tack. "For your business."

"I do. For fashion shows, for events, to meet with my counterparts in our European offices. Just what does this have to do with Tom helping you in an investigation?"

"It's part of my investigation."

"I don't —" She broke off when her pocket 'link rang. "Excuse me, that's my private line. I need to get this."

She shifted it to privacy mode, slid on a miniheadset, and angled away so Eve couldn't see the 'link's view screen.

"Julietta Gates. Yes."

Her voice warmed, several degrees, and that just-a-little-too-thin mouth tipped up in a smile.

"Absolutely. I have it on my calendar. One o'clock. Mmm-hmm. Yes, I'm in a meeting." There was a long silence as she listened, and Eve noted the faint flush that rose to her cheeks. "I'll look forward to that. Yes, I will. Goodbye."

She disconnected, slipped off the headset. "Sorry, afternoon meeting. Now —"

"Can you tell me where you were Sunday morning?"

"Oh, for heaven's sake." She let out a huff of breath. "Sundays, I let Tom sleep in and take Jed to the park, or to some other activity. I'm trying to be cooperative, Lieutenant, since Mavis has asked me to, but I'm finding this very annoying."

"Almost done. How about the night of September second, between midnight and three?"

Julietta snatched up her calendar again, keyed in. Again, Eve saw the slight change cross her face. "I had a meeting with an associate. I can't tell you precisely when I got home as I didn't make note of it, but I think it was after nine, maybe close to ten. I was tired, and went straight up to bed since Tom was working."

"So he was home the entire night."

"Why wouldn't he be? He was working. I took a pill and went to bed. I told him I was going to, so he'd hardly have left the house because of Jed. Tom's completely devoted, and somewhat overprotective of Jed. What *is* this?"

"That's it for now. Thanks for the time."

"I think I'm entitled to some sort of —"

"If you still want, we can talk about that article." Mavis popped to her feet. "I just need a minute first."

She scooted out of the office with Eve, then dropped her voice to a whisper. "So? Did she kill somebody or what?"

"Doubtful. The worst I figure she's done is cheat on her husband with whoever called her on her private 'link."

"She did? She is? How do you know?"

"Plenty of tells. Look, if you don't want to deal with her, you can leave with me and Peabody. We'll get you home."

"No, it's chilly. A spread in *Outre's* like my fantasy. And it'll give a boost to my disc sales. Won't hurt

Leonardo's biz either. It cooks for all of us. We did good, right?"

"We did good."

"Night or day, day or night. Hey, what do you think about Vignette or Vidal?"

"What are they?"

"My baby. Vignette for a girl, Vidal for a boy. They're French. We're experimenting with French names, and I ditched Fifi. I mean, who names a kid Fifi?"

Eve didn't know who might name a kid Vignette either, but made a noncommittal mouth noise.

"Somebody will call her Viggy," Peabody said. "Which rhymes with piggy, so she'll be Piggy Viggy in school."

Mavis looked horrified. "You think? Deep-six Vignette." She gave her belly a comforting rub. "Plenty of time to come up with something else. Catch you later." She swung back into Julietta's office.

"Impressions, Peabody?" Eve asked as they rode down.

"She looks great, and she'll come up with something better than Vignette or Vidal."

"About Julietta Gates, you moron."

"I know, I just wanted to annoy you. Sir," she added when Eve looked at her. "Used to running the show, and likes it. Dresses for power even more than style. Ambitious. She'd have to be to have gotten where she is at her age. Strikes me as a little cold-blooded. There's no zing when she talks about her kid. That was a good catch with the extramarital. Blew right by me. Then when you said it, and I played it back, it was right there. The way her voice changed, the body language."

"And from the way her face flushed up, I'd say the voice on the other end was letting her know a few games they'd be playing at their one o'clock today. I'm going to want to confirm the dish on the side, in case we need to push on her later."

"We going to surveil?"

"No, don't want to risk her spotting either one of us this close to our little interview. I'll see if Baxter can handle it. How much does a kid like hers talk?"

"At that age, they rarely shut up. Hardly anybody but immediate family can understand them, but it doesn't stop them from talking."

"She met her side piece on Sunday, you can take that to the vault. And she had the kid with her. Wouldn't he tattle to daddy?"

"She probably told him it was a secret."

"Huh." This was foreign territory, so she took Peabody at her word. "Kids keep secrets?"

"No, but she doesn't strike me as the type who knows her own kid very well. And the boy seems pretty tight with his dad. My best guess is he kept the secret until she was out of hearing, then blabbed. Daddy, me and Mommy and Uncle Side Dish played on the swings, but it's a secret."

Eve let it play in her head, and nodded. "And I doubt it's the first time. Daddy knows what's going on, and wouldn't that irritate him? Wouldn't he be a bit put out? Here he is, staying at home watching the kid, taking care of the house, while she's running around town — and Europe — with some other guy. Playing with some other guy with his son in tow. Yeah, that's a real pisser."

"Mother and whore," she said as they got back into the vehicle. "We keep coming back to that. No problem for him to get out of the house for either murder, and he might've picked up the writing paper — paying cash — on his spring trip to London. Hell, the paper could've been a gift from a fan for that matter. And he decided it fit the bill. He knows the prototype murders as well as the initial killers."

"Means, motive, opportunity."

"Yeah, Thomas A. just jumped to the top of our list."

CHAPTER FIFTEEN

Eve had barely disconnected with Baxter when her communicator signaled. Whitney's face filled the screen.

"He'll see you at ten forty-five. Make it good."

"Yes, sir. Thank you."

Peabody studied Eve's satisfied smile. "A person's fifteen minutes late, one time, and she's out of the loop?"

"Get me some data on Sophia DiCarlo, the Renquist's au pair, and I'll fill you in on the way to the U.N."

"We're going back to the U.N., to Renquist, and not risking federal imprisonment?"

"We're going back to apologize, grovel, and eat massive portions of crow."

"You don't know how to do those things." Peabody looked mournful. "We're going to the pen."

"Just get the data. If I don't know how to apologize, grovel, and eat crow, it's because it's rarely appropriate for me to do so. You have to be wrong first."

When there was silence, Eve glanced over. "No smart-ass comment?"

"My grandmother always says, if you can't say something positive about someone, keep your trap shut."

"Yeah, like you listen to her. Renquist is pissed, his wife is pissed, and they're in the position to crimp the investigation. Nobody knows how to tie up red tape like a politician. And since my impression of them is that they are pompous assholes, I figured slathering on the 'I'm just a public servant, ergo a bonehead' line might get me in."

"You said ergo."

"It goes with pompous."

"Sophia DiCarlo, twenty-six and single. Citizen of Italy with green card and work permit. Parents and two sibs reside in Rome. Aha, parents are domestics, employed by Angela Dysert. Bet it's a relation to Mrs. Pompous Asshole. Sophia's been employed by the Renquists as domestic, child-care position, for the past six years. No criminal on record."

"Okay, the girl — Renquist's girl, she's old enough for school, right? See what you can find on that."

"It's touchy getting data on minors, Dallas, especially foreign nationals, without more clearance."

"Get what you can."

Peabody went to work while Eve drove across town. Overhead in the hazy sky, ad blimps and tourist trams moved sluggishly. Inside the relative cool, Eve practiced groveling in her head. Even telling herself it was for the greater good, it rankled.

"They've got the kid's privacy blocked. That's pretty standard," Peabody told her. "Especially with more upscale family types. You don't want kidnappers and unsavory types knowing stuff about your kids. You're not going to get anything without clearance."

"Can't ask for clearance. I don't want the Renquists to know I'm looking at them. Doesn't matter. The au pair's bound to take the kid out sometime, or better, go out on her own. Has to have a day off."

Eve tucked her thoughts away as they approached the U.N., and prepared to go through the multiple security checks.

It took twenty minutes to get through to Renquist's outer office. It was his admin who greeted them, and invited them to wait.

Eve figured the extra twenty Renquist kept them cooling their heels was just his way to show who was in charge. Crow was already sticking in her throat when they were admitted.

"Please make it brief," Renquist said immediately. "I've made time for you out of a very busy day only due to the direct request of your chief of police. You've already infringed on my time here, and my wife's."

"Yes, sir. I'm very sorry to have intruded on you, and on Mrs. Renquist. In my zeal to further my investigation, I overstepped. I hope neither you nor Mrs. Renquist will take this offense personally, nor let it reflect on the department."

He arched his brow, and the surprise — the satisfaction — was obvious in his eyes. "Being considered a suspect in a murder is hardly usual for me, and could hardly be anything but personally offensive."

"I regret that I gave the impression you were a suspect. Investigative procedure demands that I pursue any and all possible connections. I . . ." She tried a little fumble, wished she could work up a flush. "I can only apologize again, sir, and tell you frankly that my own frustration in being unable to clear this case may have made my demeanor less than courteous to both you and Mrs. Renquist. In actuality, I'm only seeking to remove your name from any list as applies to this investigation. My interview with Mrs. Renquist, however ill-advised, did serve to confirm your whereabouts at the time of the murders."

"My wife was very distressed that the subject came up in our home, with guests on the point of arriving."

"I realize that. I apologize again for the inconvenience." *You schmuck*.

"I hardly see why my name should be on any sort of a list merely because I may have some writing paper in my possession."

She lowered her eyes. "It's the only lead I have. The killer has taunted me with these notes. It's very upsetting. But that doesn't excuse my disturbing your wife at home. Please convey my apologies to Mrs. Renquist."

He smiled now, thinly. "I will do so. However, Lieutenant, I have the impression that you wouldn't be here, offering this apology, had your superiors not insisted you do so."

She lifted her gaze, met his, and let a hint of the resentment show through. "I was doing my job as best I know how. I don't play politics well. I'm just a cop. And I follow orders, Mr. Renquist."

He nodded. "I can respect someone who follows orders, and give some leeway to a public servant who allows her zeal for duty to cloud her judgment somewhat. I hope you weren't reprimanded too harshly."

"No more than my actions warranted."

"And you remain as primary in this investigation?"

"Yes, sir, I do."

"Then I'll wish you luck with it." He rose and offered a hand. "And hope that you identify and arrest the person responsible quickly."

"Thank you." Eve took his hand, held it and his eyes. "I intend to put him into a cage, personally, very soon."

He cocked his head. "Confidence, Lieutenant, or arrogance?"

"Whatever works. Thank you again, sir, for your time and your understanding."

"I take it back," Peabody said when they were clear of the building. "You're good. Frustrated apology, with just a hint of resentment. The foot soldier who'd tried to do her job, and got shafted by her superiors. Forced to eat that crow, and swallowing it down stoically. You really sold it."

"Wasn't that far off. He could turn up a lot of heat under the department. He's got both political and media connections. Nobody ordered me to apologize, but nobody's going to be sorry I did, either. Fucking politics."

"You make rank, you've got to play them sometimes."

Eve merely shrugged and climbed back into the car. "Don't have to like it. Don't have to like him, either. In fact, every time I see him, I like him less."

"It's the snooty factor," Peabody explained. "It's really hard to like somebody who has a high snooty factor, and his is top of the scale."

She looked back at the glossy white building, the shining tower, the waving flags. "I guess dealing with diplomats and ambassadors and heads of state every day makes a high snooty factor a prerequisite."

"Diplomats, ambassadors, and heads of state are supposed to represent the people, which makes them no different than us. Renquist can take his snooty factor and shove it."

She drove away from the white walls and flags, toward the heart of the city. "Wouldn't hurt my feelings a bit if it turns out to be him. I'm going to lock the cage on this son of a bitch personally. I meant that. And I wouldn't mind seeing Renquist's snotty face on the other side of the bars when I do."

She hunkered down at Central and used the exercise of clearing her desk to let her thoughts brew. She forwarded a dozen messages and demands from reporters to the media liaison, and happily forgot about them. She imagined there was a press conference in her future, but she didn't have to think about it now.

She caught up on paperwork as much as she ever caught up on paperwork, then made some calls of her own.

She took out the notes, reread them, searching for a rhythm, phrasing, word uses, anything that clicked with the speech patterns of the people on her list.

It wasn't his voice, she thought again. Deliberately not his voice. He assumes and mimics and becomes. Who did he become when he wrote the notes?

Her desk 'link signaled an incoming, and wanting to avoid reporters she waited for the transmission location to flash on. When she read Feeney, Captain Ryan, EDD, she answered.

"You work fast," she said.

"Kid, I'm a frigging rocket. Got a pop might be your guy. Case is cold. Vic was a fifty-three-year-old female. Schoolteacher. Found strangled in her apartment by a sister. Cooked for a few days first. Raped with a piece of statuary, which he also used to bash her over the head. Strangled with a pair of those panty hose you people wear. Tied in a bow under the chin."

"Bingo. How cold and where?"

"Went down June of last year, Boston. I'll send you all the particulars. No note with this one, and he smashed her head and face pretty good with the statue. ME report says she was already on the way out when he strangled her."

"Practice makes perfect."

"Could be. I got another with enough clicks to make me wonder. Six months before Boston, out in New L.A. Fifty-six-year-old vic. This one was a squatter though, and that doesn't fit. But somebody did her in her flop, raped her with a ball bat, smashed her up with it before he strangled her with her own scarf. Got a bow there, too, which is what pulled it."

"Follows, doesn't it? A squatter's an easy hit. Not tough to get to, and nobody cares too much. It'd be a good place to perfect your technique."

"My thinking. I'll send these to you. Haven't got any hits on the mutilation. Plenty of slash and gash in the good old U.S. of A., but nothing that hums along with your guy. I'm widening to international."

"Thanks, Feeney. You got some vacation time coming, don't you?"

His mournful face drooped. "Wife's nagging my ass red about putting in for a week. Frigging holiday brochures all over the damn house. Thinks we should rent some big beach house or some shit, take the whole damn family. Kids, grandkids."

"How about Bimini?"

"Who?"

"Where, Feeney."

"Oh. *Bimini*. What about it?"

"Roarke's got a place there, big house, staffed. Beach, waterfall, blah blah. I can clear it with him, have your whole damn family fly down on one of his transports. Interested?"

"Jesus Christ, I go home and tell the wife we're taking the whole herd to Bimini for a week, she'll keel over. Shit, yeah, I'm interested, but we don't have to play payback."

"I'm not playing. Place is just sitting there. He flipped a deal to Peabody and McNab awhile back, so I figure I can flip one to you. Especially since I'm going to ask you to keep an eye on things when I do some out-of-town work."

"Sounds like I'm getting the shiny end of the deal. Data coming through."

She read it through, and felt that quick little buzz in the blood. A cop buzz. She was looking at his work. Practice strokes. Not that sort of thing that merited a signature, she thought, but a building of style and skill he preferred not to add to his credits.

He'd have been sloppier, less cautious. There'd have been mistakes, and though the trail was cold, she might still find a shadow of them.

She took the time to organize the data before taking it to Whitney for her pitch.

With her commander's go-ahead under her belt, she made tracks back to Homicide, already formulating her next pitch in her head. She breezed through the bull pen, giving Baxter a with-me signal when he called out her name.

"So, you get a look at the guy she's boinking on the side?"

"She's not boinking a guy on the side."

The rush Eve was still riding on drained. "Gotta be. Damn it, Baxter, she had big, secret affair written all over her. I could almost smell the sex."

"Please, you're giving me a woody. I'm just going to have some of your coffee and calm myself down."

"If you couldn't keep a tail on her —"

"I kept a tail on her." He ordered up an enormous mug, two sugars, splash of cream. Taking it, he leaned back against her filing cabinet to enjoy the first jolt.

"God*damn*, this is coffee. Speaking of tails, which you were, the blonde had a superior one."

"Take your woody and your idiot brain out of my office. She's screwing somebody on the side."

"Did I say she wasn't?" He smiled, sipped again, and wiggled his eyebrows at Eve over the rim. "She just ain't driving a stick."

"She's . . . Oh. Well, well, well, this is interesting." She lowered to the corner of her desk, thought it through. "Not just a side dish, a girl side dish. That has to be a real pisser for a guy."

"And the dish was prime. Tall, lanky, black, and beautiful. The kind you just want to start slurping on from the toes up. Waste from my point of view — two superior examples of the species, and they're sliding all over each other. Of course, thinking about them sliding all over each other is entertaining. I had a good time with that, and have to thank you for the duty."

"You're a sick perv."

"And proud of it."

"Do you think you could defer your lesbian fantasies until you give me a report?"

"I've already had the fantasies, and plan to have them again, but I can postpone the next act. Your girl left the office, twelve forty-five, and caught a cab. Proceeded uptown to the Silby Hotel on Park. Went straight into the lobby, where her date was waiting. Hot side dish later identified as Serena Unger through detective's charm, skill, and the fifty he passed the desk clerk."

"Fifty? Shit, Baxter."

"Hey, classy joint, classy bribe. Unger had preregistered. Both subjects proceeded to an elevator, which was, to the detective's great joy, glass-sided. In this way he was able to use his keen observation techniques to watch them exchange a big, sloppy wet one on the way up to the fourteenth floor. They entered room 1405, where they remained, engaged in activities the detective was sadly unable to witness, until fourteen hundred. At which time Julietta Gates exited the room, and the hotel, procuring another cab. She returned to her place of employment with what the detective believed was a satisfied smile on her face."

"You run Unger?"

"Had Trueheart do it while we waited for the lunchtime quickie to run its course. She's a fashion designer. Thirty-two, single. No criminal. Currently employed with Mirandi's second label arm. They're New York-based."

"Question: Your woman cheats on you with another woman. Better or worse than her diddling with a guy?"

"Oh, worse. Bad enough she's playing you, but she's doing it without a dick, which means she doesn't think too much of your equipment. It's a guy, you can maybe rationalize it some. You know, he took advantage of her, or she had a moment of weakness."

"Took advantage of her." Eve snorted. "Men are really sad and simple."

"Please, a boy needs his illusions. Anyway, it's another skirt, she had to go looking, and she had to go looking for something you don't have. Makes you a double loser."

"Yeah, that's how I see it. It's going to give you a real hard-on against women. So to speak. We're going to want to find out how long Julietta's been going girl-on-girl."

He set the empty mug down and linked his hands in a gesture of prayer. "Please, please, please, let me do it. I never get the fun stuff."

"I need subtle on this."

"My middle name."

"I thought your middle name was Horny dog."

"That's my first middle name," he said with some dignity. "Come on, Dallas, how about it?"

"Play ring-around-a-rosie with Unger. Talk to the staff at the hotel and keep the bribes to a minimum. Budget's not going to stretch if you keep slapping down fifties. Talk to her neighbors. Sniff around her place of employment. She's going to get wind of it, so keep the reason for the look-see quiet. Subtle, Baxter, seriously. I've got to do an out-of-town. If I get lucky, I'll be back in tomorrow. If not, it may take another day."

"You can leave this in my very capable hands. Oh, and I won't put in for the fifty," he said as he started out. "It was worth the price of the ticket."

He'd handle it, she thought. She couldn't be in Boston, New L.A., and poking around Serena Unger in New York at the same time. Baxter could work that angle, Feeney the like-crimes area, and she'd pursue other potential leads.

It appeared she'd put together a team without intending to.

Now, she thought, she was about to add another member. And it would be her turn to play it subtle.

She didn't expect to get through to Roarke on the first try, but the great god of meetings must have decided to cut her a break. His admin passed her on to him, with the polite comment that he'd just returned from a business lunch.

"So what'd you eat?" she asked when he came on.

"Chef's salad. How about you?"

"I'm getting something in a minute. You got any business in Boston?"

"I could have. Why?"

"I've got to make a run up there, maybe out to the West Coast. Check out some things. I don't want to take Peabody. She's got the exam day after tomorrow. She needs to stay here, plus I can't be a hundred percent I'll be back on time for her to make it. Thought you might want to tag along."

"I might. When?"

"ASAP."

"This wouldn't be a maneuver to avoid Summerset's return?"

"No, but it's a handy side benny. Look, you want to go or not?"

"I have to do some shuffling." He angled away, and she saw him dance his fingers over a small keyboard. "I need . . . two hours will do it."

"That works for me." Now came the tricky part. "I'll meet you at the Newark transpo center, say seventeen hundred. We'll grab a shuttle there."

"Public transpo? And at five o'clock? I don't think so."

She just loved the way he sneered. "Timing can't be helped," she began.

"Accommodations can. We'll take one of my shuttles."

Which was exactly what she'd expected him to say. Thank God. The last thing she wanted was to squeeze on to a commuter sweatbox and deal with the inevitable delays and poor hygiene. But she knew how to play the game, and gave him an obligatory scowl.

"Look, pal, this is police business. You're just along for the ride, and possible out-of-town nookie."

"All nookie is appreciated, but the method of transpo's a deal breaker. I'll pick you up when I arrange things here. And if you argue, you'll just put me behind." He checked his wrist unit. "I'll let you know when I'm on my way." And clicked off.

That, she thought, went perfectly.

Shortly after five she was seated comfortably in Roarke's private shuttle, nibbling on strawberries and studying her notes in the fragrant cool. As rides went, it beat the hell out of the public sardine cans.

"You can go along for the interview with Roberta Gable," she told Roarke. "But then I have to ditch you. I talked to the primary with Boston PD, and he'll take a meet with me, but he's cranky about it. I bring a civilian along, he's going to get crankier."

"I believe I can find something to occupy me." He was working manually at one of the onboard computers and didn't glance up.

"Figure you will, and I also figure that the shuffling you did had to be fast and furious. Thanks."

"I expect to be paid in out-of-town nookie at the first opportunity."

"You're a cheap date, Roarke."

He smiled, but kept on working. "We'll see about that. Oh, and by the way, your token protest about taking my shuttle lacked a certain panache. You might put a little more effort into it next time."

She bit down on a strawberry. "I don't know what you're talking about." And was saved from further comment by the beep of her 'link. "Dallas."

"Hey, kid, got a couple bumps. Figured you'd want to know while you were in transit." Feeney's droopy eyes narrowed. "You eating strawberries?"

"Maybe." She swallowed guiltily. "I missed lunch. So what? Give."

"First one's messy, maybe too messy to be our guy. Mutilated body of an LC, female, twenty-eight, fished out of the river. The Seine. That's gay Paree. Three years ago June. Cut to pieces, with liver and kidneys missing. Throat cut, and a number of defensive wounds on forearms. She was in the river too long for them to recover any trace evidence, had there been any. Investigation dead-ended, and the case remains open."

"Any suspects?"

"Investigator pushed on the last John on her books, but it didn't pan out. Did a press on her coordinator, too, who's got a known for roughing up his employees, but that fizzled out, too."

"Okay. What else?"

"Two years ago, London, Ripper-style murder in Whitechapel sector. Junked up LC who slipped through the tox screenings. She was thirty-six, had two female roommates of the same occupation. They tried to finger her on-again, off-again boyfriend for it, but he was alibied tight. Looks clear to me."

"How'd he do her?"

"Slit her throat. Went for her works again, and said works were not recovered on the scene. He also cut her up. Slashes over the breasts, palms of both hands. Investigator puts it down to lust kill. But the ME's got an interesting note here, and looking it over, I lean toward him. Says the slashes on breasts and palms were like an afterthought. No passion to them. You got one witness says he saw the vic head off with a guy dressed in a black cape and a fancy hat. Since the witness was trashed on Zoner, the investigator didn't put much faith in his statement."

"It fits," Eve told him. "You know, it fits. He dressed like DeSalvo did for the strangulations, in handyman garb. Why wouldn't he costume himself up for the Ripper? Thanks, Feeney. Shoot the files to my office unit, copy to my home unit. I'm hoping to be back within twenty-four hours."

"Done. I'm going to take this search off planet. It's got me hooked now."

She sat back, stared up at the ceiling.

"Are we going to London and Paris?" Roarke asked her.

"I don't think I can risk the time, or the energy it'd take to hack through the international red tape. I'll try to tie it in, talking to the primaries via 'link."

"If you change your mind, it wouldn't take more than one extra day."

She'd like to see where he'd been, where he'd done some of his early work. But she shook her head. "He's in New York. I need to be in New York. He's been practicing a long time," she said half to herself. "Honing his talents. That's why he can afford to kill close together now. All the prep work, all the research, all the details are in place. He doesn't have to wait because he's waited long enough."

"Practiced or not, the speed is going to make him sloppy," Roarke stated. "He may be meticulous, he may have honed his talents, but he's moving too fast for caution."

"I think you're right about that. And when he messes up, we'll get him. When we get him, when I get him in the box and break him down, we're going to find out there were more. Other bodies, hidden or destroyed, until he got better. Until he could leave them to be found, with some pride. But his early mistakes, he doesn't want to be embarrassed by them. That's the emotional reason. The other's more practical. He didn't want to leave too many like crimes on the books, draw attention until he was ready to make his splash."

"I've done some research of my own." Roarke swiveled the workstation aside. "For fifteen months between March of 2012 and May of 2013, a man named Peter Brent murdered seven police officers in the city of Chicago. Brent, unable to pass the psych screen to become a member of the CPSD, joined a fringe paramilitary group where he learned how to handle what would be his weapon of choice, a long-range blaster, already banned for civilians at that time."

"I know about Brent. He liked rooftops. He'd hunker down on a roof, wait for a cop to come into range, and take him out with a head shot. It took a fifty-man task force more than a year to bring him down."

Understanding, she leaned forward, laid her hands on Roarke's. "Brent didn't kill women, he killed cops. Didn't matter to him as long as they had the uniform he couldn't wear. He doesn't fit the profile for the prototype."

"Five of the seven dead cops were female officers. As was the chief of police who he tried, and failed, to assassinate. Don't hose me, Lieutenant," he said calmly enough. "You've thought of Brent, and you've run a probability just as I have. You know there's an eighty-eight point six probability factor that he will emulate Brent, and target you."

"He's not going to go for me," she insisted. Not yet, she thought. Not quite yet. "He needs me to pursue, so he feels more important, more successful, more satisfied. Taking me out wouldn't give him the same rush."

"So he's saving you for his final act."

There was no point in dissembling, not with Roarke. "I figure he may have that for a long-range goal. But I can promise you, he won't get there."

He took her hand, linked fingers. "I'm holding you to that promise."

CHAPTER SIXTEEN

She'd decided to hang on to Roarke for her interview with Roberta Gable. He would, she considered, provide another set of impressions. The former child-care professional had agreed to speak with Eve as long as the interview lasted no longer than twenty minutes.

"She wasn't particularly gracious about it," Eve told him as they approached the small apartment complex where Gable made her home. "Especially when I said we'd be here around six-thirty. She eats promptly at seven, and I was told I'd have to respect that."

"People of a certain age tend to develop routines."

"And she called me Miss Dallas. Repeatedly."

Companionably, Roarke swung an arm around her shoulders. "You already hate her."

"I do. I really do. But the job's the job. No snuggling on the job," she added.

"I keep forgetting that." Still he gave her a friendly squeeze before removing his arm.

Eve stepped up to the security grid, gave her name, displayed her badge, stated her business. She was cleared so quickly she assumed Gable had been waiting for her.

"I'm going to intro you as my associate," she said as they walked into the tiny foyer. One look at his gorgeous face, the elegant suit, and the shoes that probably cost more than Gable's monthly rent had Eve sighing. "And unless she's blind and senile, she won't buy it, but we'll try to brush by that."

"It shows a definite bias to assume that cops can't be well dressed."

"Your shirt lists for more than my weapon," she chided. "So once in, you keep it buttoned, the lip as well as the shirt, and look firm and stern."

"And I was counting on shooting you quiet, adoring looks."

"Burst that bubble. Second floor." They took the steps, turned into a short hall with two doors on either side.

The absolute silence told her the building had excellent soundproofing, or everyone in the place was dead.

Eve pressed the buzzer beside 2B.

"Miss Dallas?"

At the sound of the voice through the speaker, Roarke firmed his lips against a grin and stared dutifully at the door.

"Lieutenant Dallas, Ms. Gable."

"I want to see your identification. Hold it up to the peep."

After Eve complied there was a long silence. "It appears to be in order. There's a man with you. You didn't indicate there would be a man with you."

"My associate, Ms. Gable. May we come in, please? I don't want to take up any more of your time than necessary."

"Very well."

There was another stretch during which Eve assumed various locks were being turned. Roberta Gable opened the door, and scowled.

Her identification photo was, if anything, flattering. Her thin face had the sort of hard edges Eve judged came from not only avoiding any of the softer areas of life but disparaging them. The grooves around her mouth indicated that the scowl was a regular feature. Her hair was pulled back so tightly it gave Eve a headache just to look at it.

She was dressed in gray, like her hair — a crisp shirt and skirt that hung on her bony body. Her shoes were black and thick soled, with laces tied in very precise knots.

"I know you," she said to Roarke, and sucked in so much air her nostrils flared visibly. "You are not a police officer."

"No, ma'am."

"Civilian consultants are often utilized by the police department," Eve put in. "If you have any questions about this procedure, you can call my commanding officer in New York. We can wait outside until you verify."

"That won't be necessary." She stepped back until they entered the living area. It was ruthlessly clean, and spartan. None of the frilly business Eve generally expected from older women living alone was in evidence.

No pillows or dust-catchers, no framed photos or flowers. There was a single sofa, a single chair, two tables, two lamps. It was as soulless, and just as welcoming, as a cage in a high-security prison.

One would not, she was sure, hear the dulcet sounds of a Carmichael Smith CD within these walls. That, at least, was one small mercy.

"You may sit, on the sofa. I will not offer refreshments this close to mealtime."

She took the chair, sat with her back straight as a poker, her feet flat on the floor with her knees pressed so tightly together they might have been glued. She folded her hands in her lap.

"You indicated you wished to speak to me regarding one of my former charges, but refused to give me a name. I find that quite rude, Miss Dallas."

"I find murder quite rude, and that's what I'm investigating."

"There is no need for sass. If you can't conduct yourself with respect, this interview is over."

"Respect's a two-way street. My name is Lieutenant Dallas."

Gable's mouth folded in, but she inclined her head in acknowledgment. "Very well. *Lieutenant* Dallas. I assume since you've attained that rank you have some aptitude for your profession, and some sense. If you'll explain, succinctly, why you've come to speak to me, we can conclude this matter and get back to our business."

"My questions will be of a highly confidential nature. I'm asking for your discretion."

"I lived and worked in private homes, among important families, most of my life. I am nothing if not discreet."

"One of those families included a son. Niles Renquist."

Gable's eyebrows shot up, the first genuine animation she'd shown. "If you've come all the way from New York to ask me about the Renquists, you're wasting my time and your own. Mine is valuable to me."

"Valuable enough, I'd imagine, to want to avoid being transported to New York and brought into formal interview." The threat was hot air. No judge would give her the power to drag a civilian across state lines on what little she'd gathered. But the idea of the inconvenience was often enough to elicit cooperation.

"I don't believe you can have me taken to New York like a common criminal." There was more animation now as temper put an almost rosy flush in Gable's cheeks. "I have no doubt my attorney could prevent such a high-handed tactic."

"Maybe. Go ahead and contact him, if you want to go to the trouble, the time, and the expense. We'll see who wins in the end."

"I don't care for your attitude, or your demeanor."

Gable's fingers had curled on her thighs, with the knuckles going white. A pincher. Eve was sure of it.

"I get that a lot. Something about murder just gets me all irritable. You can talk to me here and now, Ms.

Gable, in the comfort of your own home. Or we can start the bureaucratic ball rolling. Up to you."

Gable had a good stare, icy and unblinking. But it was no match for a cop with eleven years under her belt. "Very well. You can ask your questions. I'll answer what I deem appropriate."

"Did Niles Renquist ever demonstrate violent or disturbing behavior under your watch?"

"Certainly not." She sniffed even the thought of it away. "He was a well-bred young man from good family. I believe his current position and circumstance bears that out."

"Does he keep in touch with you?"

"I receive flowers on my birthday and a card at Christmas, as is proper."

"So, the two of you maintain an affectionate relationship."

"Affectionate?" Gable's face drew together as if she'd scented something vaguely unpleasant. "I neither want nor expect affection from any of my charges, Lieutenant Dallas, as I doubt you expect any from your subordinates."

"What do — or did — you expect?"

"Obedience, respect, and organized, well-disciplined behavior."

Sounded more like the army than the nursery to Eve, but she nodded. "And you received same from Renquist."

"Of course."

"Did you employ corporal punishment?"

"When appropriate. My methods, which served me and my charges well, were to suit the disciplinary action to the child and the offense."

"To your memory, what disciplinary actions most usually suited Niles Renquist?"

"He responded best to denial. Denial of recreation, society, entertainment, etcetera. He could and would become argumentative or sullen during the deprivation, but would, eventually, submit. He learned, as did all my charges, that there are consequences for unacceptable behavior."

"Did he have friends?"

"He had a suitably selected number of playmates and acquaintances."

"Selected by?"

"Myself, or his parents."

"And his relationship with his parents?"

"Was all that it should be. I fail to see the pertinence of these questions."

"Nearly done. Did he have any pets?"

"There was, I recall, a family dog. A miniature terrier of some sort. Sarah, the young girl, was particularly fond of it, and nearly inconsolable when it ran away."

"How old was Renquist when it ran away?"

"Ten or twelve, I believe."

"How about the young girl, Renquist's sister? What can you tell me about her?"

"She was a model charge. Amenable, quiet, and well-mannered. A bit clumsy and prone to nightmares, but otherwise biddable and good-natured."

"Clumsy how?"

"She went through a stage where she tripped over her own feet quite often, or bumped into objects and had more than her share of bumps and scrapes. At my recommendation the Renquists had her vision checked, but her sight was quite perfect. It was simply a matter of a lack of coordination, and a slightly skittish nature. She grew out of it."

"When would you say she grew out of it?"

"At about twelve, I suppose. She developed grace at a stage when many young girls lose theirs. Puberty is a difficult period, but Sarah bloomed during hers."

"And about this time, when she developed grace and stopped turning up with cuts and bruises, her brother was sent to Eton. Would that be about right?"

"I suppose it would. Doubtless having my undivided time and attention helped her gain more poise and confidence. Now, if that's all —"

"Just one more thing. Do you recall if there were any other family pets that went missing during your time with the Renquists? Other animals in the neighborhood that ran away?"

"Other people's pets weren't my concern. I have no recollection."

"Were you following me in there?" Eve asked Roarke when they stood on the sidewalk.

"Clear enough. You're looking to establish whether or not this Renquist had an abusive female authority figure in his childhood. Whether or not he, in turn, abused his younger, female, sibling. Whether or not he may, as is often the case with serial or torture killers, killed or tortured pets."

"Textbook stuff," Eve agreed. "And what's funny is she didn't follow the dots. That tells me she's either oblivious or stupid, hiding something, or the possibility she might have helped raise a psychopath doesn't enter her tidy little world."

"What's your money on?"

"The last one. She's a pincher, all right, and worse. You get a lot of her type in the foster system. Somebody like her wouldn't consider she had a mentally or emotionally twisted *charge* as long as the kid presented the illusion of submission."

"Did you?"

"Not so much, but I could when it was worth my while. And I know a lot of kids, most kids, come through something like that and lead normal lives. Renquist could be one of them. His sister might very well have been clumsy. But I don't like coincidence. I've got to mull this over and I've got to go meet the Boston cop."

"I'll drop you."

"No, better I catch a cab or take the underground. This guy sees me show up in a hot car with a fancy piece behind the wheel, he's not going to like me."

"You know how I love being referred to as your fancy piece."

"Sometimes you're my love muffin."

He managed a strangled laugh. She could, at the oddest times, surprise him. "And I try my very best to earn the name. In any case, I've got some business I can take care of. Why don't you contact me when you've finished, and let me know what comes next?"

"You're pretty amenable for a fancy piece."

He leaned down and kissed her lightly. "I've been thoroughly disciplined."

"My ass."

"Which is certainly part of the package. No rush," he added as he slid into the car. "I'm going to be at least an hour myself."

It took Eve over a quarter of that to travel through the hideous Boston traffic. It still put her at the bar and grill a half block from Haggerty's station house ahead of time.

It was a typical cop haunt — good, cheap food and drink with no fancy notes. Booths, a scatter of two and four tops, and plenty of stools along the bar.

There were a number of off-shift cops, in and out of uniform, winding down from the day. Attention slid her way when she entered, the brief beat of observation, then recognition of breed. Cop to cop.

She'd expected Haggerty to come in early — marking his territory — and wasn't surprised by the signal from a lone man at a table.

He was toughly built — bull-chested, big-shouldered, with a ruddy, square face topped by a short crop of sandy hair. He studied her as she crossed the room.

There was a beer, half gone, in front of him.

"DS Haggerty?"

"That's me. Lieutenant Dallas."

"Thanks for making time."

They shook hands; she sat.

"Want a beer?"

"Could use one, thanks."

She let him order it, since it was his territory, and let him take his time sizing her up.

"You got an interest in one of my open cases," he said at length.

"I got a vic. A strangulation, rape with object. A run-through IRCCA for like crimes turned up yours. My theory is he was practicing, perfecting, before he did the New York job."

"He wasn't sloppy in Boston. Neither am I."

She nodded, sipped her beer. "I'm not here to bust balls, Haggerty, or to question your investigation. I need a hand. If I'm right, the guy we're both looking for is working in New York now, and he's not done. So we help each other, and we shut him down."

"And you get the collar."

She drank more beer, let it simmer. "I take him in New York, I get the collar. That's the way it works. But your boss will know if any information you share with me aided in the arrest and conviction of this son of a bitch. And you'll close your case. Your cold case," she added. "Unless you're a fuckup, you'll be able to hang another murder on him. When this goes down, there's going to be a lot of media. You'll get your share of that, too."

He sat back. "Pissed you off."

"I start off my day pissed off. My investigation has led me to believe this asshole has killed at least six people to date. I suspect there are more, and I know goddamn well there *will* be more."

He sobered. "Stand down, Lieutenant. I was testing the waters. I don't give a skinny rat's ass about the media. Not going to say I don't care about the collar. Fucking right I do. My vic was beat to shit before he tied his goddamn bow around her neck. So I want him, and I got nothing. I worked the case hard, and got nothing. Yeah, officially it's cold, but it ain't cold to me."

He took a long drink of beer. "It's under my skin, and I work it whenever I get the chance. So you tell me you got a case in New York, and it brings you back here, to mine, I want a piece of it."

Because she understood, she lowered her hackles and took the first step. "He's imitating historic serial killers. One of the reasons he hit Boston —"

"Boston Strangler?" Haggerty pursed his lips. "I played with that awhile. Copycat thing. Had enough of the same elements. I studied up on those cases, looking for an angle to work. Nothing gelled, and since he didn't hit again . . ."

"He did a homeless woman in New L.A. before Boston, and he's hit New York. He's also killed three LCs, Paris, London, New York, by emulating Jack the Ripper."

"You've got to be shitting me."

"It's the same man. He left me notes with my two."

"Nothing like that with mine," he said, answering her unspoken question. "Don't have a single witness. The security system on the building, if you can call it that, was taken out the day before he killed her. Nobody got around to fixing it. Let me get out my notes."

She took her own from his. Before she'd drained her beer they'd agreed to exchange case files.

She checked the time, calculated. A call to the West Coast netted her a meet with the primary there. Another got her Roarke.

He seemed to be in some sort of a bar himself, but from the pretty lights, the quiet hum, and the glint of what she thought was crystal, it was several steps away from Haggerty's hangout.

"I've wrapped up here," she told him. "I'm on my way to transpo. How much time do you need?"

"Another half hour on this will do me."

"Fine. Just meet me there. I've got enough to occupy myself with until you show. Any problem for you if we head straight to the West Coast from here?"

"I believe I can find something to occupy myself with there as well."

She didn't doubt it. By the time he walked onto the shuttle, she'd reread her notes and was writing a report on her Boston leg for her team and her commander.

Roarke set his briefcase aside, cleared the shuttle to take off when ready, then ordered them both a meal.

"How do you feel about basketball?" he asked her.

"It's okay. Lacks the poetry of baseball and the sheer meanness of arena ball, but it's got speed and drama. What'd you do, spend your hour buying the Celtics?"

"I did, yes."

She looked up. "Get out."

"Actually, it took a bit more than an hour. We've been in negotiations for a few months now. Since I was here, I gave it the last push and we finalized it. I thought it would be fun."

"I spend an hour drinking a lukewarm beer and talking murder, and you buy a basketball team."

"We should all play to our strengths."

She ate because it was there, and filled Roarke in.

"Haggerty's thorough. Bulldog type, not just in build. In mindset. He hasn't let go of the case, and a lot of cops would have after this amount of time. He's kept picking at it but hasn't gotten anywhere. I just can't see what he missed. Might catch something when I see the full file, but he did the steps."

"And how does that help you?"

"Knowing he was here. Being sure of it. The dates. I can backtrack there, see if anybody on my list was in Boston, or just unaccounted for on the corresponding dates. See if maybe, just maybe, there's a connection between any of them and Haggerty's victim."

"Someone else is a bulldog," Roarke commented. "Not in body type, but certainly in mindset. I could check the transportation angle for you. See if any of your names show up on public or private transpos for those dates."

"I don't have the authorization for that. Yet. I'm going to get it. I pull the New L.A. and the European murders into the mix, and I'll get it. Any and all of my current suspects are high-profile enough that if I brush too close to the line, they could use it to get evidence tossed in trial."

"That's assuming they, or their attorneys, saw the brush strokes."

They wouldn't see Roarke's, Eve knew. No one would. "I can't use the evidence if I don't have the authorization to seek the evidence." But she'd know enough to be able to narrow the list. Enough, potentially, to save a life.

"I take him down, give him any wiggle room in the courts and he gets off, he'll kill someone else down the road. He won't stop until he's stopped. Not only because he enjoys it, he needs it, but because he's been working toward this for a long, long time. If I screw this up, all I do is put a hitch in his stride. Once he gets his rhythm back, whoever he kills is on me. I can't live with that."

"All right. I understand that. But, Eve, look at me now, promise me that if he kills someone else before you're able to stop him, you won't feel the same way."

She did look at him. "I wish I could" was all she said.

Detective Sloan was a young, eager beaver who'd caught the case with his older, more experienced, and less interested partner. The partner had since retired, and Sloan was partnered with a female counterpart who'd come along for the ride for the meet with Eve.

"It was the first homicide where I was primary," Sloan told Eve over chilled juices in a health bar. New L.A.'s version, she supposed, of the cop haunt.

The place was bright and cool, done in crisp colors and boasting a cheery waitstaff who were bouncy on their feet.

Eve thanked God she lived and worked on the other coast, where waiters were appropriately surly and never felt obliged to offer you something called Pineapple-Papaya Phizz as the special of the day.

"Trent gave it to me as a training exercise," he added.

"He gave it to you so he didn't have to lift his fat ass off his desk chair," the partner put in.

Sloan grinned amiably. "Might've played into it. The victim was one of the disenfranchised. I did track some family after we identified her, but nobody cared to claim the body. I got conflictings from the witnesses I managed to convince to talk to me. Though they were impaired by some form of illegals, the most substantial described a male — race undetermined — wearing a gray or blue uniform who was seen entering the building at or around the time of the murder. Victim was squatting, and since anybody else in the building was also there illegally, everybody worked at ignoring everybody else."

"You've got a hot one back in New York with a similar MO." The new partner's name was Baker, and both she and Sloan were attractive, healthy specimens with sun-bleached hair. They looked more like a couple of professional surfers than cops.

Unless, Eve mused, you looked at the eyes.

"We, ah, did a little research after you contacted me," Sloan explained. "Get a better handle on what you were looking for, and why."

"Good, saves me time explaining myself. You could reach out on this and let me have a copy of your case files, and walk me through the steps of your investigation."

"I can do that, and I'd like quid pro quo. My first case as primary," Sloan added. "I'd sure like to close it."

"*We'd* like to close it," Baker corrected. "Trent cashed it on his twenty-five, plans to spend the rest of his life fishing. He's not in this."

"Fair enough," Eve said.

This time when she was finished, she let Roarke pick her up. To her mind, any cops who weren't embarrassed to be seen drinking papaya juice couldn't blink at a fellow officer getting into a sleek little convertible. She stashed her growing bag of notes and discs behind her seat.

"I want to run by the scene, take a look at the setup."

"We can do that."

She gave him the address, waited until he'd programmed it into the onboard computer. "So, did you buy the Dodgers?"

"I'm afraid not, but you have only to ask."

She leaned her head back, let her thoughts circle while he drove.

"Can't figure out why anybody lives out here," she said. "Just because they've had the big one doesn't mean there's not another big one just waiting to flatten them."

"Nice breeze though," Roarke commented. "And they've certainly battled back the smog and noise pollution."

"Whole place feels like a vid, you know? Or a VR program. Too much peachy, pinky, white. Too many healthy bodies with perfect smiling faces on top of them. Creeps me. And I just don't think you ought to have palm trees waving around in the middle of a city. It's just not right."

"This should please you then. The building you want appears to be suitably shabby and unkempt, and the locals seem to be satisfactorily shady."

She sat up, stifled a yawn, and looked around.

Only about half the streetlights were working, and the building itself was dead dark. Some of the windows were riot-barred, others boarded. Several people skulked and slithered around in the shadows, and in one she spotted an illegals deal winding up.

"This is more like it." Cheered, she stepped out of the car. "This thing got full security?"

"It's loaded." He put the top up, engaged locks and deflectors.

"Her flop was on the third floor. Might as well poke around since we're here."

"It's always a pleasure to poke around in a condemned building where someone might stab, bludgeon, or blast us at any moment."

"You've got your kind of fun, I've got mine." She scanned the area, selected her target. "Yo, asshole!"

The chemi-head in the long black jacket rocked to the balls of his feet.

"If I have to chase you, it's going to piss me off," Eve warned. "Then I'll probably slip so that my foot ends up planted in your balls. Just got a question. You got the answer, it's worth ten."

"Don't know nothing."

"Then you won't make the ten. How long you flopped around here?"

"While. Not bothering nobody."

"Were you around when Susie Mannery got strangled, up on three?"

"Shit. I don't kill nobody. I don't know nobody. Prolly the men in white done it."

"What men in white?"

"Shit, you know. The guys from under the world. Turn themselves into rats when they want, then kill people in their sleep. Cops know. Some prolly be cops."

"Right. Those men in white. Blow," she told him, and started into the building.

"Where my ten?"

"Wrong answers."

She didn't get any right ones on her way to the third floor. Mannery's room was occupied again, but the current resident wasn't at home. There was a ripped mattress on the floor, a box of rags, and a very old sandwich.

Like the chemi-head outside, nobody she managed to roust inside had seen anything, knew anything, done anything.

"Wasting our time," she said at length. "This isn't my turf. I don't know who to push. And if I did, I don't know what help it would be. Living like this, people think you've given up. But Mannery hadn't. Sloan gave me a list of her personal effects. She had clothes, and a cache of food, and a stuffed dog. You don't haul around a stuffed dog if you've given up. She was probably zoned out when he came in on her, but she was still breathing. And he had no right."

Roarke turned her so that she faced him in the hot, filthy room. "Lieutenant, you're tired."

"I'm okay."

When he simply stroked her cheek, she closed her eyes a moment. "Yeah, I'm tired. I know about places like this. A couple of times, when he ran thin, we'd flop in places like this. Hell, it might've been here for all I know. I don't have all of it back."

"You need to shut down for a bit."

"I'll catch some sleep in the shuttle. No point in staying out here. I probably think better in New York anyway."

"Let's go home then."

"I guess I reneged on the out-of-town nookie."

"I'll put it on your account."

She dozed in the shuttle as it flew over the country, and dreamed of rats who become men dressed in white. Of a man without a face who strangled her with a long white scarf, and tied it with a pretty bow under her chin.

CHAPTER SEVENTEEN

Marlene Cox worked the ten to two shift, three nights a week at Riley's Irish Pub. It was her uncle's place, and his name was actually Waterman, but his mother had been born a Riley, and Uncle Pete figured that was close enough.

It was a good way to help finance her post-grad work at Columbia. She was studying horticulture, though her plans for what she wanted to do with the degree once she'd earned it were vague. Mostly she simply liked college, so she remained a student at twenty-three.

She was a slight and pretty brunette with long, straight hair and a pair of guileless brown eyes. Earlier in the summer her family had worried so much about her — several college students in New York had been murdered — that she'd canceled her summer classes.

She had to admit she'd been a little scared herself. She'd known the first girl who'd been killed. Only slightly, but still, it had been a shock to have recognized the face of a fellow student in the media reports.

She'd never known anyone who'd died before, much less known anyone who'd died violently. It hadn't taken much persuasion to convince her to stick closer to home, to take extra precautions.

But the police had caught the killer. She'd actually known *him* a little, too. That had been not only a shock but also a little exciting in a weird way.

Now that things had quieted down again, Marlene didn't give much thought to the girl she'd known slightly, or the killer she'd chatted with briefly at a cyber-club. Between her family, the part-time job, and her studies, her life was as normal as normal got.

In fact, it was just a little too normal at the moment. She couldn't wait for classes to get into a serious rhythm again. She wanted to get back in full swing, spending more time with friends. And she was toying with getting a bit more serious with a guy she'd started flirting with during her aborted summer session.

She got off the subway two blocks from the apartment she shared with two of her cousins. It was a good location — family approved — with quiet streets and a neighborhood feel. The short walk didn't worry her. She'd been taking the same route for over two years, and no one had ever bothered her.

Sometimes she almost wished someone would, just so she could prove to her doting family she could handle herself.

She turned the corner and saw a mini moving van, one of the rentals from the same company she'd used when she'd moved from her parents' place to the one she shared with her cousins.

It was a weird time for somebody to be moving in or out, she thought, but she heard thumps, and a couple of breathless male curses as she came up alongside of it.

She saw the man struggling to get a small sofa into the back. He was well-built, and though his back was to her, she took him to be young enough to manage it. Then she saw the thick white cast on his right arm.

He tried to muscle it up left-handed, using his shoulder, but the weight and angle fought against him, causing the end of the sofa to thump onto the street again.

"Damn it, damn it, *damn* it." He took out a white handkerchief, mopped at his face.

She got a look at him now, and thought he was cute. Under his ball cap, curly dark hair — her favorite on a man — spilled out over the collar of his shirt.

She started to walk by. Cute or not, it wasn't smart to talk to strange men on the street in the middle of the night. But he looked so pitiful — hot, frustrated, and just a little helpless.

Her good nature had her pausing; her New York caution had her keeping her distance. "Moving in or out?" she asked.

He jolted, making her bite back a laugh. And when he turned and saw her, his already flushed face went pinker. "Ah, looks like neither. I guess I could just leave the stupid thing like this and live in the truck."

"Did a number on your arm, huh?" Curiosity had her edging a little closer. "I've never seen a cast like that."

"Yeah." He ran his hand over it. "Two more weeks. Broke it in three places rock climbing in Tennessee. Stupid."

She thought she'd caught the South in his voice, and edged a little closer. "Pretty late at night for moving day."

"Well, my girl — ex-girlfriend," he said with a grimace, "works nights. She said if I wanted my stuff, I had to haul it out when she wasn't around. Another bad break," he added with a hint of a smile. "My brother's supposed to be here, but he's late. Typical. I want to get this stuff loaded before Donna gets back, and I've only got the rental till 6a.m."

He *was* cute. A bit older than her usual type, but she liked the hint of twang in his voice. Plus he was in a jam. "Maybe I could give you a hand with it."

"Really? You wouldn't mind? I'd really appreciate it. If we could just get this bastard in, maybe Frank will show. I think I could handle some of the other stuff."

"No problem." She stepped closer. "Maybe if you get up in the back, I could push it, and you could guide it or something."

"We'll give it a shot." He climbed in, hampered somewhat by the cast.

She did her best to lift and shove, but the end of the sofa thudded on the pavement again.

"Sorry."

"It's okay." He grinned at her, though she thought he looked exhausted. "You're just a little thing, aren't you? If you've got another minute, we could try it the other way. I can take the weight. Use my back, shoulders. Maybe you could come up in here, hold it steady, sort of pull while I push."

There was a vague ring from a warning bell in the back of her mind, but she ignored it. She clambered up into the truck, warmed by his grateful smile as he slid out.

He called out instructions as he grunted and cursed his brother, Frank, in a way that made her laugh. As the sofa began to slide in, she backed up, tugging it along with a fine sense of accomplishment.

"Mission accomplished!"

"Hold on, just a minute. Let me . . ." He boosted himself in, swiping his good arm over his brow. "If we could just shove it, that way."

He started to point, and though the warning bell had pealed louder when he'd climbed in with her, into the small dark cave, she glanced over at the direction of his finger.

The first blow caught her on the side of the head, and sent her staggering. She saw lights flash, and felt a terrible and confusing pain.

She stumbled, catching her foot on the leg of the sofa and pitching to the left without any idea that the spill saved her skull from a second, brutal blow with the cast.

It smashed her shoulder instead, had her whimpering as she tried to crawl away from the attack, from the pain.

She could hear his voice through the screaming in her head, but there was something different about it. Something ripped — her clothes, her body — as he hauled her back.

No, you don't. Sneaky little twat.

She couldn't see now, there was only dark and those awful flashing lights. But she tasted blood, her own blood, in her mouth. And she could hear, just hear through the screams in her head, horrible things panted out in a horrible voice.

She was crying, making tiny animal sounds that turned to moans as more blows rained on her back. With a trembling hand, she reached into her pocket, fighting to stay conscious, fighting to make her numb fingers grip the gift her uncle had given her when she'd gone to work for him.

With blind instinct, she pointed it toward the sound of his voice.

He howled — a grotesque sound that told her the mugger spray had hit the mark. The panic siren attached to the device wailed. Sobbing — she thought she was sobbing, but it might have been him — she tried to crawl again.

Pain, more pain exploded inside her when a vicious kick hit her ribs, her jaw. She felt herself falling, falling, and the world was already dropping away when her head hit the pavement with a violent crack.

At 4a.m., Eve stood on the sidewalk studying the blood on the pavement. Marlene Cox had been transported to the hospital an hour before. Unconscious, she was not expected to live.

He'd abandoned the rental, and his props, and left his victim bleeding on the street. But he hadn't finished her.

Eve crouched, and with her sealed fingers picked up a small shard of white plaster. She'd fought back long enough, hard enough to chase him away.

She studied the ball cap and wig already sealed in evidence. Cheap models, she mused. Tough to trace. The sofa looked old, shabby, used. Something he picked up at a flea market. But they had the moving van, so maybe they'd get lucky.

And a twenty-three-year-old woman was dying.

She looked up as Peabody sprinted down the sidewalk. "Lieutenant?"

"Twenty-three-year-old female," Eve began. "Identified as Marlene Cox. Lives in that building," she said, gesturing. "Apparently on her way home from work. I've checked with the hospital where she was taken before I arrived on scene. She's in surgery, prognosis poor. She was beaten severely about the head, face, body. He used this — to start, anyway." She held up a chunk of plaster.

"What is it?"

"Plaster. I'd say from a cast, an arm cast. Poor guy's trying to haul the sofa in or out of the truck. Probably in. He'd want to get her inside. Got a busted wing, can't quite manage it. He looks harmless, helpless, so she gives him a hand. He was probably charming. Lots of smiles and aw, shucks. Then when she's inside, he hits her. Goes for the head, needs to knock her down, debilitate and disorient. Keep hitting her, hard enough to smash the cast."

She stepped up to the opening in the back of the van. Close quarters, small space. That was a mistake, Eve noted. Didn't give himself enough room to really wind up for the hits, and the props — the couch, the packing boxes — got in the way.

The imitation was good, she decided, but the stage had been cramped and spoiled his performance.

"He didn't move fast enough," she said out loud. "Or maybe he was enjoying it too much. She had some mugger spray." Eve lifted the evidence bag with the pocket bottle. "I figure she got off at least one good shot in his face or near enough to hurt him, and the panic siren tripped. So he ran. From the looks of it," she added, nodding to the blood on the pavement, "she either fell out of the truck, or he shoved her out. Uniform that briefed me said there was so much blood from her head he thought she was DOS. But she had a pulse."

"Ted Bundy. I've been boning up," Peabody said when Eve looked at her. "Especially on the serial killers you put on your hot sheet. He used this method."

"Yeah, and more successfully than our guy. That's going to piss him off. Even if she dies, he'll be pissed off. Let's run the truck, Peabody. I've got some uniforms doing the knock-on-doors, and I'm about to set the sweepers loose on the rental. Let's fucking find something on this bastard."

Marlene was still in surgery when Eve got to the hospital. The surgical waiting area was packed with people. The nurse on duty had already warned her the patient's family was there, en masse.

She recognized the mix of shock, fear, hope, grief, and anger on the faces as, nearly as one, they turned toward her.

"I'm sorry to intrude. I'm Lieutenant Dallas, NYPSD. I'd like to speak with Peter Waterman."

"That's me." He rose, a big, burly man with a military cut to his dark hair, and the shadows of worry in his eye.

"If you could step out here, Mr. Waterman."

He bent to murmur to one of the waiting women, then followed Eve into the corridor.

"I'm sorry to pull you away from your family, but my information is you were the last to speak with Ms. Cox before she left for home this morning."

"She works for me, for us. I got a bar, and Marley, she waits tables a few times a week."

"Yes, sir, I know. What time did she leave?"

"Right after two. I sprang her, did the lock up myself. Watched her walk to the subway station. It's only a few steps from the door. She's only got two blocks to go once she's off. It's a good neighborhood. My two kids, they live there with her. My own daughters live right there."

And his voice shook on the statement so that he had to stop, just stop and breathe.

"My brother, he lives half a block from them. It's a good neighborhood. Safe. Goddamn it."

"It's a good neighborhood, Mr. Waterman." And small comfort. "When the panic siren went off, people came out. They didn't burrow inside and ignore it. We've already got a couple of witnesses who saw the man who attacked her running away. He might not have run if it wasn't a good neighborhood, if people hadn't opened their windows or come outside to help."

"Okay." He swiped the heel of his hand across his cheek, the back of his hand under his nose. "Okay. Thanks. I helped them find that apartment, you see. My sister, Marley's mother, she asked me to check the place out."

"And you found her a place where people come out to help. Mr. Waterman, a guy runs a bar, he notices people, right? You get a feel. Maybe you got a feel for somebody who'd come in recently."

"People don't come into my place looking for trouble. We got sing-alongs for Christ sake. We got regulars, and there's some tourist trade. I got a deal going with a couple of hotels. It's a middle-class, neighborhood pub, Sergeant."

"Lieutenant."

"Sorry. I don't know anybody who'd do this to our Marley. I don't know anybody who'd do this to anybody's daughter. What kind of sick bastard beats a little girl like that? Can you tell me? What kind of sick bastard does something like this?"

"No, sir, I can't tell you. Did she mention anyone she met recently, or anyone she noticed around the neighborhood, around where she shopped or ate or hung out? Anything at all?"

"No. Some guy she met in school earlier this summer. I don't know his name. One of my girls might." He took out a handkerchief, blew his nose. "We pushed her to drop her summer classes, because of those kids that were killed. Those college kids a few weeks ago. She knew one of them, the first one, so it upset her. Upset all of us. I got her that mugger spray, told her to keep it in her pocket. She did. She's a good girl."

"And she used it. That means she's smart and she's tough. She drove him off, Mr. Waterman."

"The doctors won't tell us." Eve turned as a woman spoke behind her. She'd come to the door and stood there, leaning on the opening as if she couldn't bear her own weight. "They won't say, but I could see what they thought. That's my baby they've got in there. My baby, and they think she'll die. But they're wrong."

"She's going to be fine, Sela." Waterman pulled her into his arms, held her tight. "Marley's going to be just fine."

"Mrs. Cox, is there anything you can tell me that will help?"

"She'll tell you herself, when she wakes up." Sela's voice was stronger than her brother's, and absolutely sure. "Then you'll go after him, and you'll lock him up. When you do, I'm going to come in, and look right at his face and tell him it was my girl, it was my baby who put him there."

Dallas left them alone, found a corner, a cup of coffee, and waited until Peabody returned and sat down beside her.

"No luck on the rental yet, but McNab and Feeney are on it."

"Smart. Careful," Eve commented. "Rents it via computer with a bogus name and license number, and pays to have it delivered to the bogus address. Nobody sees him. He seals up, so we've got no prints, no hair, no nothing inside the van except the wig he ditched and the pieces of plaster."

"Maybe some of the blood on-scene will turn out to be his."

Eve only shook her head. "He's too smart for that. But he's not as smart as he thinks he is because he didn't get Marlene Cox. Not the way he wanted. And somebody's seen him. Somebody saw him get in that rental or park it by her building. Just the way people saw him running like a scared rabbit away from the scene."

She took a long breath, a long sip of coffee. "The moving van, that was his stage set, so he was careful there. He wanted us to find her inside the van. But he had to run, with his eyes burning, his throat on fire from the spray. Had to get to his bolt-hole."

She looked over as a doctor in surgical scrubs came down the hall. On his face she could see what Sela Cox had seen — the grimness. "Damn it."

Eve got to her feet, and waited for him to go in and speak with the family.

She heard weeping, male and female, and voices down to murmurs. She was waiting when he stepped back out.

"Dallas." She flipped out her badge. "I need a minute."

"Dr. Laurence. She can't talk to you, or anybody else."

"She's alive?"

"I don't know how she made it through surgery, and I don't expect her to last the morning. I'm letting her family go in, to say good-bye."

"I wasn't able to speak to the MTs on-scene. Can you tell me about her injuries?"

He stalked over to a vending machine, ordered coffee. "Broken ribs. I'd say he kicked her. Collapsed lung, bruised kidneys, dislocated shoulder, broken elbow. Those are just some of the minor injuries. Her skull, that's a different matter. Ever taken a hard-boiled egg, run it with your palm over a hard surface to break up the shell?"

"Yeah."

"That's about what her skull looked like. The MTs got to her fast, and they did a heroic job, but she'd lost a lot of blood before they responded. Her skull's fractured, Lieutenant, and the damage is severe. There were bone splinters in her brain. The chances of her regaining consciousness, even for a few minutes, are slim to none. The odds of her being able to speak, have a coherent thought, motor functions — should that miracle occur?" He shook his head.

"I'm told she sprayed the guy," he added.

"There was a container of mugger spray on-scene," Eve confirmed. "The siren engaged. It was identified as belonging to her. My take is she got him; otherwise, he'd have finished what he started. I'm betting she got his eyes."

"I've put the word out. Anybody comes in this ER, or any other facility I've been able to reach with the symptoms, we'll send up a flag."

"That's helpful, thanks. Any change in her condition, one way or the other, I'd appreciate it if you'd contact me. Peabody? You got a card?"

"Yes, sir."

"One more thing," Eve said when he'd slipped it into his pocket. "You have much call to use this anymore?" She offered him a shard of plaster.

"Haven't used this since my intern days," he said, turning it over in his hand. "Still see it now and then, depending on the injury and the insurance. Plaster's cheaper than the skin casts used more habitually now. A break takes longer to heal, and the cast's cumbersome, uncomfortable. More likely to see these on low-income patients."

"Where do you get it, the stuff you make it from?"

"Medical supply company, I imagine. Hell, probably pick some up at a higher end rehab place, for people who want the old stuff, want authentic plasterwork."

"Yeah, that's what I was thinking. Appreciate it."

"Medical supplies or building supplies?" Peabody asked as they walked out.

"I want both. Cash sales. He won't want a paper trail. And I'm betting there aren't that many cash sales for this sort of thing. Small amounts, self-pickup. Delivery means he had to give an address. He walked in and bought this, paid cash, walked out. Run building supplies first," she decided. "Any Joe Blow can walk into one of them and nobody notices. That's his first choice."

She checked the time as she slid into the car. "Briefing in one hour. When we're done, we're going shopping."

She walked into her office and wasn't sure if she was annoyed or amused to see Nadine Furst sitting at her desk enjoying a cup of coffee and a tiny muffin.

"Don't snap and snarl. I brought you doughnuts."

"What kind of doughnuts?"

"Cream-filled, sprinkled with colored sugar." Nadine opened the small bakery box. "Six of them, and they're all yours, fatso."

"I like a good bribe. Now get out of my chair."

She walked to the AutoChef, ordered up coffee. When she turned back Nadine was sitting in her single visitor's chair, crossing her silky legs.

"I should rephrase. Get out of my office."

"I thought we'd have breakfast together." Nadine lifted the minuscule muffin to her lips, and took a bite Eve estimated contained three crumbs. "Dallas, I appreciate your stand on playing favorites, and the bitching and moaning from other members of the Fourth Estate. I've backed off. You have to agree."

"I'm not seeing your back, but with that shirt, I'm seeing a lot of your tits."

"Pretty, aren't they? But to remain on track, I've respected your stand because you had a point. I know you've fed Quinton some information — no more, no less, than you wanted out there. I respect that as well."

"We're just loaded with respect this morning." She took a huge bite of pastry. "Bye-bye now."

"He hasn't put it together. He may, especially after I give him a good nudge. He's bright and he's eager, but he's green. As yet, he hasn't wondered why you're primary on what is now three seemingly unrelated homicides."

"Crime is running rampant in our city. Run and hide. Better yet, move to Kansas. And it's two homicides, Nadine. Marlene Cox isn't dead yet."

"Sorry, my information was she wasn't expected to make it through surgery."

"She has. Barely."

"Even more curious then. Why our stalwart homicide lieutenant is picking at the threads of an assault." She took a tiny sip of coffee, rubbed her lips together. "I say we've got one killer employing a variety of methods. And this occurred to me when I got wind of the last —"

"Cox was attacked about two-thirty this morning. Shouldn't you have been asleep, or banging your flavor of the month?"

"I was asleep, and was awakened from my virginal bed —"

"Pig's eye."

"With an anonymous tip," Nadine finished with a little cat's smile. "I started wondering, then I started working, and I started asking myself what these three women had in common, besides you. I decided, the killer. The first was, obviously, an imitation of the infamous Ripper. What if the others were also imitations of previous crimes?"

"I'm not going to comment on this, Nadine."

"Albert DeSalvo and Theodore Bundy."

"No comment."

"I don't need you to comment." She leaned forward. "I can put enough together to go on the air with a story, with supposition."

"Then what're you doing here?"

"Giving you a chance to confirm or deny, or to ask me to hold the story I'm putting together. I'll hold it if you ask me, because you won't unless you need to."

"You're also thinking I won't ask unless you're right, and then you'll have a big, sexy story with big, sexy ratings."

"That plays, too. But I'll still hold it, if you need me to. And by holding it, I'm giving competitors the chance to come to the same conclusions I have."

Eve contemplated her doughnut. "I need to think a minute, so just be quiet."

There were pros and cons here, and Eve ran through them all while Nadine sat silently, eating her muffin crumb by crumb.

"I'm not going to give you data. I'm not even going to give you hints. Because when I'm asked, and I will be, I want to be able to say honestly that I didn't. That I wasn't your source. I'm not going to confirm or deny your supposition, which is what you'll have to say if and when you break this story. Lieutenant Dallas would neither confirm nor deny. I will, however, make a personal comment, between us girls. Besides having those pretty tits, you've got a sharp brain."

"Why, thank you. I've also got great legs."

"Now if I were doing this story, which I'm not, I'd wonder why this particular bag of nuts has so little personality, power, and imagination. He has to pretend he's somebody else to do the job. And the last time out, he flubs it up so bad, a girl about half his size hurts him and he has to run away."

Eve picked a sprinkle of colored sugar from the doughnut, laid it on her tongue. "Word is the primary investigating officer has a good idea just who he is, and is, at this time, compiling the evidence so that she can make an arrest, and ensure conviction."

"Are you?"

"I will neither confirm nor deny."

"You're bluffing."

"No comment."

"Big bluff, Dallas. I go out with this, and you don't make that arrest quickly, you're going to look like an asshole."

"The story's your business. Now that I've finished my doughnut, I've got to get back to my business."

"I break this, and it goes down this way, I'm going to deserve an exclusive one-on-one."

"I'll see about that, as soon as I consult my crystal ball."

Nadine rose. "Good luck. Serious good luck."

"Yeah," Eve murmured when she was alone. "I'm about due for some."

CHAPTER EIGHTEEN

She grabbed a conference room, brought in her disc files, set up her board. As she was finishing, Peabody came in.

"Lieutenant, I'm supposed to do that. It's my job to do that. How come you're not letting me do my job?"

"Bitch, bitch, bitch. I gave you another job. Did you inform Captain Feeney and Detective McNab of the time and place of this briefing?"

"Yes, sir, I —"

"Then why aren't they here?"

"Well, I . . ." She was saved as the door opened. "They are here."

"Good job then. All right, people, take a seat. I'm going to bring you up to speed on my out-of-town interviews, and why my conclusion is our target has practiced his skills in at least three other locations to date."

When she'd finished she was sitting on the corner of the table, drinking the coffee she noted Peabody provided her without request. "I'm pushing for the authorization to check travel on my suspects for the dates in question. The commander has agreed to put the pressure on, but as my list contains some influential names, it's taking time. I've bumped Carmichael Smith to the bottom. My opinion is he's too volatile and too pampered to fit the profile."

Peabody launched up a hand like the nerdy kid in class who screwed the grading curve for everybody else. "Yes, Officer?"

"Sir, couldn't the fact that subject Smith is volatile and pampered go toward profile rather than away?"

"These traits could play in, and his travel will be checked along with the others. But he's bottom of the list for now. Fortney's ahead of him, but not by much. We —"

When Peabody's hand shot up again, Eve found herself caught between amusement and irritation. "What?"

"Sir, sorry. I'm just trying to cross all the T's like in a sim. Doesn't Fortney fit profile, almost perfectly? His upbringing, his previously documented violence against women, his current lifestyle?"

"Yeah, but he's bumped down mostly because he's just such an asshole." She waited to see if Peabody would comment, and watched her aide's brow knit as she chewed over the response. "I think our guy has more style, which is why Renquist and Breen are neck-in-neck in my mind. I'm going to corner Breen's wife's lover today, and we'll see what that nets us."

"I hear she's smoking," McNab commented and earned a frigid look from Peabody.

"Of course, one of my primary concerns is the fact that she's smoking," Eve said coolly. "I've no doubt this attribute will assist us in identifying and apprehending a man who's killed two women and brutally assaulted another in under two weeks. Moving along," she said when McNab at least pretended to look chastised. "As you EDD guys didn't come in here doing the victory shuffle, I assume we haven't locked down the rental."

"Why don't you take this, bright boy?" Feeney said. "See if you can redeem yourself."

"He used a wireless unit," McNab began. "He didn't bother to bounce or filter, so it was fairly easy to trace back. The transmission for the order originated from the Renaissance Hotel. That's the fancy place on Park. You gotta be worth minimum of a mil just to get past the doorman. The van was ordered four days ago, at fourteen thirty-six."

"Lunchtime crowd," Eve commented.

"My guess is he frequents the place, knows where to go to shoot off a quick trans. Lots of big business types cart their pricey little portables to lunch meetings. Since he had very specific requirements for the order, he either had the trans ready to go, or he sat down in one of the privacy booths, or at a nice table with a glass of wine, and generated it there."

"Good. We'll see if any of our choices lunched at the Renaissance on the order date. Not smart," she said with a satisfied nod. "Smarter would've been to dress down, use a cyber-hole somewhere. A place nobody knew him. But he likes to show off. He likes to play, so he goes to an exclusive hotel, where I just bet they know him by name. Peabody? Tell me about the plaster."

"I've got building supply places in Brooklyn, in Newark, and in Queens who did cash transactions for small quantities of plaster in the past sixty days. None in medical supply places for that substance, cash transactions."

"None?"

"No, sir. Credit or purchasing order from established accounts. Then I got a brainstorm and checked art supply outlets."

"Art supply?"

"Yes, sir. You can sculpt with plaster, and other forms of art may utilize it. I got several hits in the city, several more in the boroughs and New Jersey for cash."

"Looks like we're going to be busy then." She checked her wrist unit. "The plaster from the scene's been in the lab long enough. If they don't have an exact match on the type, they should have. Let's see if Dickhead can earn his salary and tell us if there's a difference between household, medical, and art plaster."

She looked at Feeney. "Feel like getting out of the house?"

"Wouldn't mind a little fresh air."

"Let me know if you find any out there. Want to take the hotel?"

"Long as I don't have to wear a tie."

"Peabody and I will give Dickhead a push on our way to see the side dish."

"She might hit on you," McNab commented. "Maybe we should take her. Ow!" He grabbed his side where Peabody's elbow jabbed. "Jeez, just kidding.

Since you've been studying your brains out, you've got no sense of humor."

"I'm going to laugh really hard after I kick your ass."

"Kids, kids." Eve could feel her eye starting to twitch. "Let's save all this until after we catch the mean man and send him to his room. Feeney, control your moron. Not another word, Peabody."

She gave her aide a solid push out the door.

Peabody held it in until they'd driven five blocks. Eve figured it was a new record.

"I just don't think he should talk about other women that way. Or look at them with that gleam in his eye. We signed a lease."

"Oh Jesus Christ on stilts. You've got lease fear, Peabody. Official document phobia. Get over it."

"Jesus Christ on stilts?"

"It just came to me. You're obsessing because you signed up for — what is it, a year? And now you're all, what if it doesn't work out? Who moves out? Who takes the communal salad plates or some stupid shit."

"Well, maybe. But that's normal, isn't it?"

"How the hell do I know what's normal?"

"You're married."

Sincerely shocked, Eve jerked the vehicle to a halt at a light. "That makes me normal? It just makes me married. Do you know how many abnormal married people there are out there across this great land and beyond? Just take a look at the double Ds that get called in, Manhattan borough alone. Marriage doesn't make people normal. Marriage isn't normal, probably. It just . . . is."

"Why did you get married?"

"I . . ." Her mind went blank. "He wanted to." Hearing just how lame that sounded, she shifted in her seat, and punched the gas. "It's just a promise, that's all. A promise, and you do your best not to break it."

"Like a lease."

"There you go."

"You know, Dallas, that's almost wise."

"Now I'm wise." She sighed. "Let me give you my little tidbit for the day. You want McNab to stop thinking about, looking at, talking about other women, then you'd better take him to the vet and have him fixed. He'll make a nice pet. Women are the worst. They zero in on some guy. Oh boy, he's the one, gotta get me that one. So they do. Then they spend the rest of their time trying to figure out how to change him. Then if they manage it, they're not all that interested anymore, because guess what? He's not the one anymore."

Peabody was silent for several moments. "Somewhere in there is a lot of good sense."

"If you tell me I'm sensible in addition to normal and wise, I'm going to punch you in the stomach. I'm as screwed up as the next person, and I like it that way."

"In many ways, Lieutenant, you're even more screwed up than the next person. It's what makes you, you."

"I think I'll punch you in the stomach anyway. Put it on my calendar."

She toyed with double parking, which always put her in a good mood, but found a spot on a street ramp.

The Seventh Avenue building looked ordinary, even shabby, but the security there rivaled that at the U.N.

She passed through the first post, which required her badge, a palm print, and a scan. At the second post a uniformed guard requested her business and a second scan.

She looked around the small lobby with its aging linoleum floor and bare beige walls. "What, you keep government secrets in here?"

"More vital than that, Lieutenant." The guard offered a slight grimace as he passed her back her ID. "Fashion secrets. Competitors try every damn thing to get a peak. Delivery scams mostly, trying to get up to the design floor carrying deli bags or pizza boxes. But you get some more inventive ones, too. Phoney fire inspector last month. ID cleared, too, but the scan picked up his recorder and we booted him."

"You on the job?"

"Was." And he seemed pleased she'd made him. "Put in my twenty-five, most of it out of the one-two. This pays better, and it can get pretty lively around here before the big spring and fall shows."

"I bet. You know Serena Unger, designer here?"

"I might if you draw me a picture."

"Tall, thin, black, beautiful. Thirty-two. Short black hair with a reddish overcast, sharp face, long nose. Likes the ladies."

"Yeah, I know the one you mean. Got a Caribbean accent. You got a line on her?"

"She may be a line to somebody else. There's a woman she's playing with. About the same age. Blonde, snazzy looker. Five ten, curvy, slick, and professional. Married. Gates, Julietta."

"She's cleared through here a few times. Fashion writer. Seen the two of them go out together. Lunchtime, end of business day. Hold on a minute."

He turned to his computer, called up his log. "Last, hmm, last eight months by my log, Gates checked in for Unger ten times. Six months before that, six hits for Unger. A once a month deal. Go back four more, you only get two visits."

"Eighteen months." She considered the dates of the other murders. "Thanks."

"Happy to help. Here." He unlocked a drawer and took out two lapel pins. "Put these on and you'll clear through the rest of security, no hassle. You want the east elevator bank, fifteenth floor."

"Appreciate it."

"No problem. Miss the job sometimes. The rush, you know?"

"Yeah, I know."

Fifteen was a working floor with a hive of offices and a huddle of cubes for the drones. Unger didn't keep them waiting.

"You're prompt. I appreciate that." She stepped around her desk to offer a hand. "My day's stacked."

"We'll try to let you get back to it."

She closed the door, which told Eve she was discreet. It was a corner office, which told Eve she was successful, and it was stylishly decorated with beachy prints rather than fashion posters.

She gestured to two chairs, and took her own behind the desk.

"I have to say I'm a little confused as to why the police would want to talk to me."

She was good, Eve thought. But not quite good enough. Julietta had talked to her, and she knew exactly why they were there.

"If your day's stacked, Ms. Unger, why should we waste time doing the routine? Julietta Gates would have told you we've spoken to her, and her husband. You look like a bright woman, so you've figured out that we know about your relationship with Julietta."

"I like keeping my personal life personal." Unger swiveled in her chair, her body language relaxed, her voice cool and calm. "And I don't see what my relationship with Julietta has to do with your investigation."

"You don't have to see. You just have to answer questions."

Unger's perfectly arched brows rose into her high forehead. "Well, that's moving straight to the punch."

"I've got a pretty stacked day myself. You have a sexual relationship with Julietta Gates."

"We have an intimate relationship, which is different than a sexual one."

"So you just sit up in your hotel room at the Silby during your lunch breaks and chat?"

Unger's lips pressed together as insult moved across her face. Then she hissed out a breath. "I don't like being spied on."

"I imagine Thomas Breen doesn't much like being cheated on. We all have to live with what is."

She took a long breath. "You have a point. Julietta and I have an intimate relationship that includes sex, and one that she prefers her husband remain unaware of."

"How long have you had this intimate relationship?"

"We've known each other, professionally, for about four years. Our relationship began to change about two years ago, though we didn't become intimate right away."

"That would have been more like a year and a half ago," Eve suggested, and Unger set her jaw.

"You're very thorough. We have a great deal in common, and were attracted to each other. Julietta was, and is, restless in her marriage. This was her first affair, and it remains the only time I've entered into such a relationship with a married woman, or man for that matter. I don't like cheating."

"Must be hard doing something you don't like for a couple years."

"It's not without its difficulties, or its excitement. I won't deny that. Initially, we just forgot ourselves. But rather than the one-time thing we both assumed it would be, our feelings deepened. I enjoy sex." She shrugged. "In general, I find women more interesting in bed than men. But with Julietta I found more. A kind of mate."

"You're in love with her."

"I am. I am in love with her, and it's difficult as we can't be together openly."

"She won't leave her husband."

"No, she would. But she knows that I won't be with her if she does."

"Now you've lost me."

"She has a child. A child deserves to have both of his parents when this is possible. I won't be a party to removing that child, that innocent, from the security he has now. It's not the boy's fault that his mother loves me instead of his father. We're adults, and responsible."

"And she doesn't agree with your stand on this."

"If Julietta has a flaw, it's that she's not as good a mother as she could be. Not as devoted or involved as I think she should be. I'd like to have children one day, and I expect my mate to want and care for the child as I will. From all I know, Thomas Breen is an excellent father, but he can't be the boy's mother. Only she can."

"But he's not so hot as a husband."

"As he's not mine it wouldn't be accurate or fair for me to judge. But she doesn't love him, or respect him. She finds him tedious and too easily led."

"You were with her on the night of September second."

"Yes, at my apartment. She told her husband she had a late meeting."

"And you think he's buying it?"

"She's careful. He hasn't confronted her. She would have told me. To be frank, Lieutenant, I think she wishes he would."

"And the following Sunday morning, when she took the boy out. Were you with them?"

"I met them in the park." Her voice warmed. "I enjoy the boy."

"So you've spent time with him, the three of you together."

"Once a week or so. I want him to know me, so he's comfortable. When he's older, perhaps we'll find a way to blend our relationships."

"Has Julietta ever told you her husband is violent?"

"No. Believe me, if there was violence in the home, I would urge her to take the boy and leave. His work is odd, disturbing, but he appears to leave it at that. You suspect him of killing that woman in Chinatown. Lieutenant, if I believed him capable of such a thing, I'd get my lover and her son away from him. Whatever it took."

"You know the trouble with people having extramarital affairs, Peabody?"

"Explaining why you never wear all that sexy underwear you bought at home?"

"There's that. But it's the delusion. They really believe they're getting away with it. Some do, for the short haul, but there are always tells. Too many late nights at the office, secret 'link transmissions, the friend of a friend who happens to see you having lunch with someone not your spouse in some out-of-the-way restaurant. And beyond all that, if that spouse isn't in a coma, there's a sense — a look, a smell, a change in touch. Serena Unger's no dummy, but actually believes Breen hasn't got a clue."

"And you don't."

"He knows. His wife's been playing pass the strap-on with another woman for a year and a half, he knows."

"But if he does, how can he ignore it, just go around pretending everything's fine day after day? It would have to eat away at you, make you crazy . . . Which is exactly what you're getting at. If Roarke was fooling around with somebody, what would you do?"

"They'd never find the bodies." She tapped her fingers on the wheel as she sat in traffic. "Women are ruining his happy home, threatening his family. Worse, it leaves him feeling dickless. You spend all day writing about murder. You're fascinated with it. Why not give it a try? Show those bitches who's boss. I think it's time to bring him in and press him. But first we'll check out some of your plaster outlets. Maybe we can add weight."

Peabody pulled out her PPC, did a search for the closest address. "Village Art Supplies, 14 West Broadway. Lieutenant, I know you're looking sharp at Breen and Renquist, but I've got just the opposite direction, which I sincerely hope doesn't piss you off so that you remember to punch me in the stomach. I've seen you punch, and it's gotta hurt."

"If I got pissed off at everyone who disagrees with me . . . Oh, that's right, I do. But in this case I'll make an exception."

"Big thanks for that."

"Why do you disagree?"

"Okay." Peabody scooted around in her seat to face Eve's profile. "I think Fortney fits the profile more. He has no respect for women. He hits them and hits on them because it's a way to show what a big shot he is. He's hooked up with a strong woman because she'll take care of him, and the more she takes care of him, the more he resents it, and the more he cheats on her. He's got two exes who skinned him financially because he couldn't keep it in his pants, and without Pepper, he probably wouldn't be able to get a meeting in his chosen field. He's lied in interview to protect himself. His alibis have more holes than a pound of Swiss, and he's theatrical."

"Those are all good points, and a proud tear threatens my eye."

"Really?"

"About the tear? No. However, all those points you make are why he's still on the list."

"But when you lean toward a guy like Breen, I just don't see it. A man that sweet with his kid. And if he does know about the affair, isn't it more likely he's holding it together because he loves his wife and son, and just wants it to go away? As long as he doesn't acknowledge it, it's not real. I can see how somebody'd handle it that way. He could convince himself it doesn't count because she's not with another man. She's going through a phase, experimenting, whatever."

"You could be right."

"I could?" Emboldened, Peabody pressed on. "And Renquist. He's just too prissy or something. The whole Sunday brunch at ten routine. Then there's his wife. I can see her looking the other way if he likes to try on her underwear occasionally in the privacy of their own home, but I can't see her living with a psychopath.

She's too prissy. And she'd have to know. You could tell she has her finger on the pulse of that household, so she'd have to know something."

"I think you're right about that. Nothing gets by her. But I think she could live with a psychopath just fine. As long as he doesn't drip any blood on her floors. I met the woman who raised him, Peabody. He married the same basic type, just more upscale and stylish. But you think Fortney, I'll tell you what. If we haven't closed this by the day after tomorrow, you take him."

"Take him where?"

"Work him, Peabody. Make him your focus and see what comes up."

"You think we're going to close it."

"Soon. But you may get your shot."

They checked out three outlets before Eve decided it was time to go by the hospital to check on Marlene Cox. She acknowledged the guard she'd stationed outside the door, and told him to take a ten-minute break while Peabody stood as relief.

Inside, she found Mrs. Cox reading aloud from a book beside the bed while machines kept her daughter tethered to the world.

Sela looked up, then marked her place before setting the book aside. "They know people in comas can often hear sounds, voices, and respond to them. It can be like being behind a curtain you can't quite open."

"Yes, ma'am."

"One of us takes turns reading to her." Mrs. Cox reached over, fussed with the sheet that covered

Marlene. "Last night we put in a disc. *Jane Eyre*. It's one of Marley's favorites. Have you read it?"

"No."

"It's a wonderful story. Love, survival, triumph, and redemption. I brought the book today. I think hearing me read it would be comforting for her."

"I'm sure you're right."

"You think she's already gone. That's what they think here, though they're very kind, and they're working very hard. They think she's gone. But I know she's not."

"It's not for me to say, Mrs. Cox."

"Do you believe in miracles . . . I'm sorry, I've forgotten your name."

"I'm Dallas. Lieutenant Dallas."

"Do you believe in miracles, Lieutenant Dallas?"

"I've never thought much about it."

"I believe in them."

Eve crossed to the bed and looked down. Marlene's face was colorless. Her chest moved gently up and down to the rhythm of the machine that breathed for her in constant, whooshing notes. She saw death all over her.

"Mrs. Cox, he would have raped her. He would have been brutal. He would have done his best to keep her conscious during it so she'd have felt the pain and the fear and the helplessness. He would have reveled in that, and he would have taken some time to torture her. There were . . . instruments in the van he would have used on her."

"You want me to know that because she fought, she escaped that. She stopped him from doing those terrible things to her, and that's a kind of miracle." Her breath shuddered as she fought back a sob. "Well, where there can be one, there can be another. As soon as she can open the curtain she'll tell you who it was. They told us she probably wouldn't live through the morning. It's past noon now. Can you tell me, if you believe she's done, why you came in today?"

Eve started to speak, then shook her head and looked back at Marlene. "I was going to tell you it's routine. But the fact is, Mrs. Cox, she belongs to me, too, now. That's the way it is for me."

When her communicator signaled, she excused herself and stepped out into the corridor.

"Peabody," she said the minute she ended transmission, "with me."

"Have we got something?"

"I had a man watching Renquist's place. The nanny just took a cab to the Metropolitan Museum, without the kid. I've been looking for an opening to talk to her solo."

Sophia was doing a slow walk through French impressionism. Eve spoke briefly to the shadow, dismissed her, then wandered in the au pair's direction.

"Sophia DiCarlo." Eve held up her badge and watched the woman jolt and go pale.

"I didn't do anything."

"Then you shouldn't look so guilty. Let's sit down."

"I haven't broken the law."

"Then don't start now by refusing to speak to a police officer." It was hardly a criminal offense, but she could see Sophia didn't know that.

"Mrs. Renquist said I wasn't to speak to you. How did you find me here? I could lose my job. It's a good job. I do a good job with Rose."

"I'm sure you do, and Mrs. Renquist doesn't have to know you spoke with me."

To ensure some cooperation, Eve took her arm and drew her to a bench in the center of the room. "Why do you think Mrs. Renquist doesn't want you to talk to me?"

"People gossip. If the family and the staff are questioned by the police, people will gossip. Her husband is a very important man, very important. People like to gossip about important men."

She wrung her hands as she spoke. It wasn't often Eve saw someone actually wring their hands. Nerves, and something closer to fear, shimmered around the woman like warning lights.

"Sophia, I checked with INS. You're legal. Why are you afraid to talk to the police?"

"I told you. Mr. and Mrs. Renquist brought me to America, they gave me a job. If they're displeased, they could send me away. I love Rose. I don't want to lose my little girl."

"How long have you worked for them?"

"Five years. Rose was only a one-year-old. She's such a good girl."

"What about her parents? Are they easy to work for?"

"They . . . they are very fair. I have a beautiful room and a good salary. I have one full day and one afternoon off every week. I like to come here, to the museum. I'm improving myself."

"Do they get along? The Renquists?"

"I don't understand."

"Do they argue?"

"No."

"Not ever."

Sophia went from looking terrified to desperate. "They are very proper, at all times."

"That's hard to swallow, Sophia. You've lived in their home for five years and have never witnessed an impropriety, never overheard an argument."

"It's not my place —"

"I'm making it your place." Five years, Eve thought. At the going salary rate, the woman would have a reasonable financial cushion. The vague possibility of losing her job might upset her, but not frighten her. "Why are you scared of them?"

"I don't know what you mean."

"Yes, you do." It was in her eyes now, too easily recognizable. "Does he come to your room at night, when the girl's asleep? When his wife's down the hall?"

Tears welled up, spilled over. "No. No! I won't talk this way. I'll lose my job —"

"Look at me." Eve gripped Sophia's busy hands, squeezed. "I've just left the hospital where a woman is losing her life. You will talk to me, and you'll tell me the truth."

"You won't believe me. He's a very important man. You'll say I'm a liar, and I'll be sent away."

"That's what he told you. No one will believe you. 'I can do whatever I want because no one would believe it.' He's wrong. Look at me, look at my face. I'll believe you."

The tears had to blur her vision, but she must have seen something, seen enough to have the words come flooding out. "He says I must, because his wife will not. Not since she learned she carried a child. They have separate rooms. It is . . . he says it is the civilized way of marriage, and that it's my place to let him . . . touch me."

"It's not the civilized way of anything."

"He's an important man, and I'm just a servant." Though she continued to cry, her voice held a cold finality. "If I speak of it, he'll send me away, away from Rose, in disgrace. Shame my family, ruin them. So he comes to my room, and he locks the door, and he turns off the lights. I do what he tells me to do, and he leaves me again."

"Does he hurt you?"

"Sometimes." She looked down at her hands, and the tears that dripped on them. "If he's not able . . . not able to, he becomes angry. She knows." Sophia lifted her drenched eyes. "Mrs. Renquist. There is nothing that happens in the house that she doesn't know. But she does nothing, says nothing. And I know, in my heart, she will hurt me more than he could if she finds out I spoke of it."

"I want you to think back, to the night, the early morning of September second. Was he home?"

"I don't know. I swear to you," she rushed on before Eve could speak. "My room is at the back of the house, and my door is closed. I don't hear if someone comes in or goes out. I have an intercom for Rose's room. It's always on, except . . . except when he turns it off. I never leave my room at night, unless Rose needs me."

"The following Sunday morning."

"The family had brunch, as they always do. Ten-thirty. Exactly ten-thirty. No minute sooner, no minute later."

"Earlier than that. Say eight o'clock. Was he in the house then?"

"I don't know." She bit her bottom lip as she tried to remember. "I think not. I was in Rose's room, helping her pick her dress for the day. She must wear a proper dress on Sunday. I saw, from the window, Mr. Renquist drive to the house. It was perhaps nine-thirty. He sometimes plays golf or tennis on Sunday mornings. It's part of his work, to socialize."

"What was he wearing?"

"I . . . I'm sorry. I don't remember. A golf shirt, I think. I think. Not a suit, but something casual for summer. They dress carefully, both of them. Appropriately."

"And last night? Was he home all night?"

"I don't know. He didn't come to my room."

"This morning. How did he behave this morning?"

"I didn't see him. I was instructed to give Rose her breakfast in the nursery. We do this if Mr. or Mrs.

Renquist is very busy, or unwell, or if they have appointments."

"Which was it?"

"I don't know. I wasn't told."

"Is there any place in the house where he goes that you and the child aren't allowed?"

"His office. He's a very important man, doing very important work. His office is locked, and no one is to disturb him there."

"Okay. I may need to talk to you again. In the meantime, I can help you. What Renquist is doing to you is wrong, and it's a crime. I can make it stop."

"Please. Please. If you do anything, I'll have to leave. Rose needs me. Mrs. Renquist doesn't love Rose, not the way I do, and he — he barely notices the child. The other, what he does, it's not important. It isn't so very often, not any longer. I think he loses interest."

"If you change your mind, you can contact me. I'll help you."

CHAPTER NINETEEN

A call to Renquist's office netted her the information that he'd been called out of town, and would be unavailable for the next two days. She went through the formality of making an appointment upon his return, then drove to his house.

The housekeeper gave her the same information.

"You see him leave? You personally?"

"I beg your pardon?"

"You watch him walk out the door with his suitcase?"

"I fail to see the relevance of such a question, but as it happens, I carried Mr. Renquist's luggage to the car myself."

"Where'd he go?"

"I'm not privy to that information, and would not be free to divulge it if I were. Mr. Renquist's duties often require travel."

"I bet. I'd like to see Mrs. Renquist."

"Mrs. Renquist isn't at home. Nor is she expected to be until this evening."

Eve looked past her, into the house. She'd have given a month's pay for a search warrant.

"Let me ask you something, Jeeves."

She winced. "Stevens."

"Stevens. When did the boss get this call to duty?"

"I believe he made the arrangements very early this morning."

"How'd he find out he was hitting the trail?"

"Excuse me?"

"A transmission come in, a call, a private messenger whiz by, what?"

"I'm afraid I don't know."

"Some housekeeper you are. How'd his eyes look this morning?"

Stevens looked perplexed, then simply annoyed. "Lieutenant, Mr. Renquist's eyes are not my concern nor yours. Good day."

She thought about booting the door open when it started to shut in her face, but decided it was a waste of energy.

"Peabody, start the EDD troops doing a search to find out where Renquist went, and how he's getting there."

"I guess he's the one."

"Why?"

It was Peabody's turn to look perplexed and she hurried after Eve to the vehicle. "He's molesting the nanny. He and his wife lied about him being home all morning on Sunday. He's got a private, locked room in his house, and this morning, he's conveniently called out of town."

"So you cross off Fortney, just like that. Peabody, you're an investigative slut."

"But it all fits."

"You can fit it this way, too. He's molesting the nanny because he's a royal shit and a perv. His wife's not putting out, and he's got a young, pretty girl in the house who's afraid to say no. They lied because they're both royal shits who don't want to be hassled by the police, and saying he was home is more convenient. He's got a locked home office because he's got staff who might poke into sensitive material, and a kid he doesn't want bothering him when he's working. He's called out of town this morning because his line of work demands he get up and go when the call comes."

"Well, hell."

"If you don't think it from both ends, you don't get the right answers. Now let's see how Breen holds up in formal interview."

He was waiting, examining the one-way glass when Eve stepped into Interview Room B. He turned, and sent her one of his boyish smiles.

"I know I should be pissed off, and yelling lawyer, but this is just iced."

"Happy to entertain you."

"I had to leave Jed with a neighbor though. I don't trust the droid when I'm not in the house. So I hope this isn't going to take too long."

"Then sit down, and let's get started."

"Sure."

She engaged the recorder, recited the case data, and the Revised Miranda. "Do you understand your rights and obligations, Mr. Breen?"

"Oh yeah. Look, I heard the media reports on the attack early this morning. Guy pulled a Bundy. What do you think —"

"Why don't you let me ask the questions, Tom?"

"Sorry. Habit." He flashed a grin.

"Where were you this morning at 2a.m.?"

"At home, asleep. I knocked off work about midnight. By two, I was sawing them off."

"Was your wife at home?"

"Sure. Sawing them off right beside me, but in a delicate, ladylike manner."

"You think you get points for witty remarks in here, Tom?"

"Can't hurt."

Saying nothing, Eve shifted her gaze to Peabody.

"Well, yeah," Peabody responded. "If you piss her off, it can hurt. Trust me."

"Are you going to do the good cop/bad cop gambit?" He rocked back in his chair, balancing it casually on its back legs. "I've studied all the basic interrogation techniques. I can never figure out why that one works. I mean, come on, it's the oldest one in the books."

"No, the oldest one in the books is where I take you into a private room and during our little chat you trip and somehow manage to break your face."

He continued to rock while he studied Eve. "I don't think so. You've got an attitude for sure, and some innate violent tendencies, but you don't pound on suspects. Too much integrity. You're a good cop."

He spoke earnestly now, obviously high on his own intellect and intuition. "The kind that digs in and doesn't let go because you *believe*. More than anything else you believe in the spirit of the law, maybe not the letter, but the spirit. Maybe you take shortcuts now and then, stuff that doesn't find its way into your official reports, but you're careful about the lines — the ones you cross, the ones you don't. And beating confessions out of suspects isn't one of your shortcuts."

Now he looked at Peabody. "Nailed her, didn't I?"

"Mr. Breen, you couldn't nail the lieutenant if you made the attempt your life's work. She's beyond your scope."

"Oh, come on." He gave an irritated little twist of his lips. "You just don't want to admit I'm as good at this sort of game as you are. Listen, when you study murder, you don't just study murderers, you study cops."

"And victims?" Eve put in.

"Sure, and victims."

"All that studying, researching, analyzing, writing . . . that would hone your observational skills, wouldn't it?"

"Writers are born observers. It's what we do."

"So when you're writing about crime, you're writing about who committed it, who it happened to, who investigated it, and so on. In essence, you're writing about people. You know people."

"That's right."

"An observant guy like you, you'd pick up on nuances, on habits, on what people think, how they behave, what they do."

"Right again."

"So, being so observant, so in tune with human nature and behavior, you wouldn't have missed the fact that your wife's out having chick sex while you're at home playing horsey with your kid."

That wiped the smug look off his face as if she'd hit a delete button. What replaced it was the shock that turned the skin shiny white before the heat of humiliation and rage bloomed.

"You've got no right to say something like that."

"Come on, Tom, your amazing powers of observation haven't failed you inside your own little castle where a man is king. You know what she's been up to. Or maybe I should say down on."

"Shut up."

"It's gotta be a pisser, doesn't it?" Shaking her head, Eve rose, strolled around the table to lean over his shoulder, to speak directly in his ear. "She doesn't even have the courtesy to fuck another guy while you're home playing mommy. What does that say about you, Tom? The sex was so boring she decided to see what it was like in the other end of the pool? Doesn't say much for your equipment, does it?"

"I said shut up! I don't have to listen to this kind of crap."

Fists balled, he pushed up from the chair. Eve shoved him down again. "Yeah, you do. Your wife wasn't at a meeting the night Jacie Wooton was slaughtered. She was with her lover, her female lover. You know that, don't you, Tom? You know she's been sneaking off, cheating on you for nearly two years. How do you feel about that, Tom? How does it feel to know she wants another woman, loves another woman, gives herself to another woman while you're raising the son you made together, keeping the house together, being more of a wife than she ever was?"

"Bitch." He covered his face with his hands. "Goddamn bitch."

"I've got to have some sympathy for you, Tom. Here you are, doing it all. The house, the kid, the career. An important career, too. You're *somebody*. But you go the professional father route, and that's admirable. While she spends her day in a big office, having meetings about clothes, for Christ's sake."

Eve gave a hefty sigh, slowly shook her head. "About what people are going to wear. And that's more important to her than her family. She ignores you and the kid. Your mother did the same. But Jule, she takes it another step. Lying, cheating, whoring herself with another woman instead of standing up and being a wife, being a mother."

"Shut up. Can't you just shut up?"

"You want to punish her for that, Tom, who could blame you? You want to get some of your own back, who the hell wouldn't? It eats at you. Day after day, night after night. Makes you a little crazy. Women, they're just no damn good, are they?"

She sat on the edge of the table, close, pushing into his space, knowing he could feel her pushing, even as she felt him vibrating.

"She looks me right in the eyes and lies. I love her. I hate her for that, hate her because I still love her. She doesn't think about us. She puts that woman ahead of us, and I hate her for it."

"You knew she wasn't at a meeting. Did you stew about that while she was gone? And she came home, and went up to bed. Tired, too tired to be with you because she'd been with another woman. Did you wait until she was upstairs, settled in, before you left the house? Did you take your tools down to Chinatown, imagine yourself as Jack the Ripper? Powerful and terrifying and beyond the law? Did you see your wife's face when you cut Jacie Wooton's throat?"

"I didn't leave the house."

"She wouldn't know if you went out. She doesn't pay any attention to you. She doesn't care enough."

She saw him flinch when she said it, watched his shoulders hunch as if bracing for hammering blows. "How many times did you go down to Chinatown before you did Jacie in that alley, Tom? A guy like you does his research. How many trips did it take over there to scope out the whores and junkies?"

"I don't go to Chinatown."

"Never been to Chinatown? A native New Yorker?"

"I've been there. Of course, I've been there." He was starting to sweat now, and the cockiness had been replaced by shaky nerves. "I mean I don't go there for . . . I don't use LCs."

"Tom, Tom." Eve clucked her tongue and sat across from him again. There was a pleasant smile on her face and a look of amused incredulity in her eyes. "A young, healthy man like you? You're going to tell me you never paid for a quick blow job? Your wife hasn't been inclined to give you much of a bounce for what, close to two years? And you haven't made use of a perfectly legal service? If that's true you must be pretty . . . wrought up. Or maybe you just can't get it up anymore, and that's why your wife checked out the competition."

"There's nothing wrong with me." His color came up again. "Jule's just . . . I don't know, she just has to get this out of her system. And, okay, so I've hired an LC a few times since things have gotten messed up at home. Jesus, I'm not a eunuch."

"She's making you one. She's insulted, belittled, betrayed you. Maybe you were just going out to pick up some stranger. Guy's entitled when his wife shuts him out. Maybe things got out of hand. All that anger and frustration just built up. Thinking about how she'd lied to you, how she was in your bed fresh from another woman. Lying, cheating, making you *nothing*."

She let that single word vibrate in the room, let it slap at him. "You needed some attention, goddamn it. You've got a head full of men who knew how to get attention. Knew how to make a woman stand up and take notice. Had to feel good to rip into Jacie, into the symbol of her, to cut out what made her a woman. To make her pay, make them all pay for ignoring you."

"No." He wet his lips, and his breath shuddered through them. "No. You've got to be out of your mind. Out of your mind. I'm not talking to you anymore. I want a lawyer."

"Are you going to let me beat you, too, Tom? You gonna let some female cop beat you down? Once you call the lawyer, I win the round. Start whining lawyer, and I charge you with suspicion of murder in the first, two counts. Assault with intent, one count. I get to squeeze your balls blue, that is if you've still got balls to squeeze."

His breath hissed in and out, in and out in the silence that followed. And he turned his face from hers. "I don't have anything else to say until I've consulted with my attorney."

"Looks like it's my point then. This interview is ended to allow the subject to arrange for legal representation at his request. Record off. Peabody, arrange for the standard psych exam for Mr. Breen, and escort him to holding where he can contact his legal rep."

"Yes, sir. Mr. Breen?"

He got shakily to his feet. "You think you've humiliated me," he said to Eve. "You think you've broken me down. But you're too damn late. Julietta already took care of that."

She waited until he'd gone out, then she walked over and stared at her own reflection in the mirror.

Exhausted, she went back to her office. For once she couldn't face the buzz of coffee and opted for water. Standing by her stingy window, she drank like a camel, and watched the air and street traffic.

People came, people went, she observed. They didn't know what the hell went on in here. Didn't want to know. *Just keep us safe* — that was the bottom line when they gave the cops inside the building a passing thought. *Just do your job and keep us safe. We don't care how you do it, as long as it doesn't spill over on us.*

"Lieutenant?"

Eve continued to stare out the window. "You got him tucked?"

"Yes, sir. He's contacted the lawyer, and he's clammed. He requested a second transmission, re child care. I, um, I authorized it, with supervision. He contacted the neighbor and asked if she could keep Jed for several more hours. Said he'd gotten tied up with something. He made no request to contact his wife."

Eve simply nodded.

"You were pretty rough on him in there."

"Is that an observation or a complaint?"

"An observation. I know you're going to say I'm an investigative slut, but he's starting to look good to me. The way you sprang knowledge of the wife's affair on him, he never recovered from that."

"No, he didn't."

"And pushing the LC angle. The way he fumbled it, denying any association, then breaking down and admitting it to prove to you he was still sexually capable."

"Yeah, that was stupid of him."

"You don't sound too juiced about it."

"I'm tired. I'm just tired."

"Maybe you want to take a break before you wrap him up. The lawyer's got to get here, do the consult. You've got an hour anyway if you want to grab a bunk."

Eve started to speak, started to turn, and Trueheart stepped in. "Excuse me, Lieutenant, but Pepper

Franklin is here, wants to see you. I didn't know if you wanted me to pass her through."

"Yeah, go ahead."

"Do you want me to sit in?" Peabody asked her when Trueheart left. "Or go baby-sit Breen?"

"Fortney was your pick before you decided to be fickle. Let's both hear what she has to say."

She walked to her desk, sat, and swiveled toward the door when Pepper entered. The actress was wearing enormous silver sunshades and bright red lip dye. Her glamorous hair was pulled straight back in a long, sleek tail. The sunny yellow skinsuit was in direct opposition to the murderous expression on her lovely face.

"Get us some coffee, Peabody. Have a seat, Pepper. What can I do for you?"

"You can arrest that lying, cheating son of a bitch Leo, and drop him in the deepest, darkest hole you can find until the flesh rots off his fucking bones."

"No need to stifle your emotions in here, Pepper. Tell us how you really feel."

"I'm not in the mood for jokes." She whipped off the shades and revealed an impressive shiner. It would be more impressive in a few hours, Eve judged, when the blood finished gathering in bruises.

"Bet that hurts."

"I'm too mad to feel it. I found out he's been boffing my understudy. My goddamn *understudy*. And the assistant stage manager. And Christ knows who else. When I confronted him, he denied it, just kept lying, telling me I was imagining things. Have you got any vodka?"

"No, sorry."

"Probably just as well. I woke up about three this morning. I don't know why, generally I sleep like I'm in a coma. But I woke up, and he wasn't there. I was confused, and concerned, so I did a house scan. And damned if it didn't tell me he was there, in bed. Well, he wasn't there, in bed. He'd programmed it to say so, I suppose, if I ever got suspicious and ran a replay, the system would verify that he'd never left the house. *Bastard!*"

"I guess you looked through the place to make sure it wasn't a glitch, and he was in the kitchen raiding the AutoChef."

"Of course I did. I was worried." Bitterness spewed out like acid. "That was my only thought then. I looked all over the house, and I waited, and I thought about calling the police. Then it occurred to me he might have just gone out for a walk, or a drive, or Jesus, I don't know. And the security system was faulty. I convinced myself, and I actually dozed off in the chair about six. When I woke up a couple hours later, there was a message on the 'link."

She reached into a handbag the size of Nebraska and pulled out the disc. "Do you mind? I'd like to hear it again."

"Sure." Eve took it, slid it into her own 'link, and requested message play. Leo's voice spilled out.

GOOD MORNING, SLEEPYHEAD! DIDN'T WANT TO WAKE YOU. YOU LOOKED SO BEAUTIFUL SNUGGLED UP IN BED. GOT UP EARLY, DECIDED TO HEAD

STRAIGHT TO THE HEALTH CLUB, AND ENDED UP HAVING A BREAKFAST MEETING. YOU NEVER KNOW WHO YOU'LL RUN INTO. I'VE GOT A PRETTY FULL SCHEDULE, SO I WON'T BE BACK UNTIL AFTER YOU'VE LEFT TO RECORD THAT PROMO SPOT THIS AFTERNOON. YOU'LL BE GREAT! PROBABLY WON'T SEE YOU UNTIL AFTER THE SHOW TONIGHT. I'LL WAIT UP, 'CAUSE I MISS YOU, BABY DOLL.

"Baby doll, my butt," Pepper uttered. "He sent the transmission silent, about six-fifteen. He knows I'm never up before seven-thirty, never sleep past eight. He never came home last night, but he was covering himself. I went to his office, but he'd called that bimbo he's probably been doing and told her he wouldn't be in all day. She was surprised to see me as apparently he'd told *her* that I was having some sort of emotional crisis and he needed to stay with me. I'll show him an emotional crisis."

She rose, saw there wasn't room to pace, then dropped down again. "I postponed the promo spot, went home, and went through his office. That's how I found out he's been sending flowers and tasteful little gifts to his fucking harem, and I found receipts for hotel rooms, names and dates on his personal calendar. He showed up about three, looking all surprised to see me, all delighted." Her bruised eye flashed fury. "He'd had a couple of cancellations, and wasn't this lucky? Why didn't we go upstairs to bed, and get lucky again."

"I'm assuming you told him his luck had run out."

"In spades. I hit him with not being home all night, and he tried to make me think I'd been dreaming or sleepwalking. When I showed him the copies I'd made of his personal receipts and date book, he had the nerve, the fucking *nerve*, to act hurt and insulted. If I didn't trust him, we had a serious problem."

She paused, lifted a hand to indicate she needed a moment. "I couldn't believe what I was hearing coming out of his mouth. So smooth, so practiced. Well. Well."

"I don't have any alcohol in here," Eve said into the silence. "How about a hit of coffee?"

"Thanks, but just some water, if you don't mind."

While Peabody moved to take care of it, Pepper picked up her shades by the earpiece, twirled them. "No point in going into all the ugly details, but when he realized I wasn't buying, when I explained to him that it was done, he was out — out of the house, the office, the expense account, and my life — the shit hit the fan. And his fist hit my face."

"Where is he now?"

"I have no idea. Thanks," she said when Peabody handed her some water. "I expect you to find him, Dallas, and arrest him. I'd have worse than a black eye if I hadn't had a security droid on standby. I'd done that because I wanted the droid to escort him upstairs, wait while he packed up what belonged to him, and escort him out. Instead, when I called out, it came in while Leo was coming toward me, ready to hit me again. It hauled him up and heaved him out."

She drank, slow sips, until the glass was empty.

"He said vicious things to me," Pepper continued. "Crude, vicious, horrible things. It was my fault he was seduced — his term — seduced by other women because I was so controlling, even in bed. How it was past time he showed me who was in charge around here because he was through taking orders from . . . from some bossy cunt." She shuddered. "He was screaming that sort of thing at me before the droid came in. I was terrified. I didn't know I could be terrified, not really. I didn't know he could be the way he was in those few awful minutes."

"Get her some more water, Peabody," Eve ordered when Pepper started to shake.

"I'd rather be mad than scared." She dug into the bag again, found a lace-edged handkerchief, and mopped at her streaming eyes. "I'm all right when I'm just mad. I know about the woman who was attacked last night, and the report speculated it's connected with two murders — the ones you asked me about. And I thought, Oh God, oh God, I thought, Leo could have done it. The Leo I saw today could have done it. I don't know what to do."

"You're going to file a complaint, and we're going to bring charges of assault. We'll track him down and bring him in. He won't touch you again."

This time she only stared into the water Peabody gave her, and her voice dropped to a whisper. "I'm afraid to be alone. I'm ashamed that he's made me a coward, but —"

"You're not a coward. You just had some guy who outweighs you by a good thirty sock his fist into your eye and threaten to do more. If you weren't shaken up, you'd be stupid. You're not stupid because you came in and you're bringing charges."

"What if he killed those women? I slept beside him, I made love with him. What if he did those horrible things, then came home to me?"

"Let's take it one step at a time. Once we've done the paperwork, I can arrange for an officer to stay at home with you if you'd feel safer having a cop as well as your security droid."

"I would. I very much would. But I'd need him, or her, to come to the theater. I have a performance at eight." She smiled wanly. "The show must go on."

By the time she'd sent Pepper and her police escort off to Broadway, the stress and fatigue had a headache swirling behind Eve's eyes. She'd put out an APB on Fortney, and the dragnet was already spreading.

She met with Breen's attorney, let the preliminary complaints roll off her. But when he demanded his client be allowed to return home and tend to his minor child, she didn't argue. In fact, she surprised the attorney by postponing further questioning until nine the next morning.

And she assigned two men to stake out Breen and his house overnight.

She sat back down in her office, already past the end of shift, and thought about coffee, about sleep, about work.

When McNab jogged in, he looked so bright and energetic, it hurt to look at him.

"Can't you ever wear anything that doesn't glow?" she demanded.

"Summertime, Dallas. Guy's gotta glow. Got some news should put a glow back in your cheeks. Fortney booked a first-class seat on a shuttle to New L.A. He's en route."

"Quick work, McNab."

He shot out his index finger, blew on it. "Fastest EDD man in the east. Lieutenant, you look well and truly beat."

"Nothing wrong with your vision, either. Take Peabody home. Make sure she gets a good night's sleep, which is my delicate way of saying restrain yourself from rabbiting together half the night. She needs a clear and alert mind tomorrow."

"You got it. You might try that good night's sleep yourself."

"Eventually," she mumbled, then started the process of extraditing Fortney and arranging for local authorities to meet him when he stepped off the shuttle.

Peabody bounced in. "Lieutenant, McNab said you said —"

"I should just put in a revolving door because everybody just walks in and out as they damn well please anyway."

"The door was open. It's almost always open. McNab said I was relieved, but I haven't yet contacted authorities in New L.A. re Fortney, or transmitted the warrant."

"It's done. They'll pick him up, ship him back, and have promised to take just enough time to ensure he'll spend the night in a cell. He won't wrangle a bail hearing until morning."

"It's my job to —"

"Shut up, Peabody. Go home, get a meal, get some sleep. The exam starts oh eight hundred, sharp."

"Sir, I believe it might be necessary to postpone the exam as this case is at a crucial point. Fortney — and I see that my initial instincts there were right — will have to be interviewed, and you'll want to interview Breen and try to arrange an interview with Renquist to tie the matter up. I feel it's inappropriate for me to take a half day, minimum, for personal business during this stage of the investigation."

"Got the jitters?"

"Well, yeah, that, too, but —"

"You'll take the exam, Peabody. If you have to wait another three months to take it, one of us will jump off the nearest building, or more likely, I'll just pitch you off. I think, somehow, I can muddle through the day without you."

"But I think —"

"Report at Exam Room One, oh eight hundred, Officer. That's an order."

"I don't believe you can actually order me to take . . ." She trailed off, swallowed hard when Eve lifted her gaze. "But, ah, I understand the spirit of the statement, sir. I'm going to try not to let you down."

"Jesus, Peabody, you're not going to let me down whatever you do on the exam. And you'll be —"

"Stop." Peabody squeezed her eyes closed. "Don't say anything that'll jinx it. Don't say it, or any sentence with the word luck in it."

"You'd better go take a pill."

"I might." She gave a shaky smile. "Don't wish me the 'L' word, okay, but maybe you could do like a signal or a sign. You could do this." Peabody showed her teeth in a grin, widened her eyes to show enthusiasm, and punched out her fist with her thumb sticking up.

Leaning back, Eve cocked her head. "What is that? I'm supposed to signal you to stick your thumb up your ass?"

"No! It's thumbs-up. Jeez, Dallas. Thumbs-*up*. Never mind."

"Peabody." Eve rose, halting her aide before she could stalk out of the office. "Commencing at oh eight hundred hours, I expect you to kick exam butt."

"Yes, sir. Thanks."

CHAPTER TWENTY

When Eve dragged herself home, there was one thought uppermost in her mind. To get herself horizontal on a flat surface for one blessed hour.

Fortney was on his way back to New York, under wraps, and by God he could stew in a cage for a few hours. She'd deal with Breen in the morning, and Renquist. Though Smith was down on her list, he'd be watched for the next little while. But she couldn't watch anyone with eyes that felt like a couple of burnt cinders stuck in her face.

She just needed to stretch out, she told herself, give her head a chance to clear. She walked through a fog of fatigue into the cool and gorgeous quiet of the house.

The fog shimmered and tore apart. And Summerset stepped through it.

"You are, as usual, late."

She stared for a moment while her numbed brain struggled to process. Tall, bony, ugly, annoying. Oh yeah, he was back. She found the energy to peel off her linen jacket and tossed it on the newel just to irritate him.

It was amazing how much better the act made her feel.

"How'd you get through airport security with that steel pike up your ass?" Ordering herself not to stagger, she bent to pick up the cat who was busy threading himself between her legs. She stroked Galahad's head. "Look, it's back. Didn't I tell you to change the security code?"

"The disgrace you call a vehicle does not belong in front of the house, nor," he added, picking up her jacket with two thin fingers, "is this the proper place for articles of clothing."

She started up the stairs, stifling a yawn. "Bite me."

He watched her go, smiled thinly at her back. It was good to be home.

She went straight to the bedroom, managed to make it up to the platform, where she dumped the cat on the bed seconds before she fell facedown onto it herself.

She was asleep before Galahad padded his way over and curled up on her butt.

Roarke found her there, as he'd expected from the brief report from Summerset. "Finally hit the wall, have you?" he murmured, noting she hadn't removed her weapon harness or boots. He gave the cat an absent scratch between the ears, then settled down in the sitting area to work while she slept.

She didn't dream, not at first, but simply lay at the bottom of a dark pool of exhaustion. Only when she began to surface did the dreams come, in vague shapes and muffled sounds. A hospital bed, with a pale figure on it.

Marlene Cox, then herself as a child. Both battered, both helpless. Then the darker shapes that swirled around the bed. The cop she was, staring down at the child she'd been.

There were questions to be answered. You have to wake up and answer the questions or he'll do it again, to someone else. There's always another victim.

But the figure in the bed didn't stir. The face changed: from her own to Marlene's, to Jacie Wooton's, to Lois Gregg's, then back to her own.

Something began to rise up inside her that was both anger and fear. *You're not dead, not like the others. You have to wake up. Damn it, wake up and stop him.*

One of those swirling shapes coalesced, stood on the opposite side of the bed. The man who'd battered the child, and haunted the woman.

It's never really over. His eyes were bright with humor in his bloody face. *It never ends. There's always going to be another, no matter what you do. You might as well sleep, little girl. Better to sleep than to keep walking with the dead. Keep walking, and you'll be one of them.*

He reached over, pressed his hand over the child's mouth. Her eyes opened, full of pain, full of fear. Eve could only stare, unable to move, to protect, to defend. Only stare into her own eyes as they glazed over, and died.

She woke with a strangled gasp, and in Roarke's arms.

"Ssh. You're just dreaming." His lips pressed against her temple. "I'm right here. Hold on to me. Only a dream."

"I'm okay." But she kept her face buried against his shoulder until she got her breath back. "I'm okay."

"Hold on to me anyway." For he wasn't, never really was, when she wandered through nightmares.

"No problem." She could already feel her pulse begin to level off and the ugly smear of terror over her mind fade. She could smell him — soap and skin, and there was the lovely brush of his hair against her cheek.

Her world steadied.

"What time is it? How long was I out?"

"It doesn't matter. You needed to sleep. Now you need food, and more sleep."

She wasn't going to argue. She was starving. More, she recognized that tone in his voice, and it meant he'd find a way to pour a soother down her throat if she gave him the smallest opening.

"I could use a meal. But I could use something else first."

"What?"

"You know how sometimes you get in a mood when you touch me, when you love me, and it's all tender. Like you know I'm feeling raw inside."

"I do."

She tipped her head back, touched his cheek. "Show me."

"Here now." He feathered his lips over her brow, her cheeks, her mouth as he released her weapon harness. "Will you tell me what's wrong?"

She nodded. "Just be with me first. I need . . . I just need you."

He eased her back on the bed, slipped off her boots. He hated to see the shadows under her eyes, the shadows in them. She looked so pale, as if he could pass a hand through her, and if he did, she'd vanish like one of his own dreams.

He didn't have to be told to be gentle, didn't need her long, quiet sigh to know it was love that would feed her now.

"When I came in and you were sleeping, I thought: There's my soldier, exhausted from her wars." He lifted her hand, kissed her fingers. "Now, I look, and I think: There's my woman, soft and lovely."

Her lips curved as he undressed her. "Where do you get this stuff?"

"It just comes to me. I've only to look at you, and the world comes to me. You're my life."

She reared up, threw her arms around him. The sob wanted to leap out of her throat, but she feared if she let it out, it would never stop. With her lips pressed to the warm curve of his neck, she rocked. Take me away, she silently begged. Oh God, take me away, just for a little while.

As if he heard her, he began to stroke. Gently, to soothe, to comfort. Whatever he crooned quieted her troubled soul until she relaxed in his arms, and let him lead the way.

His lips were soft, soft and warm when they found hers. He took the kiss deep, but slowly, so she could drift into it, and into him, degree by degree. He felt her surrender to it, his strong and valiant soldier until she was pliant as wax, fluid as water.

Her mind misted over. There were no nightmares here, no shadows lurking in the corners. There was only Roarke, and those almost lazy caresses, those soft and dreamy kisses that took her under, into a quiet eddy of peace. Sensations layered, each one tissue thin, coating over the fatigue and the despair she hadn't realized had bloomed inside her.

His mouth cruised over her breast, stirred up her heartbeat as his tongue circled her, tasted her. She ran her hands over his back, tracing the shape of him, the muscle and bone. Death, with its infinite faces, was a world away.

When his mouth, his hands became more demanding she was ready, ready for those first shimmers of heat. Those long, liquid pulls inside her belly turned her sigh into a moan.

He took his time, endless time, arousing, fascinating, and being fascinated. Her body was a joy to him with its long, sleek lines, the supple skin, the surprising curves. He could watch the pleasure bloom on her, feel it spread through her with little quivers and shifts.

And at last, when they were both ready, he felt it burst through her, that gorgeous throaty moan, that lovely and helpless shudder.

The orgasm was a long hot wave that flooded body, heart, mind. The sheer release of it was glorious — like life. She would have folded herself around him then, wrapped him tight, taken him in, but he linked his fingers with hers and used his mouth to give her more.

She couldn't resist. He weighed her down with tenderness. And when a sob did escape, it was one of stunned joy as she crested again.

A thousand pulses beat, thickly. Nerves danced over her skin, shivering at every brush of his lips. Her muscles had gone lax, and everything she was lay open to him.

He watched her face as his lips rubbed lightly over hers. Her fingers tightened on his, and her lips curved before she said his name. Before she rose up to meet him.

When they were still and quiet, he lay with his head on her breast. He thought she might sleep again, more peacefully now, but she lifted a hand, threading her fingers through his hair.

"I was so tired," she said quietly. "I had to put the car on auto. I felt so weighed down and punchy and stupid. I had a pretty crappy day in a really crappy case. It's not just the victims, not just the women. It's like he's pointing a finger at me when he kills them."

"And that makes you one of them."

Thank God, was all she could think. Thank God he understands. "One of them, and not . . ." she said, thinking of her dream. "One of them, and the one who's standing for them when it's too late."

"Eve." He lifted his head, looked into her eyes. "It's not, it's never too late. You know that better than anyone."

"Usually. Usually I do."

There was something in her tone that had him sitting up, drawing her with him, then cupping her face so he could study it. "You know who he is."

"Yeah, I know. But the trick's stopping him, proving it, putting him away. I knew, in my gut, from the start. I needed to clear my head out so I could start taking the right steps."

"You need to eat, and tell me about it."

"I guess I need to eat, then I have to tell you about something else." She scraped her hair back with both hands. "I want to take a shower and pull myself together first."

"All right." He knew her well enough to give her room. "We'll have something up here. I'll take care of it."

Her throat filled, and she dipped her head so her brow rested on his. "You know something handy about you? You take care."

He wanted to gather her in then, to push her to tell him what troubled her mind. But he let her go.

She would run the water too hot, he thought, as he rose to get robes for both of them, to select the sort of meal that would do her the most good. Then she would stand under the spray, willing it to beat the energy back into her.

She wouldn't waste time with a towel, but step directly into the drying tube, and more heat.

No, she wouldn't sleep again, he knew as he set the meal in the sitting area. Not yet, not for a time yet. She would fuel, then she would work, then she would collapse. It was one of the most fascinating and frustrating things about her.

She came back wearing the robe he'd hung on the bathroom door, a thin and simple black robe he doubted she knew she owned.

"What is that green stuff?"

"Asparagus. It's good for you."

She thought it looked like something you'd whack out of a cartoon garden, but the fish and rice with it looked pretty good. So did the glass of straw-colored wine.

She went for the wine first, hoping it would make the green stalks go down easier. "How come stuff that's good for you always has to be green and funny looking?"

"Because nutrition doesn't come in a candy bar."

"It ought to."

"You're stalling, Eve."

"Maybe." She stabbed one of the stalks, shoved it into her mouth. It wasn't half bad, but she made a disgusted face for form.

"That's not what I meant."

"I know." She flaked off a bite of fish. "I had a dream about my mother."

"Dream or memory?"

"I don't know. Both." She ate, scooped up rice. "I think both. I was in an apartment, or a hotel room. I don't know which, but apartment, I think. Some dump. I was three, four. How do you tell?"

"I don't know."

"Me, either. Anyway . . ."

She told him of being alone, of going into the bedroom, playing with the enhancements, the wig, though she'd been forbidden.

"Maybe kids always do what you tell them not to. I don't know. But I . . . it was irresistible. I think I wanted to look pretty. I thought all that junk would make me look pretty. Dolling up, that's what they call it, don't they? I was dolling up because once, when she was in a good mood, she told me I looked like a little doll."

"Children," Roarke said carefully, "must, I think, have an instinctive need to please their mothers. At least during those early years."

"I guess. I didn't like her, I was afraid of her, but I wanted her to like me. To tell me I was pretty or something. Hell."

She shoveled in more food. "I got so into it I didn't hear them come back. She walked in, saw me. She belted me. I think she was jonesing — that's the cop talking, but I think she was. There were works on the dresser. I didn't know what they were. I mean as a kid I didn't, but . . ."

"You don't have to explain."

"Yeah." She kept eating. She was afraid the food would stick in her throat, but she kept eating. "She was screaming at me, and I was crying. Sprawled on the floor bawling. She was going to clock me again, but he wouldn't let her. He picked me up . . ." Her stomach roiled at the memory. "Shit. Oh shit."

When her fork clattered to her plate, Roarke reached over, gently eased her head down between her knees. "All right then, long and slow. Take long, slow breaths."

His voice was gentle, as was the hand on her head. But his face was murderous.

"I can't stand him putting his hands on me. Even then, it made my skin crawl. He hadn't touched me yet, hadn't raped me yet, but some part of me must've known. How could I have known?"

"Instinct." He pressed his lips to the back of her head as his heart ripped to pieces. "A child knows a monster when she sees one."

"Maybe. Maybe. Okay. I'm okay." She sat up, let her head lean back. "I couldn't stand to have him touch me, but I sort of curled into him. Anything to get away from her. From what I saw in her eyes. She hated me, Roarke. She wanted me dead. No, more. She wanted me erased. She was a whore. It was a whore's tools on the dresser. A whore and a junkie, and she looked at me as if I were dirt. I came out of her. I think she hated me more because I did."

Though her hand wasn't quite steady, she reached for the wine, used it to wet her dry throat. "I don't understand that. I thought . . . I guess I figured she couldn't be as bad as he was. I grew inside her, so there had to be *something*. But she was as bad as he was. Maybe even worse."

"They're part of you." She jerked when he said it, and he closed his hands over hers, kept his eyes fierce on hers. "What makes you, Eve, is the fact that you are what you are despite that. In spite of them."

Her voice was strangled, but she had to speak. "I love you a hell of a lot right now."

"Then we're even."

"Roarke, I didn't know, didn't realize, I wanted there to be something, to have something from her, until I realized for certain there wasn't. Stupid."

"It's not." His heart broke a little more as he brought her hands, one at a time, to his lips. "No, it's not. Was tonight the first you've had the dream?"

He saw it, the combination of guilt and embarrassment that rushed into her face. His fingers tightened on hers before she had a chance to draw her hands away. "That wasn't what this was about tonight." His tone was flat, a warning that made her hackles rise in defense. "How long ago, Eve?"

"A while. A few days. Last week. How the hell do I know? I didn't mark it on my damn calendar. Having a few dead bodies fall at my feet tends to prey on my mind. I don't have some handy admin keeping track of my every move and thought."

"You think turning this into a fight will distract me from the fact you've kept this from me for days? Before we went to Boston." Too angry to sit, he pushed to his feet. "Before that, before I asked you what was wrong, and you brushed me off with a handy lie."

"I didn't lie, I just didn't tell you. I couldn't tell you because . . ." She trailed off, shifted gears quickly. "I wasn't ready, that's all."

"Bollocks."

"I don't even know what that means." She speared another asparagus and ate determinedly.

"You made a decision not to tell me." He sat again, crowding her. "Why?"

"You know, ace, maybe you could bag your ego for five fucking minutes so this isn't about you. It's my deal, so — hey!"

She nearly slammed him back when he gripped her chin, but he outmaneuvered her, nudging her back so he could stare into her eyes. "But it is about me, isn't it? I'm following the path of your busy brain well enough now, I think. What I found out about my mother not long ago stopped you from letting me be there for you with this."

"Look, you're still messed up about it. You don't think you are — not the big, strong man, but you are. You've got bruises all over you, and I can see them, so I didn't figure dumping this on you would do any good."

"Because thinking of your mother, who had no love for you, would only bring the grief for my own, who did love me, closer to the surface."

"Something like that. Let go."

He didn't. "That's a flawed and stupid logic." He leaned in, kissed her long and hard. "And I'd have done the same, I imagine. I do grieve for her. I don't know if I'll ever stop completely. And I don't know how I'd have begun to get through it without you. Don't shut me out."

"I was just trying to give us both some time to settle."

"Understood. Accepted. But we seem to settle better together, don't you think? Where did she hit you?"

Staring at him, she touched the back of her hand to her cheek, then felt her heart stumble when he leaned in, touched his lips gently to the spot as if it were still painful.

"Never again," he told her. "We've beaten them, darling Eve. Separately, and together, we've beaten them. For all the nightmares and the bitterness, we've still won."

She took a breath. "Are you going to be pissed off when I tell you I talked to Mira about this a few days ago?"

"No. Did it help?"

"Some. This helped more." She toyed with her food again. "Cleaned me out. Maybe my brain will start cooking again. I was so off when I got home. I couldn't fling a decent insult at Summerset. And I've been saving up."

"Hmm" was Roarke's only response.

"I had some good ones stockpiled. They'll come back to me. But my head's crowded with this business, and the case. Then there's Peabody driving me over the edge."

"It's tomorrow for her, isn't it?"

"Thank God. I'll hit Fortney and Breen tomorrow while she's in exam. I can get Feeney to team with me. And then . . . oh, speaking of hitting, Fortney socked Pepper."

"Excuse me?"

"Blackened her eye. She came in, filed charges, so that smooths the way to holding him. I've shuffled things so he won't be able to whine for bail until tomorrow. I already had round one with Breen today. He started out smirky, but I wiped that off his face. I've got him shadowed until our scheduled interview tomorrow. Renquist is reportedly out of the city on business. I thought I might tug on one of my connections and see if that's the case or just a runaround."

"Would it be my ego talking again if I assume I'm that connection."

She gave him a quick, toothy grin. "You're pretty handy to have around, even *after* sex."

"Darling, that's so touching."

"I've got Smith locked down, too. I want to know where all of them are 24/7 until I can push for a warrant."

"And how do you know which of the four is your man?"

"I recognized him," she replied, then shook her head. "But that's gut, and you can't arrest on gut. There's only one who fits the profile, right down the line. Only one who'd have needed to feed himself by writing the notes. I need to eliminate the other three, build the case on the one. Once I tie the travel to the other murders, I'll have enough for a search warrant. He's got stuff — the paper, the tools, the costumes. He's kept all that. Tomorrow, the next day, I'll get in. And I'll have him."

"Are you going to tell me who it is?"

"I think we'll work on the elimination process, do the travel and murder dates. See if you start leaning in the direction I've taken. You've got a pretty good gut yourself. For a civilian."

"Such flattery. Then it appears we're going to work."

"Yeah, I — Shit." Her pocket 'link beeped. "I've got it," she said, leaping up to scramble to the platform where the bed stood and grab her trousers from off of the floor.

She dragged it out of a pocket, flipped it on. "Dallas."

"Lieutenant." Sela Cox's tear-streaked face filled the screen and had Eve's heart dropping to her knees.

"Mrs. Cox."

"She's awake." The tears kept falling even as she smiled. Brilliantly. "The doctor's with her now, but I thought I should tell you as soon as I could."

"I'm on my way." She started to click off, stopped herself. "Mrs. Cox. Thank you."

"I'll be waiting for you."

"I just got a miracle," Eve told Roarke and dragged on her trousers. Then she found she had to sit, just give into weak legs for one moment. "I saw her face. In my dream tonight. Hers, and the others, my own. I saw her face, and I thought she was dead. That I'd been too late for her, and she was dead. I was wrong."

She took a deep breath as Roarke came over to join her. "I saw him, too. My father, standing on the other side of the hospital bed. He said it never ended anyway. There's always another victim and I might as well give up before I was dead, too."

"And he was wrong."

"You're damn right." She pushed to her feet. "I'm not tagging Peabody. I want her fresh for the exam. Want to stand in?"

"Lieutenant, I already am."

CHAPTER TWENTY-ONE

She strode down the hospital corridor. She'd hooked her badge on her belt to stop any medicals from getting in her way. Roarke wanted to tell her the fire in her eyes would have done the job, but he was afraid it might dim that fierce light.

And he enjoyed seeing it too much to take the chance.

The guard she'd placed at the door to ICU was at attention when she turned the corner. In Roarke's opinion, the uniform had likely scented her energy and whipped himself on alert.

Even as she reached for the door, it swung open. The doctor, Roarke thought, was a more courageous soul. He barred her path, folding his arms across his chest and using a frown as a shield.

"I was told you'd been notified and were en route. The patient is barely conscious and drifting in and out. Her condition is still critical. I won't risk having her interrogated at this point."

"Twenty-four hours ago, you told me she'd never regain consciousness. She has."

"Frankly, I consider it a miracle she's come out of a coma, even briefly."

Sela Cox had asked for another miracle, Eve thought. And by God, she'd gotten it. "I don't believe in wasting miracles. Somebody put her in that room, and there's a chance she can tell me who before he puts someone else in the hospital. Or the goddamn morgue." Now her voice lashed like a whip that had the uniform wincing. "You don't want to get in my face on this."

"On the contrary." Laurence kept his melodious voice low. "I *am* in your face on this, and this is my turf. My patient's welfare is paramount."

"On that last point, we're in perfect agreement. I want her alive and well."

"For her testimony."

"Goddamn right. If you think that makes me the enemy, then you're just stupid. I put her in the dead column, Laurence, just like you. But she showed us both what she's made of. Now, I want her to know the man who did this to her has been put away. I want her to know I'm going to do that for her, and that she had a part in making it happen. Right now, she's just a victim. I'm going to help make her a hero. That's something to live for. You've got two choices," she said before he could speak again. "I have this officer restrain you, or you go in with me and supervise."

"I don't like your tactics, Lieutenant."

"File a complaint." She pushed open the door, glanced at Roarke over her shoulder. "I need you to wait."

When she stepped in her heart sank again. Marlene lay still and deathly pale in the bed. Her mother stood beside her, holding her hand.

"She's just resting," Sela said quickly. "When you said you'd come, I asked my husband to go down to the chapel. They'll only let two of us in here at a time."

"Mrs. Cox, I must tell you again, Lieutenant Dallas's presence is against medical orders. Your daughter needs to remain calm and quiet."

"She's been quiet since this was done to her, and she won't be calm until he's caught and punished. I'm grateful to you, Doctor, more than I can begin to say. But Marley needs to do this. I know my child."

"Watch your step," Laurence warned Eve, "or you'll be the one restrained."

She kept her focus on Marlene as she moved to the side of the bed. "You should talk to her, Mrs. Cox. I don't want to scare her."

"I've told her you were coming." Sela leaned over the bed, touched her lips to her daughter's forehead. "Marley? Marley baby, wake up now. Lieutenant Dallas is here to talk to you."

"So tired, Mom." The words were slurred and soft.

"I know, baby. Just for a little while. The lieutenant needs your help."

"I know you've been through a lot." Eve ignored the doctor as he edged closer. "I know this is hard. I'm not going to let him get away with what he did to you. We're not going to let him get away with it, Marley. You and me. You got away from him. You stopped him once. You can help me stop him once and for all."

Her eyes fluttered open. It was painful to watch, the effort of lifting those lashes, the intense focus in those eyes. Eve recognized the look, the determination of fighting back pain.

"It's all blurred, all runs together. Can't bring it clear."

"That's all right. Tell me whatever you can. You were coming home from work. You took the subway."

"Always take the subway. Just a few blocks. Hot night. Feet hurt."

"There was a van."

"Little moving van." Marlene shifted restlessly, but before the doctor could move, Sela was stroking her daughter's hair.

"It's all right, baby. It's all over now. Nobody's going to hurt you again. You're safe. I'm right here."

"Man. Big cast on his arm. Never seen big cast like that. Couldn't, couldn't get the sofa in. Kept sliding back out, thumping against the street. Felt sorry for him. Mommy."

Deliberately Eve stepped closer, took Marlene's other hand. "He can't get to you now. He's never going to touch you again. He thinks he beat you, but he didn't. You've already won."

Her eyes fluttered again. "I can't remember much. I was going to help him, then something hit me. It hurt. I never hurt like that. I don't know after that, I don't know." Tears began to leak. "I can't remember anything after that, except Mom talking to me, or Dad or my brother. Uncle Pete? Was Uncle Pete here, and Aunt Dora?"

"Yes, honey. Everyone's been here."

"I was just floating somewhere while they talked to me, then I woke up here."

"Before he hurt you, you looked at him." Eve felt Marley's fingers twitch in hers. "I bet you hesitated a little, got an impression of him. You figured he was okay, just some guy in trouble. You're too smart to go up to someone who looked dangerous."

"He had that big cast, and he looked so upset and frustrated. He was cute. Curly dark hair. Curly hair and a ball cap. I think. I can't . . . He looked over at me and smiled."

"Can you see him now. In your head? Can you see him, Marley?"

"Yes . . . I think. It's not clear."

"I'm going to show you some pictures. I want you to look at them and tell me if one of them is the man with the cast. Just see his face in your head, and look at the pictures."

"I'll try." She wet her lips. "I'm so thirsty."

"Here you are, sweetheart." All but crooning, Sela brought a cup and straw to her daughter's lips. "Take your time. Remember you're safe now."

"Hard to stay awake. Hard to think."

"She's had enough, Lieutenant."

At Laurence's voice, Marley stirred again, struggled to look toward him. "I heard you, when I was floating I heard you. You told me not to give up. That . . . you wouldn't give up if I didn't."

"That's right." It was the compassion in his voice, on his face that had Eve stifling her impatience.

"And you didn't give up," Laurence said. "You've made me look real good around here."

"Give me one more minute," Eve pleaded with him. "Just one more minute, Marley, and we'll be all done."

"You're the police?" Marlene turned her head on the pillow and looked impossibly young, impossibly frail. "I'm sorry. I'm getting mixed up."

"I'm the police." Eve drew out photos of her suspects. "When you look at these pictures, remember he can't touch you now. You got away, you didn't give up, and he can't touch you."

She showed them to Marlene one at a time, watching her eyes for that shock of recognition. She saw it, and the fear that rode with it.

"Him. Oh God, him! Mom. Mommy."

"Lieutenant Dallas, that's enough."

She elbowed the doctor back. "Marley. Are you sure?"

"Yes, yes, yes." She turned her face into her mother's breast. "That's his face. Those are his eyes. He *smiled* at me."

"It's all right. He's gone."

"I want you out. Now."

"I'm going."

"Wait." Marlene groped for Eve's a hand again, and turned her bruised and exhausted face away from her mother. "He was going to kill me, wasn't he?"

"He didn't. You beat him. And you stopped him." She leaned over the bed, spoke very deliberately as Marlene's eyes fluttered closed again. "You're the one who stopped him, Marley. You remember that. Don't ever forget that."

She stepped back while the doctor checked the vitals, the monitors. Then she turned and left the room.

"Got that son of a bitch," she said to Roarke and kept walking toward the elevator. "I need to go to Central, put this together. I still want you to check the travel dates. I want this ice cold and locked. I'll have my warrant within two hours if I have to strangle a judge to get it."

"Lieutenant! Lieutenant, wait." Sela rushed down the corridor. "You're going after him now."

"Yes, ma'am, I am."

"Did you mean what you said, that she'd stopped him?"

"I did."

She pressed her fingers to her lids. "That's going to get her through. I know my girl, and that'll get her through this. They didn't think she'd ever wake up. I knew she would."

"You sure as hell did."

Sela laughed, then clamped a hand over her lips to hold back a sob. "Dr. Laurence, I know he was rude to you, but he's been very kind to us, and worked very hard for Marley."

"I was rude right back. We're all just looking out for her."

"I just wanted to say that I've thought of Dr. Laurence as her guardian angel, and you as her avenging one. I won't ever forget you." She rose on her toes, gave Eve a quick peck on the cheek, then hurried away.

"Avenging angel." Embarrassed, Eve hunched her shoulders as she stepped into the elevator. "Jesus." Then she straightened, grinned fiercely. "I can tell you this, when I'm finished, Niles Renquist will see me as a demon from hell."

It was a tricky business, both politically and personally. Peabody was going to be pissed, and undoubtedly sulky, that she hadn't been called in. She'd just have to suck it up, Eve thought, as she prepared to make her pitch to Commander Whitney.

He was, she imagined, none too pleased himself to have been called back into Central. When she stepped into his office and noted the tuxedo covering his big frame, she fought back a wince.

"Sir, I'm sorry to have interrupted your evening."

"I assume your reasons for doing so will be strong enough to placate my wife." As Eve wasn't quite as successful in holding back the wince this time, Whitney nodded. "You don't know the half of it. You'd better have Niles Renquist cold, Lieutenant, because before I deal with my wife, I've got the ambassador, the U.N., and the British government in line."

"Marlene Cox has positively identified Niles Renquist as her assailant. I have a statement from Sophia DiCarlo, employed as au pair in the Renquist household, which conflicts with his and Mrs. Renquist's claim that he was home during the time of one of the murders. He is in possession of the stationery used for the notes left at the murder scenes, and he fits the profile. At this time Captain Feeney and expert civilian consultant Roarke are doing a search and scan on travel. I believe we will confirm that the subject was in London, Paris, Boston, and New L.A. at the time of previous murders, which match the methods of this case. Under ordinary circumstances, this would be enough for a search warrant and a warrant to bring the subject in for questioning on suspicion."

"But these aren't ordinary circumstances."

"No, sir. The subject's diplomatic status and the political arena add a sensitivity and a level of bureaucracy. I request that you speak directly with the judge and the necessary parties to expedite the warrants. He will kill again, Commander, and soon."

"You want my head in the noose, Lieutenant?" He cocked his head. "You have the statement of a woman in severe physical and emotional distress. A woman with head trauma. You have a statement from a household employee, who in your report claims to have been sexually abused by the subject. Those are both shaky. Owning or purchasing the brand of paper used in the notes isn't enough, and you know it, or Renquist would have been in a cage before this. And there are others who fit the profile. All of this will be argued by Renquist's representatives and attorneys, and the British government. You need to lock this down."

"If I get into his house, into his office, I'll lock it down. It's him, Commander. I know it's him."

He sat in silence, wide fingers tapping on the surface of the desk. "If you've got any doubt, if there's any room for doubt, it would be best to hold off on taking these steps. We can surveil, watch his every move until there is no doubt, and the case is a noose around his neck."

Good luck watching his every move if he gets back inside the U.N., Eve thought, but tried to put it more diplomatically. "Renquist may already be in the wind. Without the search, he stays in control. He's the only one who knows the identity and whereabouts of his next target. If he beats me to her, she may not be as lucky as Marlene Cox."

"Once the calls are made and the ball starts rolling, it could flatten both of us. I can survive it. I've had more years wearing a badge than you've had breathing. I can live with retirement. The ramifications of this should you be wrong will damage your career, perhaps irrevocably. Understand that."

"Understood, sir."

"You're a solid cop, Dallas, perhaps the best under my command. Is it worth pushing this forward now? Is it worth possible reassignment, losing your status in Homicide, and your credibility?"

She thought of the dream, of the dead and the victims yet to come. *There's always another*, her father had said. And damn him, he was right. "Yes, sir. If I weighed status more heavily than the job, I shouldn't be here. I'm not wrong, but if I were, I'd take the hit."

"I'll make the calls. Get me a goddamn cup of coffee."

She blinked at the order, looked vaguely around his office. The little twinge of resentment she felt as she walked to his AutoChef told her maybe status wasn't so far down on her list after all.

"How do you want it, sir?"

"Coffee regular. Get me Judge Womack," he said into the 'link. Then barked out a "Come" at the knock on his door.

Feeney hustled in, a grim smile on his face. Roarke strolled in behind him, grinned cheekily at Eve. "I wouldn't mind a cup, while you're at it."

"I don't serve civilians."

"Serve and protect, Lieutenant," he reminded her. "Protect and serve."

"Bite me," she mumbled under her breath and carried the coffee to Whitney's desk.

"We got 'em," Feeney said.

"Hold that call. What have you got?"

"Me and the civilian here did some E-finessing. If only the budget could afford this boy." With sincere affection, he slapped Roarke's shoulder. "Devious mind and magic fingers. Ah well."

"Cut through the bullshit, Feeney, and give me some weight."

"Our suspect took diplomatic, public, and private shuttles — and the private transpo was buried deep — to Paris, to London, to Boston, and to New L.A. He was in those cities during the time of the unsolved murders preceding the ones here. He frequently travels to London, as you'd expect. Less frequently to Boston. For London he uses the diplomatic transpo. For

Boston, public, though it's first-class and pricey all the way. But for the West Coast, he went private, and alone. Two trips by this method, the first, one month before the murder of Susie Mannery, the second, two days before with a return the following day — the day after the murder. Same pattern on the other unsolveds."

He turned to Eve. "Bull's-eye, kid."

Even with the added weight, it was almost midnight before Eve had the warrants in hand. Still, her earlier fatigue had burned away in a rush of adrenaline.

"How did you know?" Roarke asked as she drove uptown. "Walk the civilian through it."

"It had to be one of them. The stationery was too pointed, too much there for it not to be. He used it purposefully, to bring himself into it. The attention, the amusement, the excitement. He needs that."

She swung in behind a Rapid Cab, and let the cabbie plow the road for her. "But he'd have to know there'd be others, in New York, viable suspects. So he wouldn't have been the first to buy it. Smith was, and Smith would be easy to track. He's public, and he likes to make a splash."

"Go on," Roarke prompted.

"There's Elliot Hawthorne with his supply of the same paper."

"Speaking of him, he's divorcing his current wife. Something about a tennis pro."

She took time to smirk. "Figured Hawthorne would get around to it. He was a toss in, never seriously on my list. Too old for the profile, and nothing there. No pop."

"But you still had to take the time to check him out, had to have him in the general mix. That would've pleased Renquist."

"There you go. Then Breen, sending him the paper, just added a nice touch for Renquist. Breen was the expert, and someone Renquist probably admired. A month's pay says we find Breen's books in Renquist's office. He's studied Breen, the work and the man."

"You never thought it was Breen."

"Didn't fit. Arrogant enough, knowledgeable enough. But this isn't a guy who hates or fears women."

She remembered his devastated face as she hammered at him, remembered the broken look in his eyes. She'd have to live with her part in putting it there.

"He loves his wife, and that makes him a sap, not a murderer. He likes being at home with the kid. Probably he'd do it whatever the mother did. But I pushed him anyway, pushed him hard."

He heard the regret in her voice, and brushed a hand over her arm. "Why?"

"In case I misjudged him. In case . . ." She blew out a breath and tried to let the guilt blow out with it. "In case I was wrong. I liked him, right off, the same way I didn't like Renquist."

"So you worried part of it was personal for you."

"Some. And Breen could've been involved, that was an angle I had to factor in. He could've provided the killer with data, pooled all of it to put into his next book. How he acted and reacted, answered, didn't answer, in interview mattered."

"He'll get through it, Eve, or he won't. It's his wife who betrayed him, not you."

"Yeah, all I did was shatter his nice fantasy shield. Anyway, anyway. Renquist's got a good line on Breen. I bet he knows about the wife's sidepiece. I'll double that bet and say we'll find unregistered equipment in his office, equipment he's used to research and track the other suspects. He lined them right up for me, the son of a bitch."

"I value my money too much to take that wager. Why not Carmichael Smith?"

"Because he's pitiful. He needs a woman to adore him, and tend to him. He doesn't kill them or who'd rub his feet and stroke his head?"

"I appreciate a good foot rub myself."

"Yeah." She snorted. "Take a number."

He reached out to twist a lock of her shaggy hair around his finger, just to touch. And asked the next question just to keep her talking. "Fortney, then."

"Peabody's favorite. Mostly she leaned toward him because he offended her sensibilities. She's soft yet, you know."

"Yes. I know."

"She'll keep some of that, the soft." Eve tried not to think about the exam in the morning, and how much of Peabody's ego and esteem was wrapped up in it. "That's good," she added. "It's good she's got the makeup to keep some of it. You get too hard, you stop feeling, then the job's just being on the clock."

You've never stopped feeling, he thought. *You never will*. "You're worried about her."

"I'm not." She shot the words out, then hissed when he chuckled. "Okay, maybe I am. A little. Maybe I'm worried she's so nervous and sweaty about this damn, stupid detective's exam that she'll blow it. Maybe I wish I'd waited another six months to put her up for it. If she blows it, it's going to set her back — inside. It's so fucking important to her."

"Wasn't it to you?"

"That was different. It was," she said with conviction when he raised an eyebrow. "I wasn't going to blow it. I had more confidence in myself than she does. Had to. I didn't have anything else."

She surprised herself by smiling, looking over at him. "Then."

It didn't surprise her to feel his hand brush her cheek. "Enough mush. Back to Fortney. He clouded Peabody's thinking. He's a putz, and just not smart enough for this. Not an organized thinker, and not cold enough. Violent tendencies toward women, but a sock in the eye isn't mutilation. You gotta be cold to mutilate. And brave, in a screwed-up way. Fortney's not brave enough to go the whole route. For him, sex is his way of humiliating women. He bought the paper second, and I imagine that gave Renquist a smile — if he was following the purchases."

"And you believe he was."

She gazed at the rearview to make sure the team was still behind her. "Dead sure, and he likely did a search on Fortney and knew he'd be in New York during this period. Takes time to put on a show, months of lead time. Renquist didn't plan this overnight."

"Keep going."

Roarke was keeping her talking, she realized, so she wouldn't lose her temper and her patience with the traffic. Which was hideous. She toyed briefly with hitting the sirens and punching it. But that violated procedure. She'd do this straight, right down the line.

"He needed time to scope out his targets, so you've got several weeks between him sending the paper to Breen and the first murder. The first in New York," she amended. "We're going to find more bodies, or what's left of them, scattered over the planet, and possibly off."

"He'll tell you," Roarke deduced.

"Oh yeah." Her face was grim as she threaded through a narrow break between bumpers. "Once we get him in, he'll tell us. He won't be able to stop himself. He wants his place in the history books."

"And you'll have yours. Care about it or not, Lieutenant," Roarke said when she scowled. "You'll have yours."

"Let's stick with Renquist. He's a perfectionist, and he's had years of practice. In his work, within the image he's built, he has to be discreet, diplomatic, often subservient. And this goes against the grain, day after day. At heart, he's an exhibitionist, a man who finds himself above others — even as he's been hammered down by females all his life. Women are inferior, yet they have power over him, so they have to be punished. He hates us, and killing us is his greatest joy, his finest accomplishment."

"You were going to be his last."

She glanced over, saw him watching her. "Yeah, he'd have gotten around to me, later rather than sooner because he'd want to string this out. I saw it in his eyes the first time I met him. Just an instant. Couldn't stand the son of a bitch. I wanted it to be him."

She pulled up in front of the Renquist home, and the search team pulled up behind her. "This is going to be fun."

She waited for Feeney, let the team file in behind. Home security scanned her badge, then the warrant, before shifting to a holding pattern. Within two minutes, the housekeeper, in a long black robe, opened the door.

"I'm sorry," she began, "there must be some mistake —"

"This warrant authorizes me and my team to enter this residence and conduct a search thereof. I am also authorized to arrest Niles Renquist on multiple counts of suspicion of murder in the first degree, and a count of first-degree assault with intent. Is Mr. Renquist on the premises?"

"No, he's away on business." She looked more baffled than annoyed. "I'll need to ask you to wait here while I inform Mrs. Renquist of these . . . circumstances."

Eve held up the warrants again. "These mean I don't have to wait. But go right ahead and tell her we're here. After you direct me to Mr. Renquist's home office."

"I'm not . . . I can hardly take the responsibility for —"

"It's my responsibility." She signaled the team behind her to enter. "Split into groups of two. I want a complete and thorough room-by-room. All recorders on. The office?" she said to the housekeeper.

"It's on the second level, but —"

"You're going to want to lead the way, Stevens, then step back. You don't want a part of this."

Without waiting for the housekeeper, Eve started up the staircase. Stevens came after her in a trot. "If you'd just let me wake Mrs. Renquist and inform her —"

"As soon as you show me his office."

"It's the last door, on the right. But it's secured."

"You got the code?"

She pokered up then, struggling for dignity as she stood in her nightrobe surrounded by cops. "Only Mr. Renquist has the code. It's his personal office, and he handles sensitive material. As an official of the British government —"

"Yeah, yeah, blah blah." Eve decided she'd been right. This *was* fun. "My warrant gives me the right to open this door, with or without the code." She pulled out her master. "I am employing that authorization at this time, and using a police master code to disengage the subject's security on this door."

The housekeeper turned and fled up to the third floor. Mrs. Renquist, Eve thought, was about to get a rude awakening.

She used the master, and wasn't the least surprised to find the police code denied.

"He's taken extra precautions." She looked over her shoulder at Roarke. "At this time I find it necessary and expedient to employ alternate methods. If the electronic experts on team are unable to disengage locks, I will utilize the battering ram."

"Let's have a look first," Feeney suggested, and Eve deliberately turned her recorder away so that it wouldn't show Roarke crouching down with burglar tools in his hands.

"Feeney, I'm going to need you to confiscate all security discs. I suspect the subject doctored them, so that he wasn't scanned when he left the house for the murders and attack."

"If he did, we'll find the shadows." He tracked his gaze toward Roarke and had to bite down on a grin. Magic hands he thought again.

"I want all 'links and transmission devices as well." She didn't look at Roarke, kept her back to him. But her mind was muttering: *Hurry up, damn it, hurry up. I can't stall much longer*.

"Lieutenant," Roarke said a moment later, "I believe the locks are now disengaged."

"Good." She turned back. "We're now entering the private home office of Niles Renquist." She opened the door, called for lights on full, then took a deep breath. "Let's get to work."

The room was meticulously organized, even elegant in its choice of furnishings and decor. The antique desk held modern communication and data equipment, and what she concluded, after a puzzled study, was an old silver ink well and quill. There was a leather-bound notebook, an electronic calendar, and deeply cushioned chairs in dark, masculine green.

There was a neat black-and-white bath attached with the towels perfectly aligned on the rack.

He would wash up there after the murders, she presumed. She could see him perfectly, cleaning, grooming, watching himself in the long mirrors that shone on the walls.

She turned back, mentally measuring the room, and gestured to what looked to be a closet door.

"There. Five gets you ten his unregistered's in there."

She crossed the room, found the door locked. Rather than waste time, she waved to Roarke, then planted her feet at the sound of rushing footsteps.

With a pale peach robe swirling around her, Pamela Renquist rushed into the room. Her face was naked of enhancements, and looked older than it had. Her color was high, her teeth were already peeled back in a snarl.

"This is outrageous! This is criminal. I want you, all of you, out of my home immediately! I'm calling the ambassador, I'm calling the consulate, *and* your superiors."

"Be my guest," Eve invited, and all but slapped the warrant in her face. "I have all the proper authorization for this search, and I will complete same with or without your cooperation."

"We'll see about that." She started to march to the desk, and Eve blocked her. "You won't be able to use this 'link, or any of the house 'links until the search is complete. If you wish to make a call or send a transmission, you are restricted to the use of your personal 'links, in the company of a duly authorized officer. Where is your husband, Mrs. Renquist?"

"Go to hell."

"He's going to beat me there, I promise you."

She caught the signal from Roarke out of the corner of her eye, and moved over to the unlocked door. She opened it.

"Well, well, well, what have we here. A little hidey-hole, complete with data and communication center. We're going to find this is unregistered, Feeney. And look at all these discs. Renquist is a big fan of Thomas A. Breen, and his ilk. All these books and data on serial killers tucked in here."

"It's hardly against the law, even in this country, to have a private space, and to own books on any subject." But Pamela was losing her furious color.

Eve eased farther in, and opened a barrel-shaped leather bag. "Not against the law to own surgical tools either, but it sure is funny. I'm sure he cleaned these very well, but I just bet we find traces of Jacie Wooton's blood on them."

She opened a long cupboard, felt her own blood pump when she studied the collection of wigs, the black cape, the city employee uniform, and other costumes. "Niles likes to play dress up?"

She booted a container of plaster with her toe. "And does his own home improvements, too. A real Renaissance man."

Opening a drawer, she felt a little hitch in her heart. Then reached in with a sealed hand and picked up a gold band, set with five small sapphires.

"Lois Gregg's ring," she murmured. "I think her family will want this back."

"Got another of that sick bastard's souvenirs."

Eve turned, saw Feeney's face was white. He held the lid of a portable cold box, and she knew before he spoke what was inside.

"Looks like we found the rest of Jacie Wooton." Feeney breathed slowly through his teeth. "Son of a bitch has it labeled, for sweet Christ's sake."

Eve made herself look, made herself take the step over and look down into the container where the icy steam was already dissipating. Within was a clear, sealed bag, with its horror meticulously labeled:

WHORE

She whirled around quickly and caught the expression on Pamela's face. "You knew. Part of you knew, and you covered for him. Don't want any scandal, don't want any smudges on your perfect little world."

"That's ridiculous. I don't know what you're talking about." There was a green tinge to her skin now, as she stepped back from the closet and its awful contents. But her chin stayed high and firm, and her tone dismissive.

"Yes, you do. You know what goes on in your house. You make it your business to know. Why don't you take a closer look." Eve took her arm, gave it a little tug, though she had no intention of letting her into the closet. "Get a good up-close at what Niles has been up to. And think about when it might have been your turn. Or your daughter's."

"You're out of your mind. Take your hand off me. I'm a British citizen. I'm not under your aegis."

"You're hip-deep in my aegis, Pam." She stepped just a little closer. "I'm going to put him away. That's priority. And after I've got him in a cage, I'm going to make it my mission in life to get you on accessory."

"You have no right to speak to me that way. In my own home. When I'm finished with you —"

"We'll see who finishes. Feeney, get her out of here. House arrest, female guard. She gets one call."

"Don't you touch me. Don't you *dare* put your hands on me. I'm not leaving this room until I'm satisfied every one of you has forfeited your badge."

Eve tucked her thumbs in her pockets, stood with hip thrust out, and hoped. "You go voluntarily with Captain Feeney, or I add resisting and have you forcibly restrained."

Pamela's hand swung out. It was a girl move, and one Eve could easily have dodged or deflected. But she let it land, and got her wish. "I was so hoping for that. There's resisting and assaulting an officer. You just made my night." In a quick move, Eve had her restraints out. As Pamela blustered, she spun the woman around, jerked her arms back, and cuffed her.

"Have her transported to Central," Eve told Feeney. "Booked on resisting and assaulting an officer. She can stay in a box until we're through here."

Pamela kicked, swore with a vehemence and creativity that had Eve's eyebrows lifting. "I like her better that way." Rolling her shoulders as Feeney muscled Pamela out, Eve turned to Roarke. "I need to verify that this is unregistered equipment, which gives me another nice ball to add to the weight against Renquist. And I need all data contained within. What are you grinning at, pal?"

"You baited her so she'd take that swipe at you."

"So?"

"So I'm surprised you didn't take her out yourself."

"She's small change. I'm going to pocket that change before I'm done, but I want him first. I'm going to update the commander." She pulled out her communicator. "Get me that data."

Within fifteen minutes she had an all-points out on Renquist and was reading over Roarke's shoulder.

"It's all here," she noted. "Carefully logged. His travel, his trolling, his selection. Every victim, with chosen method. Tools, wardrobe."

"You'll notice he has quite a file on you, Lieutenant."

"Yeah, I can read."

"And," Roarke continued in that same cool tone, "that he intended you to be his crescendo. Using Peter Brent's cop-killing method. Long-range laser blaster."

"Which means he's got one in here. Better find it."

"And him. I want him now, as much as you."

She shifted her gaze, met his. "It's not personal." She waited a beat, shrugged. "Okay, what is it you say to crap like that? Bollocks. It's personal, but it can wait. I'm not next on his list."

She looked back to the screen. "Katie Mitchell, West Village. CPA. Twenty-eight, divorced, no kids. Lives alone, works primarily out of her loft. He's got everything on her. Height, weight, habits, routines, even her fucking shopping preferences. Stores, purchases. He's a thorough bastard. He's looking to do a Marsonini on her."

"Gain initial entrance by posing as a client," Roarke said. "Clone security. Enter again, when the victim is sleeping. Restrain, torture, rape, and mutilate, leaving a single red rose on the pillow beside them."

"Marsonini got six women with that method between the late winter of 2023 and the spring of 2024. All brunettes, like Mitchell, all home workers, all between the ages of twenty-six and twenty-nine. All bearing a slight resemblance to his older sister who had, reputedly, sexually and physically abused him in childhood."

She straightened. "We'll get this Katie Mitchell under wraps. If we don't find Renquist within the next forty-eight hours, he's going to find us."

CHAPTER TWENTY-TWO

There was no choice but to risk going directly to Katie Mitchell's apartment. If Renquist had it staked, it would spook him, but Eve couldn't risk a life.

If he bolted, she'd hunt him down.

With help from EDD, she had a list of residents and a layout of the building where Mitchell had her third-floor loft. She left Feeney in charge of the ongoing search of Renquist's home, and took Roarke along.

For ballast, she told him.

"You're too good to me, darling. Really, I'll get spoiled."

"Fat chance. Anyway, you've got a good touch with women."

"Now I'm blushing."

"I'm going to laugh my ass off any minute, then where will I sit? This woman may become hysterical. You're better with hysterical females than I am."

"Excuse me, did you say something? I was busy thinking about your ass."

She whipped her vehicle up a ramp and squeezed it into a second-level spot a half block from Mitchell's loft. "I'm sure that's entertaining —"

"You have no idea."

"But let's try to keep to the program. It's possible if we go in as a couple, straight in, he won't make me if he's staking out the building. I don't think he's around tonight. I think he's in some bolt-hole, putting it all together. Odds are we've got time, but I can't be sure. Marsonini always hit his victims between 2 and 3a.m. We're plenty early if he's marked her for tonight. But I want us to walk straight to the building, and in. How fast can you get through the security?"

"Time me."

"Let's move."

"I think you should hold my hand," he said as they started down the ramp. "You'll look less like a cop."

"Take the left." She switched sides with him. "I want my weapon hand free."

"Naturally." Even as he gave her arm a playful little swing, he saw her eyes, those cop's eyes, tracking, scanning, dissecting every shadow. "I'll need my hands free at the door. You could ease behind me. It wouldn't hurt to give my butt an affectionate little pat."

"What for?"

"Because I like it."

She ignored that, but did move behind him slightly as they climbed the short flight of steps to the building's entrance.

"It's cooled off considerably. I think we're done with the worst of the heat for the year."

"Hmm. Maybe."

"Why don't you lean in a bit, nuzzle my neck?"

"For cover, or because you like it?"

"As a kind of reward," he said and opened the door.

She hadn't even seen him finesse the lock. "You're pretty fucking slick," she commented and stepped in ahead of him.

She walked straight back to the steps rather than hassle with the elevator's security system. That would open, once cleared, directly into Mitchell's loft. Less traumatizing, Eve hoped, to knock on the hall door on the third level, and gain admittance that way.

"His log shows an appointment with her here, this afternoon," Eve continued. "That tells me he's already bunged up her loft security, and plans to move in tonight, tomorrow latest. I need to get her out, but I don't want cops around yet. We'll set up a unit in the morning, early." She knocked on the door, held up her badge, then turned to smile at Roarke.

"So I'm giving her to you. You'll transport her to Central, and she'll be transferred to a safe house until this goes down."

"And you plan to stay here tonight, alone? I don't think so."

"I outrank you."

Eve heard the click of the speaker engage, and the puzzled *Yes?* that came through it.

"Police, Ms. Mitchell. We need to speak with you."

"What's this about?"

"I'd like to come in."

"It's nearly midnight." Katie opened the door a crack. "Is something wrong? Has there been a break-in?"

"I'd like to discuss this inside."

She studied Eve's badge again, then glanced at Roarke. The double take was almost comical. "I know you." It was reverent. "Oh my God."

"Ms. Mitchell." Eve had to order herself not to act annoyed as Katie brushed at her hair with her hand. "May we come in?"

"Um. Yes. Okay. I was just going to bed," she said, apology in her voice as she tugged at the belt of a thin pink robe. "I wasn't expecting . . . anybody."

The living area was spacious and simple, with an opening on one side through which Eve could see a small bedroom. And through the opening on the other side was a larger, professional-looking office.

A long, galley-style kitchen was behind a low wall. She imagined the other door, which was discreetly closed, led to the bath.

Good windows, probably let in considerable light during the day, she judged. Two exits, including the elevator.

"Ms. Mitchell, you had an appointment today with this man."

Eve took a photo of Renquist from her bag.

"No," Katie said after a quick look. Her gaze went back to, and held on Roarke's face. "Would you like to sit down?"

"Would you please look at this picture again, more carefully, and tell me if this man was your three o'clock appointment this afternoon."

"My three o'clock? No, he was . . . oh, wait. It *is* Mr. Marsonini. But he had red hair. Long red hair done in a braid. And he wore these little blue sunshades the entire time. A little affected, I thought, but he was Italian."

"Was he?"

"Yes. He had a really charming accent. He's relocating here, from Rome, though he'll still have some business interests in Europe. He's in oil. Olive oil. He needs a personal accountant to work with his corporate people. Oh my. Has something happened to him? Is that why you're here?"

"No." She was measuring Katie as she'd measured the loft. As she'd concluded from the data and ID picture, Katie Mitchell was the same general build and coloring as Peabody. That might come in handy.

"Ms. Mitchell, this man's name isn't Marsonini. It's Renquist, and he's suspected of murdering at least five women."

"Oh, you must be mistaken. Mr. Marsonini was perfectly charming. I spent nearly two hours with him today."

"There's no mistake. Posing as a potential client, Renquist gained entrance to this loft for the purposes of cloning your security, having personal contact with you, and assuring himself that you did, still, live alone. Which I assume you do."

"Well, yes, but —"

"He has stalked you for some time, as is his pattern with his victims, gathering information on your routines and habits. He intends to enter this residence within the next forty-eight hours, most likely when you're sleeping. He would then restrain you, rape and torture you before using your own kitchen utensils to mutilate and kill you in the most painful way he could devise."

Eve listened to the little choked sound that creaked in Katie's throat, than watched the brunette's eyes roll back in her head.

"All yours," she said as Roarke swore and stepped in to catch Katie before she toppled over.

"You could have done that in a more sensitive and delicate way."

"Sure. But this was quicker. When she comes to, she can pack what she needs. Then you get her out."

He hefted Katie, headed with her to a sofa. "You're not staying here alone and waiting for him to come hunting."

"That's my job," she began. "But I'm calling for backup."

"Call for it now, and I'll have her out of your way inside twenty minutes."

"Deal."

She pulled out her communicator and prepared to set up the next stage of her operation.

She spent the hours until dawn sitting in the dark, waiting. A surveillance vehicle sat outside, and two armed uniforms were stationed in the living area of the Mitchell apartment. But the watch team had its orders.

Renquist, when he came, was hers.

And he sat in his quiet room in a small apartment on the edge of the Village. He'd decorated it carefully, selecting each piece so that it would have a European feel, and a rich one, rich and colorful and sexy.

So unlike the cool, stagnant home he shared with his wife when he was Niles.

When he was in this warm, deeply toned room, he was Victor Clarence. A small, amusing joke and a play on His Royal Highness Prince Albert Victor, Duke of Clarence, who some credited with the Ripper murders of Whitechapel.

Renquist liked to believe it, enjoyed the notion of a killer prince. He considered himself no less.

A prince among men. A king among killers.

And like that famed stylist of death, he would never be caught. But he was more than his prototypes. Because he would never stop.

He drank a brandy and smoked a thin cigar laced with just a whiff of Zoner. He loved these times alone, the quiet, reflective times when all the preparation was done.

He was pleased he'd decided to feign a business trip, to get away on his own for a few days. Pamela was irritating him more than usual with her long, speculative stares, her pointed questions.

Who was she to question him, to *look* at him?

If she only knew how many times he'd imagined killing her. The many and creative ways he'd devised. She'd run screaming. The image of his cold and rigid wife running for her life made him chuckle.

Of course, he would never do it. It would bring it all too close to home, and he was no fool. Pamela was safe simply because he was stuck with her. Besides, if he killed her, who would handle all the annoying details of his social life?

No, it was enough just to have these periodic rests from her, and the female she'd saddled him with. Irritating, sneaky little brat. Children were, as he'd learned from his dear old nanny, meant to be neither seen nor heard.

If they rebelled or failed to obey smartly, they were to be put somewhere, in the dark. Where they were no longer seen, where they couldn't be heard no matter how loud they screamed.

Oh yes, he remembered — remembered the dark room. Nanny Gable had had a way about her. He would like to kill her, slowly, painfully, while she screamed and screamed as he'd once done.

But that wouldn't be wise. Like Pamela, she was safe because he was stuck with her.

In any case, she'd taught him, hadn't she? Nanny Gable had certainly taught him. Children were meant to be raised by someone paid and paid well to discipline and tutor. Not that the sly little Italian thing disciplined his girl. Spoiled her, coddled her. But she was convenient. Her fear and loathing of him gave him such a rush of pleasure.

Everything in his life had finally fallen into place. He was respected, admired, obeyed. He was comfortable financially, and had an active and rarified social life. He had a wife who presented the proper image, and a young mistress who was just fearful enough to do anything, absolutely anything, he required.

And he had the most fascinating and entertaining hobby.

Years of study, of planning, of strategy. Of practice. It was all coming to fruition now in ways even he hadn't anticipated. How could he have known how much *fun* it would be to assume the guise of one of his heroes, and follow in their bloody footsteps?

Men who took charge, who took *life*. Who did what they wished to women because they understood, as others couldn't, that women needed to be debased, hurt, killed. They asked for death with their first breath.

Trying to run the world. Trying to run *him*.

He took a slow drag of the cigar, letting the Zoner calm him before one of his rages could take over. It wasn't the time for rage, but for cool, calculating action.

He worried that he'd been too clever. But really, could one be too clever? Some might consider it a mistake to have deliberately put himself forward as a suspect. But it was so much more satisfying, so much more exciting that way. It allowed him to participate on two levels and made it all so intimate.

In a way, he'd already fucked the whore cop. What a thrill it was to watch her scramble around, unable to outthink him, to anticipate him. Being forced to come to him and *apologize*. He hugged himself as he played that scene over in his head. Oh, that had been a *moment*.

Selecting Eve Dallas had been a brilliant stroke, if he did say so himself. And oh, he did.

A man wouldn't have given him nearly the same buzz. But a woman, a woman who like most of her kind considered herself superior to a man simply because she could trap him between her legs. That added spice to the brew.

He could think about choking her, beating her, raping her, gutting her even as she watched him with those cool, flat eyes.

He would never have known the same level of excitement with a male adversary.

She would be punished, of course, when she failed to stop him. When others were killed, as the accountant bitch would be killed. The lieutenant would be punished and disciplined by her superiors, as it should be.

And she would suffer, never knowing who'd bested her, she would suffer until the laser blast struck her in the back of the head.

If only he could find a way to let her know, to tell her, reveal himself to her an instant before her death. Then it would be perfect.

There was time, of course, to work that out.

Content, he settled into bed, to dream his terrible dreams.

They had obviously been off by a night, Eve thought, as she set up the morning briefing in her home office with a small, tight team. She didn't want to risk Central, or a larger operation. A leak, even a trickle might send Renquist into the wind. Now they could tighten the trap so he'd never get away.

She used her board, the wall screens, and one of Roarke's new toys, a portable holo-unit.

"We'll have units set here, and here." She highlighted the map on-screen with a laser pointer. "They are for observation only. I want to take Renquist inside the loft where he can be contained and no civilians are at risk. We moved Mitchell's across-the-hall neighbor out at oh seven hundred on the pretext of a broken water pipe. The cooperation of the building super is ensured and we've got him under wraps in case he gets an itch to share any of this with the media. The empty loft will be Observation Post C."

She highlighted the third floor of the building blueprint on the second screen. "We're installing cameras. The loft will be under constant observation. It's unlikely Renquist will use the elevator, but we'll have cameras there as well. And once he's inside the loft, the power to the elevator will be shut down, giving him only one exit. A team will move in to block that exit, another will be set on the street below in case he decides to take a header from the windows."

"Rat in a trap," Feeney commented.

"That's the idea. I'll be inside the loft, as will Officer Peabody, who will be briefed when her examination is finished. Captain Feeney will run electronics from Mitchell's home office inside the loft, and Detective McNab will head Observation Post C."

She ordered up the holo and brought a scaled-down version of the Mitchell loft into her office. "Memorize it," she ordered. "Officer Peabody will be decoy. She and the target are approximately the same size and coloring. She'll be in the bed here, I'll be posted in this closet. Getting Renquist in the bedroom is optimum. No windows, no escape route."

"He'll be armed," McNab put in.

She nodded, noting the worry in his eyes. That was the trouble, she thought, when a cop fell for another cop. "So will we. It's possible he'll bring his own blades, or that he'll detour into the kitchen first to avail himself of Mitchell's kitchen stock. He may have a blaster or another weapon, though he has yet to utilize one. We will go into this assuming he's armed, as Marsonini habitually carried a blaster or stunner, and act accordingly."

She waited a beat. "We're working on finding him before tonight. He's in the city, and as he's emulating Marsonini, it's likely he's settled in somewhere near his target's home. Marsonini habitually had a good meal, with wine, on the evening before a murder. He dressed well, generally in suits by Italian designers, and carried his tools in an expensive briefcase. He did his work to opera, again Italian. He spoke with an accent, though it was affected as he was born in St. Louis. History, details, and a complete bio of this subject are in your packs."

She waited again while members of the team shuffled and took out the bio. "Renquist will become Marsonini, attempt and likely succeed in copying his mannerisms, habits, and routines. You also have, in your packs, the projected image of how he'll look wearing the long red hair and sunshades. Now let's go over the details. If

Renquist follows this pattern, this is going down tonight."

She spent another hour before dismissing her team. Since she'd seen McNab look at his purple-banded wrist unit three times during the briefing, she held him back.

"She's got another two hours. You'd better chill."

"Sorry. She was just so wigged this morning. She's going into the sims now. She keeps choking on the sims."

"If she chokes, she's not ready to make the grade. The timing blows on this, McNab, but the fact is we've got a lot more at stake here than Peabody getting her detective shield."

"I know it. She's so damn worried about letting you down she's turned her guts inside out."

"Jesus. It's not about me."

He pressed his lips together as if wrestling with a decision, then shrugged. "Yeah, it is. Sure it is. A big part of it. I wasn't supposed to tell you, but I figure you gotta know so if she messes up on this, you can handle it. Handle her."

"She better handle herself. She's going straight into this op when she's done, and she won't have the results. She better handle herself, and do the job."

He slipped his hands into his pockets and gave Eve a cheeky grin. "See, you know just how to handle her."

"Get out of here."

She sat on the corner of the desk for a moment, to clear Peabody out of her head. It was one thing to be responsible for lives, for justice. But it was a hell of a kick in the ass to be told you had somebody's psyche in your hands.

How the hell had it gotten there?

"Lieutenant?" Roarke stood in the doorway of their adjoining offices, watching her. "A minute of your time."

"Yeah." She rose to walk into the simulation of the Mitchell bedroom again, judging distances, angles, moves. "That's about all I've got for you. We could take him on the street," she said half to herself. "But Marsonini carried a blaster or stunner, so Renquist will have a blaster or stunner. If he gets to it, starts popping off heat . . . maybe some idiot civilian gets in the way. Potential hostage. Better do it inside. Contained and controlled inside. No place to run, no civilian targets. It should be cleaner inside."

She looked over, shrugged when she realized she'd walked in and out of the holographic bedroom closet. "Sorry."

"It's not a problem. You're worried because Peabody will be in the bed, in the open."

"She can take care of herself."

"So she can. But the fact that you're worried should help you understand I've some concerns of my own. So I'm asking you to let me in on this operation."

Deliberately she cocked her brow. "Asking? Me? Why don't you just go to your good pal Jack, or your buddy Ryan?"

"One tries to learn by one's mistakes."

"Does one?"

"I want to be there for several reasons, and one is because it's become personal for you. It's trickier when it's personal."

She turned back. "End hologram program. Screens off." There was cold coffee on her desk. She picked up the cup, put it down. Then found herself reaching for the little statue of the goddess Peabody's mother had given her.

"It's not the notes. They're just irritating on a personal level, and helpful otherwise. It's not the fact that he's marked me as a future target. That goes with the territory. It's not even that he's a vicious, arrogant, sick son of a bitch. You get that all the time. It was watching Marlene Cox fighting to come back, and more than that, seeing her mother will her back. Sitting beside that hospital bed, reading to her, holding her hand, talking to her, believing — refusing not to believe because she loved her more than . . . Well, more than anything."

She set the statue down again. "The way the mother looked at me, with this utter faith that I'd make it right. In my line, you're almost always trying to make it right for the dead. But Marlene's alive. So it's personal. It got turned on me, and yeah, it's trickier when it's personal."

"Can you use me?"

"Slick operator like you? Don't see why not. I'll give you a ride into Central. You can report to Feeney in EDD."

Her first task at Central was to arrange for Pamela Renquist to be brought to an interview room.

Renquist's high-priced lawyers were already working on her release. Eve would consider herself lucky to hold the woman another twelve hours.

Pamela came in without her attorney, but wearing her own clothes rather than prison garb. Used her pull for her priority, Eve assumed and gestured to the table.

"I've agreed to speak with you, and alone, because I don't want to give you the importance of my attorneys." Pamela sat, brushed at her soft, silk pants. "I'll be released shortly, and have already instructed my attorneys to initiate suit against you for harassment, false arrest and imprisonment, and slander."

"Gosh, I'm in big trouble now. Tell me where he is, Pam, and we'll end this without anyone else getting hurt."

"First, I don't appreciate your familiar form of address."

"Gee, now you hurt my feelings."

"Secondly," Pamela continued in a voice iced as February, "my husband is in London on business, and when he returns he will use all his influence to destroy you."

"Hey, here's a flash for you: Your husband is in New York City, finalizing his preparation to kill a female accountant using the method of Enrico Marsonini, who was infamous for the rape and torture of his victims before he cut them to pieces. He always took a finger or toe with him, as a kind of door prize."

"You're disgusting."

"*I'm* disgusting." Eve let out a baffled laugh. "You are some piece of work. To continue. Following the pattern of his latest mentor, Niles visited his intended victim in her home yesterday afternoon."

Pamela curled her fingers, examined her manicure. "That's preposterous."

"You know it's not. You know that your husband, the father of your child, the man you live with, is a psychopath. You've smelled the blood on him, haven't you, Pam? You've seen what he is when you look at his face. You have a daughter. Isn't it time for you to protect her?"

Pamela's gaze flashed up, and a hint of rage eked through. "My daughter is none of your concern."

"And apparently none of yours, either. I sent a child liaison officer to your home last evening. Rose, along with Sophia DiCarlo, has been taken into protective custody. The reason this is news to you is that you haven't bothered contacting your daughter since you were brought in yesterday."

"You had no right to remove my daughter from my home."

"I do. But it was the liaison who opted to do so after speaking with her and her au pair, and other members of your staff. If you want your daughter back, it's time to step away from the madman and stand with them against him. It's time to shield your child."

The rage, that tiny hint of emotion, was iced over again. "Lieutenant Dallas, my husband is an important man. Within a year, he will be named the new British Ambassador to Spain. It's been promised to us. You will not besmirch his reputation or mine with your horrendous and ugly fantasies."

"Go down with him then. It's a nice bonus for me." Eve rose, paused. "Eventually, he'd have done you, and your daughter. He wouldn't have been able to stop himself. You're not going to Spain, Pam, but wherever you end up, you're going to have plenty of time to think about the fact that I saved your worthless life."

She walked over, gave the steel-reinforced panel two hard thuds. "On the door," she called, and walked away.

She was heading back to her office when she heard herself being hailed. Eve kept walking, and let Peabody catch up.

"Dallas. Sir. Lieutenant!"

"There's paperwork in your cube. Deal with it. In my office in ten for a briefing. We head out in thirty."

"Sir, I've already been informed about the op. McNab nipped over to meet me when I came out of exam."

Good, Eve thought. Good for him. But she kept her cop scowl in place. "The fact that Detective Moron bypassed procedure does not negate the necessity for your briefing."

"He wouldn't have had to tell me if you had."

It was the mutter that did it. Eve swung into Homicide. "My office. Now."

"You put the thumb on Renquist last night." Peabody trotted behind Eve. "I should have been called in for the search. *You* bypassed procedure."

Eve shoved her door closed. "Are you questioning my methods or my authority, Officer?"

"Your methods, Lieutenant. Sort of. I mean, jeez. If he'd been home last night, you'd have him, and I'd've missed it. As your aide —"

"As my aide you do what you're told when you're told. If you're dissatisfied with this arrangement, put it in writing and file it."

"You worked the case last night without me. You held an op briefing this morning without me. The exam shouldn't have taken priority over my involvement in this case."

"I decide what takes priority. It's done. If you have any more bitching and complaining to do about this matter, I repeat, do so in writing and file it through the proper channels."

Peabody's chin jutted up. "I have no wish to file a complaint, Lieutenant."

"Your choice. Complete the paperwork on your desk. Meet me in the garage in twenty-five. You'll be briefed en route."

It was going to be a long day, Eve imagined, as she walked through Katie Mitchell's loft, just as she'd walked through the hologram. And a long night.

Wherever Renquist had tucked himself, he'd done a good job of it.

Your move, she thought, and gulped down more coffee.

She'd thrown a net over every hotel in the sector, but she hadn't found him. Even while she paced the loft, the search was widening.

She stepped up to the doorway of the office where Roarke and Feeney worked.

"Nothing," Roarke said, sensing her. "It's more likely he's using a private residence. Short-term rental. We're searching that area."

She checked her wrist unit once more. There were hours yet, and she couldn't risk going in and out of the building. She walked back to the kitchen, poked at Mitchell's AutoChef.

"Restless?" Roarke said from behind her.

"I hate the waiting, doing nothing but going over and over it in my head. Makes me antsy."

He leaned down to kiss the back of her head. "So does having a spat with Peabody."

"Why do men always say women have spats? Men don't have spats. It's a stupid, weenie word."

He rubbed her shoulders. Because they were like rock, he made a mental note to schedule a relaxation treatment for her. Whether she liked it or not. "Why don't you ask her how the exam went?"

"She wants me to know, she'll tell me."

He leaned down closer, brushing his lips over her hair, then speaking directly into her ear. "She thinks she tanked it."

"Shit." Eve fisted her hands. "Shit, fuck, damn." She swung to the freezer, sorted through it, and confiscated a quart of Strawberry Fields Frozen Dessert.

She found a spoon, stuck it in, then marched off toward the bedroom.

"There's my girl," Roarke murmured.

Peabody sat on the edge of the bed, studying the morning briefing on her PPC. She glanced up when Eve entered, nearly had her sulky look in place when she spotted the quart of ice cream.

"Here." Eve shoved it into her hand. "Eat this and stop pouting. I need you at a hundred percent."

"It's just . . . I think I fucked up, really bad."

"I don't want you to think. You put it out of your mind, all the way. You have to be focused. You can't afford to miss a move, miss a signal. In a few hours, you're going to be lying in that bed, in the dark. When he comes in, his whole purpose will be to kill you. He'll be wearing night-vision goggles. He likes to work in the dark. He'll see you, but you won't see him. Until we make the move, you won't see him. So you can't fuck that up, or you're going to get hurt. You get hurt, you'll really piss me off."

"I'm sorry about this afternoon." Peabody shoved in the strawberry ice cream. "I had myself all worked up. I'd kicked my own ass as many times as I could on the way back from the exam. I just needed to kick somebody else's. And I started thinking, if you'd just called me in I wouldn't have taken that stupid, goddamn exam."

"You did take it. And tomorrow you'll know the results. Now put it aside and do the job."

"I will." She held out a spoonful of ice cream to Eve.

Taking it, Eve sampled. "Christ. That's just horrible."

"I think it's pretty good." More cheerful, Peabody took the spoon back and dug in for more. "You're just spoiled because you get the real thing now. Thanks for not being mad at me anymore."

"Who says I'm not? If I liked you, I'd have sent somebody out for real ice cream instead of stealing a civilian's frozen crap."

Peabody just smiled, and licked the spoon.

CHAPTER TWENTY-THREE

He'd be getting dressed now, Eve figured, as she looked out through the privacy-screened windows of Mitchell's loft. It would be full dark soon. Marsonini had always had a long, leisurely meal, with two glasses of wine, before a kill. Always an upscale restaurant, booking a corner table.

He could spend two, even three hours over it. Savoring the food, sipping the wine. Ending with coffee and dessert. A man who enjoyed the finer things.

Renquist would appreciate that.

Eve could see him now, in her mind's eye. Buttoning a perfectly white, bespoke shirt. Watching his own fingers in the mirror. It would be a good room, well appointed. He wouldn't tolerate anything but the best — as Renquist or Marsonini.

A silk tie. Probably a silk tie. He'd like the way it felt in his fingers as he slipped it on, as he finessed the perfect knot.

He would take it off after his victim was subdued and restrained. Carefully hanging every article of clothing to avoid creasing. He wouldn't want creases any more than bloodstains.

But for now, he'd enjoy the act of dressing well, of good materials against his skin, and the anticipation of the food and wine, and what followed it.

She could see him, Renquist, turning himself into Marsonini. Grooming the long red hair that was his pride and his vanity. Would Renquist see Marsonini's face in the mirror now? She imagined he would. The darker complexion, the less even features, the fuller mouth, the pale, pale eyes that would peer out from behind tinted shades. He would need to see it or the night wouldn't have the same flavor.

Now the jacket. Something in light gray, maybe, perhaps with a faint pinstripe. A good summer suit for a man of discriminating tastes. Then the lightest splash of cologne.

He would check his briefcase. Take a long breath to draw in the scent of the leather. Would he take out all of his tools? Probably. He would run his hands along the lengths of rope. Thin, strong rope that would leave painful grooves in his victim's flesh.

He loved the thought of their pain. Then the ball gag. He preferred the humiliation of that over cloth. The condoms, for his own safety and protection. The thin cigars and slim gold lighter. He enjoyed a good smoke nearly as much as burning those tiny circles into his victim's skin and watching the agony scream in their eyes. The little antique bottle he'd filled with alcohol, to pour over the wounds for that extra panache.

A retractable bat, honed steel. Strong enough to break bones, shatter cartilage. And phallic enough to suit another purpose should he be in the mood.

Blades, of course. Smooth ones, jagged ones, in case he found the woman's kitchen knives under par.

His music discs, the night-vision goggles, the hand blaster or the ministunner, his paper-thin clear gloves. He detested the texture and scent of Seal-It or any of its clones.

His own towel. White, Egyptian cotton, and his own fresh cake of unscented soap for washing up after the job was done.

And lastly, the security codes, cloned the day before during his visit to the loft. The jammer that would disengage the cameras so that he could stroll into the building without leaving a trace.

All neatly packed now, and locked into the elegant case.

One last look in the mirror, a full-length to show himself the entire effect. It had to be perfect. A flick of the finger over a lapel to remove a minute speck of lint.

Then he would stroll out the door, to begin his evening out.

"Where were you?" Roarke asked when her eyes changed, when her shoulders relaxed.

"With him." She looked over, saw he held two mugs of coffee. "Thanks," she said, taking one.

"And where is he?"

"Heading out to dinner. Soup to nuts. He'll pay cash. He always pays cash. He'll linger over it until nearly midnight, then he'll take a long walk. Marsonini didn't drive, and rarely took cabs. He'll walk here, juicing himself up, block by block."

“How did they catch him?” He knew, but he wanted Eve to say it, to talk it out.

“His intended victim lived in a loft, not so different than this. Makes sense. One of her friends had a major fight with her boyfriend, and came over to cry on Lisel’s — that was her name — came over to cry on her shoulder or whatever women do.”

“Eat strawberry ice cream.”

“Shut up. So the friend finally cried it out and bunked on the sofa. It was the music that woke her up. She hadn’t heard him come in — apparently they’d killed a bottle of cheap wine or brew. Something. Marsonini hadn’t spotted her sleeping there, which was a break. So the friend goes toward the bedroom to see about the music. Lisel was already bound, gagged, with a broken kneecap. Marsonini was naked. His back was to the doorway. He was climbing onto the bed, getting ready to rape Lisel.”

She knew what had been in the victim’s head, swimming over the pain. She knew that the awful terror of what was to come was worse, so much worse than pain.

“The friend kept her head,” Eve continued. “She ran back to the living room, called nine-one-one, then hurried back to the bedroom, picked up this bat he’d used to break Lisel’s kneecap, and she whaled on him. Fractured his skull, broke his jaw, his nose, his elbow. By the time the cops got there, Marsonini was unconscious and in a sorry state. She’d untied Lisel, covered her up, and was holding a knife to the bastard’s throat, hoping — she said in her statement

— he'd come around so she could stick it in his gullet."

"I'd say it stuck in his gullet that a woman stopped him."

Her lips quirked a little, because she understood. "I'm counting on it. He died in prison two years later when an unidentified inmate or guard castrated him and left him lying in his own cage. Bled to death."

She breathed deep, found it had helped to talk it through. "I'm going to make the rounds. You've got two hours to stretch your legs around here, then we tuck in. And we wait."

At midnight, she hauled a stool into the closet. She kept the door open to an angle that gave her a view of the bed, and Peabody's upper half.

The apartment was full dark, and silent.

"Peabody, check your communicator every fifteen, until I order radio silence. I don't want you nodding off in there."

"Lieutenant, I couldn't fall asleep if you gave me a high-powered soother. I'm revved."

"Do the checks. Stay icy."

What if I'm wrong? she asked herself. *If he changed targets, changed methods, got a whiff of me? If he doesn't come tonight, will he kill randomly or just rabbit? Does he have a back door? An emergency route, emergency funds, and ID?*

He'll come, she assured herself. *And if he doesn't, I'll track him.*

She ran through her own checks, got the all-quiet from the street teams, the house teams. After an hour, she stood up to stretch and keep herself limber.

After two, she felt her blood begin to pump. He was coming. She knew he was coming seconds before her communicator hissed in her ear.

"Possible sighting. Lone male, proceeding south toward building. Six-two, a hundred and ninety. Light-colored suit and dark tie. He's carrying a briefcase."

"Observe only. Don't approach. Feeney, you copy?"

"Loud and clear."

"McNab?"

"We're on it."

"Looks like a false alarm. He's moving past the building, continuing south. Wait . . . He's watching, that's what he's doing. Scoping things out, checking the street. He's turning back, approaching the building again. Something in his hand. Might be a security jammer. Turning in. He's heading in, Lieutenant."

"Stay in the vehicle. Wait for my command. Peabody?"

"I'm ready."

Eve saw the slight movement in the bed, and knew Peabody had her stunner in her hand. "Feeney, you and the civilian stay behind those doors until I clear it. I want him all the way in. McNab, I want that elevator shut down the minute he's through the door, and your team out and blocking the hall a second after that. Copy?"

"You've got it. How's my sex queen?"

"I beg your pardon, Detective?"

"Um . . . Question directed at Officer Peabody, Lieutenant."

"No personal communications or stupid-ass remarks, for sweet Christ's sake. Give me a twenty on the suspect."

"He's using the stairs, sir. Moving between second and third floor. I've got a good clear view of his face, Dallas. Positive ID for Niles Renquist. Moving to your door now. Taking out a keycode. He's through, and in."

"Move now," Eve said in a whisper. "All units close in now, and hold."

She couldn't hear him. Not yet. So she brought him into her head. Marsonini always removed his shoes before entering the bedroom. Shoes and socks. He would leave them neatly beside the entrance door, then take off the shades, put on the night-vision goggles. With them, he could move through the dark like a cat. Then he could stand over the victim, watching her sleep before he pounced.

Eve drew her weapon. Waited.

She heard the faintest creak of the floorboard, and willed him to come on, come *on*, you son of a bitch.

Then with her eyes long adjusted to the dark, she saw the shape of him, saw him stroke a hand gently over Peabody's back.

She kicked the door open. "Lights!" She shouted.

He whirled, with the goggles blinding him now. The bat was in his hand, and he swung out with it, toward the sound of her voice even as he ripped the goggles away.

“Police. Drop the weapon! Drop your weapon and freeze or I will drop you.”

His eyes were huge, blinking madly. But she saw the instant he recognized her and understood. She saw all his plans, his victories, drain out of his head. “Filthy cunt.”

“Come on then.” She lowered her weapon, then stabbed a warning finger toward the doorway when Roarke shoved in with Feeney behind him. “Don’t do it,” she snapped at them.

Renquist howled, threw the bat at her, then leaped.

She shifted, let the metal glance off her shoulder. Because it was more satisfying than a stun, she used her body, tucking to drive that same shoulder into his gut, her knee to his groin. And when he started to fold, her fist found its way to the underside of his jaw.

“That last one was for Marlene Cox,” Eve muttered.

She planted her foot on the small of his back as she pulled out her restraints. “Hands behind you, you bucket of puke.”

“I’ll kill you. I’ll kill all of you.” Blood trickled out of his mouth as he struggled. His eyes went wide and wild when Eve yanked the wig away.

“Keep your hands off me, you revolting bitch. Do you *know* who I am?”

“Yeah, I know just who you are.” She flipped him over because she wanted him to see her. She wanted him to look at her face. The hate was there, the sort she’d seen before. The kind of bone-deep loathing she’d seen in the eyes of her own mother.

But seeing it now brought her only satisfaction.

"Do you know who I am, Niles? I'm the woman, the revolting bitch, the filthy cunt who's kicked your sorry ass. I'm the one who's going to lock the cage on you."

"You'll never put me away." Tears began to shimmer in his eyes. "You won't lock me in the dark again."

"You're already gone. And when Breen writes about this one, he'll make careful note that it was a woman who beat you."

He began to wail and to weep. She would've said like a woman, but it would've been an insult to her entire sex.

"Read him his rights," she told Peabody, who'd emerged from the bed in full uniform. "Have him transported to Central and booked. You know the drill."

"Yes, sir. Do you wish to accompany the prisoner?"

"I'll settle things here and follow you in. I think you should be able to handle him, Detective."

"I think a ten-year-old boy could handle him in this shape, sir." She shook her head as Renquist continued to sob and drum his feet like a child in the throes of a tantrum. Then her head snapped up. "What? What did you say?"

"Do I have to repeat a standard order for prisoner procedure?"

"No. No, sir. Did you . . . did you say 'detective'?"

"Something wrong with your ears? Oh, by the way, congratulations. Suspect is contained and in custody," she said into her communicator as she walked from the room. She paused only long enough to wink at Roarke. "All units, stand down. Nice job."

"Go ahead," Feeney said to Peabody as she stood shell-shocked with McNab's kissing noises and applause ringing in her earpiece. "I've got this bag of shit."

With a little whoop, Peabody leaped over Renquist. "Dallas! Are you sure? Really, really sure? The results aren't posted until tomorrow."

"Why aren't you following my direct order re the prisoner?"

"*Please*."

"Jesus, what a baby." But it took every ounce of will to hold back the grin. "I've got some pull. I used it. Results will be posted at oh eight hundred. You placed twenty-sixth, which isn't shabby. They're taking a full hundred, so you're in. You could've done better on the sims."

"I *knew* it."

"But you did good. All in all you did good. The standard ceremony will be at noon, day after tomorrow. You will *not* cry during the cleanup of an operation," she said when Peabody's eyes teared up.

"I won't. Okay." Peabody threw open her arms, lurched forward.

Eve backpedaled. "No kissing! Mother of God. You get a handshake. A handshake." She stuck out her hand in defense. "That's it."

"Yes, sir. Yes, sir." She took Eve's hand, pumped it. "Oh screw it," she said, and wrapped her arms tightly enough around Eve to crack ribs.

"Get off me, you maniac." But now it was touch and go whether she could hold back the laugh. "Go jump McNab. I'll transport the damn prisoner."

"Thanks. Oh man, oh boy, thanks!" She started to run for the door when it flew open. McNab caught her — and Eve had to give him credit for keeping his feet — in mid-air.

Rolling her eyes for form, she walked back into the bedroom.

"I'll load him up," Feeney told her. "Let the girl have time to do her victory dance."

"I'll be right behind you."

"You'll be sorry." Renquist's eyes were still streaming, but the fury was in them again, lighting the tears. "Very sorry."

She stepped up, into his face, let the silence hang until she saw fear eat away at the anger. "I knew it was you, the first time I saw you. I saw what you were. Do you know what you are, *Niles?* Pitiful and weak, a coward who hid behind other cowards because he didn't even have the balls to be himself when he killed innocents. Do you know why I ordered my detective to take you in? Because you're not worth another minute of my time. You're over."

She turned away when he began to weep again. "Give me a lift, sailor," she said to Roarke.

"It would be my pleasure." He took her hand when they reached the door, and tightened his grip when she hissed and tried to shake him off.

"Too late to worry about such things now. You winked at me during an operation."

"I certainly did nothing of the kind." She folded her lips, primly. "Maybe I had something in my eye."

"Let's have a look." He backed her up against the wall of the hallway, and laughed when she swore at him. "No, I don't see a thing, except those big, gorgeous cop's eyes." He kissed her between them. "Peabody's not the only one who did good today."

"I did the job. That's good enough for me."

Two days later, she read Mira's preliminary psych report on Niles Renquist. Then she leaned back, stared at the ceiling. It was an interesting ploy, she mused. If his defense team was good enough, he might just pull it off.

She looked to the vase of flowers on her desk — sent that morning by Marlene Cox, via her mother. Instead of embarrassing her as they might have done, they pleased her.

Whatever the ploy, justice would be served. Niles Renquist would never see freedom again. And she had a decent shot at nailing his wife as accessory after the fact.

At least the PA had agreed to press for it, and that would have to be enough.

If she succeeded there, she was orphaning a young girl, deliberately seeing to it that a five-year-old child was without mother or father. Rising, she walked to the window. But some children were better off, weren't they, without a certain type of parent?

How the hell did she know. She dragged a hand through her hair, scrubbed them both over her face. She could only do the job and hope when the dust settled, it was right.

It felt right.

She heard her knob turn, then the knock. She'd locked it, pointedly, and now checked the time. Rolling her shoulders, she picked up her cap, set it in place.

When she opened the door she saw the rare jolt of shock on Roarke's face, then the interest, then the gleam that had color rising up on her neck.

"What are you staring at?"

"I'm not entirely sure." He stepped in before she could step out, then closed the door behind him.

"We've got to go. The ceremony starts in fifteen."

"And it's a five-minute walk. Turn around once."

"I will not." Another few seconds, she figured, and that damn flush would hit her cheeks. Mortifying her. "You've seen a cop in uniform before."

"I've never seen my cop in uniform before. I didn't know you had one."

"Of course I've got one. We've all got one. I just never wear it. But this is . . . important, that's all."

"You look . . ." He traced one of her shiny brass buttons. ". . . amazing. Very sexy."

"Oh, get out."

"Seriously." He leaned back to take it in. That long, lanky form did wonders, he thought, for the spit and polish, the crisp formal blues.

Medals, earned in the line of duty, glinted against the stiff jacket. She'd shined her black cop shoes — which he now imagined she'd kept buried in her locker — to mirror gleams. She wore her weapon at her hip, and her cap squared off on her short hair.

"Lieutenant," he said with a purr in his voice. "You've *got* to wear that home."

"Why?"

He grinned. "Guess."

"You're a sick, sick man."

"We'll play cops and robbers."

"Out of my way, pervert."

"One thing." He had fast hands, and had dipped one down her starched collar before she could move. And pulled out, to his delight, the chain that carried the diamond he'd once given her. "That's perfect, then," he murmured, and tucked it away again.

"We're not holding hands. I'm absolutely firm on that."

"Actually, I was planning to walk a couple steps behind you, so I could see how your ass moves in that thing."

She laughed, but pulled him out with her. "Update on Renquist if you're interested."

"I am."

"He's trying for insanity — not unexpected. But he's giving it a good shot. Using multiple personality disorder. One minute he's Jack the Ripper, next he's Son of Sam or John Wayne Gacy. Trips from that to DeSalvo or back to Jack."

"Do you think it's genuine?"

"Not for a minute, and Mira doesn't buy it. He could pull it off though. His defense will hire plenty of shrinks that go along, and he's good at the game. It may keep him from a cement cage and put him in a padded cell, on the mentally defective floor."

"How would you feel about that?"

"I want the cage, but you don't always get what you want. I'm going by the hospital after shift so I can tell Marlene Cox and her family what may happen."

"I think they'll be fine with it. They're not soldiers, Eve," he said when she looked at him. "They only want him put away, and you've done that. It's payment enough for them, if not for you."

"It has to be enough for me because it's over. And there'll be another to take his place. Knowing that drags some cops under."

"Not my cop."

"No." What the hell, she took his hand anyway as they walked into the meeting room for the ceremony. "It pushes me over. You just find a seat, wherever. I have to be up on the stupid stage."

He lifted her hand to his lips. "Congratulations, Lieutenant, on a job well done."

She glanced over, as he did, to where Peabody stood with McNab in the front of the room. "She did it herself" was all Eve said.

It pleased her to see that Commander Whitney had made time to officiate. She stepped onto the stage with him, took the hand he offered.

"Congratulations, Lieutenant, on your aide's promotion."

"Thank you, sir."

"We're going to start right away. We have twenty-seven promotions this session out of Central. Sixteen detective third grades, eight second grades, and three detective sergeants." He smiled a little. "I don't believe I've seen you in uniform since you made lieutenant."

"No, sir."

She stepped back with the other trainers, stood next to Feeney.

"One of my boys made second grade," he told her. "Thought we'd have a celebration drink across the street after shift. Suit you?"

"Yeah, but the civilian's going to want in. He's soft on Peabody."

"Fair enough. Here we go. Jack'll give his standard speech. Thank God it's him and not that putz Leroy who stands in for him when he can't make it. Leroy's got the trots of the tongue. Can't stop it running."

In her assigned seat, Peabody sat with her spine straight and her stomach doing cartwheels. She was terrified she'd burst into tears, as she had when she'd called home to tell her parents. It would be mortifying to cry now, but everything was so welled up, flooding her throat, that she was afraid when she opened her mouth to speak, it would all pour out.

Her ears were buzzing, so now she was afraid she wouldn't hear her name called and would just sit there like an idiot. She concentrated on Eve, and how she stood cool and perfect at parade rest in her uniform.

When she'd seen her lieutenant walk in, in uniform, she'd nearly bawled then and there. She hadn't been able to speak to her.

But buzzing or not, she heard her name in the commander's big voice. Detective Third Grade Delia Peabody. And got to her feet. She couldn't feel her knees, but somehow she was walking to the stage, up the side steps, and across it.

"Congratulations, Detective," he said, and took her hand in his enormous one before he stepped back.

And there was Dallas, stepping forward. "Congratulations, Detective. Well done." She held out the shield, and for a moment, just a flicker, there was a smile.

"Thank you, Lieutenant."

Then Eve stepped back, and it was done.

All Peabody could think when she resumed her seat was that she hadn't cried. She hadn't cried and there was a detective's shield in her hand.

She was still moving through a daze when the ceremony was done, and McNab rushed forward to lift her off her feet. And Roarke leaned over and — oh my God! — kissed her *right on the mouth*.

But she couldn't find Eve. Through the congratulations and pats on the back, the ribbing and the noise, she didn't see Eve anywhere. Finally, still clutching her badge, she broke away.

When she tracked Eve down in her office, her lieutenant was back in street clothes, at her desk, hunched over paperwork.

"Sir. You got out of there so fast."

"I had things to do."

"You were wearing your uniform."

"Why does everybody say that like it's cause for a national holiday? Listen, congratulations. I mean it. I'm proud of you, and glad for you. But fun time's over, and I've got a shit-pile of paperwork."

"Well, I'm going to take time to thank you, and that's that. I wouldn't have this if it wasn't for you." She kept the shield cupped in her hand as if it were the finest crystal. "Because you believed in me, you pushed me, and you taught me, I've got it."

"That's not entirely untrue." Eve tipped the chair back, put the heel of one boot on the desk. "But if you hadn't believed in yourself, pushed yourself, and learned, I wouldn't have done you a damn bit of good. So you're welcome, for what part I played in it. You're a good cop, Peabody, and you'll be a better one as time goes by. Now, the paperwork."

Peabody's vision was blurry, but she blinked back the tears. "I'll get right on it, sir."

"That's not your job."

"As your aide —"

"You're no longer my aide. You're a detective, and part of this paperwork I'm slogging through is your new assignment."

The tears dried up, and the flush the excitement and joy had put in her cheeks drained away. "I don't understand."

"Detectives can't be wasted as aides." Eve spoke briskly. "You'll be reassigned. I assume you'd prefer to stay in Homicide."

"But . . . but. God! Dallas, I never considered that I couldn't stay — that we wouldn't work together. I'd never have taken the damn exam if I'd known you'd have to boot me."

"That's a ridiculous thing to say, and shows a lack of respect for your shield. I can give you a short list of choices for your reassignment." Eve flicked a key on the desk unit and had a spreadsheet coming up. "Or if you're just going to whine about it, I'll make the choice for you."

"I wasn't thinking, wasn't expecting." And now her stomach hurt all over again. "I can't take it in. Couldn't I at least take a few days to adjust? Continue as your aide until you make other arrangements? I could clear up the pending —"

"Peabody, I don't need an aide. I never needed an aide, and got along fine without one before I took you on. Now it's time for you to move along."

Eve turned back to her desk in a gesture of dismissal. With her lips pressed tightly together, Peabody nodded. "Yes, sir."

"Don't need a damn aide," Eve repeated. "Could use a partner, though."

That stopped Peabody in her tracks. "Sir?" she managed in a croak.

"If you're interested, that is. And as the ranking officer, I'd still dump most of the shitwork on you. That's the part I really like."

"Partner? Your partner." Peabody's lips trembled, and the tears won.

"Oh for God's sake! Close the door if you're going to blubber. Do you think I want the bull pen to hear crying in here? They might think it's me."

She sprang up, slammed the door herself, and then found herself caught in another of Peabody's bear hugs.

"I take this as a yes."

"This is the best day of my life." Peabody stepped back, rubbed the tears off her cheeks. "The ult. I'm going to make you a hell of a partner."

"I bet you will."

"And I won't do the hug and blubber thing except in extreme circumstances."

"Good to know. Get out of here so I can finish my work. I'll buy you a drink after shift."

"No, sir. I'm buying." She opened her hand, showed Eve her badge. "It's beautiful, isn't it?"

"Yeah. Yeah, it is."

Alone, Eve sat at her desk again, then took out her own badge and studied it. Tucking it away again, she looked up at the ceiling. But this time, she smiled.

It felt right. It felt exactly right.

Also available in ISIS Large Print:

Lean Mean Thirteen

Janet Evanovich

Her first mistake was Dickie Orr. Stephanie was married to him for about 15 minutes before she caught him cheating on her with her arch-nemesis Joyce Barnhardt. After another 15 minutes, Stephanie filed for divorce, hoping never to see either one of them again.

Her second mistake was doing favours for super bounty hunter Carlos Manoso (a.k.a. Ranger). Ranger needs her to meet with Dickie to find out if he's doing something shady. Turns out, he is. Turns out, he's also back to doing Joyce Barnhardt. And it turns out Ranger's favours always come with a price . . .

And it is downhill from there. Stephanie goes completely nuts and attempts to assault Dickie in front of the entire office. Now Dickie has disappeared and Stephanie is a suspect. Is Dickie dead? Can he be found? And can Stephanie Plum stay one step ahead in this new, dangerous game?

ISBN 978-0-7531-8324-3 (hb)
ISBN 978-0-7531-8325-0 (pb)

Portrait in Death

J. D. Robb

After a tip from a reporter, Eve Dallas finds the body of a young woman in a Delancey street dumpster. Just hours before, the news station had mysteriously received a portfolio of professional portraits of the woman. The photos seemed to be nothing out of the ordinary for a pretty young girl starting a modelling career. Except that she wasn't a model. And that these photos were taken after she had been murdered.

Now Dallas is on the trail of a killer who's a perfectionist and an artist. He carefully observes and records his victim's every move. And he has a mission: to own every beautiful young woman's innocence, to capture her youth and vitality in one fatal shot . . .

ISBN 978-0-7531-8300-7 (hb)
ISBN 978-0-7531-8301-4 (pb)

A L I S
1845642